DEAD LIKE YOU

Peter James was educated at Charterhouse then at film school. He lived in North America for a number of years, working as a screenwriter and film producer before returning to England. His novels, many of which have been *Sunday Times* Top 10 bestsellers, have been translated into thirty languages and three have been filmed. All his novels reflect his deep interest in the world of the police, with whom he does in-depth research, as well as science, medicine and the paranormal. He has produced numerous films, including *The Merchant Of Venice*, starring Al Pacino, Jeremy Irons and Joseph Fiennes. He divides his time between his homes in Notting Hill in London and near Brighton in Sussex.

www.peterjames.com

DEAD LIKE YOU

PETER JAMES

PAN BOOKS

First published in the UK 2010 by Macmillan

First published in paperback 2010 by Pan Books
an imprint of Pan Macmillan, a division of Macmillan Publishers Limited
Pan Macmillan, 20 New Wharf Road, London N1 9RR
Basingstoke and Oxford
Associated companies throughout the world
www.panmacmillan.com

ISBN 978-1-4472-2294-1

1 3 5 7 9 8 6 4 2

A CIP catalogue record for this book is available from
the British Library.

Typeset by SetSystems Ltd, Saffron Walden, Essex
Printed and bound by CPI Group (UK) Ltd, Croydon CR0 4YY

Visit **www.panmacmillan.com** to read more about all our books
and to buy them. You will also find features, author interviews and
news of any author events, and you can sign up for e-newsletters
so that you're always first to hear about our new releases.

TO ANNA-LISA LINDEBLAD-DAVIES

1997

1

We all make mistakes, all of the time. Mostly trivial stuff, like forgetting to return a phone call, or to put money in a parking meter, or to pick up milk at the supermarket. But sometimes – luckily very rarely – we make the big one.

The kind of mistake that could cost us our life.

The kind of mistake Rachael Ryan made.

And she had a long time to reflect on it.

If . . . she had been less drunk. If . . . it hadn't been so sodding freezing cold. If . . . it hadn't begun to rain. If . . . there hadn't been a queue of a hundred equally drunk revellers at the taxi rank in Brighton's East Street at 2 a.m. on Christmas Eve, or, rather, Christmas morning. If . . . her flat had not been within walking distance, unlike her equally drunk companions, Tracey and Jade, who lived far away, on the other side of the city.

If . . . she had listened to Tracey and Jade telling her not to be so bloody stupid. That there were plenty of taxis. That it would only be a short wait.

*

His whole body stiffened with excitement. After two hours of watching, finally the woman he had been waiting for was turning into the street. She was on foot and alone. Perfect!

3

She was wearing a miniskirt with a shawl around her shoulders and looked a little unsteady on her legs, from drink and probably from the height of the heels. She had nice legs. But what he was really looking at was her shoes. His kind of shoes. High-heeled with ankle straps. He liked ankle straps. As she came closer, approaching beneath the sodium glare of the street lights, he could see, through his binoculars, through the rear window, that they were shiny, as he had hoped.

Very sexy shoes!

She was his kind of woman!

*

God, was she glad she had decided to walk! What a queue! And every taxi that had gone past since was occupied. With a fresh, windy drizzle on her face, Rachael tottered along past the shops on St James's Street, then turned right into Paston Place, where the wind became stronger, batting her long brown hair around her face. She headed down towards the seafront, then turned left into her street of Victorian terraced houses, where the wind and the rain played even more havoc with her hairdo. Not that she cared any more, not tonight. In the distance she heard the wail of a siren, an ambulance or a police car, she thought.

She walked past a small car with misted windows. Through them she saw the silhouette of a couple snogging, and she felt a twinge of sadness and a sudden yearning for Liam, whom she had dumped almost six months ago now. The bastard had been unfaithful. OK, he had pleaded with her to forgive him, but she just knew he would stray again, and again – he was that sort. All the same, she missed him a lot at times, and she wondered where he was now. What he was doing tonight. Who he was with. He'd be with a girl for sure.

Whereas she was on her own.

She and Tracey and Jade. *The Three Saddo Singles*, they jokingly called themselves. But there was a truth that hurt behind the humour. After two and a half years in a relationship with the man she had really believed was the one she would marry, it was hard to be alone again. Particularly at Christmas, with all its memories.

God, it had been a shitty year. In August, Princess Diana had died. Then her own life had fallen apart.

She glanced at her watch. It was 2.35. Tugging her mobile phone from her bag, she rang Jade's number. Jade said they were still waiting in the queue. Rachael told her she was almost home. She wished her a merry Christmas. Told her to wish Tracey a merry Christmas too, and said she'd see them New Year's Eve.

'Hope Santa's good to you, Rach!' Jade said. 'And tell him not to forget the batteries if he brings you a vibrator!'

She heard Tracey cackling in the background.

'Sod off!' she said with a grin.

Then she slipped the phone back into her bag and stumbled on, nearly coming a purler as one high heel of her incredibly expensive Kurt Geigers, which she'd bought last week in a sale, caught between two paving stones. She toyed for a moment with the idea of taking them off, but she was almost home now. She tottered on.

The walk and the rain had sobered her up a little, but she was still too drunk, and too coked up, not to think it was odd that at almost three on Christmas morning a man in a baseball cap a short distance in front of her was trying to lug a fridge out of a van.

He had it half out and half in as she approached. She

could see he was struggling under its apparent weight and suddenly he cried out in pain.

Instinctively, because she was kind, she ran, stumbling, up to him.

'My back! My disc! My disc has gone! Oh, Jesus!'

'Can I help?'

It was the last thing she remembered saying.

She was hurled forward. Something wet slapped across her face. She smelt a sharp, acrid reek.

Then she blacked out.

NOW

2

Wednesday 31 December

Yac spoke into the metal thing on the tall brick wall. 'Taxi!' he said.

Then the gates opened, swanky wrought-iron ones, painted black, with gold spikes along the top. He climbed back into his white and turquoise Peugeot estate and drove up a short, twisting drive. There were bushes on either side, but he did not know what kind they were. He hadn't got to bushes in his learning yet. Only trees.

Yac was forty-two. He wore a suit with a neatly pressed shirt and a carefully chosen tie. He liked to dress smart for work. He always shaved, combed his short dark hair forward to a slight peak and rolled deodorant under his armpits. He was aware that it was important not to smell bad. He always checked his fingernails and his toenails before leaving home. He always wound up his watch. He always checked his phone for messages. But he had only five numbers stored on the phone and only four people had his, so it wasn't often that he received any.

He glanced at the clock on the dashboard: 6.30 p.m. Good. Thirty minutes to go before he needed to have any tea. Plenty of time. His Thermos sat on the seat beside him.

At the top the drive became circular, with a low wall in the middle enclosing a fountain that was lit up in green. Yac steered carefully around it, past a quadruple garage door and one wall of the huge house, coming to a halt by steps leading up to the front door. It was a big, important-looking door and it was closed.

He began to fret. He didn't like it when passengers weren't already outside, because he never knew how long he would have to wait. And there were so many decisions.

Whether to switch the engine off. And if he switched the engine off, should he switch the lights off? But before he switched the engine off he needed to do some checks. *Fuel.* Three-quarters of a tank. *Oil.* Pressure normal. *Temperature.* Temperature was good. So much to remember in this taxi. Including to switch the meter on if they did not come out in five minutes. But most important of all, his drink of tea, on the hour, every hour. He checked the Thermos was still there. It was.

This wasn't actually *his* taxi, it belonged to someone he knew. Yac was a journeyman driver. He drove the hours the guy who owned it did not want to drive. Mostly nights. Some nights longer than others. Tonight was New Year's Eve. It was going to be a very long one and he had started early. But Yac didn't mind. Night was good. Much the same as day to him, but darker.

The front door of the house was opening. He stiffened and took a deep breath, as he had been taught by his therapist. He didn't really like passengers getting into his taxi and invading his space – except ones with nice shoes. But he had to put up with them until he could deliver them to their destination, then get them out again and be free.

They were coming out now. The man was tall and slim, his hair slicked back, wearing a tuxedo with a bow tie and holding his coat over his arm. She had a furry-looking jacket on, red hair all done nicely, flowing around her head. She looked beautiful, as if she might be a famous actress, like the ones he saw pictures of in the papers that people left in his taxi or on television of stars arriving at premieres.

But he wasn't really looking at her; he was looking at her shoes. Black suede, three ankle straps, high heels with glinting metal around the edges of the soles.

'Good evening,' the man said, opening the door of the taxi for the woman. 'Metropole Hotel, please.'

'Nice shoes,' Yac said to the woman, by way of reply. 'Jimmy Choo. Uh-huh?'

She squealed in proud delight. 'Yes, you're right. They are!'

He recognized her intoxicating scent too, but said nothing. *Oscar de la Renta Intrusion*, he thought to himself. He liked it.

He started the engine and quickly ran through his mental checks. *Meter on. Seat belts. Doors closed. Into gear. Handbrake off.* He had not checked the tyres since dropping off the last fare, but he had done so half an hour ago, so they might still be all right. *Check in mirror.* As he did, he caught another glimpse of the woman's face. Definitely beautiful. He would like to see her shoes again.

'The main entrance,' the man said.

Yac did the calculation in his head as he steered back down the drive: 2.516 miles. He memorized distances. He knew most of them within this city because he had memorized the streets. It was 4,428 yards to the Hilton Brighton Metropole, he recalculated; or 2.186 nautical miles, or 4.04897 kilometres, or 0.404847 of a Swedish mile. The fare would be approximately £9.20, subject to traffic.

'Do you have high-flush or low-flush toilets in your house?' he asked.

After a few moments of silence while Yac pulled out into the road, the man glanced at the woman, raised his eyes and said, 'Low flush. Why?'

'How many toilets do you have in your house? I bet you've got a lot, right? Uh-huh?'

'We have enough,' the man said.

'I can tell you where there's a good example of a high-flush toilet – it's in Worthing. I could take you there to see it if you're interested.' Hope rose in Yac's voice. 'It's a really good example. In the public toilets, near the pier.'

'No, thank you. They're not my thing.'

The couple in the back fell silent.

Yac drove on. He could see their faces in the glow of the street lights, in his mirror.

'With your low-flush toilets, I bet you have some push-button ones,' he said.

'We do,' the man said. 'Yes.' Then he put his mobile phone to his ear and answered a call.

Yac watched him in the mirror before catching the woman's eyes. 'You're a size five, aren't you? In shoes.'

'Yes! How did you know?'

'I can tell. I can always tell. Uh-huh.'

'That's very clever!' she said.

Yac fell silent. He was probably talking too much. The guy who owned the taxi told him there had been complaints about him talking too much. The guy said people didn't always like to talk. Yac did not want to lose his job. So he kept quiet. He thought about the woman's shoes as he headed down to the Brighton seafront and turned left. Instantly the wind buffeted the taxi. The traffic was heavy and it was slow going. But he was right about the fare.

As he pulled up outside the entrance to the Metropole Hotel, the meter showed £9.20.

The man gave him £10 and told him to keep the change.

Yac watched them walk into the hotel. Watched the woman's hair blowing in the wind. Watched the Jimmy Choo shoes disappearing through the revolving door. Nice shoes. He felt excited.

Excited about the night ahead.

There would be so many more shoes. Special shoes for a very special night.

3

DEAD LIKE YOU

Wednesday 31 December

Detective Superintendent Roy Grace stared out of his office window into the dark void of the night, at the lights of the ASDA superstore car park across the road and the distant lights of the city of Brighton and Hove beyond, and heard the howl of the gusting wind. He felt the cold draught that came though the thin pane on his cheek.

New Year's Eve. He checked his watch: 6.15. Time to go. Time to quit his hopeless attempt at clearing his desk and head home.

It was the same every New Year's Eve, he reflected. He always promised himself that he would tidy up, deal with all his paperwork and start the next year with a clean slate. And he always failed. He would be coming back in tomorrow to yet another hopeless mess. Even bigger than last year's. Which had been even bigger than the one the year before.

All the Crown Prosecution files of the cases he had investigated during this past year were stacked on the floor. Next to them were small, precarious tower blocks of blue cardboard boxes and green plastic crates crammed with unresolved cases – as cold cases were now starting to be called. But he preferred the old title.

Although his work was predominantly concerned with current murders and other major crimes, Roy Grace cared about his cold cases very much, to the point that he felt a personal connection with each victim. But he had been unable to dedicate much time to these files, because it had been a strangely busy year. First, a young man had been buried alive in a coffin on his stag night. Then a vile snuff-movie ring had been busted. This had been followed by a complex case of a homicidal identity thief, before he'd successfully potted a double-killer who had faked his disappearance. But he'd had precious little acknowledgement for getting these results from his departing boss, Assistant Chief Constable Alison Vosper.

Perhaps next year would be better. Certainly it was filled with promise. A new ACC, Peter Rigg, was starting on Monday – five days' time. Also starting on Monday, which would greatly relieve his workload, was a brand-new Cold Case Team comprising three former senior detectives under his command.

But most important of all, his beloved Cleo was due to give birth to their child in June. And some time before then, at a date still to be sorted out, they would be getting married, so long as the one obstacle standing in their way could be removed.

His wife, Sandy.

She had disappeared nine and a half years ago, on his thirtieth birthday, and, despite all his efforts, no word had been heard from her since. He did not know whether she had been abducted or murdered, or had run off with a lover, or had had an accident, or had simply, elaborately, faked her disappearance.

For the past nine years, until his relationship with Cleo Morey had begun, Roy had spent almost all of his free time in a fruitless quest to discover what had happened to Sandy. Now he was finally putting her into the past. He had engaged a solicitor to have her declared legally dead. He hoped the process could be fast-tracked so they would be able to get married before the baby was born. Even if Sandy did turn up out of the blue, he would not be interested in resuming a life with her, he had decided. He had moved on in his own mind – or so he believed.

He shovelled several piles of documents around on his desk. By stacking one heap on top of another, it made the desk look tidier, even if the workload remained the same.

Strange how life changed, he thought. Sandy used to hate New Year's Eve. It was such an artifice, she used to tell him. They always spent it with another couple, a police colleague, Dick Pope, and his wife, Leslie. Always in some fancy restaurant. Then afterwards Sandy would invariably analyse the entire evening and pull it apart.

With Sandy, he had come to view the advent of New Year's Eve with decreasing enthusiasm. But now, with Cleo, he was looking forward to it hugely. They were going to spend it at home, alone together, and feast on some of their favourite foods. Bliss! The only downer was that he was the duty Senior Investigating Officer for this week, which meant he was on twenty-four-hour call – which meant he could not drink. Although he had decided he would allow himself a few sips of a glass of champagne at midnight.

He could hardly wait to get home. He was so in love with Cleo that there were frequent moments in every day when he was overcome by a deep yearning to see her, hold her, touch her, hear her voice, see her smile. He had that feeling now, and wanted nothing more than to leave and head for her house, which had now, to all intents and purposes, become his home.

Just one thing stopped him.

All those damned blue boxes and green crates on the floor. He needed to have everything in order for the Cold Case Team on Monday, the first official working day of the New Year. Which meant several hours of work still ahead of him.

So instead he sent Cleo a text with a row of kisses.

For a time, this past year, he had managed to delegate all these cold cases to a colleague. But that hadn't worked out and now he had inherited them all back. Five unsolved major crimes out of a total number of twenty-five to be reinvestigated. Where the hell did he begin?

The words of Lewis Carroll's *Alice's Adventures in Wonderland* came into his head suddenly: 'Begin at the beginning and go on till you come to the end: then stop.'

So he began at the beginning. Just five minutes, he thought, then he would quit for the year and head home to Cleo. As if echoing his thoughts, his phone pinged with an incoming text. It was an even longer row of kisses.

Smiling, he opened the first file and looked at the activity report. Every six months the DNA labs they used would run checks on the DNA from their cold-case victims. You just never knew. And there had been several offenders who must have long thought they had got away with their crimes but who had successfully been brought to trial and were now in prison because of advances in DNA extraction and matching techniques.

The second file was a case that always touched Roy Grace deeply. Young Tommy Lytle. Twenty-seven years ago, at the age of eleven, Tommy had set out from school on a February afternoon to walk home. The one lead in the case was a Morris Minor van, spotted near the scene of the boy's murder, which was later searched. From the files, it was obvious that the Senior Investigating Officer at the time was convinced the owner of the van was the offender, but they were unable to find that crucial forensic evidence that would have linked the boy to the van. The man, a weirdo loner with a history of sexual offences, was released – but, Grace knew, still very much alive.

He turned to the next file: *Operation Houdini.*
Shoe Man.

Names of operations were thrown up randomly by the CID computer system. Occasionally they were apt. This one was. Like a great escapologist, this particular offender had so far avoided the police net.

The Shoe Man had raped – or attempted to rape – at least five women in the Brighton area over a short period of time back in 1997, and in all likelihood had raped and killed a sixth victim whose body had never been found. And it could have been a lot more – many women are too embarrassed or traumatized to report an attack. Then suddenly the attacks appeared to have stopped. No DNA evidence had been recovered from any of the victims who had come forward at the time. But techniques for obtaining it were less effective then.

All they had to go on was the offender's MO. Almost every criminal had a specific modus operandi. A way of doing things. His or her particular 'signature'. And the Shoe Man had a very distinct one: he took his victim's panties and one of her shoes. But only if they were classy shoes.

Grace hated rapists. He knew that everyone who became a victim of crime was left traumatized in some way. But most victims of burglaries and street crimes could eventually put it behind them and move on. Victims of sexual abuse or sexual assault, particularly child victims and rape victims, could never ever truly do that. Their lives were changed forever. They would spend the rest of their days living with the knowledge, struggling to cope, to hold down their revulsion, their anger and their fear.

It was a harsh fact that most people were raped by someone they knew. Rapes by total strangers were exceedingly rare, but they did happen. And it was not uncommon for these so-called 'stranger rapists' to take a souvenir – a trophy. Like the Shoe Man had.

Grace turned some of the pages of the thick file, glancing through comparisons with other rapes around the country. In particular, there was one case further north, from the same time period, that bore striking similarities. But that suspect had been eliminated, as evidence had established that it definitely could not have been the same person.

So, *Shoe Man*, Grace wondered, *are you still alive? If so, where are you now?*

4

Wednesday 31 December

Nicola Taylor was wondering when this night of hell would end, little knowing that the hell had not yet even begun.

'Hell is other people', Jean-Paul Sartre once wrote, and she was with him on that. And right now hell was the drunken man with the wonky bow tie on her right who was crushing every bone in her hand, and the even drunker man on her left, in a green tuxedo jacket, whose sweaty hand felt as slimy as pre-packed bacon.

And all the other 350 noisy, drunken people around her.

Both men were jerking her arms up and down, damned nearly pulling them out of their sockets as the band in the Metropole Hotel function room struck up 'Auld Lang Syne' on the stroke of midnight. The man on her right had a plastic Groucho Marx moustache clipped to the inside of his nostrils and the one on her left, whose slimy hand had spent much of the evening trying to work its way up her thigh, kept blowing a whistle that sounded like a duck farting.

She so totally did not want to be here. So wished to hell she had stuck to her guns and stayed home, in her comfort zone, with a bottle of wine and the television – the way she had most evenings this past year, since her husband had dumped her in favour of his twenty-four-year-old secretary.

But oh no, her friends Olivia and Becky and Deanne had all insisted there was *no way* they were going to allow her to get away with spending New Year's Eve moping at home on her own. Nigel was not coming back, they assured her. The slapper was pregnant. Forget him, kiddo. There were plenty more fish in the sea. Time to get a life.

This was getting a life?

Both her arms were jerked up in the air at the same time. Then she was dragged forward in a huge surge, her feet almost falling out of her insanely expensive Marc Jacobs heels. Moments later she found herself being dragged, tripping, backwards.

Should auld acquaintance be forgot . . . the band played.

Yes, they bloody well should. And current ones too!

Except she could not forget. Not all those midnights on New Year's Eve when she had stared into Nigel's eyes and told him she loved him, and he'd told her he loved her as well. Her heart was heavy, too damned heavy. She wasn't ready for this. Not now, not yet.

The song finally ended and Mr Pre-packed Bacon now spat his whistle out, gripped both her cheeks and planted a slobbery, lingering kiss on her lips. 'Happy New Year!' he burbled.

Then balloons fell from the ceiling. Paper streamers rained down on her. Jolly smiling faces surrounded her. She was hugged, kissed, fondled from every direction she turned. It went on and on and on.

Nobody would notice, she thought, if she escaped now.

She struggled across the room, weaving through the

sea of people, and slipped out into the corridor. She felt a cold draught of air and smelt sweet cigarette smoke. God, how she could do with a fag right now!

She headed along the corridor, which was almost deserted, turned right and walked along into the hotel foyer, then crossed over to the lifts. She pressed the button and, when the door opened, stepped in and pressed the button for the fifth floor.

Hopefully, they'd all be too drunk to notice her absence. Maybe she should have drunk more too and then she'd have been in a better party mood. She was feeling stone cold sober and could easily have driven home, but she'd paid for a room for the night and her stuff was in there. Perhaps she'd call up some champagne from room service, watch a movie and get quietly smashed on her own.

As she stepped out of the lift, she pulled her plastic room key-card out of her silver lamé Chanel evening bag – a copy she'd bought in Dubai on a trip there with Nigel two years ago – and made her way along the corridor.

She noticed a slender blonde woman – in her forties, she guessed – a short distance ahead. She was wearing a full-length, high-necked evening dress with long sleeves and appeared to be struggling to open her door. As she drew level with her, the woman, who was extremely drunk, turned to her and slurred, 'I can't get this sodding thing in. Do you know how they work?' She held out her key-card.

'I think you have to slip it in and then out quite quickly,' Nicola said.

'I've tried that.'

'Let me try for you.'

Nicola, helpfully, took the card and slipped it into the

slot. As she pulled it out, she saw a green light and heard a click.

Almost instantaneously, she felt something damp pressed across her face. There was a sweet smell in her nostrils and her eyes felt as if they were burning. She felt a crashing blow on the back of her neck. Felt herself stumbling forward. Then the carpet slammed into her face.

1997

5

Rachael Ryan heard the snap of the man's belt buckle in the darkness. A clank. The rustle of clothes. The sound of his breathing – rapid, feral. She had a blinding pain in her head.

'Please don't hurt me,' she begged. 'Please don't.'

The van was rocking in the frequent gusts of wind outside and occasionally a vehicle passed, bright white light strobing through the interior from its headlamps, as terror strobed through her. It was in those moments that she could see him most clearly. The black mask tight over his head, with tiny slits for his eyes, nostrils and mouth. The baggy jeans and the tracksuit top. The small, curved knife that he gripped in his left, gloved hand, the knife he said he would blind her with if she shouted out or tried to get away.

A musty odour, like old sacks, rose from whatever thin bedding she was lying on. It mingled with the faint smell of old plastic upholstery and the sharper reek of leaking diesel oil.

She saw his trousers come down. Stared at his white underpants, his lean, smooth legs. He pushed his pants down. Saw his small penis, thin and stumpy like the head of a snake. Saw him rummage in his pocket with his right hand and pull something out which glinted. A square foil packet. He sliced it open with his knife, breathing even harder and squeezed something out. A condom.

Her brain was racing with wild thoughts. A condom? Was he being considerate? If he was considerate enough to use a condom, would he really use his knife on her?

'We're going to get the rubber on,' he panted. 'They can get DNA now. They can get you from DNA. I'm not leaving you a present for the police. Make me hard.'

She shuddered with revulsion as the head of the snake moved closer to her lips and saw his face suddenly lit up brightly again as another car passed. There were people outside. She heard voices in the street. Laughter. If she could just make a noise – bang on the side of the van, scream – someone would come, someone would stop him.

She wondered for a moment whether she should just try to arouse him, to make him come, then maybe he would let her go and he would disappear. But she felt too much revulsion, too much anger – and too much doubt.

Now she could hear his breathing getting even deeper. Hear him grunting. See that he was touching himself. He was just a pervert, just a weirdo fucking pervert and this was not going to happen to her!

And suddenly, fuelled by the courage from the alcohol inside her, she grabbed his sweaty, hairless scrotum and crushed his balls in both hands as hard as she could. Then, as he recoiled, gasping in pain, she tore the hood off his head and jammed her fingers into his eyes, both eyes, trying to gouge them out with her nails, screaming as loudly as she could.

Except, in her terror, as if she were trying to scream in a nightmare, only a faint croak came out instead.

Then she felt a crashing blow on the side of her head.

'You bitch!'

He smashed his fist into her again. The mask of pain and fury that was his face, all blurred, was inches from her own. She felt the fist again, then again.

Everything swam around her.

And suddenly she felt her panties being pulled off, and then he was entering her. She tried to move back, to push away, but he had her pinned.

This is not me. This is not my body.

She felt totally detached from herself. For an instant she wondered if this was a nightmare from which she could not wake. Lights flashed inside her skull. Then fused.

NOW

6

Today was New Year's Day. And the tide was in!

Yac liked it best when the tide was in. He knew the tide was in because he could feel his home moving, rising, gently rocking. Home was a Humber keel coaler called *Tom Newbound*, painted blue and white. He did not know why the boat had been given that name, but it was owned by a woman called Jo, who was a district nurse, and her husband, Howard, who was a carpenter. Yac had driven them home one night in his taxi and they had been kind to him. Subsequently they'd become his best friends. He adored the boat, loved to hang about on it and to help Joe with painting, or varnishing, or generally cleaning her up.

Then one day they told him they were going to live in Goa in India for a while, they did not know how long. Yac was upset at losing his friends and his visits to the boat. But they told him they wanted someone to look after their houseboat, and their cat, for them.

Yac had been here for two years now. Just before Christmas he'd had a phone call from them, telling him they were going to stay for another year at least.

Which meant he could stay here for another year at least, which made him very happy. And he had a prize from last night, a new pair of shoes, which also made him very happy . . .

Red leather shoes. Beautifully curved with six straps and a buckle and six-inch stilettos.

They lay on the floor beside his *bunk*. He had learned nautical terms. It was a bed, really, but on a ship it was called a bunk. Just like the way the toilet wasn't called a toilet, but the *heads*.

He could navigate from here to any port in the UK – he had memorized all the Admiralty charts. Except the boat had no engine. One day he would like to have a boat of his own, with an engine, and then he would sail to all those places that he had stored inside his head. Uh-huh.

Bosun nuzzled his hand, which was hanging over the side of his bunk. Bosun, the big, slinky ginger tom, was the boss here. The true master of this boat. Yac knew that the cat regarded him as its servant. Yac didn't mind. The cat had never thrown up in his taxi, like some people had.

The smell of expensive new shoe leather filled Yac's nostrils. Oh yes. Paradise! To wake up with a new pair of shoes.

On a rising tide!

That was the best thing of all about living on the water. You never heard footsteps. Yac had tried to live in the city, but it had not worked for him. He could not stand the tantalizing sound of all those shoes clacking all around him when he was trying to sleep. There were no shoes here, out on the moorings on the River Adur at Shoreham Beach. Just the slap of water, or the silence of the mudflats. The cry of gulls. Sometimes the cry of the eight-month-old baby on the boat next door.

One day, hopefully, the infant would fall into the mud and drown.

But for now, Yac looked forward to the day ahead. To getting out of bed. To examining his new shoes. Then to cataloguing them. Then perhaps to looking through his collection, which he stored in the secret places he had found and made his own on the boat. It was where he kept, among other things, his collection of electrical wiring diagrams. Then he would go into his little office up in the bow and spend time on his laptop computer, online.

What better way could there be to start a New Year?

But first he had to remember to feed the cat.

But before doing that he had to brush his teeth.

And before that he had to use the *heads*.

Then he would have to run through all the checks on the boat, ticking them off from the list the owners had given him. First on the list was to check his fishing lines. Then he had to check for leaks. Leaks were not good. Then he needed to check the mooring ropes. It was a long list and working through it made him feel good. It was good to be needed.

He was needed by Mr Raj Dibdoon, who owned the taxi.

He was needed by the nurse and the carpenter, who owned his home.

He was needed by the cat.

And this morning he had a new pair of shoes!

This was a good start to a New Year.

Uh-huh.

7

Thursday 1 January

Carlo Diomei was tired. And when he was tired he felt low, as he did right now. He did not like these long, damp English winters. He missed the crisp, dry cold of his native Courmayeur, high up in the Italian Alps. He missed the winter snow and the summer sunshine. He missed putting on his skis on his days off and spending a few precious hours alone, away from the holidaying crowds on the busy pistes, making his own silent tracks down parts of the mountains that only he and a few local guides knew.

He had just one more year of his contract to run and then, he hoped, he would return to the mountains and, with luck, to a job managing a hotel there, back among his friends.

But for now the money was good here and the experience in this famous hotel would give him a great step up his career ladder. But, shit, what a lousy start to the New Year this was!

Normally as Duty Manager of the Brighton Metropole Hotel he worked a day shift, which enabled him to spend his precious evenings at home in his rented sea-view apartment with his wife and children, a two-year-old son and a four-year-old daughter. But the Night Manager had picked yesterday, New Year's Eve of all nights, to go down with flu. So he'd had to come back and take over, with just a two-hour break in which to dash home, put his kids to bed, toast his wife a Happy New Year with mineral water, instead of the champagne night at home they had planned, and hurry back to work to supervise all the New Year celebrations the hotel had been hosting.

He'd now been on duty for eighteen hours straight and was exhausted. In half an hour he would hand over to his deputy and would finally go home, and celebrate by smoking a badly needed cigarette, then falling into bed and getting some even more badly needed sleep.

The phone rang in his tiny, narrow office on the other side of the wall to the front desk.

'Carlo,' he answered.

It was Daniela de Rosa, the Housekeeping Manager, another Italian, from Milano. A room maid was concerned about room 547. It was 12.30, half an hour past check-out time, and there was a *Do Not Disturb* sign still hanging on the room door. There had been no response when she knocked repeatedly, nor when she phoned the room.

He yawned. Probably someone sleeping off a night of overindulgence. Lucky them. He tapped his keyboard to check on the room's occupant. The name was Mrs Marsha Morris. He dialled the room number himself and listened to it ringing, without answer. He called Daniela de Rosa back.

'OK,' he said wearily, 'I am coming up.'

Five minutes later, he stepped out of the lift on the fifth floor and walked along the corridor, to where the Housekeeping Manager was standing, and knocked hard on the door. There was no response. He knocked again. Waited. Then, using his pass key, he opened the door slowly and stepped in.

'Hello!' he said quietly.

The heavy curtains were still drawn, but in the semi-darkness he could make out the shape of someone lying on the wide bed.

'Hello!' he said again. 'Good morning!'

He detected the faintest movement on the bed. 'Hello!' he said again. 'Good morning, Mrs Morris. Hello! Happy New Year!'

There was no response. Just a little more movement.

He felt on the wall for the light switches and pressed one. Several lights came on at once. They revealed a slender, naked woman with large breasts, long red hair and a dense triangle of brown pubic hair, spread-eagled on the bed. Her arms and legs were outstretched in a crucifix position and held in place with white cords. The reason there was no response from her was instantly clear as he stepped closer, feeling a growing spike of unease in his gullet. Part of a face towel protruded either side of duct tape pulled tight across her mouth.

'Oh, my God!' the Housekeeping Manager cried out.

Carlo Diomei hurried over to the bed, his tired brain trying to make sense of what he was looking at and not entirely succeeding. Was this some strange sex game? Was her husband, or boyfriend or whoever, lurking in the bathroom? The woman's eyes looked at him in desperation.

He ran to the bathroom and flung open the door, but it was empty. He'd seen some strange things going on in hotel rooms and had to deal with some weird shit in his time, but for a moment, for the first time in his career to date, he was uncertain what he should do next. Had they interrupted some kinky sex game? Or was something else going on?

The woman looked at him with small, frightened eyes. He felt embarrassed looking down at her nakedness. Overcoming it, he tried to remove the duct tape, but as he gave the first tentative pull the woman's head thrashed violently. Clearly it was hurting her. But he had to get it off, he was certain. Had to speak to her. So he pulled it away from her skin as gently as he could, until he was able to pluck the towel out of her mouth.

Instantly the woman began burbling and sobbing incoherently.

8

Thursday 1 January

It had been a long time, Roy Grace reflected, since he had felt this good on a New Year's Day. For as far back as he could remember, except for the times when he had been on duty, the New Year always began with a blinding headache and the same overwhelming sensation of doom that accompanied his hangovers.

He had drunk even more heavily on those first New Year's Eves since Sandy's disappearance, when their close friends Dick and Leslie Pope would not hear of him being on his own and insisted he join in their celebrations. And, almost as if it was a legacy from Sandy, he had started to intensely dislike the festivity too.

But now, this particular New Year's Eve had been totally different. Last night's had been the most sober – and the most enjoyable – he could remember in his entire life.

For a start, Cleo passionately loved the whole idea of celebrating the New Year. Which made it all the more ironic that she was pregnant and therefore could not really drink very much. But he hadn't minded; he was just happy to be with her, celebrating not just the coming year, but their future together.

And, quietly, he celebrated the fact that his irascible boss, Alison Vosper, would no longer be there to dampen his spirits on an almost daily basis. He looked forward to his first meeting with his new boss, Assistant Chief Constable Peter Rigg, on Monday.

All he had managed to glean about the man so far was that he was a stickler for detail, liked to be hands-on involved and had a short fuse with fools.

To his relief, it had been a quiet morning in the CID HQ at Sussex House, so he'd spent the time steadily working through his paperwork and making brisk progress, while keeping a regular eye on the serials – the log of all reported incidents in the city of Brighton and Hove – on the computer.

As expected, there had been a few incidents in the bars, pubs and clubs, mostly fights and a few handbag thefts. He noted a couple of minor road traffic collisions, a *domestic* – a couple fighting – a complaint about noise from a party, a lost dog, a stolen moped and a naked man reported running down Western Road. But now a serious entry had appeared. It was a reported rape, at Brighton's smart Metropole Hotel, which had popped on to the screen a few minutes ago, at 12.55 p.m.

There were four principal categories of rape: *stranger, acquaintance, date* and *partner*. At this moment there was no mention on the serial of which this might be. New Year's Eve was the kind of time when some men got blind drunk and forced themselves on their dates or partners, and in all likelihood this incident would be in one of those categories. Serious enough, but not something likely to involve Major Crime.

Twenty minutes later he was about to head across the road to the ASDA supermarket, which doubled as the CID HQ canteen, to buy himself a sandwich for lunch, when his internal phone rang.

It was David Alcorn, a detective inspector he knew and liked a lot. Alcorn was based at the city's busy main police station in John Street, where Grace himself had spent much of his early career as a detective, before moving to the CID HQ at Sussex House.

'Happy New Year, Roy,' Alcorn said in his usual blunt, sardonic voice. From the tone of his voice, *happy* had just fallen off a cliff.

'You too, David. Did you have a good night?'

'Yeah. Well, it was all right. Had to keep off the booze a bit to be here for seven this morning. You?'

'Quiet, but nice – thanks.'

'Thought I'd better give you a heads-up, Roy. Looks like we might have a stranger rape at the Metropole.'

He filled him in on the sketchy details. A Uniform Response Team had attended the hotel and called in CID. A Sexual Offences Liaison Officer or SOLO was now on her way over to accompany the victim to the recently opened specialist rape unit, the Sexual Assault Referral Centre or SARC, in Crawley, a post-war town located in the geographical centre of Sussex.

Grace jotted down the details, such as Alcorn could give him, on a notepad. 'Thanks, David,' he said. 'Keep me updated on this. Let me know if you need any help from my team.'

There was a slight pause and he sensed the hesitation in the DI's voice. 'Roy, there's something that could make this a bit politically sensitive.'

'Oh?'

'The victim had been at a do last night at the Metropole. I'm informed that a number of police brass were at a table at this same function.'

'Any names?'

'The Chief Constable and his wife, for starters.'

Shit, Grace thought, but did not say.

'Who else?'

'The Deputy CC. And one assistant chief constable. You get my drift?'

Grace got his drift.

'Maybe I should send someone from Major Crime up to accompany the SOLO. What do you think? As a formality.'

'I think that would be a good plan.'

Grace quickly ran through his options. In particular he was concerned about his new boss. If ACC Peter Rigg was truly a stickler for detail, then he damned well had to start off on the right footing – and to cover himself as best he could.

'OK. Thanks, David. I'll send someone up there right away. In the meantime, can you get me a list of all attendees of that event?'

'That's already in hand.'

'And all the guests staying there, plus all the staff – I would imagine there might have been extra staff drafted in for last night.'

'I'm on to all of that.' Alcorn sounded just slightly miffed, as if Grace was doubting his abilities.

'Of course. Sorry.'

Immediately after he ended the call, he rang DC Emma-Jane Boutwood, one of the few members of his team who was in today. She was also one of the detectives he had tasked with working through the mountains of bureaucracy required by the Crown Prosecution Service for *Operation Neptune*, a large and harrowing human-trafficking investigation he had been running in the weeks before Christmas.

It took her only a few moments to reach him from her desk in the large, open-plan Detectives' Room just beyond his door. He noticed she was limping a little as she came into his office – still not fully recovered from the horrific injuries she had sustained in a pursuit last summer, when she had been crushed against a wall by a van. Despite multiple fractures and losing her spleen, she had insisted on cutting short her advised convalescence period to get back to work as quickly as possible.

'Hi, E-J,' he said. 'Have a seat.'

Grace had just begun to run through the sketchy details David Alcorn had given him and to explain the delicate political situation when his internal phone suddenly rang again.

'Roy Grace,' he answered, raising a finger to E-J to ask her to wait.

'Detective Superintendent Grace,' said a chirpy, friendly voice with a posh, public-school accent. 'How do you do? This is Peter Rigg here.'

Shit, Grace thought again.

'Sir,' he replied. 'Very nice to – er – um – hear from you. I thought you weren't actually starting until Monday, sir.'

'Do you have a problem with that?'

Oh boy, Roy Grace thought, his heart sinking. The New Year was barely twelve hours old and they had their first serious crime. And the new ACC hadn't even officially started and he'd managed to piss him off already.

He was conscious of E-J's eyes on him, and her ears scooping this all up.

'No, sir, absolutely not. This is actually fortuitous timing. It would seem we have our first critical incident of the year. It's too early to tell at this moment, but it has potential for a lot of unwelcome media coverage.'

Grace then signalled to E-J that he needed privacy and she left the room, closing the door.

For the next couple of minutes he ran through what was happening. Fortunately, the new Assistant Chief Constable continued in a friendly vein.

When Grace had finished, Rigg said, 'You're going up there yourself, I take it?'

Roy hesitated. With the highly specialized and skilled team at Crawley, there was no actual need for him to be there at this stage, and his time would be far better employed here in the office, dealing with paperwork and keeping up to speed on the incident via the phone. But he decided that was not what the new ACC wanted to hear.

'Yes, sir. I'm on my way shortly,' he replied.

'Good. Keep me informed.'

Grace assured him he would.

As he hung up, thinking hard, his door opened and the morose face and shaven dome of Detective Sergeant Glenn Branson appeared. His eyes, against his black skin, looked tired and dulled. They reminded Grace of the eyes of fish that had been dead too long, the kind Cleo had told him he should avoid on a fishmonger's slab.

'Yo, old-timer,' Branson said. 'Reckon this year's going to be any less shitty than last?'

'Nope!' Grace said. 'The years never get less shitty. All we can do is try to learn to cope with that fact.'

'Well, you're a sack-load of goodwill this morning,' Branson said, slumping his huge frame down into the chair E-J had just vacated.

Even his brown suit, garish tie and cream shirt looked

tired and rumpled, as if they'd also been on a slab too long, which worried Grace about his friend. Glenn Branson was normally always sharply dressed, but in recent months his marriage breakup had sent him on a downward spiral.

'Wasn't the best year for me last year, was it? Halfway through I got shot and three-quarters of the way through my wife threw me out.'

'Look on the bright side. You didn't die and you got to trash my collection of vinyls.'

'Thanks a bunch.'

'Want to take a drive with me?' Grace asked.

Branson shrugged. 'A drive? Yeah, sure. Where?'

Grace was interrupted by his radio phone ringing. It was David Alcorn calling again to give him an update.

'Something that might be significant, Roy. Apparently some of the victim's clothes are missing. Sounds like the offender might have taken them. In particular her shoes.' He hesitated a moment. 'I seem to remember there was someone doing that a few years back, wasn't there?'

'Yes, but he took just one shoe and the underwear,' Grace replied, his voice quiet all of a sudden. 'What else has been taken?'

'We haven't got much out of her. I understand she's in total shock.'

No surprise there, he thought grimly. His eyes went down to one of the blue boxes on the floor – the one containing the cold-case file on the Shoe Man. He pondered for a moment.

That was twelve years ago. Hopefully it was just a coincidence.

But even as he thought that a wintry gust rippled through his veins.

1997

9

They were moving. Driving somewhere. Rachael Ryan could hear the steady, dull boom of the exhaust and she was breathing in lungfuls of its fumes. She could hear the sound of the tyres sluicing on the wet road. Could feel every bump jarring her through the sacking on which she lay trussed up, arms behind her back, unable to move or speak. All she could see was the top of the back of his baseball cap in the driver's cab up front and his ears sticking out.

She was frozen with cold, with terror. Her mouth and throat were parched and her head ached terribly from when he had hit her. Her whole body hurt. She felt nauseous with disgust – dirty, filthy. She desperately wanted a shower, hot water, soap, shampoo. Wanted to wash herself inside and out.

She felt the van going around a corner. She could see daylight. Grey daylight. Christmas morning. She should be in her flat, opening the stocking her mother had posted to her. Every year of her childhood and still now, at twenty-two, she had a Christmas stocking.

She began crying. She could hear the clunk-clop of windscreen wipers. Suddenly, Elton John's 'Candle in the Wind' began playing loudly and crackly on the radio. She could see the man's head swaying to the music.

Elton John had sung that song at Princess Diana's funeral, with new lyrics. Rachael remembered that day so vividly. She had been one of the hundreds of thousands of mourners outside Westminster Abbey, listening to that song, watching the funeral on one of the huge television screens. She had camped the night on the pavement, and the day before had spent a big part of her week's wages from her job on the help desk in the customer relations department of American Express in Brighton on a bouquet of flowers that she had placed, alongside the thousands of others, in front of Kensington Palace.

She had idolized the Princess. Something had died inside her the day Diana died.

Now a new nightmare had begun.

The van braked sharply to a halt and she slid forward a few inches. She tried again to move her hands and her legs, which were agonizingly cramped. But she could move nothing.

It was Christmas morning and her parents were expecting her for a glass of champagne and then Christmas lunch – followed by the Queen's speech. A tradition, every year, like the stocking.

She tried again to speak, to plead with the man, but her mouth was taped shut. She needed to pee and had already once, some time ago, soiled herself. She could not do that again. There was a ringing sound. Her mobile phone; she recognized the Nokia ringtone. The man turned his head for an instant, then looked to the front again. The van moved forward. Through her blurry eyes and the smeared windscreen she saw a green traffic light pass by. Then she saw buildings on her left that she recognized. Gamley's, the toyshop. They were on Church Road, Hove. Heading west.

Her phone stopped. A short while later she heard a beep-beep, signalling a message.

From whom?

Tracey and Jade?

Or her parents calling to wish her Happy Christmas? Her mother anxious to know if she liked her stocking?

How long before they started to worry about her?

Oh, Christ! Who the hell is this man?

She rolled over to her left as the van made a sharp right turn. Then a left turn. Then another turn. And stopped.

The song stopped. A cheery male voice began talking about where the wonderful Elton John was spending his Christmas.

The man got out, leaving the engine running. The fumes and her fear were making her more and more nauseous. She was desperate for water.

Suddenly he came back into the van. They moved forward, into increasing darkness. Then the engine was switched off and there was a moment of complete silence as the radio went off too. The man disappeared.

There was a metallic clang as the driver's door shut.

Then another metallic clang, cutting out all light.

She lay still, whimpering in fear, in total darkness.

10

Suited and booted and proudly wearing the smart red paisley tie that Sandy had given him yesterday for Christmas, Roy passed on his left the blue door marked *Superintendent* and on his right the one marked *Chief Superintendent*. Roy often wondered whether he'd ever get to make Chief Superintendent.

The whole building felt deserted this Boxing Day morning, apart from a few members of the *Operation Houdini* team in the Incident Room on the top floor. They were still working around the clock to try to catch the serial rapist known as the Shoe Man.

As he waited for the kettle to boil, he thought for a moment about the Chief Superintendent's cap. With its band of silver to distinguish it from the lesser ranks, it was, no question, very covetable. But he wondered if he was smart enough to rise to such a rank – and doubted it.

One thing Roy Grace had learned about Sandy, in their years of marriage, was that she had at times a perfectionist view of how she wanted her particular world to be – and a very short fuse if any aspect failed her expectations. On a number of occasions, her sudden flare of temper at an inept waiter or shop assistant had left him feeling acutely embarrassed. But that spirit in her was part of what had attracted him to her in the first place.

She had all the support and enthusiasm in the world for success, however big or small, but he just had to remember that, for Sandy, failure was never an option.

Which explained, in part, her deep resentment, and occasional outbursts of anger, that, after years of trying almost every fertility treatment possible, she was still unable to conceive the baby they both so desperately wanted.

Humming the words of Eric Clapton's 'Change the World' – which for some reason had popped into his head – Roy Grace carried his mug of coffee down to his desk in the deserted open-plan Detectives' Room on the second floor of Brighton's John Street police station, with its rows of partitioned desks, its manky blue carpet, its crammed pigeonholes and its view to the east of the white walls and gleaming blue windows of the American Express headquarters. Then he logged on to the clunky, slow computer system to check the overnight serials. While he waited for it to load, he took a sip of coffee and fancied a cigarette, silently cursing the ban on smoking in police offices which had recently been introduced.

An attempt had been made, as it was every year, to bring some Christmas cheer into the place. There were paper-chains hanging from the ceiling. Bits of tinsel draped along the tops of the partitions. Christmas cards on several desks.

Sandy was deeply unimpressed that this was the second Christmas in three years that he had found himself on duty. And, as she quite rightly pointed out, it was a lousy week to be working. Even most of the local villains, off their trolleys with drink or off their faces with drugs, were in their homes or their lairs.

Christmas was the peak period for sudden deaths and for suicides. It might be a happy few days for those with friends and families, but it was a desperate, wretched time for the lonely, particularly the elderly lonely ones who didn't even have enough money to heat their homes properly. But it was a quiet period for serious crimes – the kind that could get an ambitious young detective sergeant like himself noticed by his peers and give him the chance to show his abilities.

That was about to change.

Very unusually, the phones had been quiet. Normally they rang all around the room constantly.

As the first serials appeared, his internal phone suddenly rang.

'CID,' he answered.

It was a Force Control Room operator, from the centre which handled and graded all enquiries.

'Hi, Roy. Happy Christmas.'

'You too, Doreen,' he said.

'Got a possible misper,' she said. 'Rachael Ryan, twenty-two, left her friends on Christmas Eve at the cab rank on East Street to walk home. She did not show up for Christmas lunch at her parents and did not answer her home phone or mobile. Her parents visited her flat in Eastern Terrace, Kemp Town, at 3 p.m. yesterday and there was no response. They've informed us this is out of character and they are concerned.'

Grace took down the addresses of Rachael Ryan and her parents and told her he would investigate.

The current police policy was to allow several days for a missing person to turn up before assigning any resources, unless they were a minor, an elderly adult or someone identified as being vulnerable. But with today promising to be quiet, he decided he'd rather be out doing something than sitting here on his backside.

The twenty-nine-year-old Detective Sergeant got up and walked along a few rows of desks to one of his colleagues who was in today, DS Norman Potting. Some fifteen years his senior, Potting was an old sweat, a career detective sergeant who had never been promoted, partly because of his politically incorrect attitude, partly because of his chaotic domestic life, and partly because, like many police officers, including Grace's late father, Potting preferred frontline work rather than taking on the bureaucratic responsibilities that came with promotion. Grace was one of the few here who actually liked the man and enjoyed listening to his 'war stories' – as police tales of past incidents were known – because he felt he could learn something from them; and besides, he felt a little sorry for the guy.

The Detective Sergeant was intently pecking at his keyboard with his right index finger. 'Bloody new technology,' he grumbled in his thick Devon burr as Grace's shadow fell over him. A reek of tobacco smoke rose from the man. 'I've had two lessons, still can't make sodding head nor tail of this. What's wrong with the old system we all know?'

'It's called progress,' Grace said.

'Hrrr. Progress like allowing all sorts into the force?'

Ignoring this, Grace replied, 'There's a reported misper that I'm not very happy about. You busy? Or got time to come with me to make some enquiries?'

Potting hauled himself to his feet. 'Anything to break the mahogany, as my old auntie would say,' he replied. 'Have a good Christmas, Roy?'

'Short and sweet. All six hours of it that I spent at home, that is.'

'At least you *have* a home,' Potting said morosely.

'Oh?'

'I'm living in a bedsit. Threw me out, didn't she? Not much fun, wishing your kids a merry Christmas from a payphone in the corridor. Eating an ASDA Christmas Dinner for One in front of the telly.'

'I'm sorry,' Grace replied. He genuinely was.

'Know why women are like hurricanes, Roy?'

Grace shook his head.

'Because when they arrive they're wet and wild. When they leave they take your house and car.'

Grace humoured him with a thin, wintry smile.

'It's all right for you – you're happily married. Good luck to you. But just watch out,' Potting went on. 'Watch out for when they turn. Trust me, this is my second bloody disaster. Should have learned my lesson first time around. Women think coppers are dead sexy until they marry 'em. Then they realize we're not what they thought. You're lucky if yours is different.'

Grace nodded but said nothing. Potting's words were uncomfortably close to the truth. He had never been interested in opera of any kind. But recently Sandy had dragged him to an amateur operatic society performance of *The Pirates of Penzance*. She had nudged him continually during the song 'A Policeman's Lot is not a Happy One'.

Afterwards she had asked him, teasing, if he thought those words were wrong.

He'd replied that yes, they were wrong. He was very happy with his lot.

Later, in bed, she'd whispered to him that perhaps the lyrics needed to be changed. That they should have sung, 'A policeman's *wife's* lot is not a happy one.'

NOW

11

Several of the houses in the residential street outside the hospital had Christmas lights in the windows and wreaths on the front door. They'd be coming down soon for another year, Grace thought a little sadly, slowing as they approached the entrance to the squat slab of stained concrete and garishly curtained windows of Crawley Hospital. He liked the magical spell that the Christmas break cast on the world, even when he had to work through it.

The building had no doubt looked a lot more impressive under the sunny blue sky of the architect's original impression than it did on a wet January morning. Grace thought that the architect had probably failed to take into account the blinds blocking half of its windows, the dozens of cars parked higgledy-piggledy outside, the plethora of signs and the weather stains on the walls.

Glenn Branson normally liked to terrify him by showing off his driving skills, but today he had allowed his colleague to drive here, freeing him to concentrate on giving Roy the full download on his lousy Christmas week. Glenn's marriage, which had hit new lows in the weeks building up to Christmas, had deteriorated even further on Christmas Day itself.

Already livid that his wife, Ari, had changed the locks on their house, his temper had boiled over on Christmas morning when he'd arrived laden with gifts for his two young children and she'd refused to let him in. A massively powerful former nightclub bouncer, Glenn kicked open the front door, to find, as he suspected, her new lover ensconced in *his* house, playing with *his* children, in front of *his* Christmas tree, for God's sake!

She had dialled the nines and he had narrowly escaped being arrested by the Response Team patrol car that had turned up from East Brighton Division – which would have put paid to his career.

'So what would you have done?' Glenn said.

'Probably the same. But that doesn't make it OK.'

'Yeah.' He was quiet for a moment, then said, 'You're right. But when I saw that dickhead personal trainer playing the X-Box with *my* kids, I could have fucking ripped his head off and played basketball with it.'

'You're going to have to keep a lid on it somehow, matey. I don't want you screwing your career up over this.'

Branson just stared through the windscreen at the rain outside. Then he said bleakly, 'What does it matter? Nothing matters any more.'

Roy Grace loved this guy, this big, well-meaning, kind-hearted man-mountain. He'd first encountered him some years back, when Glenn was a freshly promoted detective constable. He had recognized in him so many aspects of himself – drive, ambition. And Glenn had that key element it took to make a good policeman – high emotional intelligence. Since then, Grace had mentored him. But now, with his disintegrating marriage and his failing control of his temper, Glenn was dangerously close to losing the plot.

He was also dangerously close to damaging their deep

friendship. For the past few months Branson had been his lodger, at his home just off the Hove seafront. Grace did not mind about that, as he was now effectively living with Cleo in her town house in the North Laine district of central Brighton. But he did mind Branson's meddling with his precious record collection and the constant criticism of his taste in music.

Such as now.

In the absence of having his own car – his beloved Alfa Romeo, which had been destroyed in a chase some months earlier and was still the subject of an insurance wrangle – Grace was reduced to using pool cars, which were all small Fords or Hyundai Getzs. He had just mastered an iPod gadget that Cleo had given him for Christmas which played his music through any car's radio system and had been showing off to Branson on the way here.

'Who's this?' Branson asked, in a sudden change of focus as the music changed.

'Laura Marling.'

He listened for a moment. 'She's so derivative.'

'Of whom?'

Branson shrugged.

'I like her,' Grace said defiantly.

They listened in silence for a few moments, until he spotted an empty slot and steered into it. 'You're soft in the head for women vocalists,' Branson said. 'That's your problem.'

'I do actually like her. OK?'

'You're sad.'

'Cleo likes her too,' he retorted. 'She gave me this for Christmas. Want me to tell her you think she's sad?'

Branson raised his huge, smooth hands. 'Whoahhhh!'

'Yeah. Whoahhhh!'

'Respect!' Branson said. But his voice was almost quiet and humourless.

All three spaces reserved for the police were taken, but as today was a public holiday there were plenty of empty spots all around. Grace pulled into one, switched off the ignition and they climbed out of the car. Then they hurried through the rain around the side of the hospital.

'Did you and Ari ever argue over music?'

'Why?' Branson asked.

'Just wondering.'

Most visitors to this complex of buildings would not even have noticed the small white sign with blue lettering saying SATURN CENTRE, pointing along a nondescript pathway bordered by the hospital wall on one side and bushes on the other. It looked as if it might be the route to the dustbins.

In fact it housed Sussex's first Sexual Assault Referral Centre. A dedicated unit, recently opened by the Chief Constable, like others around England it showed a marked change in the way rape victims were treated. Grace could remember a time, not so long ago, when traumatized rape victims had to walk through a police station and frequently be interviewed by cynical male officers. All that had now changed and this centre was the latest development.

Here the victims, who were in a deeply vulnerable state, would be seen by trained same-sex officers and psychologists – professionals who would do their very best to comfort them and put them at their ease, while at the same time having to go through the brutal task of establishing the truth.

One of the hardest things facing Sexual Offences

Liaison Officers was the fact that the victims actually had to be treated as crime scenes themselves, their clothes and their bodies potentially containing vital trace evidence. Time, as in all investigations, was crucial. Many rape victims took days, weeks or even years before they went to the police, and many never reported their attacks ever, not wanting to relive their most tormented experience.

*

Branson and Grace hurried past a black wheelie bin, then a row of traffic cones incongruously stacked there, and reached the door. Grace pressed the bell and moments later the door was opened. They were ushered in, and out of the elements, by a woman staff member he knew, but whose name he had momentarily forgotten.

'Happy New Year, Roy!' she said.

'You too!'

He saw her looking at Glenn and desperately racked his brains for her name. Then it came to him!

'Glenn, this is Brenda Keys – Brenda, this is DS Glenn Branson, one of my colleagues in the Major Crime Branch.'

'Nice to meet you, Detective Sergeant,' she said.

Brenda Keys was a trained interviewer who had processed victims in Brighton and other parts of the county before this facility was established. A kind, intelligent-looking woman with short brown hair and large glasses, she was always dressed quietly and conservatively, as she was today, in her black slacks and a grey V-neck over a blouse.

You could tell you were inside one of the modern generation of interview suites with your eyes shut, Grace thought. They all smelt of new carpets and fresh paint and had a deadened, soundproofed atmosphere.

This one was a labyrinth of rooms behind closed pine doors, with a central reception area carpeted in beige. The cream-painted walls were hung with framed, brightly coloured and artily photographed prints of familiar Sussex scenes – beach huts on the Hove promenade, the Jack and Jill windmills at Clayton, Brighton Pier. It all felt well intentioned, but as if someone had tried just a bit too hard to distance the victims who came here from the horrors they had experienced.

They signed themselves in and Brenda Keys brought them up to speed. As she did so, a door opened along the corridor and a heavily built female uniformed constable with spikes of short black hair rising from her head, as if she had stuck her fingers into an electrical socket, ambled towards them with a genial smile

'Constable Rowland, sir,' she said. 'Detective Super-intendent Grace?'

'Yes – and this is DS Branson.'

'They're in Interview One – only just started. The SOLO, DC Westmore, is talking to the victim and DS Robertson's observing. Would you like to go into the observation room?'

'Is there room for us both?'

'I'll put another chair in. Can I get you anything to drink?

'I'd murder a coffee,' Grace said. 'Muddy, no sugar.'

Branson asked for a Diet Coke.

They followed the constable down the corridor, past doors marked *Medical Examination Room*, *Meeting Room*, then *Interview Room*.

A short distance along she opened another door with

no sign on it and they went in. The observation room was a small space, with a narrow white worktop on which sat a row of computers. A flat-screen monitor was fixed to the wall, displaying the CCTV feed from the adjoining interview room. The Detective Sergeant who had first attended at the Metropole Hotel, a boyish-looking man in his late twenties with a shaven fuzz of fair hair, was seated at the desk, an open notebook in front of him and a bottle of water with the cap removed. He was wearing an ill-fitting grey suit and a purple tie with a massive knot, and he had the clammy pallor of a man fighting a massive hangover.

Grace introduced himself and Glenn, then they sat down, Grace on a hard secretarial swivel chair which the Constable had wheeled in.

The screen gave a static view of a small, windowless room furnished with a blue settee, a blue armchair and a small round table on which sat a large box of Kleenex. It was carpeted in a cheerless dark grey and the walls were painted a cold off-white. A second camera and a microphone were mounted high up.

The victim, a frightened-looking woman in her thirties, in a white towelling dressing gown with the letters MH monogrammed on the chest, sat, hunched up like a ball on the sofa, arms wrapped around her midriff. She was thin, with an attractive but pale face, and streaked mascara. Her long red hair was in a messy tangle.

Across the table from her sat DC Claire Westmore, the Sexual Offences Liaison Officer. She was mirroring the victim, sitting with the same posture, arms wrapped around her midriff too.

The police had learned, over the years, the most effective ways to obtain information from victims and witnesses during interviews. The first principle concerned dress code. Never wear anything that might distract the subject, such as stripes or vivid colours. DC Westmore was dressed appropriately, in a plain blue open-neck shirt beneath a navy V-neck jumper, black trousers and plain black shoes. Her shoulder-length fair hair was swept back from her face and cinched with a band. A simple silver choker was the only jewellery she was wearing.

The second principle was to put the victim or witness in the dominant position, to relax them, which was why the interviewee – Nicola Taylor – was on the sofa, while the DC was on the single chair.

Mirroring was a classic interview technique. If you mirrored everything that the subject did, sometimes it would put them at ease to such an extent that they began to mirror the interviewer. When that happened, the interviewer then had control and the victim would acquiesce, relating to the interviewer – and, in interview parlance, start to *cough*.

Grace jotted down occasional notes as Westmore, in her gentle Scouse accent, slowly and skilfully attempted to coax a response from the traumatized, silent woman. A high percentage of rape victims suffer immediate post-traumatic stress disorder, their agitated state limiting the time they are able to concentrate and focus. Westmore was intelligently making the best of this by following the guidelines to go to the most recent event first and then work backwards.

Over his years as a detective Grace had learned, from numerous interviewing courses he had attended, something that he was fond of telling team members: there is no such thing as a bad witness – only a bad interviewer.

But this DC seemed to know exactly what she was doing.

'I know this must be very difficult for you to talk about, Nicola,' she said. 'But it would help me to understand what's happened and really help in trying to find out who has done this to you. You don't have to tell me today if you don't want to.'

The woman stared ahead in silence, wringing her hands together, shaking.

Grace felt desperately sorry for her.

The SOLO began wringing her hands too. After some moments, she asked, 'You were at a New Year's Eve dinner at the Metropole with some friends, I understand?'

Silence.

Tears were rolling down the woman's cheeks.

'Is there anything at all you can tell me today?'

She shook her head suddenly.

'OK. That's not a problem,' Claire Westmore said. She sat in silence for a short while, then she asked, 'At this dinner, did you have very much to drink?'

The woman shook her head.

'So you weren't drunk?'

'Why do you think I was drunk?' she snapped back suddenly.

The SOLO smiled. 'It's one of those evenings when we all let our guard down a little. I don't drink very much. But New Year's Eve I tend to get wrecked! It's the one time of year!'

Nicola Taylor looked down at her hands. 'Is that what you think?' she said quietly. 'That I was wrecked?'

'I'm here to help you. I'm not making any assumptions, Nicola.'

'I was stone cold sober,' she said bitterly.

'OK.'

Grace was pleased to see the woman reacting. That was a positive sign.

'I'm not judging you, Nicola. I'd just like to know what happened. I honestly do understand how difficult it is to speak about what you have been through and I want to help you in any way I can. I can only do that if I understand exactly what's happened to you.'

A long silence.

Branson drank some of his Coke. Grace sipped his coffee.

'We can end this chat whenever you want, Nicola. If you would rather we leave it until tomorrow, that's fine. Or the next day. Whatever you feel is best. I just want to help you. That's all I care about.'

Another long silence.

Then Nicola Taylor suddenly blurted out the word, 'Shoes!'

'Shoes?'

She fell silent again.

'Do you like shoes, Nicola?' the SOLO probed. When there was no response she said chattily, 'Shoes are my big weakness. I was in New York before Christmas with my husband. I nearly bought some Fendi boots – they cost eight hundred and fifty dollars!'

'Mine were Marc Jacobs,' Nicola Taylor said, almost whispering.

'Marc Jacobs? I love his shoes!' she replied. 'Were they taken with your clothes?'

Another long silence.

Then the woman said, 'He made me do things with them.'

'What kind of things? Try – try to tell me.'

Nicola Taylor started to cry again. Then, in between her sobs, she began talking in graphic detail, but slowly, with long periods of silence in between, as she tried to compose herself, and sometimes just plain let go, waves of nausea making her retch.

As they listened in the observation room, Glenn Branson turned to his colleague and winced.

Grace acknowledged him, feeling very uncomfortable. But as he listened now, he was thinking hard. Thinking back to that cold-case file on his office floor, which he had read through only very recently. Thinking back to 1997. Recalling dates. A pattern. An MO. Thinking about statements given by victims back then, some of which he had re-read not long ago.

That same wintry gust he had felt earlier was rippling through his veins again.

1997

12

'Thermometer says *tonight*!' Sandy said, with that twinkle in her brilliant blue eyes that got to Roy Grace every time.

They were sitting in front of the television. Chevy Chase's *Christmas Vacation* had become a kind of ritual, a movie they traditionally watched every Boxing Day night. The sheer stupidity of the disasters normally made Roy laugh out aloud. But tonight he was silent.

'Hello?' Sandy said. 'Hello, Detective Sergeant! Anyone home?'

He nodded, crushing out his cigarette in the ashtray. 'I'm sorry.'

'You're not thinking about work, are you, my darling? Not tonight. We didn't have a proper Christmas, so let's at least enjoy what's left of Boxing Day. Let's make something special out of it.'

'I know,' Roy said. 'It's just—'

'It's always, *It's just* . . .' she said.

'I'm sorry. I had to deal with a family who didn't have a Christmas or a Boxing Day celebration, OK? Their daughter left her friends early on Christmas morning and never arrived home. Her parents are frantic. I – I have to do what I can for them. For her.'

'So? She's probably busy shagging some bloke she met in a club.'

'No. Not her pattern.'

'Oh, sod it, Detective Sergeant Grace! You told me yourself about the number of people who get reported missing by loved ones every year. Around two hundred and thirty thousand in the UK alone, you said, and most of them turn up within thirty days!'

'And eleven thousand, five hundred don't.'

'So?'

'I have a feeling about this one.'

'Copper's nose?'

'Uh-huh.'

Sandy stroked his nose. 'I love yours, Copper!' She kissed it. 'We have to make love tonight. I checked my temperature and it seems like I might be ovulating.'

Roy Grace grinned and stared into her eyes. When colleagues, off duty, got wrecked in the bar upstairs at Brighton nick or out in pubs, and talk turned, as it always did among men, to football – something in which he had little interest – or to birds, the girls got divided fifty-fifty into those that blokes fancied because of their tits and those that blokes fancied because of their legs. But Roy Grace could honestly say that the first thing he had fancied about Sandy was her mesmerizing blue eyes.

He remembered the first time they met. It was a few days after Easter and his father had just been diagnosed with terminal bowel cancer. His mother had just been diagnosed with secondaries from breast cancer. He was a probationary police officer and feeling about as low as it was possible to feel. Some colleagues had encouraged him to join them for an evening at the dogs.

With little enthusiasm he'd turned up to the Brighton and Hove greyhound stadium and found himself seated across from a beautiful, bubbly young woman whose name he failed to clock. After some minutes busily chatting to a guy sitting beside her, she had leaned across the table to Grace and said, 'I've been given a tip! Always bet on any dog that does its business before it races!'

'You mean watch and see if it has a crap?'

'Very sharp,' she'd said. 'You must be a detective!'

'No,' he'd replied, 'not yet. But I'd like to be one day.'

So, while eating his prawn cocktail, he'd carefully watched the dogs for the first race being paraded out towards the starting gate. No. 5 had stopped for a serious dump. When the woman from the Tote had come round, the girl had bet a fiver on it and, to show off, he'd bet a tenner on it that he could ill afford to lose. The dog had romped home last by about twelve lengths.

On their first date, three nights later, he had kissed her in the darkness to the sound of the echoing roar of the sea beneath Brighton's Palace Pier. 'You owe me a tenner,' he'd then said.

'I think I got a bargain!' she replied, fumbling in her handbag, pulling out a banknote and dropping it down the inside of his shirt.

*

He looked at Sandy now, in front of the television. She was even more beautiful than when they had first met. He loved her face, the smells of her body and of her hair; he loved her humour, her intelligence. And he loved the way she took all life in her stride. Sure, she had been angry that he'd been on duty over Christmas, but she understood because she wanted him to succeed.

That was his dream. Their dream.

Then the phone rang.

Sandy answered it, said coldly, 'Yes he is,' and handed the receiver to Roy.

He listened, jotted down an address on the back of a Christmas card, then said, 'I'll be there in ten minutes.'

Sandy glared at him and shook a cigarette out of the packet. Chevy Chase continued his antics on the screen.

'It's *Boxing Night*, for Christ's sake!' she said, reaching for the lighter. 'You don't make it easy for me to quit, do you?'

'I'll be back as quickly as I can. I have to go and see this witness – a man who claims he saw a man pushing a woman into a van in the early hours.'

'Why can't you see him tomorrow?' she demanded petulantly.

'Because this girl's life may be at risk, OK?'

She gave him a wry smile. 'Off you go, Detective Sergeant Grace. Go and save the sodding world.'

NOW

13

'You seem very distracted tonight. Are you OK, my love?' Cleo said.

Roy Grace was sitting on one of the huge red sofas in the living room of her town house in a converted warehouse development, and Humphrey, getting larger and heavier by the day, was sitting on him. The black puppy, nestled comfortably in his lap, was pulling surreptitiously at the strands of wool of his baggy jumper as if his game plan was to unravel it entirely before his master noticed. The plan was working, because Roy was so engrossed in the pages of case-file notes on *Operation Houdini* he was reading that he had not noticed what the dog was doing.

The first reported sexual assault in *Operation Houdini* had been on 15 October 1997. It was a botched attack on a young woman late one evening in a twitten – a narrow alleyway – in the North Laine district of Brighton. A man walking his dog had come to her rescue before her assailant had removed her panties, but he had run off with one of her shoes. The next was, unfortunately, more successful. A woman who had attended a Halloween ball at the Grand Hotel at the end of the month had been seized in the corridor of the hotel by a man dressed as a woman and was not found by hotel staff until the morning, bound and gagged.

Cleo, curled up on the sofa opposite him, wrapped in a camel poncho over woollen black leggings, was reading a tome on the ancient Greeks for her Open University philosophy degree studies. Pages of her typed and hand-written notes, all plastered with yellow Post-its, were spread out around her. Her long blonde hair tumbled across her face and every few minutes she would sweep it back with her hand. Grace always loved watching her do that.

A Ruarri Joseph CD was playing on the hi-fi and on the muted television screen Sean Connery, in *Thunderball*, held a beautiful woman in an urgent clinch. During the past week, since Christmas, Cleo had developed a craving for king prawn kormas and they were waiting for the delivery of tonight's meal – their fourth curry in five days. Grace didn't mind, but tonight he was giving his system a rest with some plain tandoori chicken.

Also on the table sat one of Grace's Christmas presents to Cleo, a big new goldfish bowl, replacing the one that had been smashed by an intruder the previous year. Its incumbent, which she had named Fish-2, was busily exploring its environment of weed and a miniature submerged Greek temple in sharp, nervy darts. Next to it was a stack of three books that had been Glenn Branson's Christmas present to him. *Bloke's 100 Top Tips for Surviving Pregnancy*, *The Expectant Father* and *You're Pregnant Too, Mate!*

'Yup, I'm fine,' he said, looking up with a smile.

Cleo smiled back and he felt a sudden rush of such intense happiness and serenity that he wished he could just stop the clock now and freeze time. Make this moment last forever.

'And I'd rather share your company,' Ruarri Joseph was singing to his acoustic guitar, and yes, Grace thought,

I'd rather share your company, my darling Cleo, than anyone else's on this planet.

He wanted to stay here, on this sofa, in this room, staring longingly at this woman he loved so deeply, who was carrying their child, and never, ever leave it.

'It's New Year's Day,' Cleo said, raising her glass of water and taking a tiny sip. 'I think you should stop working now and relax! We'll all be back in the fray on Monday.'

'Right, like the example you're setting, working on your degree. Is that relaxing?'

'Yes, it is! I love doing this. It's not work for me. What you're doing *is* work.'

'Someone should tell criminals they're not permitted to offend during public holidays,' he said with a grin.

'Yep, and someone should tell old people they shouldn't die over the Christmas break. It's very antisocial! Morticians are entitled to holidays too!'

'How many today?'

'Five,' she said. 'Poor sods. Well, actually three of them were yesterday.'

'So they had the decency to wait for Christmas.'

'But couldn't face the prospect of another year.'

'I hope I never get like that,' he said. 'To the point where I can't face the prospect of another year.'

'Did you ever read Ernest Hemingway?' she asked.

Grace shook his head, acutely aware of how ignorant he was compared to Cleo. He'd read so little in his life.

'He's one of my favourite writers. I'm going to make you read him one day! He wrote, "The world breaks everyone and afterward many are strong at the broken places." That's you. You're stronger, aren't you?'

'I hope so – but I sometimes wonder.'

'You have to be stronger than ever now, Detective Superintendent.' She patted her stomach. 'There are two of us who need you.'

'And all the dead people who need you!' he retorted.

'And the dead who need you too.'

That was true, he thought ruefully, glancing at the file again. All those blue boxes and green crates on his office floor. Most of them representing victims who were waiting from beyond the grave for him to bring their assailants to justice.

Would today's rape victim, Nicola Taylor, get to see the man who did this brought to justice? Or would she end up one day as just a name on a plastic tag on one of those cold-case files?

'I'm reading about a Greek statesman called Pericles,' she said. 'He wasn't really a philosopher, but he said something very true. "What you leave behind is not what is engraved in stone monuments, but what is woven into the lives of others." That's one of the many reasons I love you, Detective Superintendent Grace. You're going to leave good things woven into the lives of others.'

'I try,' he said, and looked back down at the files on the Shoe Man.

'You poor love, your mind really is somewhere else tonight.'

He shrugged. 'I'm sorry. I hate rapists. It was pretty harrowing today up in Crawley.'

'You haven't really talked about it.'

'Do you want to hear about it?'

'Yes, I do. I really do want to hear about it. I want to know everything you learn about the world that our child is going to be born into. What did this man do to her?'

Grace picked up his bottle of Peroni from the floor,

took a long pull on it, draining it, and could have done with another. But instead he put it down and thought back to this morning.

'He made her masturbate with the heel of her shoe. It was some expensive designer shoe. Marc Joseph or something.'

'Marc Jacobs?' she asked.

He nodded. 'Yes. That was the name. Are they expensive?'

'One of the top designers. He made her masturbate? You mean using the heel like a dildo?'

'Yes. So, do you know much about shoes?' he asked, a little surprised.

He loved the way Cleo dressed, but when they were out together she rarely looked in shoe-shop or fashion-shop windows. Whereas Sandy used to all the time, sometimes driving him to distraction.

'Roy, darling, *all* women *know* about shoes! They're part of a woman's femininity. When a woman puts on a great pair of shoes, she feels sexy! So, he just watched her doing this to herself?'

'Six-inch stilettos, she said,' he replied. 'He made her push the heel all the way in repeatedly, while he touched himself.'

'That's horrible. Sick bastard.'

'It gets worse.'

'Tell me.'

'He made her turn over, face down, then he pushed the heel right up her back passage. OK? Enough?'

'So he didn't actually rape her? In the sense that I understand it?'

'Yes, he did, but that was later. And he had problems getting an erection.'

After some moments' silent thought she said, 'Why, Roy? What makes someone like that?'

He shrugged. 'I talked to a psychologist this afternoon. But he didn't tell me anything I didn't already know. Stranger rape – which this one looks like – is rarely about sex. It's more about hatred of women and power over them.'

'Do you think there's a connection between whoever did this and your file on the Shoe Man?'

'That's why I'm reading it. Could be coincidence. Or a copycat. Or the original rapist reoffending.'

'So what do you think?'

'The Shoe Man did the same things to some of his victims. He also had problems getting an erection. And he always took one of his victim's shoes.'

'This woman today – did he take one of her shoes?'

'He took both, and all her clothes. And from what the victim has said so far, it sounds like he might be a transvestite.'

'So there's a slight difference.'

'Yes.'

'What's your instinct? What does your copper's nose tell you?'

'Not to jump to conclusions. But . . .' He fell silent.

'But?'

He stared at the file.

14

Saturday 3 January

Ask people to recall where they were and what they were doing at the moment – *the exact moment* – they heard about the planes striking the Twin Towers on 9/11, or about Princess Diana's death, or that John Lennon had been shot or, if they are old enough, that John F. Kennedy had been assassinated in Dallas, Texas, and most will be able to tell you, with crystal clarity.

Roxy Pearce was different. The defining moments in her life came on those days when she finally bought the shoes that she had been lusting after. She could tell you exactly what was happening in the world on the day she acquired her first Christian Louboutins. Her first Ferragamos. Her first Manolo Blahniks.

But today, all those gleaming leather treasures languishing in her cupboards paled into insignificance as she strutted around the grey-carpeted floor of Brighton's Ritzy Shoes emporium.

'Oh yes! Oh, God, yes!'

She looked at her ankles. Pale, slightly blue from the veins beneath the surface, they were too thin and bony. Never before her best feature, today they were transformed. They were, she had to admit, one pair of drop-dead-beautiful ankles. The thin black straps wrapped themselves like sensuous, living, passionate fronds around the white skin either side of the protruding bone.

She was sex on legs!

She stared in the mirror. Sex on legs stared back at her! Sleek black hair, a great figure, she definitely looked a lot younger than a woman three months short of her thirty-seventh birthday.

'What do you think?' she said to the assistant, staring at her reflection again. At the tall stilettos, the curved sole, the magical black gloss of the leather.

'They were made for you!' the confident thirty-year-old salesgirl said. 'They were just absolutely made for you!'

'I think so!' Roxy squealed. 'You think so too?'

She was so excited that several people in the shop glanced round at her. Brighton was busy this first Saturday morning of the new year. The bargain hunters were out in force as the Christmas sales headed into their second week and some prices came down even more.

One customer in the shop did not glance round. Anyone looking would have seen an elegantly dressed middle-aged woman with a long dark coat over a high roll-neck jumper and expensive-looking high-heeled boots. Only if they peeled back the top of the roll-neck would they have spotted the giveaway Adam's apple.

The man in drag did not glance round, because he was already looking at Roxy. He had been observing her discreetly from the moment she'd asked to try on those shoes.

'Jimmy Choo just has it!' the assistant said. 'He really knows what works.'

'And you really do think these look good on me? They're not very easy to walk in.'

Roxy was nervous. Well, £485 was a lot of money, particularly at the moment, when her husband's software solutions business was in near meltdown and her own small PR agency was barely washing its face.

But she had to have them!

OK, £485 could buy an awful lot of things.

But none would give her the pleasure of these shoes!

She wanted to show them off to her friends. But more than anything she wanted to wear them for Iannis, her crazily sexy lover of just six weeks. OK, not the first lover she'd had in twelve years of marriage, but the best, oh yes. Oh yes!

Just thinking about him brought a big grin to her face. Then a twist of pain in her heart. She had been through it all twice before and knew she should have learned from experience. Christmas was the worst time for lovers having an affair. It was when workplaces shut down and most people got drawn into family stuff. Although they had no kids of their own – neither she nor Dermot had ever wanted any – she'd been forced to accompany her husband to his family in Londonderry for four whole days over Christmas, and then another four, following straight on, with her parents – *the ageing Ps*, as Dermot called them – in the remote wilds of Norfolk.

On the one day they had planned to meet, before the end of the year, Iannis, who owned two Greek restaurants in Brighton and a couple more in Worthing and East-bourne, had had to fly unexpectedly to Athens to visit his father, who'd had a heart attack.

This afternoon they were going to be seeing each other for the first time since the day before Christmas Eve – and it felt more like a month. Two months. A year. Forever! She longed for him. Yearned for him. Craved him.

And, she had now decided, she wanted to wear these shoes for him!

Iannis was into feet. He loved to take off her shoes, breathe in their scents, smell them all over, then inhale, as if he was tasting a fine wine in front of a proud sommelier. Maybe he'd like her to keep her Jimmy Choos on today! The thought was turning her on so much she was feeling dangerously moist.

'You know the great thing with these shoes is you can dress up or down with them,' the assistant continued. 'They look terrific with your jeans.'

'You think so?'

It was a stupid question. Of *course* the assistant thought so. She was going to say they looked good on her if she came in wrapped in a bin liner full of sardine heads.

Roxy was wearing these leg-hugging, ripped DKNYs because Iannis said she had a great arse in jeans. He liked to unzip them and pull them slowly down, telling her in that rich, deep accent of his that it was like unpeeling beautiful ripe fruit. She liked all the romantic tosh he spoke. Dermot never did anything sexy these days. His idea of foreplay was to walk across the bedroom in his socks and Y-fronts and fart twice.

'I do!' the assistant said earnestly.

'I don't suppose there's any discount on these? Not part of the sale or anything?'

'I'm afraid not, no. I'm sorry. They are new stock, only just in.'

'That's my luck!'

'Would you like to see the handbag that goes with them?'

'I'd better not,' she said. 'I daren't.'

But the assistant showed it to her anyway. And it was

gorgeous. Roxy rapidly reached the conclusion that, having seen the two together, the shoes now looked quite naked without the bag. If she didn't buy that bag, she would regret it later, she knew.

Because the shop was so busy, and because her thoughts were totally on how she could keep the receipt concealed from Dermot, she took no notice at all of any of the other customers, including the one in the roll-neck jumper, who was examining a pair of shoes a short distance behind her. Roxy was thinking she'd have to grab her credit card statement when it came in and burn it. And anyway, it was her own money, wasn't it?

'Are you on our mailing list, madam?' the assistant asked.

'Yes.'

'If you could let me have your postcode I'll bring your details up.'

She gave it to the assistant, who tapped it into the computer beside the till.

Behind Roxy, the man jotted something down quickly on a small electronic notepad. Moments later her address appeared. But the man didn't need to read the screen.

'Mrs Pearce, 76 Droveway Avenue?'

'That's right,' Roxy said.

'Right. That's a total of one thousand, one hundred and twenty-three pounds. How would you like to pay?'

Roxy handed over her credit card.

The man in drag slipped out of the shop, swinging his hips. He actually had developed, with much practice, quite a sexy walk, he thought. He was absorbed into the teeming mass of shoppers in the Brighton Lanes within moments, his heels clicking on the dry, cold pavement.

15

It was always quiet in these anticlimactic days following New Year's Eve. It was the end of the holidays, people were back to work, and more broke this year than usual. It was hardly surprising, thought PC Ian Upperton of the Brighton and Hove Road Policing Unit, that there weren't many people out and about on this freezing January Saturday afternoon, despite the sales being in full swing.

His colleague, PC Tony Omotoso, was behind the wheel of the BMW estate, heading south in the falling darkness, past Rottingdean pond and then on down towards the seafront, where he turned right at the lights. The south-westerly wind, straight off the Channel, buffeted the car. It was 4.30 p.m. One final cruise along above the cliffs, past St Dunstan's home for blind servicemen and Roedean school for posh girls, then along the seafront and back up to their base for a cup of tea, and wait there on the radio for the remainder of their shift.

There were some days, Upperton felt, when you could almost feel electricity in the air and you knew things were going to happen. But he felt nothing this afternoon. He looked forward to getting home, seeing his wife and kids, taking the dogs for a walk, then a quiet evening in front of the telly. And to the next three days, which he had off.

As they drove up the hill, where the 30-mph limit

gave way to a 50-mph one, a little Mazda MX-2 sports car roared past them in the outside lane, way too fast.

'Is the driver effing blind?' Tony Omotoso said.

Drivers usually braked when they saw a police patrol car, and not many dared to pass a police car, even when it was being driven at several miles per hour under the limit. The Mazda driver had either stolen it, was a head-case or had simply not seen them. It was pretty hard not to see them, even in the gloom, with the luminous Battenberg markings and POLICE in high-visibility lettering covering every panel of the car.

The tail lights were rapidly pulling away into the distance.

Omotoso floored the accelerator. Upperton leaned forward, switched on the flashing lights, siren and onboard speed camera, then tugged on his shoulder strap, to take the slack out of it. His colleague's pursuit-driving always made him nervous.

They caught up with the Mazda rapidly, clocking it at 75 mph before it slowed going down the dip towards the roundabout. Then, to their astonishment, it accelerated away again, hard, as it left the roundabout. The ANPR fixed to the dashboard, which automatically read all number plates in front of it and fed the information into the government-licensing computer, remained silent, indicating that the car had not been reported stolen and that its paperwork was in order.

This time the speed camera dial showed 81 mph.

'Time for a chat,' said Upperton.

Omotoso accelerated directly behind the Mazda, flashing his headlights. This was a moment when they always wondered whether a car would try to do a runner, or be sensible and stop.

Brake lights came on sharply. The left-hand indicator began winking, then the car pulled over. From the silhouette they could see through the rear window, there appeared to be just one occupant, a female driver. She was looking over her shoulder anxiously at them.

Upperton switched the siren off, left the blue lights flashing and switched on the emergency red hazard flashers. Then he got out of the car and, pushing against the wind, walked around to the driver's door, keeping a wary eye out for cars coming along the road behind them.

The woman wound down the window part-way and peered out at him nervously. She was in her early forties, he guessed, with a mass of frizzed hair around a rather severe, but not unattractive, face. Her lipstick seemed to have been put on clumsily and her mascara had run, as if she had been crying.

'I'm sorry, Officer,' she said, her voice sounding edgy and slurred. 'I think I might have been going a bit fast.'

Upperton knelt to get as close to her face as possible, in order to smell her breath. But he didn't need to. If he'd lit a match at this moment, flames would have probably shot out of her mouth. There was also a strong smell of cigarette smoke in the car.

'Got bad eyesight, have you, madam?'

'No – er – no. I had my eyes tested quite recently. My vision's near perfect.'

'So you always overtake police cars at high speed, do you?'

'Oh, bugger, did I? I didn't see you! I'm sorry. I've just had a row with my ex-husband – we've got a business together, you see. And I—'

'Have you been drinking, madam?'

'Just a glass of wine – at lunchtime. Just one small glass.'

It smelt more like she'd drunk an entire bottle of brandy to him.

'Could you switch your engine off, madam, and step out of the car. I'm going to ask you to take a breath test.'

'You're not going to book me, are you, Officer?' She slurred even more than before now. 'You see – I need the car for my business. I've already got some points on my licence.'

No surprise there, he thought.

She unclipped her seat belt, then clambered out. Upperton had to put his arm out to stop her staggering further into the road. It was unnecessary to get her to blow into the machine, he thought. All he needed to do was hold it within a twenty-yard radius and the reading would go off the scale.

1979

16

'Johnny!' his mother bellowed from her bedroom. 'Shut up! Shut that noise up! Do you hear me?'

Standing on the chair in his bedroom, he removed another of the nails clenched between his lips, held it against the wall and struck it with his claw hammer. *Blam! Blam! Blam!*

'JOHNNY, BLOODY WELL STOP THAT NOISE! NOW! STOP IT!' She was screaming now.

Lying neatly on the floor, exactly the same distance apart, were each of his prized collection of high-flush lavatory chains. All fifteen of them. He'd found them in skips around Brighton – well, all except two, which he had stolen from toilets.

He took another nail from his mouth. Lined it up. Began hammering.

His mother ran into the room, reeking of Shalimar perfume. She wore a black silk camisole, fish-net stockings with suspenders not yet fastened, harsh make-up and a wig of blonde ringlets that was slightly askew. She was standing on one black stiletto-heeled shoe and holding the other in her hand, raised, like a weapon.

'DO YOU HEAR ME?'

Ignoring her, he began hammering.

'ARE YOU BLEEDIN' DEAF? JOHNNY?'

'I'm not Johnny,' he mumbled through the nails, continuing to hammer. 'I am *Yac*. I have to hang my chains up.'

Holding the shoe by the toe, she slammed the stiletto into his thigh. With a yelp like a whipped dog, he fell sideways and crashed to the floor. Instantly she was kneeling over him, raining down blows on him with the sharp tip of the heel.

'You are not Yac, you are Johnny! Understand? Johnny Kerridge.'

She hit him again, then again. And again.

'I am Yac! The doctor said so!'

'You stupid boy! You've driven your father away and now you're driving me crazy. The doctor did not say so!'

'The doctor wrote Yac!'

'The doctor wrote *YAC – Young Autistic Child* – on his sodding notes! That's what you are. Young, *useless*, sodding pathetic autistic child! You are Johnny Kerridge. Got it?'

'I am Yac!'

He curled himself up in a protective ball as she brandished the shoe. His cheek was bleeding from where she had struck him. He breathed in her dense, heady perfume. She had a big bottle on her dressing table and she once told him it was the classiest perfume a woman could wear, and that he should appreciate he had such a high-class mother. But she wasn't being classy now.

Just as she was about to strike him again the front doorbell rang.

'Oh shit!' she said. 'See what you've done? You've made me late, you stupid child!' She hit him again on the thigh, so hard it punctured his thin denim trousers. 'Shit, shit, shit!'

She ran out of the room, shouting, 'Go and let him in. Make him wait downstairs!'

She slammed her bedroom door.

Yac picked himself up, painfully, from the floor and limped out of his room. He walked slowly, deliberately, unhurriedly down the staircase of their terraced two-up, two-down on the edge of the Whitehawk housing estate. As he reached the bottom step, the doorbell rang again.

His mother shouted, 'Open the door! Let him in! I don't want him going away. We need it!'

With blood running down his face, seeping through his T-shirt in several places and through his trousers, Yac grumpily limped up to the front door and reluctantly pulled it open.

A plump, perspiring man in an ill-fitting grey suit stood there, looking awkward. Yac stared at him. The man stared back and his face reddened. Yac recognized him. He'd been here before, several times.

He turned and shouted back up the stairs, 'Mum! It's that smelly man you don't like who's come to fuck you!'

1997

17

Rachael was shivering. A deep, dark terror swirled inside her. She was so cold it was hard to think. Her mouth was parched and she was starving. Desperate for water and for food. She had no idea what the time was: it was pitch black in here, so she could not see her watch, could not tell whether it was night or day outside.

Had he left her here to die or was he coming back? She had to get away. Somehow.

She strained her ears for traffic noise that might give her a clue as to whether it was day or night, or for the caw of a gull that might tell her if she was still near the sea. But all she could hear was the occasional, very faint wail of a siren. Each time her hopes rose. Were the police out looking for her?

They were, weren't they?

Surely her parents would have reported her missing? They would have told the police that she hadn't turned up for Christmas lunch. They'd be worried. She knew them, knew they would have gone to her flat to find her. She wasn't even sure what day it was now. Boxing Day? The day after?

Her shivering was getting worse, the cold seeping deep inside her bones. It was all right, though, she thought, so long as she was shivering. Four years ago, when she had left school, she'd worked for a season as a washer-upper in a ski resort in France. A Japanese skier had taken the last chairlift up one afternoon in a snow-storm. There was a mistake by the lift attendants, who thought the last person had already gone up and been counted at the top, so they turned the lift off. In the morning, when they switched it back on, he arrived at the top, covered in ice, dead, stark naked, with a big smile on his face.

No one could understand why he was naked or smiling. Then a local ski instructor she'd had a brief fling with explained to her that during the last stages of hypo-thermia people hallucinated that they were too hot and would start removing their clothes.

She knew that somehow she had to keep warm, had to ward off hypothermia. So she did the only movements she could, rolling, left and then right on the hessian matting. Rolling. Rolling. Totally disoriented by the dark-ness, there were moments when she lay on her side and toppled on to her face and others when she fell on to her back.

She had to get out. Somehow. Had to. How? Oh, God, how?

She couldn't move her hands or her feet. She couldn't shout. Her naked body was covered in goose pimples so sharp they felt like millions of needle points piercing her flesh.

Oh, please God, help me.

She rolled again and crashed into the side of the van. Something fell over with a loud, echoing clangggggg.

Then she heard a gurgling noise.

Smelt something foul, rancid. Diesel oil, she realized. Gurgling. Glug . . . glug . . . glug.

She rolled again. And again. Then her face pressed into it, the sticky, stinking stuff, stinging her eyes, making her cry even more.

But, she figured, it must be coming from a can!

If it was pouring out, then the top had come off. The neck of the can would be round and thin! She rolled again and something moved through the stinking wet slimy stuff, clattering, scraping.

Clatter . . . clatter . . . clangggg.

She trapped it against the side of the van. Wriggled around it, felt it move, made it turn, forced it to turn until it was square on, spout outwards. Then she pressed against the sharpness of the neck. Felt its rough edge cutting into her. She wormed her body against it, jigging, slowly, forcefully, then felt it spin away from her.

Don't do this to me!

She wriggled and twisted until the can moved again, until she felt the rough neck of the spout again, then she pressed against it, gently at first, then applying more pressure, until she had it wedged firmly. Now she moved slowly, rubbing right, left, right, left, for an eternity at whatever was binding her wrists. Suddenly, the grip around them slackened, just a fraction.

But enough to give her hope.

She kept on rubbing, twisting, rubbing. Breathing in and out through her nose. Breathing in the noxious, dizzying stink of the diesel oil. Her face, her hair, her whole body soaked in the stuff.

The grip on her wrists slackened a tiny bit further.

Then she heard a sudden loud metallic clang and she froze. *No, please no.* It sounded like the garage door opening. She rolled on to her back and held her breath. Moments later she heard the rear doors of the van opening. A flashlight beam suddenly blinded her. She blinked into it. Felt his stare. Lay in frozen terror wondering what he was going to do.

He just seemed to be standing in silence. She heard heavy breathing. Not her own. She tried to cry out, but no sound came.

Then the light went out.

She heard the van doors clang shut. Another loud clang, like the garage door closing.

Then silence.

She listened, unsure whether he was still in here. She listened for a long time before she began to rub against the neck once more. She could feel it cutting into her flesh, but she didn't care. Each time she rubbed now, she was certain the bonds holding her wrists were slackening more and more.

NOW

18

Garry Starling and his wife, Denise, had gone to the China Garden restaurant most Saturday nights for the past twelve years. They favoured the table just up the steps, to the right of the main part of the restaurant, the table where Garry had proposed to Denise almost twelve years ago.

Separated from the rest of the room by a railing, it had a degree of privacy, and with Denise's increasingly heavy drinking, they could sit here without the rest of the diners being privy to her frequent tirades – mostly against him.

She was usually drunk before they had even left home, particularly since the smoking ban, when she would quaff the best part of a bottle of white wine and smoke several cigarettes, despite his nagging her for years to quit, before tottering out to the waiting taxi. Then, at the restaurant, Denise would polish off one and often two Cosmopolitans in the bar area before they got to their table.

At which point she usually kicked off and began complaining about defects she perceived in her husband. Sometimes the same old ones, sometimes new ones. It was water off a duck's back to Garry, who remained placid and unemotional, which usually wound her up even more. He was a control freak, she told her girlfriends. As well as being a sodding fitness freak.

The couple they normally came here with, Maurice and Ulla Stein, were heavy drinkers too and, long used to Denise's tirades, they tended to humour her. Besides, there were plenty of undercurrents in their own relationship.

Tonight, the first Saturday of the New Year, Denise, Maurice and Ulla were in particularly heavy drinking mode. Their hangovers from New Year's Eve, which they had celebrated together at the Metropole Hotel, were now distant memories. But they were also a little tired and Denise was in an uncharacteristically subdued mood. She was even drinking a little water – which, normally, she rarely touched.

The third bottle of Sauvignon Blanc had just been poured. As she picked her glass up, Denise watched Garry, who had stepped out to take a phone call, walking back towards them and slipping his phone into his top pocket.

He had a slight frame and a sly, studious face topped with short, tidy black hair that was thinning and turning grey. His big, round, staring eyes, set beneath arched eyebrows, had earned him the nickname *Owl* at school. Now, in middle age, wearing small, rimless glasses, a neat suit over a neat shirt and sober tie, he had the air of a scientist quietly observing the world in front of him with a look of quizzical disdain, as if it was an experiment he had created in his laboratory with which he was not entirely happy.

In contrast to her husband, Denise, who had been a slender blonde with an hourglass figure when they had first met, had ballooned recently. She was still blonde, thanks to her colourist, but years of heavy drinking had taken their toll. With her clothes off, in Garry's opinion – which he had never actually voiced to her because he was too reserved – she had the body of a flabby pig.

'Lizzie – my sister,' Garry announced apologetically, sitting down again. 'She's been at the police station for the last few hours – she's been done for drink-driving. I was just checking that she's seen a solicitor and that she's getting a lift home.'

'Lizzie? Stupid woman, what's she gone and done that for?' said Denise.

'Oh, sure,' Garry said. 'She did it deliberately, right? Give her a break, for God's sake! She's been through the marriage from hell and now she's going through the divorce from hell from that bastard.'

'Poor thing,' said Ulla.

'She's still way over the limit. They won't let her drive home. I wonder if I should go and—'

'Don't you dare!' Denise said. 'You've been drinking too.'

'You have to be so damned careful, drinking and driving now,' Maurice slurred. 'I just won't do it. I'm afraid I don't have much sympathy with people who get caught.' Then, seeing his friend's darkening expression, he said, 'Of course, except for Lizzie.' He smiled awkwardly.

Maurice had made gazillions out of building sheltered homes for the aged. His Swedish wife, Ulla, had become heavily involved in animal rights in recent years and not long ago had led a blockade of Shoreham Harbour – Brighton's main harbour – to stop what she considered to be the inhumane way that sheep were exported. Garry had noticed, particularly in the past couple of years, that the two of them had less and less in common.

Garry had been Maurice's best man. He'd secretly lusted after Ulla in those days. She had been the classic flaxen-haired, leggy Swedish blonde. In fact he'd continued to lust after her until quite recently, when she had begun to let her looks go. She too had put on weight, and had taken to dressing like an Earth Mother, in shapeless smocks, sandals and hippy jewellery. Her hair was wild and she seemed to apply make-up as if it was warpaint.

'Do you know about the Coolidge effect?' Garry said.

'What's that?' Maurice asked.

'When Calvin Coolidge was president of the United States he and his wife were being taken around a chicken farm. The farmer got embarrassed when a rooster began shagging a hen right in front of Mrs Coolidge. When he apologized the President's wife asked him how many times a day the rooster did this and the farmer replied that it was dozens. She turned to him and whispered, "Would you mind telling my husband?"'

Garry paused while Maurice and Ulla laughed. Denise, who had heard it before, remained stony-faced.

He continued, 'Then a little later Coolidge asked the farmer more about the rooster. "Tell me, does it always screw the same hen?" The farmer replied, "No, Mr President, always a different one." Coolidge whispered to the man, "Would you mind telling my wife?"'

Maurice and Ulla were still laughing when crispy duck and pancakes arrived.

'I like that one!' Maurice said, then winced as Ulla kicked him under the table.

'A bit close to home for you,' she said acidly.

Maurice had confided to Garry, over the years, about a string off affairs. Ulla had found out about more than one of them.

'At least the rooster has proper sex,' Denise said to her husband. 'Not the weird stuff you get off on.'

Garry's mask smiled implacably at her, humouring her. They sat in awkward silence as the pancakes and spring onions and hoisin sauce appeared, and while the waiter shredded the duck before retreating.

Helping himself to a pancake and rapidly changing the subject, Maurice asked, 'So, how's business looking going into the New Year, Garry? Think people are going to cut down?'

'How would he know?' Denise butted in. 'He's always on the sodding golf course.'

'Of course I am, my darling!' Garry retorted. 'That's where I get my new leads. That's how I built my business. I got the police as customers through playing golf with an officer one day.'

Garry Starling had started in life as an electrician, working for Chubb Alarms, doing installations. Then he had left and taken the gamble of forming his own company, operating at first from a tiny office in central Brighton. His timing had been perfect, as it was just when the security business began to boom.

It was a winning formula. He used his membership of his golf club, of the Round Table and then the Rotary Club to work on everyone he met. Within a few years of opening his doors, he had built up Sussex Security Systems and its sister company, Sussex Remote Monitoring Services, into one of the major security businesses in the Brighton area for home and commercial premises.

Turning back to Maurice, he said, 'Actually, business is OK. We're holding our own. How about you?'

'Booming!' Maurice said. 'Incredible, but it is!' He raised his glass. 'Well, cheers, everyone! Here's to a brilliant year! Never actually got to toast you on New Year's Eve, did we, Denise?'

'Yep, well, sorry about that. Don't know what came over me. Must be the bottle of champagne we had in our room while we were getting changed!'

'That *you* had,' Garry corrected her.

'Poor thing!' Ulla said.

'Still,' Maurice said, 'Garry did his best to make up for you by drinking your share, didn't you, old son?'

Garry smiled. 'I made a sterling effort.'

'He did,' Ulla said. 'He was well away!'

'Hey, did you see the *Argus* today?' Maurice said with an abrupt change of tone.

'No,' Garry said. 'Haven't read it yet. Why?'

'A woman was raped in the hotel! Right while we were partying! Incredible!'

'In the Metropole?' Denise said.

'Yes! In a bedroom. Can you believe it?'

'Great,' she said. 'Terrific to know your caring husband is getting shit-faced while his wife's in bed alone, with a rapist at large.'

'What did it say in the paper?' Garry said, ignoring the comment.

'Not much – just a few lines.'

'Don't look so guilty, darling,' Denise said. 'You couldn't keep it up long enough to rape a flea.'

Maurice busied himself with his chopsticks, lifting strands of duck on to his pancake.'

'Unless of course she was wearing some high – ouch!' she cried out.

Garry had kicked her hard under the table. Silencing her.

1997

19

Rachael was beyond caring about the pain she was in. Her wrists, behind her back, were numb from cold as she sawed, desperately, back and forward against the sharp rim of the fuel can spout. Her bum was numb and a sharp, cramping pain shot down her right leg every few moments. But she ignored it all. Just sawing. Sawing. Sawing in utter desperation.

It was desperation that kept her going. Desperation to get free before he came back. Desperation for water. Desperation for food. Desperation to speak to her parents, to hear their voices, to tell them she was OK. She was crying, shedding tears as she sawed, writhed, wriggled, struggled.

Then, suddenly, to her utter joy, the gap between her wrists widened a fraction. She could feel the bonds slackening. She sawed even harder and now they were becoming slacker by the second.

Then her hands were free.

Almost in disbelief, she moved them further and further apart in the darkness, as if they might suddenly be propelled back together and she would wake to find it was all an illusion.

Her arms ached terribly, but she did not care. Thoughts were racing through her mind.

I'm free.
He's going to come back.
My phone. Where's my phone?

She needed to phone for help. Except, she realized, she did not know where she was. Could they locate you from where your phone was? She didn't think so. Which meant all she could tell them, until she got out of the door and found her bearings, was that she was in a van in a garage somewhere in Brighton or Hove, perhaps.

He might come back at any moment. She needed to free her legs. In the darkness she felt the area around her for her phone, her bag, anything. But there was just slimy, stinky diesel oil. She reached forward, to her ankles, and felt the PVC tape around them, wound so tight it was as hard as a plaster cast. Then she reached up to her face, to see if she could free her mouth and at least shout for help.

But would that be smart?

The tape was just as tight around her mouth. She got a grip on it with difficulty, her fingers slippery with the diesel oil, and tore it off, almost oblivious to the pain in her urgency. Then she tried to get a grip on an edge of the tape around her legs, but her fingers were shaking so much she couldn't find one.

Panic rose.

Must escape.

She tried to get to her feet but, with them bound together, at her first attempt she fell over sideways, striking her forehead hard on something. Moments later she felt liquid trickle down into her eye. Blood, she guessed. Snorting air, she rolled over, sat back against the side of the van and then, trying to grip the floor with her bare feet, began pushing herself up the side. But her feet kept slipping on the damned diesel oil, which had turned the floor into a skating rink.

She scrabbled around until she found the hessian she had been lying on, then put her feet on that and tried again. This time she got more grip. Steadily, she began to rise. She made it all the way up on to her feet, her head striking the roof of the van. Then, totally disoriented by the pitch darkness, she fell sideways with a jarring crash. Something slammed into her eye with the force of a hammer.

NOW

20

Saturday 3 January

There was a ping from the data unit on the dashboard. It startled Yac, who was parked up in a meter bay on the blustery seafront, close to Brighton Pier, drinking a mug of tea. His 11 p.m. mug of tea. He was actually ten minutes late drinking it, because he had been so absorbed reading the newspaper.

He looked at the screen. It was a call from the dispatcher that read:

China Garden rest. Preston St. 2 Pass. Starling. Dest. Roedean Cresc.

The China Garden restaurant was just around the corner. He knew the destination. He could visualize it now, the way he could visualize every street and every dwelling in Brighton and Hove. Roedean Crescent sat high up above the cliffs to the east of the city. All the houses were big, detached and individual, with views out across the Marina and the Channel. Rich people's homes.

The sort of people who could afford nice shoes.

He hit the acknowledge button, confirming that he would make the pick-up, then continued to sip his tea and read the newspaper that had been left in his taxi.

They'd be finishing their meal still. When people ordered a taxi in a restaurant, they expected to wait a while, certainly a quarter of an hour or so on a Saturday night in downtown Brighton. And besides, he could not stop reading and then re-reading the story about the rape of the woman in the Metropole on New Year's Eve. He was riveted.

In his mirrors he could see the twinkly lights of the pier. He knew all about those lights. He used to work on the pier as an electrical engineer, part of the team maintaining and repairing the rides. But he got the sack. It was for the same reason he usually got the sack, because he lost his temper with someone. He hadn't yet lost his temper with anyone in his taxi, but he had once got out and shouted at another driver who'd pulled on to a rank in front of him.

He finished his tea, reluctantly folded the newspaper and put the mug back in the plastic bag alongside his Thermos, then placed the bag on the front seat.

'Vocabulary!' he said aloud. Then he began his checks.

First check the tyres. Next start the engine, then switch on the lights. Never the other way around, because if the battery was low, the lights might drain the energy that the starter motor needed. The owner of the taxi had taught him that. Especially in winter, when there were heavy loads on the battery. It was winter now.

As the engine idled, he checked the fuel gauge. Three-quarters of a tank. Then the oil pressure. Then the temperature gauge. The interior temperature was set to twenty degrees, as he had been instructed. Outside, a digital display told him, it was two degrees Celsius. Cold night.

Uh-huh.

He looked in his mirror, checked his seat belt was on,

indicated, pulled out into the road and drove up to the junction, where the lights were red. When they changed to green he turned right into Preston Street and almost immediately pulled over to the kerb, halting outside the front door of the restaurant.

Two very drunk yobs staggered down the hill towards him, then knocked on his window and asked if he was free to take them to Coldean. He wasn't free, he was waiting for passengers, he told them. As they walked away he wondered whether they had high-flush or low-flush toilets in their homes. It suddenly became very important to him to know. He was about to get out and hurry after them, to ask them, when finally the restaurant door opened.

Two people emerged. A slim man in a dark coat, with a scarf wound around his neck, and a woman who was clinging to him, teetering on her heels; she looked like she'd fall over if she let go. And from the height of the stilettos she was wearing, that would be a long fall.

They were nice heels. Nice shoes.

And he had their address! He always liked to know where women who had nice shoes lived.

Uh-huh.

Yac lowered his window. He didn't want the man knocking on it. He didn't like people knocking on his window.

'Taxi for Starling?' the man said.

'Roedean Crescent?' Yac replied.

'That's us!'

They climbed in the back.

'Sixty-seven Roedean Crescent,' the man said.

'Sixty-seven Roedean Crescent,' Yac repeated. He had been told always to repeat the address clearly.

The car filled with smells of alcohol and perfume. *Shalimar*, he recognized instantly. The perfume of his childhood. The one his mother always wore. Then he turned to the woman.

'Nice shoes,' he said. 'Bruno Magli.'

'Yesh,' she slurred.

'Size four,' he added.

'An expert on shoes, are you?' the woman asked him sourly.

Yac looked at the woman's face in the mirror. She was all uptight. She did not have the face of a woman who had had a good time. Or who was very nice. The man's eyes were closed.

'Shoes,' Yac said. 'Uh-huh.'

1997

21

Rachael woke with a start. Her head was throbbing. Disoriented, for a cruel, fleeting instant she thought she was at home in bed with a mighty hangover. Then she felt the hard metal floor. The hessian matting. Breathed in the stink of diesel oil. And reality gate-crashed her consciousness, kicking her wide awake, sending dark dread spiralling through her.

Her right eye hurt like hell. God, it was agony. How long had she been lying there? He could come back at any moment, and if he did he would see that she'd freed her wrists. He would tape them up again and probably punish her. She had to free her legs and run, now, while she had the chance.

Oh, God. Please help me.

Her lips were so parched they cracked painfully when she tried to move them. Her tongue felt like a ball of fur in her mouth. She listened for an instant, to make sure she was still alone in here. All she could hear was a distant siren and again she wondered, with the faintest uplift of hope, whether that might be the police out looking for her.

But how would they find her in here?

She rolled over until she felt the side of the van, then hauled herself upright and began picking at the tape binding her ankles with her fingernails. Trying to find a join on the slippery, diesel-coated PVC where she could get a grip.

Finally she found one and slowly, carefully, worked it free, until she had a whole wide strip of it. She began to unwind it, jerking it free with a series of sharp ripping noises. Then she winced in pain as the last of it came away from the skin of her ankles.

Grabbing the sodden hessian matting, she got to her feet, stretched and rubbed her legs to get feeling back into them, and stumbled her way, weakly, to the back of the van, crying out in pain, suddenly, as she stood on something sharp in her bare feet – a nut or a bolt. Then she felt her way across the rear doors for the handle. She found a vertical metal rod and ran her hands up it until she reached the handle. She tried to pull it down. Nothing happened. She tried to move it upwards and it would not budge.

It was locked, she realized, her heart sinking.

No. Please, no. Please, no.

She turned and made her way down to the front, her fast, rasping breaths echoing in the metallic cavern of the van's interior. She found the back of the passenger seat, climbed over clumsily, then ran her finger along the sill of the passenger window until she found the lock pin. She gripped it as hard as she could with her slippery fingers and pulled.

To her relief, it popped up easily.

Then she groped for the handle, pulled it and shoved as hard as she could on the door, almost tumbling out on to the concrete floor as it opened, and simultaneously the interior light in the van came on.

Now, in its dim glow, she could see the inside of her prison. But there wasn't much. Just some tools hanging on hooks on the bare wall. A tyre. Grabbing the matting, she hurried along the side of the van towards the garage door, her heart thudding with fear. Suddenly the matting snagged on something and, when she tugged it, there was a loud metallic crash as several objects fell to the floor. She winced but carried on, until she reached the up-and-over door.

There was a two-sided handle in the centre, attached to wires to the mechanism at the top of the door. She tried to turn the handle, first to the right, then to the left, but it would not move. It must be locked from the outside, she realized. With panic increasing inside her, she grabbed the wire and pulled. But her fingers slipped on it, not getting any purchase.

In desperation, Rachael bashed the door with her shoulder, oblivious to the pain. But nothing happened. Whimpering in fear and increasing desperation, she tried again. There was a loud, echoing, metallic booommmmm.

Then another.

And another.

Please, God, somebody must hear this. Please, God. Please.

Then suddenly the door swung up, startling her, almost knocking her over backwards.

In the stark glare of the street lighting outside he stood there, looking at her inquisitively.

She stared back at him in utter terror. Her eyes darted, desperately hoping there might be a passer-by, wondering if she could find the strength to dodge by him and run.

But before she had a chance, he hit her, slamming his fist up beneath her chin, snapping her head back so hard it bashed with a loud crack against the rear of the van.

22

Monday 29 December

Detective Sergeant Roy Grace was surprised at the number of people packed into the top-floor conference room of Brighton's John Street police station, on this December morning. Despite the cold outside, it was feeling stuffy in here.

Mispers never usually attracted much attention, but this was a quiet time of the year for news. A bird flu epidemic in Hong Kong was one of the few big stories that the national headline writers could use as a shocker in between the Christmas festivities and the upcoming New Year's celebrations.

But the story of the missing young woman, Rachael Ryan, in the wake of the series of rapes that had occurred in the city in the past couple of months, had caught the imagination of the press and media not only locally but nationally. And the *Argus*, of course, was having a field day with Brighton heading into a new year with the Shoe Man still at large.

Newspaper, radio and television reporters occupied all the chairs, and the standing room as well, in the cramped windowless space. Grace sat suited and booted behind a table on the raised platform facing them, next to Chief Inspector Jack Skerritt, in full dress uniform, reeking of pipe tobacco, and the Police Press Officer, Tony Long.

A blue back board carrying the Sussex Police crest stood behind them, next to which was a blow-up photograph of Rachael Ryan, and the table was covered in microphones and tape recorders. Cables led down from the table and across the floor to TV cameras from BBC South Today and Meridian.

With cameras clicking and the constant strobing of flash, Skerritt first introduced his colleagues on the top table, then read in his blunt voice from a prepared statement: 'A twenty-two-year-old resident of Brighton, Ms Rachael Ryan, was reported missing by her family on the evening of Christmas Day, after she failed to turn up for Christmas dinner. No word has been heard from her since. Her parents have informed us that this is completely uncharacteristic behaviour. We are concerned for the safety of this young lady and would ask her, or anyone with information about her, to contact the Incident Room at Brighton police station urgently.'

A tenacious, balding, bespectacled crime reporter from the *Argus*, Phil Mills, dressed in a dark suit, sitting hunched over his notepad, asked the first question. 'Chief Inspector, do Brighton police suspect that the disappearance of this young lady might be connected with *Operation Houdini* and the rapist you have nicknamed the Shoe Man?'

Both Skerritt and Grace reacted to this in silent fury. Although the police knew him as the Shoe Man, his MO had been kept secret from the public, as was usual. This was in order to weed out time-wasters who either confessed to the crime or phoned in purporting to have knowledge of the perpetrator. Grace could see Skerritt wrestling with whether or not to deny the nickname. But he clearly decided that it was out in the open now and they were stuck with it.

'We have no evidence to suggest that,' he replied curtly and dismissively.

Jack Skerritt was a popular and diligent member of the CID. A tough, blunt, no-nonsense copper of nearly twenty years' experience, he had a lean military bearing and a hard face, topped with a slick of brown hair clipped short. Grace liked him, although Skerritt made him a little nervous because he was intensely demanding of his officers and did not treat mistakes lightly. But he had learned a lot working under him. Skerritt was the kind of detective he would like to be himself one day.

A female reporter immediately raised her hand. 'Chief Inspector, can you explain more about what you mean by "Shoe Man"?'

'We believe the offender who has been preying on women in the Brighton area for several months now has an abnormal interest in women's shoes. It is one of a number of lines of enquiry we are pursuing.'

'But you haven't mentioned this publicly before.'

'We haven't, no,' Skerritt replied. 'As I said, it is one line.'

Mills came straight back at him. 'The two friends Rachael was out with on Christmas Eve say that she had a particular obsession with shoes and spent a disproportionate amount of her income on them. I understand that the Shoe Man specifically targets women wearing so-called *designer* shoes.'

'On a night like Christmas Eve, every young lady in Brighton and Hove would have been out in her finery,' Skerritt retorted. 'I repeat that, at this stage of our investigations, we have no evidence to suggest there is any connection to the so-called Shoe Man rapes that have occurred in this vicinity.'

A woman reporter Grace did not recognize raised her hand. Skerritt nodded at her.

'You have assigned the name *Operation Sundown* to Rachael Ryan's disappearance. Creating a formal operation tells us you are taking this more seriously than a normal missing persons inquiry. Is that correct?'

'We take all missing persons inquiries seriously. But we have elevated the status of this particular inquiry to a major incident.'

A local radio reporter raised his hand. 'Chief Inspector, do you have any leads in your search for the Shoe Man?'

'At this stage, as stated, we are pursuing several lines of enquiry. There has been a substantial response from the public and all calls to our Incident Room are being followed up by my team.'

'But you are not close to an arrest?'

'At this stage, that is correct.'

Then a journalist Grace recognized as a stringer for several national papers raised his hand. 'What steps are Brighton police currently taking to find Rachael Ryan?'

'We have forty-two officers deployed in the search for her. They are carrying out house-to-house enquiries in her immediate neighbourhood and along the route we believe she took home. We are searching all garages, warehouses and empty buildings in the vicinity. We have been given particularly good information by a witness who lives near Ms Ryan's residence in Kemp Town, who believes he saw a young lady forced into a white van in the early hours of Christmas morning,' Skerritt said, then studied the journalist for some moments, as if eyeing him up as a suspect, before once more addressing everyone present.

'Unfortunately we have only part of the registration number for this van, which we are working on, but we would urge anyone who thinks they might have seen a white van in the vicinity of Eastern Terrace on Christmas Eve or early Christmas morning to contact us. I will give out the Incident Room phone number at the end of this briefing. We are also anxious to hear from anyone who may have seen this young lady on her way home.' He pointed at the screen behind him, on which were displayed a series of photographs of Rachael Ryan, obtained from her parents.

He paused for a moment and patted his pocket, as if checking his pipe was there, then continued: 'Rachael was wearing a black mid-length coat over a miniskirt, and black patent-leather shoes with high heels. We are trying to trace her precise route home from the time she was last seen, at the taxi rank in East Street, shortly after 2 a.m.'

A diminutive, rotund man, his face largely obscured by an unkempt beard, raised a stubby, chewed finger. 'Chief Inspector, do you actually have any suspects in your Shoe Man enquiries?'

'All I can say at this stage is that we are following some good leads and we are grateful to the public for their response.'

The tubby man got in a second question quickly. 'Your enquiry into Rachael Ryan seems to be a departure from police policy,' he said. 'You don't normally react so quickly to missing-person reports. Would I be correct in assuming you think there may be a link here to the Shoe Man – *Operation Houdini* – even if you are not publicly announcing this?'

'No, you would not be correct,' Skerritt said bluntly.

A woman reporter raised her hand. 'Can you tell us some of the other lines of enquiry you are pursuing on Rachael Ryan, Chief Inspector?'

Skerritt turned to Roy Grace. 'My colleague DS Grace is organizing a reconstruction of the parts of Rachael's journey home that we can be reasonably certain of. This will take place at 7 p.m. on Wednesday.'

'Does this mean you don't believe you are going to find her before then?' Phil Mills asked.

'It means what it says,' retorted Skerritt, who had had several run-ins with this reporter before. Then he nodded at his colleague.

Roy Grace had never spoken at a press briefing before and suddenly he was nervous as all hell. 'We have a WPC who is of similar height and build to Rachael Ryan, who will be dressed in similar clothing and will walk the route we believe Rachael took on the night – or rather early morning – of her disappearance. I would urge all people who might have been out early on Christmas morning to spare the time to retrace their steps and see if it jogs their memories.'

He was perspiring when he finished. Jack Skerritt gave him a brief nod of approval.

These reporters were after a story that would sell their papers, or bring listeners to their radio stations or viewers to their channels. He and Skerritt had a different agenda. To keep the streets of Brighton and Hove safe. Or at least to make the citizens *feel* they were safe in a world that never had been safe and never would be. Not with the kind of human nature he had come to know as a police officer.

There was a predator out on the streets of this town. As a result of the Shoe Man's reign of terror, there was not a woman in Brighton who felt comfortable right now. Not a single woman who did not look over her shoulder, did not ram home her door chain, did not wonder if she might be next.

Roy Grace was not involved in the Shoe Man investigation. But he had an increasingly certain feeling that *Operation Houdini* and the search for Rachael Ryan were one and the same thing.

We're going to get you, Shoe Man, he promised silently.

Whatever it takes.

23

Monday 29 December

Rachael was in a helicopter with Liam. With his long, spiky hair and his sulky, boyish face he looked so much like Liam Gallagher of Oasis, her favourite group. They were swooping low through the Grand Canyon. Crimson rocks of the cliff face were passing either side, so close, dangerously close. Below them, a long, long way down, the metallic blue water snaked along through jagged grey-brown contours.

She gripped Liam's hand. He gripped hers back. They couldn't speak to each other because they had headsets on, listening to the pilot's commentary. She turned and mouthed *I love you* to him. He grinned, looking funny with the microphone partially obscuring his mouth, and mouthed *I love you* back.

Yesterday they'd walked past a wedding chapel. For a joke he'd suddenly dragged her through the door, into the tiny golden-coloured interior. There were rows of pews either side of the aisle and two tall vases of flowers acting as a kind of cheesy non-denominational altar. Fixed to the wall behind was a glass display cabinet containing on one shelf a bottle of champagne and a white handbag with a floral handle, and on another an empty white basket and big white candles.

'We could get married,' he said. 'Right now. Today!'

'Don't be daft,' she'd replied.

'I'm not being daft. I'm serious! Let's do it! We'll go back to England as Mr and Mrs Hopkirk!'

She wondered what her parents would think. They'd be upset. But it was tempting. She felt so intensely happy. This was the man she wanted to spend the rest of her life with.

'Mr Liam Hopkirk, are you proposing to me?'

'No, not exactly – but I'm thinking, you know, screw all the crap and bridesmaids and stuff that goes with a wedding. It would be fun, wouldn't it? Surprise them all?'

He was being serious and that shocked her. He meant it! Her parents would be devastated. She remembered sitting on her father's knee when she was a child. Her father telling her how beautiful she was. How proud he would be one day to walk her down the aisle on her wedding day.

'I couldn't do this to my parents.'

'They mean more to you than me?'

'No. It's just . . .'

His face darkened. Sulking again.

The sky darkened. Suddenly the helicopter was sinking. The walls turning dark and rushing past the big bubble window. The river beneath rushing up towards them.

She screamed.

Total darkness.

Oh, Christ.

Her head was pounding. Then a light came on. The feeble glow of the dome lamp of the van. She heard a voice. Not Liam, but the man, glaring down at her.

'You stink,' he said. 'You're making my van stink.'

Reality crashed through her. The coils of terror spiralling through every cell in her body. *Water. Please. Water.* She stared up at him, parched and weak and dizzy. She tried to speak but could only make a feeble deep whine in her throat.

'I can't have sex with you. You revolt me. Know what I'm saying?'

A faint ray of hope lifted her. Perhaps he would let her go. She tried again to make a coherent sound. But her voice was just a hollow rumbling mumble.

'I should let you go.'

She nodded. *Yes. Yes, please. Please. Please.*

'I can't let you go, because you saw my face,' he said.

She pleaded with her eyes. *I won't tell anyone. Please let me go. I won't tell a soul.*

'You could put me behind bars for the rest of my life. Do you know what they do to people like me in prison? It's not nice. I can't take that chance.'

The knot of fear in her stomach spread like poison through her blood. She was trembling, quaking, whimpering.

'I'm sorry,' he said, and he really did sound sorry. Really apologetic, like a man in a crowded bar who had just accidentally stepped on her foot. 'You're in the papers. You are on the front page of the *Argus*. There's a photograph of you. *Rachael Ryan.* That's a nice name.'

He stared down at her. He looked angry. And sulky. And genuinely apologetic. 'I'm sorry you saw my face,' he said. 'You shouldn't have done that. It wasn't clever, Rachael. It could all have been so very different. Know what I'm saying?'

NOW

24

The newly formed Cold Case Team was part of Roy Grace's Major Crime Branch responsibility. It was housed in an inadequate office within the Major Incident Suite on the first floor of Sussex House, with views across a yard cluttered with wheelie bins, emergency generator housings and SOCO vehicles to the custody block, which cut out much of the natural light.

There were few things in the world, Roy Grace always thought, that could create as much paperwork as a Major Crime investigation. The grey-carpeted floor was piled high with stacks of large green crates and blue cardboard boxes, all labelled with operation names, as well as reference books, training manuals and a doorstop of a tome sitting on its own, *Practical Homicide.*

Almost every inch of the desktop space of the three workstations was covered by computers, keyboards, phones, racks of box files, crammed in trays, Rolodex files, mugs and personal effects. Post-it notes were stuck on just about everything. Two free-standing tables visibly sagged beneath the weight of files piled on them.

The walls were plastered with news cuttings of some of the cases, and photographs and old wanted posters of suspects still at large. One was a picture of a smiling dark-haired teenager, with the wording above:

HAVE YOU SEEN THIS WOMAN?

£500 reward

Another was a black-and-white Sussex Police poster featuring an amiable-looking man with a big smile and a shock of unruly hair. It was captioned:

SUSSEX POLICE

MURDER of JACK (John) BAKER.

Mr Baker was murdered at Worthing, Sussex
on 8/9 January 1990.

Did you know him? Have you seen him before?

IF YOU HAVE ANY INFORMATION
PLEASE CONTACT THE MURDER INCIDENT ROOM

telephone no. 0903-30821,

OR ANY POLICE STATION.

There were hand-drawn sketches of victims and suspects, computer-generated E-Fits, one of a rape suspect shown with different hats and hoods, with and without glasses.

In charge of this entire new cold case initiative, and answering to Roy Grace, was Jim Doyle, a former detective chief superintendent with whom Grace had worked many years back. Doyle was a tall, studious-looking man, whose appearance belied his mental – and physical – toughness. He had about him more the courteous air of a distinguished academic than a police officer. Yet with his firm, unflappable manner, his enquiring mind and a precision in the way he approached everything, he had been a devastatingly effective detective, involved in solving many of the county's most serious violent crimes during his thirty-year career. His nickname in the force had been *Popeye*, after his namesake, Jimmy 'Popeye' Doyle in the film *The French Connection*.

Doyle's two colleagues were similarly experienced. Eamon Greene, a quiet, serious man, was a former Sussex under-16 chess champion and was now a grand master, still playing and winning tournaments. Before retiring at just forty-nine, and then returning to the force as a civilian, he had reached the rank of detective superintendent in Sussex CID, Major Crime Branch. Brian Foster, a former detective chief inspector known as *Fossy*, was a lean sixty-three-year-old, with close-cropped hair and still, despite his age, boyishly handsome features. In the previous year he had run four marathons in four consecutive weeks in different countries. Since retiring from Sussex CID at the age of fifty-two, he had worked for the past decade in the prosecutor's office of the International War Crimes Tribunal in The Hague, and had now returned home eager to start a new phase in his career.

Roy Grace, wearing a suit and tie for his first meeting with the new Assistant Chief Constable later that morning, cleared a space on one of the work surfaces and sat down on it, cradling his second mug of coffee of the day. It was 8.45 a.m.

'OK,' he said, swinging his legs. 'It's good to have the three of you. Actually, let me rephrase that – it is bloody brilliant!'

They all grinned.

'Popeye, you taught me just about everything I know, so I don't want to sit here and teach you how to suck eggs. The "Chief" – ' by which he meant Chief Constable Tom Martinson – 'has given us a generous budget, but we're going to have to deliver if we want the same again next year. Which is shorthand for saying if you guys still want your jobs next year.'

Turning to the others, he said, 'I'm just going to tell you something Popeye told me when I first worked with him. As part of his work-load back in the 1990s he had just been given responsibility for cold cases – or whatever they were called then!'

That raised a titter. All three retired officers knew the headaches caused by the ever-changing police termin-ology.

Grace pulled a sheet of paper from his pocket and read from it. 'He said, and I quote, "Cold-case reviews utilize the forensic technology of today to solve the crimes of the past, with a view to preventing the crimes of the future."'

'Glad all those years with you weren't wasted, Roy,' Jim Doyle said. 'At least you remembered something!'

'Yep. Impressive to have learned anything from an *old sweat*!' quipped Foster.

Doyle did not rise to the bait.

Roy Grace went on: 'You've probably seen it on the serials or in the *Argus* that a woman was raped on New Year's Eve.'

'In the Metropole Hotel?' Eamon Greene said.

'That's the one.'

'I attended the initial interview of the victim last Thursday, New Year's Day,' Grace said. 'The offender, apparently disguised in drag, appears to have forced the victim into a hotel room on the pretext of asking for help. Then, wearing a mask, he tied her up and sexually assaulted her vaginally and anally with one of her stiletto shoes. He then attempted to penetrate her himself, with only partial success. This has similarities to the MO of the

Shoe Man cold case back in 1997. In those cases, the Shoe Man adopted a series of different disguises and pretexts for requiring help to lure his victims. Then he stopped offending – in Sussex at any rate – and was never apprehended. I have a summary of this case file which I'd like you all to read as a priority. You will each have your own individual cases to review, but for now I want you all to work on this one, as I think it could help with the case I'm investigating now.'

'Was there any DNA evidence, Roy?' Jim Doyle asked.

'There was no semen from any of the women, but three of his victims said that he wore a condom. There were clothing fibres, but nothing conclusive from those. No nail scrapings, no saliva. A couple of his victims reported that he had no pubic hair. This man was clearly very forensically aware, even back then. No DNA was ever found. There was just one common link – each of the victims was seriously into shoes.'

'Which covers about 95 per cent of the female population – if my wife is anything to go by,' Jim Doyle said.

'Precisely.' Grace nodded.

'What about descriptions?' asked Brian Foster.

'Thanks to the way in which rape victims were treated back then, not much. We have a slightly built man, with not a lot of body hair, a classless accent and a small dick.

'I've spent the weekend reading through the files of those victims, and all other major crimes committed during this same period,' Grace went on. 'There is one more person that I suspect might have been a victim of the Shoe Man – possibly the last victim. Her name is Rachael Ryan. She disappeared in the early hours of Christmas Eve – or rather Christmas Day, 1997. What has brought her to my attention is that I was a DS back then on the day she was reported missing. I went to interview her parents. Respectable people, completely mystified that she never turned up for Christmas dinner. By all accounts she was a decent young woman of twenty-two, sensible, although low after having split up with a boy-friend.'

He nearly added, but did not, that she had vanished off the face of the earth, just like his own wife, Sandy, had vanished.

'Any theories?' asked Foster.

'Not from the family,' Grace said. 'But I interviewed the two friends she was out with on Christmas Eve. One of them told me that she was a bit obsessed with shoes. That she bought shoes which were way beyond her means – designer shoes at upwards of a couple of hundred quid a pop. All the Shoe Man's victims wore expensive shoes.' He shrugged.

'Not much of a peg to hang your coat on there, Roy,' said Foster. 'If she'd split up with her boyfriend she could have topped herself. Christmas, you know, that's a time when people feel pain like this. I remember my ex walking out on me three weeks before Christmas. I damned near topped myself over that Christmas holiday – 1992, it was. Had Christmas dinner on my own in a bloody Angus Steak House.'

Grace smiled. 'It's possible, but from all I learned about her at that time I don't think so. Something I do think is significant is that one of her neighbours happened to be looking out of his window at three o'clock on Christmas morning – the timing fits perfectly – and saw a man pushing a woman into a white van.'

'Did he get the registration?'

'He was shit-faced. He got part of it.'

'Enough to trace the vehicle?'

'No.'

'You believed him?'

'Yes. I still do.'

'Not a lot to go on, is it, Roy?' said Jim Doyle.

'No, but there's something strange. I came in early this morning to look up that particular file before this meeting – and do you know what?' He stared at each of them.

They all shook their heads.

'The pages I was looking for were missing.'

'Who would remove them?' Brian Foster said. 'I mean – who would have access to them to be able to remove them?'

'You used to be a copper,' Grace said. 'You tell me. And then tell me why?'

25

Maybe it was time to quit.

Prison aged you. Ten years it put on – or took off – your life, depending on which way you looked at it. And right now Darren Spicer wasn't too happy about either of the ways he was looking at it.

Since he was sixteen, Spicer had spent much of his life inside. *Doing bird*. A *revolving-door prisoner*, they called him. A career criminal. But not a very successful one. He'd only once, since becoming an adult, spent two consecutive Christmases as a free man, and that had been in the early years of his marriage. His birth certificate – his real one – told him he was forty-one. His bathroom mirror told him he was fifty-five – and counting. Inside he felt eighty. He felt dead. He felt . . .

Nothing.

Lathering up, he stared at the mirror with dull eyes, grimacing at the lined old geezer staring back at him. He was naked, his gangly, skinny body – which he liked to think of as just plain lean – toned up from daily workouts in the prison gym.

Then he set to work on his hard stubble with the same blunted blade he had been using for weeks in prison before his release and which he had taken with him. When he had finished, his face was as clean-shaven as the rest of his body, which he had shaved last week. He always did that when he came out of prison, as a way of cleansing himself. One time, in the early days of his now long-dead marriage, he'd come home with lice in his pubes and chest hair.

He had two small tattoos, at the top of each arm, but no more. Plenty of his fellow inmates were covered in the things and had a macho pride in them. Macho pride equalled mucho stupidity, in his view. Why make it easy for someone to identify you? Besides, he had enough identifying marks already – five scars on his back, from stab wounds when he'd been set on in prison by mates of a drug dealer he'd done over some years back.

This last sentence had been his longest yet – six years. He was finally out on licence now after three of them. Time to quit, he thought. Yeah, but.

The big *but*.

You were supposed to feel free when you left prison. But he still had to report to his probation officer. He had to report for retraining. He had to obey the rules of the hostels he stayed in. When you were released, you were supposed to go home.

But he had no home.

His dad was long dead and he'd barely spoken a dozen words to his mum in twenty-five years – and that was too many. His only sibling, his sister Mags, had died from a heroin overdose five years back. His ex-wife was living in Australia with his kid, whom he hadn't seen in ten years.

Home was wherever he could find a place to doss down. Last night it was a room in a halfway house just off the Old Steine in Brighton. Shared with four pathetic, stinking winos. He'd been here before. Today he was going to try to get into a better place. St Patrick's night shelter. They had decent grub, a place you could store things. You had to sleep in a big dormitory but it was clean. Prison was meant to help your rehabilitation back into the community after serving your time. But the reality was that the community didn't want you, not really. Rehabilitation was a myth. Although he played the game, went along with the concept.

Retraining!

Ha! He wasn't interested in retraining, but he had shown willing while he had been at Ford Open Prison these past six months in preparation for his release, because that had enabled him to spend days out of prison on their work placement scheme. *Working Links*, they were called. He had chosen the hotel handyman course, which enabled him to spend time in a couple of different Brighton hotels. Working behind the scenes. Understanding the layouts. Getting access to the room keys and to the electronic room-key software. Very useful indeed.

Yeah.

His regular prison visitor at Lewes, a pleasant, matronly lady, had asked him if he had a dream. If he could ever see a life for himself beyond the prison walls. And what was it?

Yeah, sure, he'd told her, he had a dream. To be married again. To have kids. To live in a nice house – like one of those fancy homes he burgled for a living – and drive a nice car. Have a steady job. Yep. Go fishing at the weekends. That was his dream. But, he told her, that was never going to happen.

'Why not?' she had asked him.

'I'll tell you why not,' Darren had replied. 'Cos I've got one hundred and seventy-two *previous*, right? Who's gonna let me stay in a job when they find that out? And they always do find out.' He'd paused before adding, 'Anyhow, it's all right here. Got me mates. The grub's good. The electricity's paid for. Got me television.'

Yeah, it was all right. Except . . .

No women. That's what he missed. Women and cocaine were what he liked. Could get the drugs in prison, but not the women. Not very often, anyway.

The Guv had let him stay in over Christmas, but he'd been released two days after Boxing Day. To what?

Shit.

Tomorrow hopefully he'd move. If you played by the rules at St Patrick's for twenty-eight days, you could get yourself into one of their MiPods. They had these strange plastic pods in there, like space capsules, taken from some Japanese hotel idea. You could stay in a MiPod for another ten weeks. They were cramped, but they gave you privacy; you could keep your things safe.

And he had things he needed to keep safe.

His mate, Terry Biglow – if he could call the shifty little weasel a mate – was safeguarding the only possessions he owned in the world. They were inside a suitcase, with three padlocked chains holding its contents a secret – the chains and padlocks were a mark of how much he could trust Biglow not to open it up.

Maybe this time he could stay out of jail. Get enough money together, from burgling and drug dealing, to buy himself a little flat. And then what? A woman? A family? One moment that seemed attractive, the next it was all too much. Too much hassle. Truth was, he had grown used to his way of life. His own company. His own secret kicks.

His dad had been a roofer and as a kid he'd helped

him out. He'd seen some of the posh houses in Brighton and Hove his dad worked on – and the tasty women with their beautiful clothes and their flash cars who lived in them. His dad fancied that kind of lifestyle. Fancied a posh house and a classy-looking woman.

One day his dad fell through a roof, broke his back and never worked again. Instead he just drank his compensation money all day and night. Darren didn't fancy roofing, that wasn't ever going to make you rich, he figured. Studying could. He liked school, was good at maths and science and mechanical things, loved all that. But he had problems at home. His mother was drinking too. Some time around his thirteenth birthday she clambered into his bed, drunk and naked, told him his father couldn't satisfy her any more, now it was his job as the man in the family.

Darren went to school every day, ashamed, increasingly disconnected from his friends. His head was all messed up and he couldn't concentrate any more. He didn't feel a part of anything, and took to spending more and more time alone, fishing, or in really bad weather hanging about in his uncle's locksmith's shop, watching him cut keys, or running errands, and occasionally standing behind the counter while his uncle nipped along to the bookie. Anything to escape from home. From his mother.

He liked his uncle's machinery, liked the smell, liked the mystery of locks. They were just puzzles, really. Simple puzzles.

When he was fifteen his mother told him it was time he started supporting her and his dad, that he needed to learn a skill, get a job. His uncle, who had no one to take over the business when he retired, offered him an apprenticeship.

Within a couple of months, Darren could solve any problem anyone had with a lock. His uncle told him he was a bloody genius!

There was nothing to it, Darren figured. Anything that was made by a man could be figured out by another man. All you had to do was think your way inside the lock. Imagine the springs, the tumblers – imagine the inside of the lock, put yourself into the mind of the man who designed it. After all, there were basically only two kinds of domestic lock – a Yale, which operated with a flat key, and a Chubb, which operated with a cylindrical key. Mortises and rim locks. If you had a problem, you could see inside most locks with a simple bit of medical kit, a proctoscope.

Then he graduated to safes. His uncle had developed a bit of a niche business, opening safes for the police. Given a bit of time, there wasn't any mechanical safe his nephew could not open. Nor any door lock.

He'd burgled his first house, up in Hollingdean, when he was sixteen. He got busted and spent two years in an approved school. That was where he developed a taste for drugs for the first time. And where he learned his first valuable lesson. It was the same risk to burgle a shitty little house for a stereo system as it was to burgle a ritzy pad where there might be jewellery and cash.

When he came out his uncle didn't want him back – and he had no inclination to get a low-paid labouring job, which was his only choice. Instead he burgled a house in Brighton's secluded Withdean Road. Took seven grand from a safe. Blew three of it on cocaine, but invested four of it in heroin, which he traded and made a twenty-grand profit.

He did a string of large houses after then, made himself almost a hundred Gs. Sweet. Then he met Rose in a club. Married her. Bought a little flat in Portslade. Rose didn't approve of him burgling, so he tried going straight. Through a bloke he knew, he faked a new ID and got a job working for a company that installed alarm systems called Sussex Security Systems.

They had a top-end clientele. Half of the city's big homes. Being in them was like being a kid in a sweetshop. It did not take him long to miss the buzz of burgling. Particularly the kick he got out of it. But even more particularly the money he could make.

The best of all of it was being alone in a posh bedroom. Smelling the scent of a rich woman. Inhaling her perfumes, the perspiration on her underwear in the wash baskets, her expensive clothes hanging in her wardrobe, her silks, cottons, furs, leathers. He liked rifling through her things. Particularly her underwear and her shoes. Something about these places aroused him.

These women were from a different world to the one he knew. Women beyond his means. Beyond his social skills.

Women with their stuffy husbands.

These kinds of women were gagging for it.

Sometimes a scent of cologne or a sour odour on a soiled garment would remind him of his mother, and something erotic would burn inside him for a brief instant, before he suppressed it with a flash of anger.

For a while he'd been able to fool Rose by telling her he was going fishing – night fishing, mostly. Rose asked him why he never took the kid fishing. Darren told her he would, when the kid was older. And he would have done, he really would.

But then one February evening, burgling a house in Tongdean, the owner came home, surprising him. He legged it out the back, across the garden and straight into the deep end of an empty sodding swimming pool, breaking his right leg, his jaw and his nose, and knocking himself out cold.

Rose only visited him once in prison. That was to tell him she was taking the kid to Australia and she never wanted to see him again.

Now he was out and free again, he had nothing. Nothing but his suitcase at Terry Biglow's place – if, of course, Terry was still there and not dead or back inside. And nothing else but his hard, scarred body, and the urges from three years of lying on his narrow bunk, dreaming of what he would do when he was back out . . .

1997

26

'I *can* forget that I saw your face,' Rachael said, staring up at him.

In the yellow glow of the interior light he looked jaundiced. She tried to make eye contact, because in the dim, distant, terror-addled recesses of her mind, she remembered reading somewhere that hostages *should* try to make eye contact. That people would find it harder to hurt you if you established a bond.

She was trying, through her parched voice, to bond with this man – this monster – this *thing*.

'Sure you can, Rachael. When do you think I was born? Yesterday? Last week on Christmas fucking Day? I let you go, right, and one hour later you'll be in a police station with one of those E-Fit guys, describing me. Is that about the size of it?'

She shook her head vigorously from side to side. 'I promise you,' she croaked

'On your mother's life?'

'On my mother's life. Please can I have some water? Please, something.'

'So I could let you go, and if you do cheat me and go to the police, it would be OK for me to go round to your mother's house, in Surrenden Close, and kill her?'

Dimly, Rachael wondered how he knew where her

163

mother lived. Perhaps he had read it in the papers? That gave her a glimmer of hope. *If* he had read it in the papers, then it meant she was in the news. People would be out looking for her. Police.

'I know everything about you, Rachael.'

'You can let me go. I'm not going to risk her life.'

'I can?'

'Yes.'

'In your dreams.'

NOW

27

He liked to be inside nice big houses. Or, more accurately, to be inside the *inside* of these houses.

Sometimes, squeezed into narrow cavities, it felt as if he was wearing the house like a second skin! Or squeezed into a wardrobe, surrounded by hanging dresses and the tantalizing smells of the beautiful woman who owned them, and of the leather of her shoes, he would feel on top of the world, as if he owned the woman.

Like the one who owned the dresses all around him now. And who owned racks and racks full of some of his favourite designer shoes.

And for a while, soon now, he would own her! Very soon.

He already knew a lot about her – far more than her husband did, he was sure about that. It was Thursday. He'd watched her for the past three nights. He knew the hours she came home and went out. And he knew the secrets on her laptop – so obliging of her to have no password! He'd read the emails to and from the Greek man she was sleeping with. The files with the photographs she had taken of him, some of them very rude indeed.

But for a while, if he got lucky, *he* would be her lover tonight. Not Mr Hairy Designer Stubble, with his massive, indecently big pole.

He would have to be careful not to move an inch when she came home. The hangers were particularly clanky – they were mostly those thin metal ones that came from dry-cleaners. He'd removed some, the worst offenders, and laid them on the wardrobe floor, and he'd wrapped tissues around the ones nearest him. Now all he had to do was wait. And hope.

It was like fishing. A lot of patience was required. She might not come home for a long time, but at least there was no danger of her husband returning tonight.

Hubby had gone on a jet plane far, far away. To a software conference in Helsinki. It was all there on the kitchen table, the note from him to her telling her he'd see her on Saturday, and signed off, *Love you XXXX*, with the name of the hotel and the phone number.

Just to be sure, as he'd had time to kill, he'd phoned the hotel using the kitchen phone and asked to speak to Mr Dermot Pearce. He was told in a slightly sing-song voice that Mr Pearce was not picking up and asked if he would like to leave a message on his voicemail.

Yes, I am about to have sex with your wife, he was tempted to say, getting caught up in the thrill of the moment, the joy at the way it was all dropping into his lap. But sensibly he hung up.

The photographs of two teenage children, a boy and a girl, displayed downstairs in the living room were a slight worry. But their two bedrooms were immaculate. Not the bedrooms of children who were living here. He concluded they were the husband's children by a former marriage.

There was a cat, one of those nasty-looking Burmese things that had glared at him in the kitchen. He'd given it a kick and it had disappeared through the flap. All was quiet. He was happy and excited.

He could feel some houses living and breathing around him. Especially when the boilers rumbled into life and the walls vibrated. Breathing! Yes, like him now, breathing so hard with excitement he could hear the sound of it in his ears, and he could hear the pounding of his heart, the roaring of his blood coursing through his veins like it was in some kind of a race.

Oh, God, this felt so good!

28

Thursday 8 January

Roxy Pearce had been waiting all week for tonight. Dermot was away on a business trip and she had invited Iannis over for a meal. She wanted to make love to him here in her own home. The idea felt deliciously wicked!

She hadn't seen him since Saturday afternoon, when she'd strutted around his apartment naked in her brand-new Jimmy Choos, and they'd screwed with her still wearing them, which had driven him wild.

She'd read somewhere that the female mosquito gets so crazed for blood that she will do anything, even if she knows she will die in the process, to get that blood.

That's how she felt about being with Iannis. She had to see him. *Had* to have him, whatever the cost. And the more she had him, the more she needed him.

I am not a good person, she thought guiltily, as she drove home, accelerating her silver Boxster through the street-lit darkness up swanky Shirley Drive, past the Hove recreation ground. She turned right into Droveway Avenue, then right again into their drive and up to the big, square, modern house they'd had built, a secluded paradise within the city, with its rear garden backing on to the playing fields of a private school. The security lights popped on as she headed along the short drive.

I am SO not a good person.

This was the kind of thing you could rot in hell for. She'd been brought up a good Catholic girl. Brought up to believe in sin and eternal damnation. And she'd got herself both the T-shirt and the one-way ticket to damnation with Dermot.

He had been married when they'd met. She'd lured him away from his wife, and the kids he adored, after an intensely passionate affair that had become stronger and stronger over two years. They'd been crazily in love. But then, when they'd got together, the magic between them had steadily evaporated.

Now those same deep passions had exploded inside her all over again with Iannis. Just like Dermot, he was married, with two much younger children. Her best friend, Viv Daniels, had not approved, warning her she was going to get a reputation as a marriage wrecker. But she couldn't help it, could not switch off those feelings.

She reached up to the sun visor for the garage clicker, waited for the door to rise, drove into the space which seemed cavernous without Dermot's BMW and switched off the engine. Then she grabbed the Waitrose bags off the passenger seat and climbed out.

She had first met Iannis when Dermot had taken her to dinner at Thessalonica in Brighton. Iannis had come and sat at their table when their meal was finished, plying them with ouzo on the house and staring constantly at her.

It was his voice she'd fallen for first. The passionate way he spoke about food and about life, in his broken English. His handsome, unshaven face. His hairy chest, visible through a white shirt opened almost to the navel. His ruggedness. He seemed to be a man without a care in the world, relaxed, happy in his skin.

And so intensely sexy!

As she opened the internal door, then tapped out the code on the touch pad to silence the beeping alarm warning, she did not notice that a different light on the panel was on from the usual one. It was the night-setting warning for downstairs only, isolating the upstairs. But she was totally preoccupied in an altogether different direction. Would Iannis like her cooking?

She'd opted for something simple: mixed Italian hors d'oeuvres, then rib-eye steak and salad. And a bottle – or two – from Dermot's prized cellar.

Shutting the door behind her she called out to the cat, 'Sushi! Yo Sushi! Yo! Mummy's home!'

The cat's stupid name had been Dermot's idea – taken from the first restaurant they had gone to, in London, on their first date.

Silence greeted her, which was unusual.

Normally the cat would stride over to meet her, rub against her leg and then look up at her expectantly, waiting for dinner. But he wasn't there. Probably out in the garden, she thought. Fine.

She looked at her watch, then at the kitchen clock: 6.05. Less than an hour before Iannis was due to arrive.

It had been another shitty day at the office, with a silent phone and the overdraft on fast-track towards its limit. But tonight, for a few hours, she was not going to care. Nothing mattered but her time with Iannis. She would savour every minute, every second, every nano-second!

She emptied the contents of the bags on to the kitchen table, sorted them out, grabbed a bottle of Dermot's prized Château de Meursault and put it in the fridge to chill, then she opened a bottle of his Gevrey

Chambertin 2000 to let it breathe. Next she prised the lid off a can of cat food, scooped its contents into the bowl and placed it on the floor. 'Sushi!' she called out again. 'Yo Sushi! Supper!'

Then she hurried upstairs, planning to shower, shave her legs, spray on some Jo Malone perfume, then go back down and get the meal ready.

*

From inside her wardrobe, he heard her calling out, and he pulled his hood on over his head. Then he listened to her footsteps coming up the stairs. Everything inside him tightened with excitement. With anticipation.

He was in a red mist of excitement. Hard as hell! Trying to calm his breathing. Watching her from behind the silk dresses, through the curtained glass-fronted wardrobe doors. She looked so beautiful. Her sleek black hair. The careless way she kicked off her black court shoes. Then stepped wantonly out of her navy two-piece. As if she was doing it for him!

Thank you!

She removed her white blouse and her bra. Her breasts were smaller than he had imagined they might be, but that did not matter. They were OK. Quite firm, but with small nipples. It didn't matter. Breasts were not his thing.

Now her undies!

She was a shaver! Bald and white, down to a thin strip of a Brazilian! Very hygienic.

Thank you!

He was so aroused he was dripping perspiration.

Then she walked, naked, through into the bathroom. He listened to the hiss of the shower. This would be a good moment, he knew, but he didn't want her all wet

173

and slippery with soap. He liked the idea that she dried herself for him and perhaps put on some perfume for him.

After a few minutes she came back out into the bedroom, swathed in a big towel, a smaller white towel wrapped around her head. Then suddenly, as if she was giving him a private performance, she let the towel drop from her body, opened a wardrobe door, and selected from the racks a pair of elegant, gleaming black shoes with long stiletto heels.

Jimmy Choos!

He could barely contain his excitement as she slipped them on, placed one foot, then the other on the small armchair beside the bed and tied the straps, four on each shoe! Then she paraded around the room eyeing herself, naked, pausing to pose from every angle in the large mirror on the wall.

Oh yes, baby. Oh yes! Oh yes! Thank you!

He stared at the trim narrow strip of black pubic hair beneath her flat stomach. He liked it trim. He liked women who looked after themselves, who took care of the details.

Just for him!

She was coming towards the wardrobe now, towel still around her head. She reached out a hand. Her face was inches from his own, through the curtained glass.

He was prepared.

She pulled open the door.

His surgically gloved hand shot out, slamming the chloroform pad into her nose.

Like a striking shark, he glided out through the hanging dresses, grabbing the back of her head with his free arm, keeping up the pressure against her nose for a few seconds until she went limp in his arms.

1997

29

Rachael Ryan lay motionless on the floor of the van. His fist hurt from where he had hit her on the head. It hurt so damned much he worried he had broken both his thumb and a finger. He could hardly move them.

'*Shit*,' he said, shaking it. '*Shit, fuck, shit. Bitch!*'

He peeled off his glove so he could examine them, but it was hard to see anything in the feeble glow of the van's interior light.

Then he knelt beside her. Her head had gone back with a loud snap. He didn't know if it was a bone breaking in his own hand or her jaw. She did not seem to be breathing.

He laid his head against her chest anxiously. There was movement, but he wasn't sure if it was his movement or hers.

'Are you OK?' he asked, feeling a sudden surge of panic. 'Rachael? Are you OK? Rachael?'

He worked his glove back on, gripped her shoulders and shook her. 'Rachael? Rachael? Rachael?'

He pulled a small torch out of his pocket and shone it in her face. Her eyes were closed. He pulled one lid open and it closed again when he let go.

His panic was increasing. 'Don't die on me, Rachael! Do not die on me, do you hear me? Do you fucking hear me?'

Blood was trickling from her mouth.

'Rachael? Do you want something to drink? Want me to get you something to eat? You want a McDonald's? A Big Mac? A Cheeseburger? Or maybe a submarine? I could get you a submarine. Yeah? Tell me, tell me what filling you'd like in it. Spicy sausage? Something with melted cheese? They're really good those. Tuna? Ham?'

NOW

30

Yac was hungry. The chicken-n-melted cheese submarine had been tantalizing him for over two hours. The bag rolled around on the passenger seat, along with his Thermos flask every time he braked or went around a corner.

He'd been planning to pull over and eat it during his on-the-hour tea break, but there were too many people around. Too many fares. He'd had to drink his 11 p.m. cup while driving. Thursday nights were normally busy, but this was the first Thursday after the New Year. He had expected it to be quiet. However, some people had recovered and were out partying again. Taking taxis. Wearing nice shoes.

Uh-huh.

That was fine by him. Everyone had their own way of partying. He was happy for them all. Just so long as they paid what was on the meter and didn't try to do a runner, as someone did every now and then. Even better when they tipped him! All tips helped. Helped towards his savings. Helped towards building up his collection.

That was growing steadily. Very nicely. Oh yeah!

A siren wailed.

He felt a sudden prick of alarm. Held his breath.

Flashing blue lights filled his mirrors, then a police car shot past. Then another police car moments later, as if following in its wake. Interesting, he thought. He was out all night most nights and it wasn't often he saw two police cars together. Must be something bad.

He was approaching his regular spot on Brighton seafront, where he liked to pull over every hour, on the hour, during the night and drink his tea, and now, also, to read his paper. Since the rape in the Metropole Hotel last Thursday he had started to read the paper every night. The story excited him. The woman's clothes had been taken. But what excited him most of all was reading that her shoes had been taken.

Uh-huh!

He brought the taxi to a halt, switched off the engine and picked up the carrier bag with the submarine inside, but then he put it down again. It did not smell good any more. The smell made him feel sick.

His hunger was gone.

He wondered where those police cars were headed.

Then he thought about the pair of shoes in the boot of his taxi and he felt good again.

Really good!

He tossed the submarine out of the window.

Litter lout! he chided himself. *You bad litter lout!*

31

One good thing, or rather, one of the *many* good things about Cleo being pregnant, Grace thought, was that he was drinking a lot less. Apart from the occasional glass of cold white wine, Cleo had been dutifully abstemious, so he had cut down too. The bad thing was her damned craving for curries! He wasn't quite sure how many more of those his system could take. The whole house was starting to smell like an Indian fast-food joint.

He longed for something plain. Humphrey was unimpressed too. After just one lick, the puppy had decided that curries were not going to provide him with any tasty leftover scraps in his bowl that he would want to eat.

Roy endured them because he felt duty-bound to keep Cleo company. Besides, in one of the pregnancy-formen books Glenn Branson had given him, there was a whole passage about indulging and sharing your partner's cravings. It would make your partner feel happy. And if your partner felt happy, then the vibes would be picked up by your unborn child, and it would be born happy and not grow up to become a serial killer.

Normally, he liked to drink lager with curry, Grolsch preferably or his favourite German beer, Bitberger, or the weissbier he'd developed a taste for through his acquaintance with a German police officer, Marcel Kullen, and from his visits last year to Munich. But this week it was his rota turn to be the Major Crime Branch's duty Senior Investigating Officer, which meant he was on call 24/7, so he was reduced to soft drinks.

Which explained why he felt bright as a button, sitting in his office at 9.20 a.m. this Friday, sipping his second coffee, switching his focus from the serials to the emails that poured in as if they were coming out of a tap that had been left running, then to the paper mountain on his desk.

Just two and a bit more days to go until midnight Sunday, then another detective superintendent or detective chief inspector on the rota would take over the mantle of Senior Investigating Officer and it would be another six weeks before his turn came round again. He had so much work to get through, preparing cases for trial, as well as supervising the new Cold Case Team, that he really did not need any new cases to consume his time.

But he was out of luck.

His phone rang and as soon as he answered he instantly recognized the blunt, to-the-point voice of DI David Alcorn from Brighton CID.

'Sorry, Roy. Looks like we've got another stranger rape on our hands.'

Up until now, Brighton CID had been handling the Metropole Hotel rape, although keeping Roy informed. But now it sounded as if the Major Crime Branch was going to have to take over. Which meant him.

And it was a sodding Friday. Why on Fridays? What was it about Fridays?

'What do you have, David?'

Alcorn summed up briefly and succinctly: 'The victim is deeply traumatized. From what Uniform, who attended, have been able to glean, she arrived home alone last night

– her husband is away on a business trip – and was attacked in her house. She rang a friend, who went around this morning, and she was the one who called the police. The victim was seen by an ambulance crew but did not need medical attention. She's been taken up to the rape centre at Crawley accompanied by a SOLO and a CID constable.'

'What details do you have?'

'Very sketchy, Roy. As I said, I understand she's deeply traumatized. It sounds like a shoe was involved again.'

Grace frowned. 'What do you have on that?'

'She was violated with one of her shoes.'

Shit, Grace thought, scrabbling through the mess of papers on his desk for a pen and his notepad. 'What's her name?'

'Roxanna – or Roxy – Pearce.' Alcorn spelled the surname out in full. 'Address 76 Droveway Avenue, Hove. She has a PR agency in Brighton and her husband's in IT. That's all I really know at this stage. I've been in contact with Scenes of Crime and I'm going to the house now. Want me to pick you up on the way?'

His office was hardly on the way to the address for someone at Brighton nick, Roy thought, but he didn't argue. He could use the time in the car to get any more information on the Metropole rape that might have surfaced and to discuss the transfer of all information to the Major Crime Branch.

'Sure, thanks.'

When he terminated the call, he sat still for a moment, collecting his thoughts.

In particular, his mind went back to the Shoe Man. All this week, the Cold Case Team had been focusing on him as a priority to see what links, if any, they could establish in the MOs between the known cases, back in 1997, and the assault on Nicola Taylor at the Metropole on New Year's Eve.

Her shoes had been taken. That was the first possible link. Although back in 1997 the Shoe Man took just one shoe and the woman's panties. Both Nicola Taylor's shoes had been taken, along with all her clothes.

Somewhere beneath his paper mountain was the massively thick folder containing the offender profile, or rather, as these were now known, the Behavioural Investigator Report. It had been written by a distinctly oddball forensic psychologist, Dr Julius Proudfoot.

Grace had been sceptical of the man when he first encountered him back in 1997 on his investigations into Rachael Ryan's disappearance, but had consulted him on a number of cases since.

He became so absorbed in the report that he did not notice the click of his door opening and the footfalls across the carpet.

'Yo, old-timer!'

Grace looked up with a start to see Glenn Branson standing in front of his desk and said, 'What's your problem?'

'Life. I'm planning to end it all.'

'Good idea. Just don't do it here. I've got enough shit to deal with.'

Branson walked around his desk and peered over his shoulder, reading for some moments before saying, 'You know that Julius Proudfoot's seriously off his trolley, don't you? His reputation, right?'

'So what's new? You have to be seriously off your trolley to join the police force.'

'And to get married.'

'That too.' Grace grinned. 'What other great pearls of wisdom do you have for me?'

Branson shrugged. 'Just trying to be helpful.'

What would be really helpful, Grace thought, but did not say, would be if you were about a thousand miles from here right now. If you stopped trashing my house. If you stopped trashing my CD and vinyl collections. That's what would be *really* helpful.

Instead, he looked up at the man he loved more than any man he had ever met before and said, 'Do you want to fuck off, or do you want to really help me?'

'Sweetly put – how could I resist?'

'Good.' Grace handed him Dr Julius Proudfoot's file on the Shoe Man. 'I'd like you to summarize that for me for this evening's briefing meeting, into about two hundred and fifty words, in a form that our new ACC can absorb.'

Branson lifted the file up, then flipped through the pages.

'Shit, two hundred and eighty-two pages. Man, that's a fucker.'

'Couldn't have put it better myself.'

32

Roy Grace's father had been a true copper's copper. Jack Grace told his son that to be a police officer meant that you looked at the world differently from everyone else. You were part of a *healthy culture of suspicion*, he'd called it.

Roy had never forgotten that. It was how he looked at the world, always. It was how he looked, at this moment, at the posh houses of Shirley Drive on this fine, crisp, sunny January morning. The street was one of hilly Brighton and Hove's backbones. Running almost into the open countryside at the edge of the city, it was lined with smart detached houses way beyond the pocket of most police officers. Wealthy people lived here: dentists, bankers, car dealers, lawyers, local and London business people, and of course, as with all the smartest addresses, a smattering of successful criminals. It was one of the city's aspirational addresses. If you lived in Shirley Drive – or one of its tributaries – you were a *somebody*.

At least, you were to anyone driving by who did not have a copper's jaundiced eye.

Roy Grace did not have a jaundiced eye. But he had a good, almost photographic memory. As David Alcorn, in a smart grey suit, drove the small Ford up past the recreational ground, Grace clocked the houses one by one. It was routine for him. The London protection racketeer's Brighton home was along here. So was the Brighton brothel king's. And the crack cocaine king's was just one street away.

In his late forties, short, with cropped brown hair and smelling permanently of cigarette smoke, David Alcorn looked outwardly hard and officious, but inside he was a gentle man.

Turning right into Droveway Avenue he said, 'This is the street the missus would like to live in.'

'So,' Grace said, 'move here.'

'I'm just a couple of hundred grand short of being a couple of hundred grand short of the down payment,' he replied. 'And then some.' He hesitated briefly. 'You know what I reckon?'

'Tell me.'

Grace watched each of the detached houses slide by. On his right, they passed a Tesco convenience store. On his left, a dairy with an ancient cobbled wall.

'Your Cleo would like it here. Suit a classy lady like her, this area would.'

They were slowing now. Then Alcorn braked sharply. 'That's it there on the right.'

Grace looked for any signs of a CCTV camera as they drove down the short, laurel-lined driveway, but saw none. He clocked the security lights.

'All right, isn't it?' David Alcorn said.

It was more than sodding all right, it was totally stunning. If he had the money to design and build his dream house, Grace decided, this might be one he'd copy.

It was like a piece of brilliant white sculpture. A mixture of crisp, straight lines and soft curves, some played off against each other in daring geometric angles.

The place seemed to be built on split levels, the windows were vast and solar panels rose from the roof. Even the plants strategically placed around the walls looked as if they had been genetically modified just for this property. It wasn't a huge house; it was on a liveable scale. It must be an amazing place to come home to every night, he thought.

Then he focused on what he wanted to get from this crime scene, running through a mental checklist as they pulled up behind a small marked police car. A uniformed constable, a solid man in his forties, stood beside it. Behind him, a chequered blue-and-white crime scene tape closed off the rest of the driveway, which led up to a large integral garage.

They climbed out and the Constable, a respectful old-school officer, briefed them pedantically on what he had found earlier this morning when he had attended, and informed them that SOCO was on its way. He was not able to add much more to the details Alcorn had already given Grace, other than the fact that the woman had arrived home and apparently had deactivated the burglar alarm when she entered.

While they were talking, a small white van pulled up and a senior SOCO, a Crime Scene Manager called Joe Tindall with whom Grace had worked many times and found more than a tad tetchy, climbed out.

'Friday,' the Crime Scene Manager muttered by way of a greeting. 'What's with you and sodding weekends, Roy?' He gave Grace a smile that was incubating a leer.

'I keep asking offenders to stick to Mondays, but they're not an obliging lot.'

'I've got tickets to Stevie Wonder at the O_2 Arena tonight. If I miss that my relationship is kaput.'

'Every time I see you, you've got tickets to something, Joe.'

'Yeah. I like to think I have a life outside of this job, unlike half my colleagues.'

He gave the Detective Superintendent a pointed stare, then produced a clutch of white paper suits and blue overshoes from the rear of the van and handed them out.

Roy Grace sat on the rear sill of the van and slowly levered himself into the one-piece. Every time he did this, he cursed the designer as he wriggled to get his feet down through the trousers without tearing them, then worked himself into the arms. He was glad not to be in a public place, because the suit was almost impossible to put on without making a spectacle of yourself. Finally, grunting, he stooped down and pulled on the protective overshoes. Then he snapped on some latex gloves.

The Constable led the way inside and Grace was impressed that he'd had the good sense to mark on the ground with tape a single entry and exit route.

The open-plan hall, with polished parquet flooring, elegant metal sculptures, abstract paintings and tall, lush plants, was something that Cleo would love, he thought. There was a strong, pleasant smell of pine and a slightly sweeter, muskier scent, probably from pot-pourri, he thought. It made a refreshing change not to walk into a house that smelt of curry.

The Constable said he would come upstairs, to be available to answer questions, but he would not enter the bedroom, to minimize the disturbance in there.

Grace hoped that the officer, being this forensically aware, hadn't trampled all over it when he had responded to the emergency call earlier. He followed Alcorn and Tindall up a glass spiral staircase, along a short galleried landing and into a huge bedroom that smelt strongly of perfume.

The windows had curtains like a fine white gauze and the walls were lined with fitted wardrobes with curtained glass panels. The double doors of one of them were open and several dresses on their hangers lay fallen on the carpeted floor.

The centrepiece of the room was a king-sized bed with four tapered wooden columns rising from it. An unwound dressing gown cord lay around one of them, and a striped man's tie, knotted to a plain tie, around another. Four more ties, knotted together into two doubles, lay on the floor. The cream satin duvet was badly rumpled.

'Mrs Pearce was left gagged and tied by her wrists and ankles to each of those posts,' the Constable said from the doorway. 'She managed to free herself at about half past six this morning, and then she called her friend.' He checked his notebook. 'Mrs Amanda Baldwin. I have her number.'

Grace nodded. He was staring at a photograph on a glass-topped dressing table. It was of an attractive woman, with sleek black hair clipped up, wearing a long evening dress, standing next to a sharp-looking guy in a dinner suit.

Pointing at it, he said, 'Presume this is her?'

'Yes, chief.'

David Alcorn studied her too.

'What state was she in?' Grace asked the Constable.

'Pretty bad shock,' he replied. 'But quite compos mentis, considering her ordeal, if you know what I mean.'

'What do we know about her husband?'

'He went away yesterday on a business trip to Helsinki.'

Grace thought for a moment, then looked at David Alcorn. 'Interesting timing,' he said. 'Might be significant. I'd like to find out how often he goes away. It could be someone who knows her, or who's been stalking her.'

Turning to the Constable, he said, 'He was wearing a mask, right?'

'Yes, sir, he was – a hood with slits cut in.'

Grace nodded. 'Has the husband been contacted?'

'He's going to try to get a flight back today.'

Alcorn went out to check the other rooms.

Joe Tindall was holding a compact camera up to his eye. He took a 360-degree video of the scene, then zoomed in on the bed.

'Did you attend alone?' Grace asked the Constable.

He cast his eyes around the room as he spoke. On the floor lay a pair of cream undies, a white blouse, a navy skirt and top, tights and a bra. They weren't strewn around the room as if they had been torn off the woman; they looked as if they had been stepped out of carelessly and left where they fell.

'No, sir, with Sergeant Porritt. He's accompanied her and the SOLO to the Saturn Centre.'

Grace made a brief sketch plan of the room, noting the doors – one to the hallway, one to the en-suite bathroom – and the windows, all as possible entry/exit areas. He would require careful combing of the room for fingerprints, hair, fibres, skin cells, saliva, semen, possible lubricant traces from a condom, if one had been used, and footprints. The outside of the house would need to be searched carefully also, especially for footprints, and for clothing fibres that might have come off on a wall or a frame if the offender escaped via a window, as well as for cigarette butts.

He would need to write out and give Tindall his recovery policy on how much of the contents of the room and the house and surroundings he might want bagged and tagged for lab testing. The bedding, for sure. Towels in the bathroom in case the offender had dried his hands or any parts of his body. The soap.

He made notes, padding around the room, looking for anything out of the ordinary. There was a huge fixed mirror facing the bed, put there for kinky purposes he thought, not disapprovingly. On one bedside table were a diary and a chick-lit novel and on the other a pile of IT magazines. He opened each of the wardrobe doors in turn. There were more dresses hanging here than he had ever seen in his life.

Then he opened another and, breathing in a luxurious rich scent of leather, he encountered an Aladdin's cave of shoes. They were racked floor-to-ceiling on slide-out drawers. Grace was no expert on ladies' footwear, but he could tell at a glance that these were serious and classy. There had to be more than fifty pairs in here. The next door he opened revealed another fifty pairs. Followed by the same behind the third door.

'Looks like she's a high-maintenance lady!' he commented.

'I understand she has her own business, Roy,' David Alcorn said.

Grace silently chided himself. It had been a stupid comment, the kind of sexist assumption he might have expected from someone like Norman Potting.

'Right.'

He walked over to the window and peered out at the rear garden, a handsomely landscaped plot, with an oval swimming pool, beneath its winter cover, as its centre-piece.

Beyond the garden, visible through dense shrubs and young trees, were school playing fields. Rugby posts were up on two pitches and netted football goals on a third. This would have made a possible access route for the offender, he thought.

Who are you?

The Shoe Man?

Or just another creep?

33

'Yer could have fucking knocked,' Terry Biglow whined.

Knocking had never been Darren Spicer's style. He stood in the small room, in the semi-darkness from the drawn window blind, clutching his holdall and trying to breathe in as little as possible of the fetid air. The room reeked of ingrained cigarette smoke, old wood, dusty carpet and rancid milk.

'Thought you was still inside.' The elderly villain's voice was small and reedy. He lay, blinking into Spicer's torch beam. 'Anyhow, what the fuck you doing here at this hour?'

'Been shagging,' Spicer replied. 'Thought I'd pop by and tell you all about her, and pick up my stuff while I was at it.'

'Like I need to know. My days of shagging are over. Can hardly get it to piss. What do you want? Stop shining that bleedin' thing in my face.'

Spicer flicked the beam around the walls, found a wall switch and clicked it on. A gloomy overhead light in an even gloomier tasselled shade came on. He wrinkled his face in disgust at the sight of this room.

'You gone over the wall again?' Biglow said, still blinking.

He looked terrible, Spicer thought. Seventy, going on ninety.

'Good behaviour, mate, yeah? I'm on early release licence.' He tossed a wristwatch on to Biglow's chest. 'Brought you a present.'

Biglow grabbed it with his gnarled little hands and peered at it greedily. 'Wossis? Korean?'

'It's real. Nicked it last night.'

Biglow hauled himself up a little in the bed, scrabbled on the table beside him and put on some reading glasses that were unfashionably large. Then he studied the watch. 'Tag Heuer Aquaracer,' he announced. 'Nice one. Thieving and shagging?'

'Other way around.'

Biglow gave him a thin smile, revealing a row of sharp little teeth the colour of rusty tin. He was wearing a filthy-looking T-shirt that might once have been white. Beneath it he was all skin and bone. He smelt of old sacks.

'Nice,' he said. 'Very nice. Wot yer want for it?'

'A grand.'

'Yer having a laugh. Might get yer a monkey if I can find a buyer – and if it's kosher and not some copy. Otherwise, a one-er now. I could give yer a one-er now.'

A monkey was £500; a one-er £100.

'It's a two-grand watch,' Spicer said.

'And we're in a bleedin' recession and all.' Biglow looked at the watch again. 'You're lucky you didn't come out much later.' He fell silent, then when Spicer said nothing he went on. 'I ain't got long, see?' He coughed, a long, harsh, racking cough that made his eyes water, and spat some blood into a grimy handkerchief. 'Six months they gimme.'

'Bummer.'

Darren Spicer cast his eyes around the basement bedsit. It shook as a train thundered close by outside, emitting an eerie howl. A cold draught of air blew through the room. The place was a tip, just like he remembered it when he had last been here, over three years ago. A threadbare carpet covered some of the floorboards. Clothes hung from the dado rail on wire hangers. An old wooden clock on a shelf said it was 8.45. A crucifix was nailed to the wall just above the bed and a Bible lay on the table beside Biglow, along with several labelled bottles of medication.

This is going to be me in thirty years' time, if I get that far.

Then he shook his head. 'This it, Terry? This where you're ending your days?'

'It's all right. It's convenient.'

'Convenient? Convenient for what? The fucking funeral parlour?'

Biglow said nothing. A short distance away, across the Lewes Road, adjacent to the cemetery and the mortuary, was a whole line of undertakers.

'Ain't yer got running water?'

'Course I have,' Biglow spluttered, through another fit of coughing. He pointed across the room at a washbasin.

'Don't you ever wash? It smells like a toilet in here.'

'You want a cup of tea? Coffee?'

Spicer looked at a corner shelf on which sat a kettle and some cracked mugs. 'No thanks. Not thirsty.'

He shook his head as he looked down at the old villain. *You were a big player in this city. Even I was shit scared of you as a lad. Just the name Biglow put the fear into most people. Now look at you.*

The Biglows had been a crime family to be reckoned with, running one of the major protection rackets, controlling half of Brighton and Hove's drug scene, and Terry had been one of the scions. He wasn't a man you messed with, not if you didn't want a razor scar across your cheek or acid thrown in your face. He used to dress mean and sharp, with big rings and watches, and drive fancy cars. Now, ruined by booze, his face was all sallow and shrunken. His hair, which used to be freshly coiffed, even at midnight, now looked more worn than the carpet, and was the colour of nicotine from some off-the-shelf dye.

'On the nonce's wing, were you, in Lewes, Darren?'

'Screw you. I was never no *nonce*.'

'Not what I heard.'

Spicer looked at him defensively. 'I told you it all before, right? She was gagging for it. You can tell a woman that's gagging for it. Threw herself at me, didn't she? I had to push her away.'

'Funny the jury didn't believe yer.'

Biglow pulled a packet of cigarettes out of a drawer, shook out a cigarette and put it in his mouth.

Spicer shook his head. 'Lung cancer and you're lighting up?'

'Big lot of difference that's going to make now, nonce.'

'Fuck you.'

'Always nice to see yer, Darren.'

He lit his cigarette using a plastic lighter, inhaled and was then lost in a coughing fit.

Spicer knelt down, rolled back the carpet, removed some floorboards, then extricated the old, square leather suitcase which had three chains around it, each secured with a heavy-duty padlock.

Biglow held up the watch. 'Tell you what. I always been a fair man and don't want you thinkin' ill of me

after I gone. We got three years' left-luggage fee to negotiate and all. So what I'll do is give you thirty quid for the
watch. Can't say fairer than that.'

'A fucking carpet?'

In a fit of fury, Spicer grabbed Terry Biglow's hair
with his left hand and jerked him up, out of bed, and held
him in front of his face, dangling him like a ventriloquist's
dummy. He was surprised how light the man was. Then
he slammed a rising punch under his chin as hard as he
could, with his right hand. So hard it hurt like hell.

Terry Biglow went limp. Spicer released him and he
fell to the floor in a crumpled heap. He took a few steps
forward and trampled out the cigarette that was burning.
Then he looked around the squalid bedsit for anything
that might be worth taking. But other than recovering the
watch, there was nothing. Nothing at all. There really
wasn't.

Lugging the heavy suitcase under one arm, and his
holdall containing all his basics, he let himself out of the
door, hesitating for one moment, in which he turned back
to the crumpled heap.

'See you at your funeral, mate.'

He closed the door behind him, then climbed the
stairs and went out into the freezing, blustery Brighton
Friday morning.

34

For the second time in just over a week, the Sexual Offences Liaison Officer, DC Claire Westmore, was back at the Saturn Centre, the Sexual Assault Referral Centre attached to Crawley Hospital.

She knew from experience that no two victims ever reacted the same way, and nor did their conditions remain static. One of the difficult tasks facing her right now was to keep abreast of the changing state of mind of the woman she was with. But while treating her sensitively and sympathetically, and trying to make her feel as safe as possible, she could not lose sight of the cruel fact that Roxy Pearce, like it or not, was a crime scene from whom every possible scrap of forensic evidence needed to be obtained.

When that was completed, she would let the woman rest – safe here in this suite – and with the help of medication get some sleep. Tomorrow, when hopefully the woman would be in a better state, the interview process could start. For Roxy Pearce, as with most victims, that was likely to mean three gruelling days of reliving what had happened, with Westmore extracting from her a harrowing narrative that would eventually fill thirty pages of her A4 notebook.

At this moment she was going through the most

distressing part of all for the victim – and for herself. They were alone with a female Forensic Medical Examiner, or FME, as Police Surgeons were now called, in the sterile Forensic Room. Roxy Pearce was wearing only the white towelling dressing gown and pink slippers in which she had travelled here. She'd had a blanket wrapped around her for warmth in the police car, but now that had been removed. She sat, hunched and silent and forlorn, on the blue examining couch, her head bowed, eyes staring blankly at nothing, her long black hair matted and partially obscuring her face. From being hyper-talkative when the police had first arrived at her house, she had now become almost catatonic.

Claire Westmore had heard victims say that being raped was like having their souls murdered. Just as with murder, there was no going back. No amount of therapy would restore Roxy Pearce to the person she had previously been. Yes, in time she would recover a little, enough to function, to live a seemingly normal life. But it would be a life constantly stalked by the shadow of fear. A life in which she would find it hard ever to trust anyone or any situation.

'You're safe here, Roxy,' Claire said to her with a bright smile. 'You're in the safest possible place. He can't get to you here.'

She smiled again. But there was no response. It was like talking to a waxwork.

'Your friend Amanda is here,' she went on. 'She just went out for a ciggie. She's going to stay with you all day.' Again she smiled.

Again the blank expression. The dead eyes. Blank. As blank as everything in here around her. As blank and numb as her insides.

Roxy Pearce's eyes registered the magnolia-coloured walls of the small room. Recently painted. The round, institutional clock showing the time as 12.35. A rack of boxes containing blue latex gloves. Another rack of blue and red crates containing syringes, swabs and vials, all sealed in sterile wrappers. A pink chair. Weighing scales. A basin with a moisturizer dispenser on one side and sterile handwash on the other. A telephone sitting on a bare white work-surface like some unused lifeline in a television quiz game. A foldaway screen on castors.

Tears welled in her eyes. She wished Dermot was here. She wished, in her addled mind, that she hadn't been unfaithful to him, hadn't had this crazy thing with Iannis.

Then suddenly she blurted out, 'It's all my fault, isn't it?'

'Why do you think that, Roxy?' the SOLO asked, jotting down her words in the log she was keeping in her notepad. 'You mustn't blame yourself at all. That's not right.'

But the woman lapsed back into silence.

'OK, my love. Don't worry. You don't have to say anything to me. We don't have to talk today if you don't want to, but what I do need to do is obtain forensic evidence from you, to help us try to catch the man who did this to you. Is that all right with you?'

After some moments, Roxy said, 'I feel dirty. I want to take a shower. Can I do that?'

'Of course, Roxy,' the Forensic Medical Examiner said. 'But not just yet. We don't want to wash away any evidence, do we?' She had a slightly bossy tone, Claire Westmore thought, a little too officious for the victim's fragile state.

Silence again. Roxy's mind went off on a tangent. She had taken out two of Dermot's best bottles. Left them somewhere. One open on the kitchen table, the other in the fridge. She would have to buy a bottle somewhere to replace the opened one, and go to the house before Dermot came back and replace them in the cellar. He'd go loopy otherwise.

The FME snapped on a pair of latex gloves, walked over to the plastic crates and removed the first item from its sterile wrapping. A small, sharp implement for taking scrapings from underneath fingernails. It was possible the woman had scratched her attacker and that crucial skin cells containing his DNA might be trapped beneath her nails.

This was just the start of a long ordeal for Roxy Pearce in this room. Before she would be permitted to take a shower, the FME would have to take swabs from every part of her body where contact with her assailant might have occurred, looking for saliva, semen and skin cells. She would comb her pubic hair, take her blood alcohol and a urine sample for toxicology tests, and sketch in the Medical Examination Book any damage to the genital area.

As the FME worked her way through each of the woman's nails, bagging the scrapings separately, the SOLO tried to reassure Roxy.

'We're going to get this man, Roxy. That's why we're doing this. With your cooperation, we'll be able to stop him from doing this to anyone else. I know it must be hard for you, but try to hold on to that.'

'I don't know why you're bothering,' Roxy suddenly said. 'Only 4 per cent of rapists ever get convicted. Right?'

Claire Westmore hesitated. She'd heard that nationwide it was actually only 2 per cent, because just 6 per cent of rapes were ever reported. But she didn't want to make things worse for the poor woman.

'Well, that's not entirely true,' she answered. 'But the figures are low, yes. That's because so few victims have your guts, Roxy. They don't have the courage to come forward like you are doing.'

'Guts?' she retorted bitterly. 'I don't have *guts*.'

'Yes, you do. You really do have guts.'

Roxy Pearce shook her head bleakly. 'It's my fault. If I'd had guts, I'd have stopped him. Everyone'll think I must have wanted him to do this, that I must have encouraged him somehow. Anyone else might have managed to stop him, knee him in the nuts or something, but I didn't, did I? I just lay there.'

35

Darren Spicer's morning was getting better. He'd recovered his things from Terry Biglow and now he had a place to store them, a tall, cream metal locker with a key of his own at St Patrick's night shelter. And he hoped, in a few weeks, he'd get a MiPod there.

The big Neo-Norman church at the end of a quiet residential street in Hove had adapted to the changing world. With its shrinking congregation, much of St Patrick's cavernous interior had been partitioned off and placed in the hands of a charity for the homeless. Part of it was a fourteen-bed dormitory where people could doss down for a maximum of three months. Another part, the MiPod Room, was a sanctuary. It was where people who showed real intentions of retraining could stay for a further ten weeks in the hope of giving them a stable base.

The MiPod Room was modelled on Japanese capsule hotels. It was a self-contained space, with six plastic pods, a kitchen area and a living area with television. Each of the pods was large enough to sleep in and to store a couple of suitcases.

To become eligible for one, first Spicer had to convince the management here that he was a model resident. He hadn't thought beyond those ten weeks in the pod, but by then, with luck, he'd have plenty of cash to rent a flat or house again.

Being a model resident meant obeying the rules, such as having to be out by 8.30 a.m. and not returning until dinnertime at 7.30 p.m. During the hours in between he was meant to be retraining. Yeah, well, that's what they would all think he was doing. He'd report to the retraining centre and sign on, and hopefully get a job in the maintenance department of one of Brighton's posh hotels. There'd be some easy pickings in the rooms from that. Should be able to build himself a nice stash. And stumble across a willing woman or two, like he had last night.

Shortly after midday, dressed in a windcheater over a sweater, jeans and sneakers, he left the retraining centre. The interview had gone fine and he now possessed a stamped form and the address of the swanky Grand Hotel on the seafront, where he would start on Monday. He had the rest of today to kill.

As he mooched along Western Road, the wide shopping street connecting Brighton with Hove, his hands were dug into his pockets against the cold. He had just £7 in his pocket – all that was left from his £46 prison discharge allowance, plus the small amount of cash he'd had on him when he'd last been arrested. And he had his emergency stash in the suitcase he had retrieved from Terry Biglow.

In his head he was making out a shopping list of stuff he needed. He was given basic necessities here, like new razor blades, shaving cream, toothpaste. But he needed a few treats. He walked past a bookshop called City Books, then stopped, turned back and peered at the display in the window. Dozens of books, some by authors whose names he knew, others by authors he'd never heard of.

It was still a novelty being out. To smell the salty sea air. To walk freely among women. To hear the hum and buzz and roar of vehicles and occasional snatches of music. Yet although he felt free, he felt vulnerable and exposed too. Life *inside*, he realized, had become his comfort zone. He didn't know this other world so well any more.

And this street seemed to have changed in the past three years. It was much more vibrant than he remembered. As if the world, three years on, was a party he had not yet been invited to.

It was lunchtime and the restaurants were starting to get busy. Filling up with strangers.

Just about everyone was a stranger to him.

Sure, there were a few friends he could contact, and would in time. But he didn't have a lot to say to them at the moment. Same old same old. Yeah. He'd call them when he needed to score some coke. Or when he had some brown to sell.

A police car was coming past in the opposite direction and automatically he turned and peered in through an estate agent's window, pretending to be interested.

Most of the police in this city knew his face. Half of them had nicked him at one time or another. He had to remind himself that he was permitted to walk down this street now. That he wasn't a fugitive. He was a citizen of Brighton and Hove. He was like everyone else!

He stared at some of the houses on display. A nice one opposite Hove Park caught his eye. It looked familiar and he had a feeling he'd burgled it some years ago. Four bedrooms, conservatory, double garage. A nice price too: £750,000. Yeah, a bit above his bracket. Like £750,000 above his bracket.

The huge Tesco supermarket was a short distance ahead of him now. He crossed the road and walked in past the queue of waiting cars at the car-park barriers. Plenty of smart ones. A convertible Beemer, a nice Merc sports and several huge, in-your-face off-roader jobs – Brighton and Hove ladies doing their shopping. Yummy mummies with infants strapped smugly into their child seats in the rear.

People with folding money, with credit cards, debit cards, Tesco Club Cards.

How obliging some of them were!

He stopped outside the front entrance, watching the stream of people coming out with their bags or with laden trolleys. He ignored the ones holding just a couple of bags; they were of no interest to him. It was the laden trolleys he focused on. The mummies and daddies and rest-home proprietors doing their big shop for the week-end ahead. The ones who would have had £200 and more swiped from their MasterCards, or Barclaycards, or Amex.

Some had infants strapped into the buggy seats in their trolleys, but he wasn't interested in those. Who the fuck wanted baby food?

Then he saw her coming out.

Oh yes! Perfect!

She looked rich. She looked arrogant. She had the kind of figure he'd lain on the top bunk of his cell dreaming about for three years. She had a trolley piled so high that the top layer defied gravity. And she was wearing really nice boots. Snakeskin, with five-inch heels, he guessed.

But it wasn't the shoes that interested him at this moment. It was the fact that she paused by the dustbins, screwed up her receipt and tossed it in. He strolled nonchalantly over to the bin, keeping an eye on her, while she pushed her trolley towards a black Range Rover Sport.

Then he slipped his hand inside the top of the bin and pulled out a clutch of receipts. It only took a moment to find hers – it was a good two feet long, with a checkout time of just two minutes ago.

Well, well – £185! And, a real bonus, it was a cash receipt, which meant he would not have to produce any credit card or ID. He read down the items: wine, whiskey, prawn cocktail, moussaka, apples, bread, yoghurt. So much stuff. Razor blades! Some of the stuff he didn't want, but hey, this was not the time to be fussy ... Fantastic! He gave her a little wave, which she never saw. At the same time, he clocked her car's registration number – well, she was a looker with nice shoes, you never knew! Then, grabbing a trolley, he entered the store.

*

It took Spicer half an hour to go through her list, item by item. He was aware of the checkout time printed at the bottom, but he had his story ready, that one of the eggs was broken so he'd gone to replace it, and then he'd stopped for a coffee.

There was some stuff, such as a dozen tins of cat food, that he really did not need, and two tins of smoked oysters he could have done without, but he decided it was better to match the items on the list exactly, in case he was challenged. Six frozen steak and kidney pies he truly blessed her for. His kind of grub! And the half a dozen tins of Heinz Baked Beans. He had no stomach for fancy stuff. He approved of her choice of Jameson's Irish Whiskey, but wished she had chosen something more to his taste than Baileys. She was big into organic eggs and fruit. He could live with that.

He would take his shopping home and chuck or maybe flog or barter for cigarettes the stuff he did not want. Then he would go out on the hunt.

Life was looking good. Only one thing could improve it for him at the moment. Another woman.

1998

36

Friday 2 January

It was now eight days since Rachael Ryan had been reported missing by her parents.

Eight days in which there had been no proof of life.

Roy Grace had worked doggedly on the case since Christmas Day, increasingly certain something was very wrong, until Chief Inspector Jack Skerritt had insisted that the Detective Sergeant take New Year's Eve off to spend with his wife.

Grace had done so reluctantly, torn between his concern to find Rachael and his need to keep the peace at home with Sandy. Now, after a two-day absence, he returned on this Friday morning to a briefing update by Skerritt. The Chief Inspector told his small team of detectives of his decision, made in consultation with his ACC, to upgrade *Operation Sundown* to an Incident Room. A HOLMES – Home Office Large Major Enquiry System team – had been requisitioned, and six additional detectives from other parts of the county were being drafted in.

The Incident Room was set up on the fourth floor of John Street police station, next to the CCTV department and across the corridor from the busy *Operation Houdini* Incident Room, where the investigation into the Shoe Man continued.

Grace, who was convinced that the two operations

should be merged, was allocated his present desk, where he was to be based for the duration of the inquiry. It was by the draughty window, giving him a bleak view across the car park and the grey, rain-soaked rooftops towards Brighton Station and the viaduct.

Seated at the next desk along was DC Tingley, a bright, boyish-looking twenty-six-year-old police officer whom he liked. In particular, he liked the man's energy. Jason Tingley, sleeves rolled up, was on the phone, pen in hand, dealing with one of the dozens of calls that had come in following their reconstruction, three days earlier, of Rachael's journey from the East Street taxi rank back home.

Grace had a thick file on Rachael Ryan on his desk. Already, despite the holidays, he had her bank and her credit-card details. There had been no transactions during the past week, which meant he could effectively rule out that she had been mugged for the contents of her handbag. There had been no calls from her mobile phone since 2.35 on Christmas morning.

However, there was something useful he had gleaned from the mobile phone company. There were mobile phone base stations, or mini masts, located around Brighton and Hove, and every fifteen minutes, even in standby mode, the phone would send a signal to the nearest mast, like a plane radioing its current position, and receive one back.

Although no further calls had been made from Rachael Ryan's phone, it had remained switched on for three more days, until the battery died, he guessed. According to information he'd received from the phone company, shortly after her last phone call, she had suddenly moved two miles east of her home – in a vehicle of some kind, judging from the speed at which it had happened.

She had remained there for the rest of the night, until 10 a.m. on Christmas Day. Then she had travelled approximately four miles west, into Hove. Again the speed of the journey indicated that she was travelling in a vehicle. Then she had stopped and remained static until the last signal received, shortly after 11 p.m. on Saturday.

On a large-scale map of Brighton and Hove on the Incident Room wall, Grace had drawn a red circle around the maximum area that would be covered by this particular beacon's range. It included most of Hove as well as part of Brighton, Southwick and Portslade. Over 120,000 people lived within its radius – an almost impossible number for house-to-house enquiries.

Besides, the information was only of limited value, he realized. Rachael could have been separated from her phone. It was just an indicator of where she *might* be, but no more. But so far it was all they had. One line he would try, he decided, was to see if anything had been picked up on CCTV cameras on the routes matching the signal information. But there was only coverage on major routes and that was limited.

Rachael did not own a computer and there was nothing on the one in her office at American Express to give any clue as to why she might have disappeared.

At the moment it was if she had fallen through a crack in the earth.

Tingley put down the phone and drew a line through the name he had written a couple of minutes earlier on his pad. 'Tosser!' he said. 'Time waster.' Then he turned to Roy. 'Good New Year's Eve, mate?'

'Yeah, it was all right. Went with Dick and Leslie Pope to Donatello's. You?'

'Went up to London with the missus. Trafalgar

Square. It was brilliant – until it started pissing with rain.'
He shrugged. 'So what do you think? She still alive?'

'Not looking good,' he replied. 'She's a homebody.
Still sore about the bust-up with her ex. Into shoes, big
time.' He looked at his colleague and shrugged. 'That's
the bit I keep coming back to.'

Grace had spent an hour earlier in the day with
Dr Julius Proudfoot, the behavioural analyst *Operation
Houdini* had drafted into their team. Proudfoot told him
that, in his view, Rachael Ryan's disappearance could not
be connected to the Shoe Man. He still did not understand how the arrogant psychologist had arrived at that
conclusion, since he had so little evidence.

'Proudfoot insists this isn't the Shoe Man's style. He
says the Shoe Man attacks his victims and then leaves
them. Because he's used the same MO for five victims,
Proudfoot doesn't accept that he would suddenly have
changed and kept one.'

'Similar MO, Roy,' Jason Tingley said. 'But he takes
them in different places, right? He tried that first one in
an alley. One in a hotel room. One in her home. One
under the pier. One in a multi-storey car park. Clever if
you want to look at it that way – makes it hard for anyone
to second-guess him.'

Grace looked down at his notes, thinking hard. There
was one common denominator with each of the Shoe
Man's victims. All of them were into designer shoes. Each
one had bought a new pair of shoes, from different shops
in Brighton, shortly before they were attacked. But so far
interviews with staff in the shops had revealed nothing
helpful.

Rachael Ryan had bought a new pair of shoes too.
Three days before Christmas. Expensive for a girl of her

means – £170. She had been wearing them the night she vanished.

But Proudfoot had dismissed that.

Grace turned to Tingley and told him this.

Tingley nodded, looking pensive suddenly. 'So if it isn't the Shoe Man, who's taken her? Where has she gone? If she's OK, why isn't she contacting her parents? She must have seen the appeal in the *Argus* or heard it on the radio.'

'Doesn't make any sense. She normally phones her parents every day and chats to them. Eight days of silence? And at this time of year – Christmas and New Year? No call to wish them Happy Christmas or Happy New Year? Something's happened to her, for sure.'

Tingley nodded. 'Abducted by aliens?'

Grace looked back down at his notes. 'The Shoe Man took his victims in a different place each time, but what he did to them was consistent. And even more important was what he did to his victims' lives. He didn't need to kill them. They were already dead inside by the time he had finished with them.'

Are you a victim of the Shoe Man, Rachael? Or has some other monster got you?

NOW

37

MIR-1, the larger of the two Major Incident Rooms at Sussex House, had an atmosphere that Roy Grace always found energizing.

Located in the heart of the Major Crime Suite at the CID headquarters, it would have looked to a casual observer like any other large administrative office. It had cream walls, functional grey carpeting, red chairs, modern wooden workstations, filing cabinets, a water dispenser and several large whiteboards on the walls. The windows were high up, with permanently closed blinds across them, as if to discourage anyone from wasting one second of their time looking out of them.

But to Roy Grace this was much more than an office. MIR-1 was the very nerve centre of his current investigation, as it had been with the previous ones he had run from here, and to him it had an almost hallowed atmosphere. Many of the worst crimes committed in Sussex in the past decade had been solved, and the offenders locked up, thanks to the detective work that had been carried out in this room.

The red, blue and green marker-pen scrawlings on the whiteboards in any other office out in the commercial world might have been performance figures, sales targets, market penetrations. Here they were timelines of the crimes, family trees of the victims and suspects, along with photographs and any other key information. When they got an E-Fit of the offender, hopefully soon, that would go up too.

The place instilled in everyone a sense of purpose, of racing against a clock, and, except during briefings, there was little of the chat and banter between colleagues that was usual in police offices.

The only frivolity was a photocopied cartoon of a fat blue fish from the film *Finding Nemo* which Glenn Branson had stuck on the inside of the door. It had become a tradition in Sussex CID for a jokey image to be found for each operation, to provide a little light relief from the horrors that the team had to deal with, and this was the movie-buff Detective Sergeant's contribution to *Operation Swordfish*.

There were three other dedicated Major Crime Suites around the county, also housing similar rooms, the most recent being the purpose-built one at Eastbourne. But this location was more convenient for Roy Grace, as well as being well sited, because the two crimes he was now investigating had occurred only a couple of miles away.

There were all kinds of repeating patterns in life, he had noticed, and it seemed that recently he was on a run of crimes that took place – or were discovered – on Fridays, thus ensuring his and everyone else's weekend was wiped out.

He was meant to be going to dinner with Cleo at one of her oldest friend's tomorrow night – Cleo wanted to show him off, as she grinningly told him. He had been looking forward to a further insight into the life of this woman he was so deeply in love with and still knew so little about. But that was now down the khazi.

Fortunately for him, unlike Sandy, who had never understood or got used to his frequent crazy working hours, Cleo was regularly on call herself 24/7, having to go out at all hours to recover bodies from wherever they were found. Which made her much more sympathetic – although not always totally forgiving.

It was the case in the early stages of any major crime investigation that everything else had to be instantly dropped. The first task of the Senior Investigating Officer's assistant was to clear the SIO's diary.

It was the first twenty-four hours after the crime had been discovered that were the most crucial. You needed to protect the crime scene to preserve the forensic evidence as much as possible. The perpetrator would be at his most heightened state of anxiety, the *red mist* that people tended to be in after committing a serious crime, in which they might behave erratically, drive erratically. There would be possible eyewitnesses for whom it was all fresh in their minds, and a chance to reach them quickly through the local press and media. And all CCTV cameras within a reasonable radius would still retain footage for those past twenty-four hours.

Grace looked down at the notes typed by his assistant – his MSA – which lay beside his fresh Policy Book for this case.

'It is 6.30 p.m., Friday, 9 January,' he read out. 'This is the first briefing of *Operation Swordfish*.'

The Sussex Police computer threw up operation names at random, most of them totally irrelevant to the case on which they were working. But here, he thought wryly, it was just a tad appropriate, fish being slippery creatures.

Grace was pleased that all but one of the trusted key CID members he wanted for his core team were available. Seated around the workstation with him were DC Nick Nicholl, still looking bleary-eyed from recent father-hood, DC Emma-Jane Boutwood, highly effective DS Bella Moy, an open box of Maltesers, as ever, in front of her, belligerent DS Norman Potting, and Grace's mate and protégé DS Glenn Branson. Absent was DS Guy Batchelor, who was away on annual leave. Instead he had a detective constable he'd worked with some while back and had been very impressed with, Michael Foreman, a lean, quietly authoritative man, with gelled dark hair, who had an air of calm about him that made people naturally turn to him, even when he wasn't the senior officer present at a situation. For the past year, with a temporary promotion to acting sergeant, Foreman had been on secondment to the team at the Regional Intelligence Office. Now he was back at Sussex House, in his old rank, but Grace did not think it would be long before the man became a full sergeant. And, no question, he was heading for a much higher things than that.

Also present among Grace's regulars was HOLMES analyst John Black, a mild, grey-haired man who could have been a backroom accountant, and DC Don Trotman, a Public Protection Officer, who would be tasked with checking on MAPPA, the Multi-Agency Public Protection Arrangements, whether any recently released prisoners who were sexual offenders fitted the MO of the current offender.

New to the team was an analyst, Ellen Zoratti, who would be working closely with Brighton division and the

HOLMES analyst, progressing the intelligence leads, checking with the National Police Crime Database and SCAS, the Serious Crime Analysis Section, as well as carrying out instructions from Roy Grace.

Also new was a female press officer, Sue Fleet, from the revamped Police Public Relations Team. The pleasant thirty-two-year-old redhead, who had been a trusted and popular member of the Central Brighton John Street team, had replaced the previous public relations officer, Dennis Ponds, a former journalist who had never had an easy relationship with many members of this force, including Grace himself.

Grace wanted Sue Fleet present to organize an immediate media strategy. He needed to get a quick public response to help in the task of finding the offender and to alert the female population to the possible dangers they now faced, but at the same time he did not want to throw the city into panic. It was a delicate PR balance and would be a challenging task for her.

'Before I start,' Grace said, 'I want to remind you all of some statistics. In Sussex we have a good clear-up rate for homicide – with 98 per cent of all murders in the past decade solved. But in rape we've fallen behind the national average of 4 per cent to just above 2 per cent. This is not acceptable.'

'Do you think that's down to the attitude of some police officers?' asked Norman Potting, dressed in one of the tired old tweedy jackets that reeked of pipe smoke that he always seemed to wear. In Grace's view they made him look more like an elderly geography teacher than a detective. 'Or that some victims are just not reliable witnesses – because of other agendas?'

'Other agendas, Norman? Like that old attitude police

officers used to have that women who got raped asked for it? Is that what you mean?'

Potting grunted, non-committally.

'For God's sake, what planet are you on?' Bella Moy, who had never liked him, rounded on him furiously. 'It's like living a real *Life on Mars* working with you.'

The DS shrugged defensively and then mumbled, barely audibly, as if he wasn't convinced enough to say whatever he had on his mind more boldly, 'We know that some women cry rape out of guilt, don't they? It does make you wonder.'

'Makes you wonder what?' Bella demanded.

Grace was glaring at him, scarcely able to believe his ears. He was so angry he was tempted to kick the man off his investigation right now. He was beginning to think he had made a mistake bringing this tactless man in on such a sensitive case. Norman Potting was a good policeman, with a range of detective skills that were, unfortunately, not matched by his social skills. Emotional intelligence was one of the major assets of a good detective. On a scale of one to a hundred, Potting would have rated close to zero on this score. Yet he could be damned effective, particularly on outside enquiries. Sometimes.

'Do you want to stay on this investigation, Norman?' Grace asked him.

'Yes, Chief, I do. I think I could contribute to it.'

'Really?' Grace retorted. 'Then let's get something straight, from the start.' He glanced around the assembled company. 'I hate rapists as much as I hate murderers. Rapists destroy their victims' lives. Whether it is a stranger rape, a date rape or a rape by someone the victim knew and thought they trusted. And there's no difference in that, whether it's female rape or male rape, OK? But at this moment we happen to be dealing with attacks on women, which are more common.'

He stared pointedly at Norman Potting, then went on: 'Being raped is like being in a bad car crash that leaves you disabled for life. One moment a woman is going about her day or her night, in her comfort zone, the next moment she is shattered, and she's all smashed up in the wreckage. She faces years of counselling, years of terror, nightmares, mistrust. No matter how much help she receives, she will never be the same again. She will never lead what we know as a *normal* life again. Do you understand what I'm saying, Norman? Some women who are raped end up maiming themselves afterwards. They scrub their vaginas with wire wool and bleach because they have such a need to get rid of what happened. That's just a small part of what being raped can do to someone. Do you understand?' He looked around. 'Do you all understand?'

'Yes, chief,' Potting mumbled in his thick burr. 'I'm sorry. I didn't mean to be insensitive.'

'Does a man with four failed marriages know the meaning of the word *insensitive*,' Bella Moy asked, angrily snatching a Malteser from the box, popping it in her mouth and crunching it.

'OK, Bella, thank you,' Grace said. 'I think Norman knows where I'm coming from.'

Potting stared at his notepad, his face a dark shade of beetroot, and nodded, chastened.

Grace looked back down at his notes. 'We have another slightly sensitive issue. The Chief Constable, the Deputy Chief Constable and two of our four Assistant Chief Constables were all at the same dinner dance at the Metropole Hotel on New Year's Eve which Nicola Taylor, the first rape victim, attended.'

There was a moment of silence as everyone reflected on this.

'Are you saying that makes them suspects, boss?' DC Michael Foreman asked.

'Everyone who was in the hotel is a potential suspect, but I think I'd prefer to call them at this point *material witnesses to be eliminated from our enquiries*,' Grace replied. 'They're going to have to be interviewed along with everyone else. Any volunteers?'

No one raised a hand.

Grace grinned. 'Looks like I'll have to allocate that task to one of you. Could be a good opportunity to get noticed for promotion, or screw up your career permanently.'

There were a few uncomfortable smiles in the room.

'Perhaps I can recommend our master of tact, Norman Potting,' Bella Moy said.

There was a titter of laughter.

'I'd be happy to take that on,' Potting said.

Grace, deciding that Potting was the last person in this room he would allocate that task to, scribbled a note in his Policy Book, then studied his briefing notes for a moment.

'We have two stranger rapes within eight days, with enough similarity in the MO to assume for the moment it is the same offender,' he went on. 'This charmer made both his victims perform sexual acts on themselves with their shoes, then penetrated them anally with the heels of their shoes, then raped them himself. From what we have been able to establish – and the second victim has so far only given us a little information – he was unable to maintain an erection. This may have been due to premature ejaculation or because he is sexually dysfunctional.

There is one significant difference in his MO. Back in 1997, the Shoe Man took only one shoe, and his victim's panties. In the Metropole rape of Nicola Taylor he took all her clothes, including both her shoes. With Roxy Pearce, he took just her shoes.'

He paused to look down at his notes again, while several members of his team made notes also.

'Our offender appears to be forensically aware. In each case he wore a black hood and surgical gloves and used a condom. He either shaved his bodily hair or naturally had none. He is described as being of medium to small height, thin and softly spoken, with a neutral accent.'

Potting put up his hand and Grace nodded.

'Chief, you and I were both involved with *Operation Sundown*, the disappearance of a woman back in 1997 which may or may not have been connected to a similar case then, the Shoe Man – *Operation Houdini*. Do you think there's a possible link?'

'Apart from the differences in the trophies he took, the Shoe Man's MO is remarkably similar to the current offender's.' Grace nodded at the Analyst. 'This is one reason I've brought Ellen in.'

Sussex CID employed forty analysts. All but two of them were female, most of them with social sciences backgrounds. Male analysts were so rare that they were nicknamed *manolysts*. Ellen Zoratti was a very bright woman of twenty-eight, with dark hair just off her shoulders, cut in a sharp, modern style, and was elegantly dressed in a white blouse, black skirt and zebra-striped tights.

She would alternate round-the-clock twelve-hour shifts with another analyst and could play a crucial role over the coming days. Between them they would carry out subject profiles on the two victims, providing the team with information on their family backgrounds, their lifestyles, their friends. They would be researching them with the same depth of detail as if they were offenders.

Additional and possibly crucial information would be provided by the High-Tech Crime Unit, down on the ground floor, which had begun the process of analysing the mobile phones and computers of the two victims. They would be studying all the calls and texts made and received by the two women, from information on their phones and from their phone companies. They would look at their emails and at any chatlines either of them might have engaged with. Their address files. The websites they visited. If they had any electronic secrets, Grace's investigation team would soon know of them.

In addition, the High-Tech Crime Unit had deployed a Covert Internet Investigator to log into shoe- and foot-fetish chat rooms and build up relationships with other visitors, in the hope of finding some with extreme views.

'Do you think it could be a copycat, Ellen?' Michael Foreman asked her. 'Or the same offender from 1997 again?'

'I've started work on a comparative case analysis,' she replied. 'One of the crucial pieces of information withheld from the press and the public in *Operation Houdini* was the MO of the offender. It's too early to give you anything definitive, but from what I have so far – and it is very early days – it's looking possible that it's the same offender.'

'Do we have any information on why the Shoe Man stopped offending, sir?' Emma-Jane Boutwood asked.

'All we do know from *Operation Houdini*,' Grace said,

'is that he stopped offending at the same time as Rachael Ryan – possibly his sixth victim – disappeared. I was involved in her case, which is still open. We have no proof – or even evidence – that she was a victim, but she fitted one of his patterns.'

'Which was?' Michael Foreman asked.

'She had bought an expensive pair of shoes from a shop in Brighton approximately a week before she disappeared. Each of the Shoe Man's victims had bought a new, expensive pair of shoes shortly before they were attacked. One line of enquiry that *Operation Houdini* pursued at the time was questioning customers in Brighton and Hove's shoe shops. But no leads came from that.'

'Was there CCTV analysis then?' Bella Moy asked.

'Yes,' Grace replied. 'But the quality wasn't so good, and the city didn't have anything like the networked coverage it has now.'

'So what are the theories on why the Shoe Man stopped?' Michael Foreman asked.

'We don't know. The profiler – behavioural analyst – at the time, Julius Proudfoot, told us he might have moved away, to a different county or overseas. Or that he could be in prison for some other offence. Or that he could have died. Or it was possible he could have entered into a relationship that satisfied his needs.'

'If it is the same person, why would he stop for twelve years and then start offending again?' Bella Moy asked. 'And with a slightly different MO?'

'Proudfoot doesn't attach much importance to the difference in the trophies from 1997 to now. He is more interested that the overall MO is so similar. His view is that there could be a number of explanations why someone starts to reoffend. If it is the Shoe Man, he could simply have moved back into the area, thinking enough time has lapsed. Or the relationship he got into has changed and no longer satisfies his desires. Or he has been released from prison, where he's been for some other offence.'

'A pretty serious one if he's done twelve years,' Glenn Branson said.

'And easy to research,' Grace said. Then he turned to Ellen Zoratti. 'Ellen, have you found any other rapes with similar MOs around the country? Or where someone has been banged up for twelve years?'

'Nothing matching the Shoe Man other than a character in Leicester called James Lloyd, who raped women and then took their shoes, sir. He's currently doing life. I've checked back on all his offences and his movements, and eliminated him. He was in Leicester at the time these offences in Brighton were committed, and I have confirmation that he is currently in prison.' She paused and glanced at her notes. 'I have made a list of all sexual offenders who went inside no earlier than January 1998 and who were released prior to this past New Year's Eve.'

'Thanks, Ellen, that's very helpful,' Grace said. Then he addressed his whole team. 'It's a fact that a high percentage of stranger rapists tend to start with more minor offences. Flashing, frotting – rubbing themselves up against women – masturbating in public. That sort of thing. It's quite possible our offender was arrested for some minor offence at quite a young age. I've asked Ellen to check the local and national police databases for offenders and offences that might fit with this timeline before his first rapes in 1997 – and during the period in between. Checking for instances of theft or acts of indecency with ladies' shoes, for example. I also want every prostitute and dominatrix in the area questioned about any clients they might have with foot or shoe fetishes.'

Then he turned to Glenn Branson. 'Related to this, DS Branson's been studying Dr Proudfoot's report on the Shoe Man. What do you have for us, Glenn?'

'It's a real page-turner!' Glenn picked up a heavy-looking document. 'Two hundred and eighty-two pages of behavioural analysis. I've only had a chance to speed read it, since the chief tasked me with it earlier today, but there is something very interesting. There were five reported offences linked directly to the Shoe Man but Dr Proudfoot believes he could have committed a lot more that weren't reported.'

He paused for a moment. 'Many rape victims are so traumatized they cannot face the process of reporting it. But here's the really interesting thing: the first of the Shoe Man's reported rapes, back in 1997, occurred in the Grand Hotel, following a Halloween ball there. He lured a woman into a room. Does that sound familiar?'

There was an uncomfortable silence in the room. The Grand Hotel was next door to the Metropole.

'There's more,' Branson went on. 'The room at the Grand was booked by a woman – in the name of Marsha Morris. She paid cash and all efforts to trace her at the time failed.'

Grace absorbed the information in silence, thinking hard. The room at the Metropole, where Nicola Taylor was raped on New Year's Eve, was booked by a woman, according to the manager. Her name was Marsha Morris too. She paid in cash. The address she wrote in the register was false.

'Someone's having a laugh,' Nick Nicholl said.

'So does this mean it's the same perp,' Emma-Jane

Boutwood said, 'or a copycat with a sick sense of humour?'

'Was any of this information released to the public?' Michael Foreman asked.

Grace shook his head. 'No. The name Marsha Morris was never public knowledge.'

'Not even to the *Argus*?'

'Especially not to the *Argus*.' Grace nodded for Branson to continue.

'Here's where it gets even more interesting,' the DS said. 'Another of the victims was raped in her home, in Hove Park Road, exactly two weeks later.'

'That's a very smart address,' Michael Foreman said.

'Very,' Grace agreed.

Branson continued. 'When she arrived home, the burglar alarm was switched on. She deactivated it, went up into her bedroom and the offender struck – coming at her from out of a wardrobe.'

'Just like Roxy Pearce's attacker last night,' Grace said. 'From what we know so far.'

No one spoke for several moments.

Then Branson said, 'The Shoe Man's next victim was raped on the beach, beneath the Palace Pier. The one after that in the Churchill Square car park. His final one – if the chief's assumption is right – was taken walking home from a Christmas Eve piss-up with her friends.'

'So what you're saying, Glenn,' Bella said, 'is that we should be taking a close look at car parks in a week's time.'

'Don't go there, Bella,' Grace said. 'We're not going to let this get that far.'

He put on a brave, confident smile for his team. But inside he felt a lot less sure.

1998

38

'Does it work?' he asked.

'Yeah, course it works. Wouldn't be selling it other-wise, would I?' He glared at the lean man in the brown boiler suit as if he had just insulted his integrity. 'Every-thing in here works, mate, all right? If you want rubbish I can point you up the street. In here I only do quality. Everything works.'

'It had better.' He stared down at the white chest freezer that was tucked away between the upturned desks, swivel office chairs and upended settees at the rear of the vast second-hand furniture emporium in Brighton's Lewes Road.

'Money-back guarantee, all right? Thirty days, any problems, bring it back, no quibble.'

'Fifty quid you're asking?'

'Yeah.'

'What's your trade price?'

'Everything here's trade price.'

'Give you forty.'

'Cash?

'Uh-huh.'

'Taking it away with you? I'm not delivering for that price.'

'Gimme a hand out with it?'

'That your van outside?'

'Yeah.'

'Better get a move on. There's a warden coming.'

*

Five minutes later he jumped into the cab of the Transit, a few seconds ahead of the traffic warden, started the engine and drove it with a bump off the pavement and away from the double yellow lines. He heard the clang of his new purchase bouncing on the hessian matting on the otherwise bare metal floor behind him and moments later heard it sliding as he braked hard, catching up the congested traffic around the gyratory system.

He crawled passed Sainsbury's, then made a left turn at the lights, up under the viaduct, and then on, heading towards Hove, towards his lock-up garage, where the young woman lay.

The young woman whose face stared out at him from the front page of the *Argus*, on every news-stand, beneath the caption HAVE YOU SEEN THIS PERSON? Followed by her name, Rachael Ryan.

He nodded to himself. 'Yes. Yep. I've seen her!'

I know where she is!

She is waiting for me!

39

Shoes are your weapons, ladies, aren't they? You use them to hurt men in so many ways, don't you?

Know what I'm saying? I'm not talking about the physical, about the bruises and cuts you can make on a man's skin by hitting him with them. I'm talking about the sounds you make with them. The clack-clack-clack of your heels on bare floorboards, on concrete paving stones, on floor tiles, on brick paths.

You're wearing those expensive shoes. That means you're going somewhere – and you're leaving me behind. I hear that clack-clack-clack getting fainter. It's the last sound of you I hear. It's the first sound of you I hear when you come back. Hours later. Sometimes a whole day later. You don't talk to me about where you've been. You laugh at me, sneer at me.

Once when you came back and I was upset, you walked over to me. I thought you were going to kiss me. But you didn't, did you? You just stamped your stiletto down hard on my bare foot. You drilled it right through the flesh and bone and into the floorboard.

NOW

40

He'd forgotten how good it had felt. How addictive it had been! He'd thought that maybe just one, for old times' sake. But that *one* had immediately given him the taste for *another*. And now he was raring to go again.

Oh yes!

Make the most of these winter months, when he could wear a coat and a scarf, hide that Adam's apple, strut around freely, just like any other elegant Brighton lady! He liked the dress he had chosen, Karen Millen, and the camel Prada coat, the Cornelia James shawl around his neck, the big shiny shoulder bag and the slinky black leather gloves on his hands! But most of all he liked the feel of his wet-look boots. Yep. He felt sooooo good today! Almost, dare he say it, *sexy*!

He made his way through the Lanes, through the light drizzle that was falling. He was all wrapped up and snug against the rain and the cold wind, and, yes, sooooo *sexy*! He cast constant sideways glances at himself in shop windows. Two middle-aged men strode towards him, and one gave him an appreciative glance as they passed. He gave a coy smile back, snaking his way on through the throng of people in the narrow streets. He passed a modern jewellery shop, then an antiques shop that had a reputation for paying good prices for stolen valuables.

He walked down past the Druid's Head pub, the Pump House, then English's restaurant, crossed East Street and turned right towards the sea, heading towards Pool Valley. Then he turned left in front of the restaurant that had once been the ABC cinema and arrived outside his destination.

The shoe shop called Last.

It was a specialist designer-shoe shop and stocked a whole range of labels to which he was particularly partial: Esska, Thomas Murphy, Hetty Rose. He stared at Last's window display. At pretty, delicate, Japanese patterned Amia Kimonos. At a pair of Thomas Murphy Genesis petrol court shoes with silver heels. At brown suede Esska Loops.

The shop had wooden floorboards, a patterned sofa, a footstool and handbags hanging from hooks. And, at the moment, one customer. An elegant, beautiful woman in her forties with long, flyaway blonde hair who was wearing Fendi snakeskin boots. Size five. A matching Fendi handbag hung from a shoulder strap. She was dressed to kill, or to shop!

She had on a long black coat, with a high collar turned up and a fluffy white wrap around her neck. A pert snub nose. Rosebud lips. No gloves. He clocked her wedding band and her big engagement rock. She might still be married, but she could be divorced. Could be anything. Difficult to tell from here. But he knew one thing.

She was his type. Yep!

She was holding up a Tracey Neuls TN_29 Homage button shoe. It was in white perforated leather with a taupe trim. Like something Janet Leigh might have worn in the office before she stole the money in the original *Psycho*. But they weren't sexy! They were sort of retro

Miss America preppy, in his view. *Don't buy them*, he urged silently. *No, no!*

There were so many other much sexier shoes and boots on display. He cast his eye over them, looking appreciatively at each of their shapes, their curves, their straps, their stitches, their heels. He imagined this woman naked, wearing just these. Doing what he told her to do with them.

Don't buy those!

Good as gold, she put the shoe back. Then she turned and walked out of the shop.

He smelt her dense cloud of Armani Code perfume, which was like her own personal ozone layer, as she walked past him. Then she stopped, pulled a small black umbrella from her bag, held it up and popped it open. She had style, this lady. Confidence. She really, very definitely, could be his kind of lady. And she was holding up an umbrella, like a tour guide, just for him, so he could more easily spot her through the crowd!

Oh yes, my kind of lady!

The thoughtful kind!

He followed her as she set off at a determined stride. There was something predatory about her walk. She was on the hunt for shoes. No question. Which was good.

He was on the hunt too!

She stopped briefly in East Street to peer in the window of Russell and Bromley. Then she crossed over towards L. K. Bennett.

An instant later he felt a violent blow, heard a loud oath and he crashed, winded, down on to the wet pavement, feeling a sharp pain across his face, as if a hundred bees had stung him all at once. A steaming polystyrene Starbucks cup, its dark brown liquid spewing out, rolled past him. His head felt a rush of cold air and he realized, with panic, that his wig had become dislodged.

He grabbed it and jammed it back on his head, not caring for a moment how it looked, and found himself staring up at a shaven-headed tattooed man-mountain.

'Faggot! Why don't you look where you're frigging going?'

'Screw you!' he shouted back, totally forgetting for an instant to mask his voice, scrambled to his feet, one hand clutching his blonde wig, and stumbled on, aware of the smell of hot coffee and the unpleasant sensation of hot liquid running down his neck.

'Fucking fairy!' the voice called after him as he broke into a run, weaving through a group of Japanese tourists, fixated on the bobbing umbrella of the woman striding into the distance. To his surprise, she did not stop to look in L.K. Bennett, but headed straight into the Lanes.

She took a left fork and he followed her. Past a pub and then another jewellery shop. He dug into his handbag, pulled out a tissue and dabbed the coffee from his smarting face, hoping it had not smeared his make-up.

Blondie crossed busy Ship Street and turned right, then immediately left into the pedestrian precinct of expensive clothes shops: Duke's Lane.

Good girl!

She entered Profile, the first shop on the right.

He peered into the window. But he wasn't looking at the row of shoes and boots displayed on the shelves, he was looking at his own reflection. As subtly as he could, he adjusted his wig. Then he peered more closely at his face, but it seemed all right; no big, weird smears.

Then he checked on Blondie. She was sitting on a chair, hunched over her BlackBerry, pecking away at the keys. An assistant appeared with a shoebox, opened it the way a proud waiter might lift the lid from a tureen, and presented the contents for her inspection.

Blondie nodded approvingly.

The assistant removed a tall, high-heeled, blue satin Manolo Blahnik shoe with a square diamanté buckle.

He watched Blondie put the shoe on. She stood up and walked around the carpeted floor, peering at her foot's reflection in the mirrors. She seemed to like it.

He entered the shop and began browsing, breathing in the heady cocktail of tanned leather and Armani Code. He watched Blondie out of the corner of his eye, watched and *listened*.

The assistant asked her if she would like to try on the left foot as well. Blondie said she would.

As she strutted around the deep-pile carpeting, he was approached by the assistant, a young, slender girl with a dark fringe of hair and an Irish accent, asking if she could help her. He told her in his softest voice that he was *just looking, thank you.*

'I have to give an important speech next week,' Blondie said, in an American accent, he noticed. 'It's an after-lunch thing. I've bought the most divine blue dress. I think blue's good for daytime. What do you think?'

'Blue's a good colour on you, madam. I can tell from the shoes. Blue's a very good colour for daytime.'

'Yeah, um-umm. I think so too. Um-umm. I should have brought the dress along, but I know these are going to match.'

'They'll go with a wide range of blues.'

'Um-umm.'

Blondie stared down at the reflection of the shoes in the mirror for some moments and tapped her teeth with her fingernail. Then she said the magic words, '*I'll take these!*'

Good girl! Manolos were cool. They were beautiful. They were just so much a class act. Most importantly, they had five-inch heels.

Perfect!

And he liked her accent. Was it Californian?

He sidled up towards the counter as the purchase took place, listening intently, while pretending to study a pair of brown mules.

'Are you on our mailing list, madam?'

'I don't think so, no.'

'Would you mind if I entered you on it – we can let you know in advance of our sales. You can get some privileged bargains.'

She shrugged. 'Sure, why not?'

'If I could have your name?'

'Dee Burchmore. Mrs.'

'And your address?'

'Fifty-three Sussex Square.'

Sussex Square. In *Kemp Town*, he thought. One of the city's most beautiful squares. Most of its terraced houses were divided into flats. You had to be rich to have a whole house there. You had to be rich to buy the Manolos. And the handbag that went with it, which she was now fondling. Just the way he would soon be fondling her.

Kemp Town, he thought. That was an old stomping ground!

Happy memories.

41

Every time she bought a pair of shoes, Dee Burchmore got a guilty thrill. There was no need to feel guilty, of course. Rudy encouraged her to dress smart, to look great! As a senior executive of American & Oriental Banking, over here at its lavish new Brighton headquarters on a five-year posting to establish a foothold for the company in Europe, money was no object at all to her husband.

She was proud of Rudy and she loved him. She loved his ambitions to show the world that, in the wake of the financial scandals that had dogged US banking in recent years, it was possible to show a caring face. Rudy was attacking the UK mortgage market with zeal, offering deals to first-time buyers that none of the British lenders, still smarting from the financial meltdown, was prepared to consider. And she had an important role in this, in public relations.

In the time Dee had in between taking their two children, Josh, aged eight, and Chase, aged six, to school and then collecting them, Rudy had tasked her with networking as hard as she could within the city. He wanted her to find charities to which American & Oriental could make significant contributions – and, of course, gain significant publicity as benefactors to the city. It was a role she relished.

A respectable golfer, she had joined the ladies' section of the city's most expensive golf club, the North Brighton. She had become a member of what she had gleaned was the most influential of Brighton's numerous Rotary Clubs and she had volunteered for the committees of several of the city's major charitable institutions, including the Martlet's Hospice. Her most recent appointment was to the fund-raising committee of Brighton and Hove's principal hostel for the homeless, St Patrick's, where they had a unique facility, offering Japanese-style pods to homeless people, including prisoners out on licence who were actively involved in retraining.

She stood in the small shop, watching the assistant wrap her beautiful blue Manolos in tissue, then carefully lay them in the box. She could not wait to get home and try her dress on with these shoes and bag. She knew they were going to look sensational. Just the thing to give her confidence next week.

Then she glanced at her watch: 3.30. Shit! It had taken longer than she thought. She was late for her appointment at the Nail Studio in Hove, on the other side of the city. She hurried out of the shop, barely clocking the weird-looking woman with lopsided blonde hair who was staring at something on display in the shop window.

She never once looked behind her all the way to the car park.

If she had, she might just have noticed this same woman following her.

1998

42

It was shortly after 10 p.m. when Roy Grace flicked the right-turn indicator. Driving faster than was sensible in the pelting rain because he was so late, he nearly lost the back end of the car on the slippery tarmac as he swung off wide, quiet New Church Road into the even quieter residential street that led down to Hove seafront, where he and Sandy lived.

The elderly 3-Series BMW creaked and groaned, and the brakes made a scraping noise in protest. The car was months overdue for a service, but he was even more broke than ever, thanks in part to an insanely expensive diamanté tennis bracelet he had bought Sandy for a surprise for Christmas, and the service was going to have to wait a few more months yet.

Out of habit, he clocked each of the vehicles parked in the driveways and on the street, but there was nothing that seemed out of place. As he neared his home, he carefully checked those isolated patches of darkness where the orange haze of the street lighting did not quite reach.

One thing about being a copper, arresting villains and usually facing them in court months later, you never knew who might harbour a grudge against you. It was rare that revenge attacks happened, but Grace knew a couple of colleagues who had received anonymous hate mail, and one whose wife had found a death threat against her carved on a tree in her local park. It was not a worry you lost sleep over, but it was an occupational hazard. You tried to keep your address a secret, but villains had ways of finding out such things. You could never, ever totally let your guard down, and that was something Sandy resented about him.

It particularly irked her that Roy always picked a pub or restaurant table that gave him the best possible view of the room and the door, and that he always tried to sit with his back against the wall.

He smiled as he saw the downstairs lights of his house were on, which meant Sandy was still up, although he was a little sad to see the Christmas lights were now gone. He turned right on to the driveway and stopped in front of the integral garage door. Sandy's even more clapped-out little black Golf would be parked inside, in the dry.

This house was Sandy's dream. Shortly before she had found it, she had missed a period and their hopes had risen, only to be dashed a few weeks later. It had plunged her into a deep depression – so much so that he had become seriously worried about her. Then she rang him at the office, to say she had found a house. It was beyond their budget, she'd told him, but it had such great potential. He would love it!

They'd bought the four-bedroom semi just over a year ago. It was a big jump up the property ladder from the small flat in Hangleton where they had first lived after their marriage, and a financial stretch for both of them. But Sandy had set her heart on the house, and she'd convinced Roy they should go for it. He'd agreed against his better judgement, and knew the real reason he had said yes. It was because he could see how desperately unhappy Sandy was because of her inability to conceive and he wanted so much to please her, somehow.

Now he switched off the engine and climbed out into the freezing, pelting rain, feeling exhausted. He leaned in again, lifted the bulging attaché case containing a ton of files he needed to read through tonight off the passenger seat, hurried up to the front door and let himself in.

'Hi, darling!' he called out as he entered the hallway. It looked strangely bare without the Christmas decorations.

He heard the sound of voices from the television. There was a tantalizing aroma of cooking meat. Ravenous, he shrugged off his mackintosh, hung it on an antique coat rack they'd bought from a stall on the Kensington Street market, plonked his case down and walked into the living room.

Sandy, in a thick dressing gown and covered in a blanket, was lying on the sofa, cradling a glass of red wine and watching the news. A reporter was standing, holding a microphone, in a gutted, torched village.

'I'm sorry, darling,' he said.

He smiled at her. She looked so beautiful, with her damp hair carelessly hanging around her face, and no make-up. That was one of the things he loved most of all about her, that she looked just as good without make-up as with it. Always an early riser, he loved some mornings to lie awake in bed for a few minutes, just watching her face.

'Sorry about what's happening in Kosovo?' she retorted.

He bent down and kissed her. She smelt of soap and shampoo.

'No, for being so late. I was going to help you with the decorations.'

'Why aren't you sorry about Kosovo?'

'I am sorry about Kosovo,' he said. 'I'm also sorry about Rachael Ryan, who's still missing, and I'm sorry for her parents and her sister.'

'Are they more important to you than Kosovo?'

'I need a drink,' he said. 'And I'm starving.'

'I've already eaten, I couldn't wait any longer.'

'I'm sorry. I'm sorry I'm late. I'm sorry about Kosovo. I'm sorry about every damned problem in the world that I can't deal with.'

He knelt and pulled a bottle of Glenfiddich from the drinks cabinet, then, as he carried it out to the kitchen, she called after him, 'I've left you a plate of lasagne in the microwave and there's salad in the fridge.'

'Thanks,' he called back.

In the kitchen he poured himself four fingers of whisky, popped in some ice cubes, retrieved his favourite glass ashtray from the dishwasher and went back into the living room. He pulled off his jacket, then removed his tie and plonked himself down in his armchair as she was taking up the whole sofa. He lit a Silk Cut cigarette.

Almost instantly, like a Pavlovian reaction, Sandy batted away imaginary smoke.

'So, how was your day?' he asked. Then he reached down and picked a pine needle off the floor.

A young, attractive woman with spiky black hair and wearing battle fatigues appeared on the screen, against a background of burnt buildings. She was holding a microphone and talking to camera about the terrible human cost of the war in Bosnia.

'That's the Angel of Mostar,' Sandy said, nodding at

the screen. 'Sally Becker – she's from Brighton. She's doing something about the war there. What are you doing about it, Detective Sergeant, hoping soon to be *Detective Inspector*, Grace?'

'I'll start dealing with the war in Bosnia, and all the other problems of the world, when we've won the war in Brighton, which is the one I'm paid to fight.' He put the pine needle in the ashtray.

Sandy shook her head. 'You don't get it, do you, my love? That young woman, Sally Becker, is a hero – rather, a *heroine*.'

He nodded. 'She is, yes. The world needs people like her. But—'

'But what?'

He dragged on his cigarette and then sipped his whisky, feeling the burning, warming sensation deep in his gullet.

'No one person can solve all the problems in the world.'

She turned towards him. 'OK, so talk me through the one you've been solving.' She turned the volume on the television down.

He shrugged.

'Come on, I want to hear. You never tell me about your work. You always ask me about my day and I tell you about all the weirdo people I have to deal with who come into the medical centre. But every time I ask you, I get some crap about confidentiality. So, *soon-to-be Detective Inspector*, tell me about *your* day for a change. Tell me why for ten nights running you've left me to eat on my own, yet again. Tell me. Remember our wedding vows. Wasn't there something about not having secrets?'

'Sandy,' he said. 'Come on! I don't need this!'

'No, you *come on* for a change. Tell me about your day. Tell me how the search for Rachael Ryan is going.'

He took another deep drag on his cigarette. 'It's going bloody nowhere,' he said.

Sandy smiled. 'Well, there's a first! Don't think I've ever heard you be so honest in all the years we've been married. Thank you, *soon-to-be Detective Inspector*!'

He grinned. 'Shut up about that. I might not get through.'

'You will. You're the force's blue-eyed boy. You'll get the promotion. You know why?'

'Why?'

'Because it means more to you than your marriage.'

'Sandy! Come on, that's—'

He laid his cigarette in the ashtray, jumped up from his chair, sat on the edge of the sofa and tried to put an arm around her, but she resisted.

'Go on. Tell me about your day,' she said. 'I want every detail. If you truly love me, that is. I've never actually heard a minute-by-minute account of your day before. Not once.'

He stood up again and crushed the cigarette out, then moved the ashtray to the table beside the sofa and sat back down.

'I've spent the whole day looking for this young woman, all right? Just as I've been doing for the past week.'

'Yeah, fine, but what did that entail?'

'You really want to know the details?'

'Yes, I do. I really want to know the details. You have a problem with that?'

He lit another cigarette and inhaled. Then, with the smoke jetting from his mouth, he said, 'I went round with a detective sergeant – a guy called Norman Potting, he's not the most tactful officer in the force – to see the missing woman's parents again. They're in a terrible state, as you can imagine. We tried to reassure them about all we were doing, and took down every detail they could give us about their daughter that they might not already have done. Potting managed to upset them both.'

'How?'

'By asking a lot of awkward questions about her sex life. They needed to be asked – but there are ways of doing it . . .'

He took another sip of his drink and another drag, then laid the cigarette down in the ashtray. She was looking at him inquisitively.

'And then?'

'You really want to hear everything else?'

'I do, I really want to hear everything else.'

'OK, so we've been trying to prise out of them everything about Rachael's life. Did she have any friends or close work colleagues we haven't already talked to? Had anything like this ever happened before? We tried to build up a picture of her habits.'

'What were her habits?'

'Phoning her parents every day, without fail. That's the most significant one.'

'And now she hasn't phoned them for ten days?'

'That's right.'

'Is she dead, do you think?'

'We've checked her bank accounts to see if any money's been withdrawn and it hasn't. She has a credit card and debit card, and no transactions have taken place since the day before Christmas Eve.'

He drank some more whisky and was surprised to

find that he'd emptied the glass. Ice cubes tumbled against his lips as he drained the last drops.

'She's either being held against her will or she's dead,' Sandy said flatly. 'People don't just vanish off the face of the earth.'

'They do,' he said. 'Every day. Thousands of people every year.'

'But if she had that close connection to her parents, she wouldn't want to hurt them deliberately, like this, surely?'

He shrugged.

'What does your copper's nose tell you?'

'That it doesn't smell good.'

'What happens next?'

'We're widening the search, the house-to-house enquiries are expanding to cover a bigger area, we're drafting in more officers. We're searching the parks, the waste dumps, the surrounding countryside. CCTV footage is being examined. Checks are being made at all stations, harbours and airports. Her friends are being questioned and her ex-fiancé. And we're using a criminal psychologist – a profiler – to help.'

After some moments Sandy asked, 'Is this the shoe rapist again, do you think? The Shoe Man?'

'She's mad about shoes, apparently. But this is not his MO. He's never taken one of his victims.'

'Didn't you once tell me that criminals get bolder and more violent – that it's an escalating thing?'

'That's true. The guy who starts out as a harmless flasher can turn into a violent rapist. So can a burglar, as he gets bolder.'

Sandy sipped her wine. 'I hope you find her quickly and that she's OK.'

Grace nodded. 'Yup,' he said quietly. 'I hope so too.'

'Will you?'

He had no answer. Not, at least, the one she wanted to hear.

NOW

43

Yac did not like drunk people, especially drunk slappers, especially drunk slappers who got into his taxi. Especially this early on a Saturday night, when he was busy reading the latest on the Shoe Man in the *Argus*.

There were five drunk girls, all without coats, all in skimpy dresses, all legs and flesh, displaying their breasts and tattoos and pierced belly buttons. It was January! Didn't they feel the cold?

He was only licensed to carry four of them. He'd told them that, but they'd been too drunk to listen, all piling in at the rank on East Street, shouting, chattering, giggling, telling him to take them to the pier.

The taxi was full of their scents: Rock 'n Rose, Fuel for Life, Red Jeans, Sweetheart, Shalimar. He recognized them all. Uh-huh. In particular, he recognized the Shalimar.

His mother's perfume.

He told them it was only a short walk, that with the Saturday-night traffic they'd be quicker to walk. But they insisted he take them.

'It's bleedin' freezing, for Christ's sake!' one of them said.

She was a plump little thing, wearing the Shalimar, with a mass of fair hair and half-bared breasts that looked

267

like they'd been inflated with a bicycle pump. She reminded him a little of his mother. Something in the coarseness, the shape of her figure and the colour of her hair.

'Yeah,' said another. 'Sodding bleedin' freezing!'

One of them lit a cigarette. He could smell the acrid smoke. That was against the law too, he told her, staring at her crossly in the mirror.

'Want a drag, gorgeous?' she said, pouting, holding out the cigarette to him.

'I don't smoke,' he said.

'Too young, are you?' said another, and they broke into peals of squeaky laughter.

He nearly took them to the skeletal remains of the West Pier, half a mile further along the coast, just to teach them a lesson not to risk a taxi driver's livelihood. But he didn't, for one reason only.

The shoes and the perfume the plump one was wearing.

Shoes that he particularly liked. Black and silver sparkly Jimmy Choos. Size four. Uh-huh. His mother's size.

Yac wondered what she would look like naked, just wearing those shoes. Would she look like his mother?

At the same time, he wondered if she had a high- or low-flush loo in her home. But the problem with people who were drunk was that you couldn't have a proper conversation with them. Waste of time. He drove in silence, thinking about her shoes. Smelling her perfume. Watching her in the mirror. Thinking more and more how much she looked like his mother had once looked.

He made a right turn into North Street and crossed over Steine Gardens, waited at the lights, then turned right and queued at the roundabout before coming to a halt in front of the gaudy lights of Brighton Pier.

Just £2.40 showed on the meter. He'd been sitting in the queue at the cab rank for thirty minutes. Not much for it. He wasn't happy. And he was even less happy when someone handed him £2.50 and told him to keep the change.

'Huh!' he said. 'Huh!'

The man who owned the taxi expected big money on a Saturday night.

The girls disgorged themselves, while he alternated between watching the Jimmy Choos and glancing anxiously around for any sign of a police car. The girls were cursing the cold wind, clutching their hair, tottering around on their high heels, then, still holding the rear door of the taxi open, began arguing among themselves about why they'd come here and not stayed in the bar they'd just left.

He reached across, called out, 'Excuse me, ladies!' then pulled the door shut and drove off along the sea-front, the taxi reeking of Shalimar perfume and cigarette smoke and alcohol. A short distance along, he pulled over on to the double yellow lines, beside the railings of the promenade, and switched off the engine.

A whole bunch of thoughts were roaring around inside his head. Jimmy Choo shoes. Size four. His mother's size. He breathed deeply, savouring the Shalimar. It was coming up to 7 p.m. His on-the-hour, every hour, mug of tea. That was very important. He needed to have that.

But he had something else on his mind that he needed more.

Uh-huh.

44

Saturday 10 January

Despite the cold and the biting wind, several groups of people, mostly youngsters, milled around the entrance to the pier. Garish lights sparkled and twinkled all along the structure, which stretched almost a third of a mile out into the inky darkness of the English Channel. A Union Jack crackled in the wind. A giant sandwich-board hoarding in the middle of the entrance advertised a live band. The ice-cream stall wasn't doing much business, but there were ragged queues at the Southern Fried Chicken, Doughnut, Meat Feast and Fish and Chips counters.

Darren Spicer, wearing a donkey jacket, jeans, woollen mittens and a baseball cap pulled low, was flying high, totally oblivious to the cold, as he stood in the queue to buy a bag of chips. The aroma of frying batter was tantalizing and he was hungry. He stuck his bent roll-up in his mouth, rubbed his hands together and checked his watch. Eight minutes to seven. He needed to be back at the St Patrick's night shelter by 8.30, lock-up time, or he would lose his bed, and it was a brisk twenty-five minutes' walk from here, unless he jumped on a bus or, more extravagantly, took a taxi.

Tucked into one of his big inside poacher's pockets was a copy of the *Argus* he'd pulled out of a wheelie bin at the Grand Hotel, where he had registered earlier, to start work on Monday, doing a job that would utilize his electrical skills. The hotel was replacing its wiring, a lot of which did not appear to have been touched for decades. On Monday he would be in the basement, running new cables from the emergency generator to the laundry room.

It was a big area and they were short-staffed. Which meant not many people would be there to keep an eye on him. Which meant he'd pretty much have the run of the place. And all its rich pickings. And he'd have access to the computer system. Now all he needed was a pay-as-you-go mobile phone. That wouldn't be a problem.

He felt good! He felt terrific! At this moment he was the most powerful man in this whole city! And probably the horniest!

A gaggle of scantily clad girls disgorging from a taxi caught his eye. One of them was a plump little thing, with her tits almost falling out of her blouse and pouting, bee-stung lips. She tottered around on the tiles at the entrance in sparkly high heels, clutching at her hair, which was being batted by the wind. She looked as if she was a little the worse for wear from alcohol.

Her miniskirt blew up and he saw a sudden flash of the top of her thigh. It gave him a sharp prick of lust. She was his kind of girl. He liked a bit of flesh on a woman. Yeah, she was definitely his kind of tottie.

Yeah.

He liked her.

Liked her shoes.

He took a deep drag of his cigarette.

The taxi drove off.

The girls were arguing about something. Then they all headed to the back of the queue behind him.

He got his bag of chips, then stepped away a short distance, leaned against a stanchion and watched the girls in the queue, still arguing and joshing each other. But in particular he watched the plump one, that prick of lust growing inside him, thinking again and again of the flash of her thigh he had seen.

He had finished his chips and lit another cigarette by the time the girls had all got their bags and had fumbled in their purses for the right change to pay for them. Then they set off up the pier, the plump one trailing behind them. She was hurrying to catch up but struggling on her heels.

'Hey!' she called out to the two at the rear. 'Hey, Char, Karen, not so fast. I can't keep up with yer!'

One of the four turned round, laughing, keeping up her pace, staying level with her friends. 'Come on, Mandy! It's cos yer too bleedin' fat, in't yer!'

Mandy Thorpe, her head spinning from too many Sea Breezes, broke into a run and caught up with her friends briefly. 'Sod off about my weight! I am so not fat!' she shouted in mock anger. Then, as the tiled entrance gave way to the wooden boardwalk of the pier itself, both her heels stuck in a slat, her feet came flying out of them and she fell flat on her face, her handbag striking the ground and spewing out its contents, her chips scattering across the decking.

'Shit!' she said. 'Shit, shit, shit!'

Scrambling back upright, she ducked down and jammed each of her feet back into the shoes, bending down even lower to lever them in with her fingers, cursing these cheap, ill-fitting Jimmy Choo copies which she had bought on holiday in Thailand and which pinched her toes.

'Hey!' she called out. 'Char, Karen, hey!'

Leaving the mess of ketchup-spattered chips, she stumbled on after them, watching the slats in the decking carefully now. She followed her friends past a toy locomotive and into the bright lights and noise of the amusement arcade. Music was playing, and there were chimes from machines and the clatter of coins, and shouts of joy and angry cusses. She passed a giant illuminated pink cracker, then a glass-fronted machine filled with teddy bears, a sign flashing £35 CASH JACKPOTS, and a cash booth in the shape of a Victorian tram shelter.

Then they were outside in the biting cold again. Mandy caught up with her friends just as they passed a row of stalls, each blaring out music. HOOK A DUCK! LOBSTER POT – 2 BALLS FOR £1! HENNA TATTOOS!

In the distance to her left, across the black void of the sea, were the lights of the elegant town houses of Kemp Town. They walked on past the DOLPHIN DERBY, heading towards the carousel, helter-skelter, dodgems, the CRAZY MOUSE rollercoaster and the TURBO SKYRIDE, which Mandy had been on once – and it had left her feeling sick for days.

To their right now were the ghost train and the HORROR HOTEL.

'I want to go on the ghost train!' Mandy said.

Karen turned, pulling a cigarette pack out of her handbag. 'It's pathetic. The ghost train's shit. It's like nothing. I need another drink.'

'Yeah, me too!' said Char. 'I need a drink.'

'What about the Turbo?' said another girl, Joanna.

'No fear!' Mandy said. 'I want to go on the ghost train.'

Joanna shook her head. 'I'm scared of that.'

'It's not *really* scary,' Mandy said. 'I'll go on me own if you won't come.'

'You're not brave enough!' Karen taunted. 'You're a scaredy cat!'

'I'll show you!' Mandy said. 'I'll bloody show you!'

She tottered over to a booth that sold tokens for the rides. None of them noticed the man standing a short distance back from them, carefully crushing his cigarette out underfoot.

1998

45

He had never seen a dead body before. Well, apart from his mum, that was. She'd been all skeletal, wasted away from the cancer that had been on a feeding frenzy inside her, eating up just about everything except her skin. The little bastard cancer cells would probably have eaten that too if the embalming fluid hadn't nuked them.

Although they were welcome to her. It had seemed a shame to hurt them.

His mum had looked like she was asleep. She was all tucked into bed, in her nightdress, in a room in the undertaker's Chapel of Rest. Her hair all nicely coiffed. A bit of make-up on her face to give her some colour, and her skin had a slightly rosy hue from the embalming fluid. The funeral director had told him that she'd come up really nice.

Much nicer in death.

Dead, she couldn't taunt him any more. Couldn't tell him, as she climbed into his bed, that he was as useless as his drunken father. That his *thing* was pathetic, that it was shorter than the heels of her shoes. Some nights she brought a stiletto-heeled shoe into the bed with her and made him pleasure her with that instead.

She began calling him *Shrinky*. It was a name that quickly got around at his school. 'Hey, Shrinky,' other boys and girls would call out to him. 'Has it grown any longer today?'

He'd sat beside her, on the chair next to her bed, the way he'd sat beside her in the ward of the hospital in the days when her life was slipping away. He'd held her hand. It was cold and bony, like holding the hand of a reptile. But one that couldn't harm you any more.

Then he'd leaned over and whispered into her ear, 'I think I'm supposed to tell you that I love you. But I don't. I hate you. I've always hated you. I can't wait for your funeral, because afterwards I'm going to get that urn with your ashes and throw you into a fucking skip, where you belong.'

But this new woman now was different. He didn't hate Rachael Ryan. He looked down at her, lying naked on the bottom of the chest freezer he had bought this morning. Staring up at him through eyes that were steadily frosting over. That same glaze of frost that was forming all over her body.

He listened for a moment to the hum of the freezer's motor. Then he whispered, 'Rachael, I'm sorry about what happened, you know? Really I am. I never wanted to kill you. I've never killed anything. That's not me. I just want you to know that. Not me at all. Not my style. I'll look after your shoes for you, I promise.'

Then he decided he didn't like her eyes looking at him all hostile like that. As if she was still able to accuse him, even though she was dead. Able to accuse him from some other place, some other dimension she'd now arrived at.

He slammed the lid shut.

His heart was thumping. He was running with perspiration.

He needed a cigarette.

Needed to think very, very calmly.

He lit a cigarette and smoked it slowly, thinking. Thinking. Thinking.

Her name was everywhere. Police were looking for her all over the city. All over Sussex.

He was shaking.

You stupid dumb woman, taking off my mask!

Look what you've done. To both of us!

They mustn't find her. They'd know who she was if they found the body. They had all kinds of techniques. All kinds of science. If they found her, then at some point they were going to find him.

At least by keeping her cold he'd stopped the smell that had started to come from her. Frozen stuff didn't smell. So now he had time. One option was just to keep her here, but that was dangerous. The police had put in the paper that they were looking for a white van. Someone might have seen his van. Someone might tell the police that there was a white van that sometimes drove in and out of here.

He needed to get her away.

Throwing her in the sea might be an option, but the sea might wash her body ashore. If he dug a grave somewhere out in a wood, someone's dog might sniff her. He needed a place where no dog would sniff.

A place where no one was going to come looking.

NOW

46

Maybe this wasn't such a good idea after all, Mandy thought to herself, her courage suddenly deserting her as she handed her token to the man in the booth of the ghost train ride.

'Is it scary?' she asked him.

He was young and good-looking, with a foreign accent – maybe Spanish, she thought.

'No, is not really scary. Just a little!' He smiled. 'Is OK!'

'Yeah?'

He nodded.

She tottered along inside the railings to the first car. It looked like a wood-panelled Victorian bathtub on rubber wheels. She clambered in unsteadily, her heart in her throat suddenly, and sat down, putting her bag on the seat beside her.

'Sorry, you can't take bag. I look after for you.'

Reluctantly she handed it to him. Then he pulled down the metal safety bar and clicked it home, committing her.

'Smile!' he said. 'Enjoy! Is OK, really!'

Shit, she thought. Then she called out to her friends. 'Char! Karen!'

But the wind whipped her voice away. The car rumbled

283

forward, without warning crashing through double doors into darkness. The doors banged shut behind her and the darkness was total. In contrast to the blustery sea air, in here it was dry and smelt faintly of hot electrical wiring and dust.

The darkness pressed in all around her. She held her breath. Then the car swung sharply right, picking up speed. She could hear the roar of its wheels echoing around the walls; it was like being on a tube train. Streaks of light shot past her on both sides. She heard a ghostly laugh. Tendrils brushed her forehead and her hair, and she screamed in terror, clenching her eyes shut.

This is dumb, she thought. *This is so stupid. Why? Why did I do this?*

Then the car crashed through more double doors. She opened her eyes to see a long-dead, dusty old man rise up from behind a writing desk and swing head first towards her. She ducked, covering her eyes, her heart pounding, all the courage the alcohol had given her deserting her now.

They went down a sharp incline. She uncovered her eyes to see that the light was fading rapidly and she was back in pitch darkness again. She heard a hissing sound. A hideous, luminous, skeletal snake reared out of the darkness and spat at her, cold droplets of water striking her face. Then a brightly lit skeleton swung out of the darkness and she ducked in terror, convinced it would hit her.

They crashed through more doors. *Oh, God, how long was this going to go on for?*

They were travelling fast, downhill, in darkness. She heard a screech, then a horrible cackle of laughter. More tendrils touched her, like a spider crawling through her hair. They crashed through more doors, swung sharply left and, quite suddenly, stopped. She sat for a moment in the pitch darkness, shaking. Then suddenly she felt an arm around her neck.

A human arm. She smelt warm breath on her cheek. Then a voice whispered into her ear. A voice she had never heard before.

She froze in blind panic.

'Got a little extra for you, darling.'

Was this some prank from Char and Karen? Were they in here messing around?

Her brain was racing. Something was telling her this was not part of the ride. That something was badly wrong. The next instant she heard a clang as the safety bar jerked up. Then, whimpering in terror, she was jerked out of the car and dragged quickly over a hard surface. Something sharp bashed into her back and she was pulled through curtains into a room which smelt of oil. She was dropped on her back on to a hard surface. Then she heard the door clang shut. Heard a click that sounded like a switch, followed almost immediately by the grinding sound of heavy machinery. Then a torch was shining into her face, temporarily blinding her.

She stared up, almost paralysed by utter terror and confusion. Who was this? The ride operator she'd met outside?

'Please don't hurt me,' she said.

Through the beam of light she saw the silhouette of a man's face inside what looked like a nylon stocking with slits in it.

As she opened her mouth and tried to scream, something soft and foul-tasting was rammed into it. She heard a ripping sound and the next instant felt sticky tape being pressed over her lips and around each side of her face. She tried to scream again, but all that came out was a muffled choking sound that seemed to shimmy around inside her head.

'You're gagging for it, aren't you, doll? Dressed like that? Dressed in those shoes!'

She lashed out at him with her fists, pummelling him, trying to scratch him. Then she saw something glint in the darkness. It was the head of a large claw hammer. He was holding it in a latex-gloved hand.

'Keep still or I'll fucking hit you.'

She still in terror, staring at the dull metal.

Suddenly she felt a crashing blow to the side of her head. Her brain filled with sparks.

Then silence.

She never felt him entering her or removing her shoes afterwards.

47

Garry Starling entered the packed China Garden restaurant shortly after 9 p.m. and hurried towards his table,
pausing only to order a Tsingtao beer from the manager,
who stepped across to greet him.

'You are late tonight, Mr Starling!' the jovial Chinese
man said. 'I don't think your wife is a very happy lady.'

'Tell me something new!' Garry replied, palming him
a £20 note.

Then he hurried up the steps to his regular table and
noticed that the gannets had almost finished the mixed
starters. There was one solitary spring roll left in the huge
bowl, and the tablecloth was littered with shreds of seaweed and stains from the spilt sauces. All three of them
looked like they'd had a good few drinks.

'Where the sodding hell have you been?' his wife,
Denise, said, greeting him with her customary acidic
smile.

'Actually I've been *sodding* working, my darling,' he
said, giving Maurice's barmy-looking Earth Mother wife,
Ulla, a perfunctory kiss, shaking Maurice's hand and then
sitting in the empty seat between them. He didn't kiss
Denise. He'd stopped greeting her with a kiss back in the
year dot.

Turning and staring pointedly at his wife, he said,

'Working. Right? *Working*. A word that's not in your lexicon. Know what it means? To pay for the sodding mortgage. Your sodding credit-card bill.'

'And your sodding camper van!'

'Camper van?' said Maurice, sounding astonished. 'That's not your style, Garry.'

'It's a VW. The original split-windscreen one. They're fine investments, very collectable. Thought it would be good for Denise and me to experience the open road, sleeping out in the wild every now and then, get back to nature! I would have bought a boat, but she gets seasick.'

'It's midlife crisis, that what it is,' Denise said to Maurice and Ulla. 'If he thinks he's taking me on holiday in a sodding van he can think again! Just like last year, when he tried to get me on the back of his motorbike to go on a blooming camping holiday in France!'

'It's not a sodding van!' Garry said, grabbing the last spring roll before anyone else could get it, dipping it by mistake in the hot sauce and cramming it into his mouth.

A small thermonuclear explosion took place inside his head, rendering him temporarily speechless. Denise took good advantage of it.

'You look like shit!' she said. 'How did you get that scratch on your forehead?'

'Crawling up in a sodding loft, trying to replace an alarm wire bloody mice had eaten. A nail sticking out of a rafter.'

Denise suddenly leaned closer to him and sniffed. 'You've been smoking!'

'I was in a taxi where someone had been smoking,' he mumbled a little clumsily, chewing.

'Oh, really?' She gave him a disbelieving look, then turned to their friends. 'He keeps pretending he's quit, but he thinks I'm stupid! He goes out to take the dog for a walk, or a bike ride, or to take his motorbike for a spin, and comes back hours later stinking of fags. You can always smell it on someone, can't you?' She looked a Ulla, then at Maurice and swigged some Sauvignon Blanc.

Garry's beer arrived and he took a long pull, glancing first at Ulla, thinking that her mad hair looked even madder than usual tonight, and then at Maurice, who looked more like a toad than ever. Both of them, and Denise as well, looked strange, as if he was seeing them through distorting glass. Maurice's black T-shirt stretched out over his pot belly, his eyes bulged out of their sockets and his expensive, hideous checked jacket, with its shiny Versace buttons, was too tight. It looked like a hand-me-down from an older brother.

Defending his friend, Maurice shook his head. 'Can't smell anything.'

Ulla leaned across and sniffed Garry, like a dog on heat. 'Nice cologne!' she said evasively. 'Smells quite feminine, though.'

'Chanel Platinum,' he replied.

She sniffed again, giving a dubious frown, and raised her eyebrows at Denise.

'So where the hell have you been?' Denise demanded. 'You look a mess. Couldn't you at least have brushed your hair?'

'It's blowing a hooley out there, in case you haven't noticed!' Garry replied. 'I had to deal with an irate client – we're short-staffed tonight – one down with flu, one down with something else, and a bolshy Mr Graham Lewis in Steyning, whose alarm keeps going off for no reason, was threatening to change suppliers. So I had to go and sort him out. OK? Turns out it was damned mice.'

She tilted her glass into her mouth, to drain it, then realized it was already empty. At that moment a waiter appeared with a fresh bottle. Garry pointed at his own wine glass, draining his beer at the same time. His nerves were shot to hell and he needed drink right now. Lots of it.

'Cheers, everyone!' he said.

Maurice and Ulla raised their glasses. 'Cheers!'

Denise took her time. She was glaring at Garry. She just did not believe him.

But, Garry thought, when had his wife last believed him about anything? He drained half of the sharp white wine in just one gulp, momentarily relieving the burning sensation in the roof of his mouth. If the truth be known, the last time she had believed him was probably on the day they got married, when he said his vows.

Although . . . he hadn't even been sure then. He could still remember the look she had given him in front of the altar, as he'd slipped the ring on to her finger and got prompted through the wording by the vicar. It was not the love in her eyes that he might have expected, more the smug satisfaction of a hunter returning home with a dead animal over their shoulder.

He had nearly bailed out then.

Twelve years later, there was not a day that went by when he didn't wish he had.

But hey. There were advantages to being married. It was important never to forget that.

Being married gave you respectability.

48

'I've had a go at the wording on the wedding invites,' Cleo called out from the kitchen.

'Great!' Roy Grace said. 'Want me to take a look?'

'We'll go through it when you've had supper.'

He smiled. One thing he was learning about Cleo was that she liked to plan things well in advance. It was going to be touch and go for the wedding to take place before their child was born. They couldn't even set a firm date yet because of all the bureaucracy that had to be dealt with to have Sandy declared legally dead first.

Humphrey lay contentedly beside him now on Cleo's living-room floor with a goofy grin, head flopped over, his tongue half out. Roy ran his palm back and forward across the happy creature's soft, warm belly, while a Labour politician on the flat-screen TV on the wall pontificated on *News at Ten*.

But he wasn't listening. With his suit jacket removed and his tie loosened, his thoughts were on the evening briefing and the pages of work he had brought home, which were spread out on the sofa beside him. In particular, he was poring over the similarities between the Shoe Man and the new offender. A number of unanswered questions were going around his mind.

If the Shoe Man was back, where had he been for the

past twelve years? Or if he had remained in the city, why had he stopped offending for so long? Was it possible that he had raped other victims who had not reported it?

Grace doubted that he could have raped repeatedly for twelve years without someone reporting it. Yet so far there were no rapists showing up on the national database with a comparable MO. He could of course have gone abroad, which would take a massive amount of time and resourcing to establish.

However, this evening it emerged that there was one potential suspect in the city, following the Analyst's search of the ViSOR and MAPPA databases, ViSOR being the Violent and Sex Offender Register and MAPPA the Multi-agency Public Protection Arrangements.

Having been set up to manage the release of violent and sexual offenders back into the community after their release from prison on licence, MAPPA graded these offenders into three categories. Level 1 was for released prisoners who were considered to have a low risk of reoffending and were monitored to ensure that they complied with the terms of their licence. Level 2 was for those considered to be in need of moderately active inter-agency monitoring. Level 3 was for those considered to have a high risk of reoffending.

Zoratti had discovered that there was a Level 2 who had been released on licence, from Ford Open Prison, having served three years of a six-year sentence, mostly at Lewes, for burglary and indecent assault – a career burglar and drugs dealer, Darren Spicer. He'd attempted to kiss a woman in a house he had broken into, then run off when she'd fought back and had pressed a hidden panic button. Later, she'd picked him out in an identity parade.

Spicer's current place of residence was being traced

urgently tonight through the Probation Service. But while
he was worth interviewing, Grace wasn't convinced Darren Spicer ticked many boxes. He had been in and out of
jail several times in the past twelve years, so why had he
not offended in the interim? More important, in his view,
was the fact that the man had no previous record of
sexual assaults. The last offence that had contributed to
Spicer's sentence appeared to be a one-off – although, of
course, there was no certainty of that. With the grim
statistic that only 6 per cent of rape victims ever reported
the crimes, it was quite possible he had committed previous such offences and got away with them.

Next he turned his mind to the copycat theory. One
thing that was deeply bothering him was the missing
pages from the Rachael Ryan file. Sure, it was possible
that they had simply been misfiled somewhere else. But
there could be a much darker reason. Could it be that the
Shoe Man himself had accessed the file and removed
something that might incriminate him? If he had access
to that file, he would have had access to all the Shoe
Man's files.

Or was it someone else altogether who had gained
access to them? Someone who had decided, for whatever
sick reason, to copy the Shoe Man's MO.

Who?

A member of his trusted team? He didn't think so,
but of course he couldn't discount that. There were plenty
of other people who had access to the Major Crime Suite
– other police officers, support staff and cleaning staff.
Solving that mystery, he realized, was now a priority for
him.

'Are you nearly ready to eat, darling?' Cleo called out.

Cleo was grilling him a tuna steak. Roy took this as a

sign that maybe, finally, she was starting to wean herself off curries. The reek of them had gone and there was now a strong smell of wood smoke from the crackling fire that Cleo had lit in the grate some time before he had arrived, and the welcoming aroma of scented candles burning in different parts of the room.

He took another long sip of the deliciously cold vodka martini she had mixed, enviously, for him. He now had to drink for both of them, she'd told him – and tonight he did not have a problem with that. He felt the welcoming buzz of the alcohol and then, still mechanically stroking the dog, he lapsed back into his thoughts.

A car had been seen leaving the Pearce house in Droveway Avenue at 9 p.m. on Thursday, which fitted perfectly with the timing of the attack. It had been travelling at speed and nearly ran over a local resident. The man was so angry he tried to take a note of the number plate, but could only be certain of two digits and one letter of the alphabet. Then he did nothing about it until he read of the attack in the *Argus*, which prompted him to phone the Incident Room this evening.

According to him, the driver was male, but with the vehicle's tinted windows he had not been able to get a clear look at his face. Somewhere in his thirties or forties with short hair was the extent of his description. He did much better with the car, asserting it was a light-coloured old-model Mercedes E-Class saloon. Just how many of those Mercedes were there around, Grace wondered? Loads of them. It was going to take a while to sift through all the registered keepers when they didn't have a full registration number to work from. And he did not have the luxury of time.

With the rising frenzy in the media after two stranger

rapes in the city in a little over a week, the news stories were ramping up fear in the public. The call handlers were being inundated with queries from anxious women about whether it was safe to go out and he was aware that his immediate superiors, Chief Superintendent Jack Skerritt and ACC Peter Rigg, were anxious to see rapid progress with this case.

The next press conference was scheduled for midday on Monday. It would calm everything down greatly if he could announce they had a suspect and, even better, that they had made an arrest. OK, they had Darren Spicer as a possible. But nothing made the police look more inefficient than having to release a suspect because of lack of evidence, or because it was the wrong person. The Mercedes was more promising. But the driver wasn't necessarily the offender. There could be an innocent explanation – perhaps a family friend who had popped round for a visit to the Pearce household, or simply someone delivering a package?

The fact that the car was being driven recklessly was a good indicator that it might have been the suspect. It was a known fact that offenders often drove badly immediately after committing a crime – because they were in a heightened state of anxiety, the *red mist.*

He'd sent all his team home for the night to get some rest, except for the two Analysts, who were working a 24/7 rota between them. Glenn Branson had asked him for a quick pint on the way home, but he'd apologetically excused himself, having barely seen Cleo this weekend. With his mate's marital woes spiralling from bad to worse, he was running out of sympathetic things to say to Glenn. Divorce was a grim option, especially for someone with young kids. But he could no longer see much alternative for his friend – and wished desperately that he could. Glenn was going to have to bite the bullet and move on. An easy thing to tell someone else, but an almost impossible thing to accept oneself.

He felt a sudden craving for a cigarette, but resisted, with difficulty. Cleo was not bothered if he smoked in here, or anywhere, but he was mindful of the baby she was carrying, and all the stuff about passive smoke, and the example he needed to try to set. So he drank some more, ignoring the craving.

'Ready in about five minutes!' she called out from the kitchen. 'Need another drink?' She popped her head around the door.

He raised his glass to show it was nearly empty. 'I'll be under the table if I have another!'

'That's the way I like you!' she replied, coming over to him.

'You're just a control freak!' he said with a big grin.

He would take a bullet for this woman. He would die for Cleo gladly, he knew. Without an instant's hesitation.

Then he felt a sudden strange pang of guilt. Wasn't this how he'd felt once about Sandy?

He tried to answer himself truthfully. Yes, it had been total hell when she disappeared. That morning on his thirtieth birthday, they had made love before he went to work, and that same evening, when he returned home, looking forward to their celebration, she had not been there – that had been total hell.

So had the days, weeks, months and then years after. Imagining all the terrible things that might have happened to her. And sometimes imagining what might still be happening to her in some monster's lair. But that was just one of many scenarios. He'd lost count of the number of psychics he'd had consultations or sittings with over these past ten years – and not one of them had said she was in the spirit world. Despite all of them, he was reasonably certain that Sandy was dead.

In a few months' time it would be ten years ago that she had disappeared. An entire decade, in which he'd gone from a young man to a middle-aged fart.

In which he'd met the loveliest, smartest, most incredible woman in the world.

Sometimes he woke up and imagined he must have dreamed it all. Then he would feel Cleo's warm, naked body beside him. He would slip his arms around her and hold her tightly, the way someone might try to hold on to their dreams.

'I love you so much,' he would whisper.

'Shit!' Cleo broke away from him, breaking the spell.

There was a smell of burning as she dashed back over to the hob. 'Shit, shit, shit!'

'It's OK! I like it well done. I don't like fish with its heart still beating!'

'Just as well!'

The kitchen filled with black smoke and the stink of burning fish. The smoke alarm started beeping. Roy opened the windows and the patio door and Humphrey raced outside, barking furiously at something in his squeaky puppy bark, then raced back inside and tore around barking at the alarm.

A few minutes later, Grace sat at the table and Cleo placed a plate in front of him. On it lay a blackened tuna steak, a lump of tartare sauce, some limp-looking mangetout, and a mess of disintegrated boiled potatoes.

'Eat that,' she said, 'and you are proving it's true love!'

The television above the table was on, with the sound turned down. The politician had gone and now Jamie Oliver was energetically demonstrating how to slice the coral from scallops.

Humphrey nudged his right leg, then tried to jump up.

'Down! No begging!' he said.

The dog looked at him uncertainly, then slunk away.

Cleo sat down beside him and gave him a wide-eyed frown.

'You don't have to eat it if it's really horrible.'

He forked some fish into his mouth. It tasted even worse than it looked, but only marginally. No question, Sandy was a better cook than Cleo. A thousand times better. But it did not matter to him one jot. Although he did glance a tad enviously at the dish Jamie Oliver was preparing.

'So how was your day?' he asked, dubiously forking another section of burnt fish into his mouth, thinking that the curries really had not been so bad after all.

She told him about the body of a forty-two-stone man she'd had to recover from his home. It had required the help of the fire brigade.

He listened in astounded silence, then ate some salad, which she put down on a side plate. At least she had managed not to burn that.

Switching subjects she said, 'Hey, something occurred to me about the Shoe Man. Do you want my thoughts?'

He nodded.

'OK, your Shoe Man – *if* it is the same offender as before and *if* he stayed in this area – I can't see that he would have just totally stopped getting his kicks.'

'Meaning what?'

'If he stopped offending, for whatever reason, he must still have had urges. He would need to satisfy them. So maybe he'd go to dominatrix dungeons – or places like that – weird sex places, fetishes and stuff. Put yourself in his shoes, as it were – forgive the pun! You're a creep who gets off on women's shoes. OK?'

'That's one of our lines of enquiry.'

'Yes, but listen. You've found a fun way of doing it – raping strangers in classy shoes and then taking those shoes. OK?'

He stared at her, without reacting.

'Then, oooops! You go a bit too far. She dies. The media coverage is intense. You decide to lie low, ride it out. But . . .' She hesitated. 'You want the *but*?'

'We don't know for sure that anyone died. All we know is that he stopped. But tell me?' he said

'You still get your rocks off on women's feet. OK? You following me?'

'In your footsteps? In your shoes?'

'Sod off, Detective Superintendent!'

He raised his hand. 'No disrespect!'

'None taken. OK, so you are the Shoe Man, you are still turned on by feet, or by shoes. Sooner or later that thing inside you, that *urge*, is going to ride to the top. You're going to need that. Where do you go? The Internet, that's where you go! So you type in *feet* and *fetish* maybe and *Brighton*. Do you know what you come up with?'

Grace shook his head, impressed with Cleo's logic. He tried to ignore the horrible stench of burnt fish.

'A whole bunch of massage parlours and dominatrix dens – just like the ones I sometimes have to recover bodies from. You know – old geezers who get too excited—'

Her mobile phone rang.

Apologizing to Roy, she answered it. Instantly her expression switched to work mode. Then, when she ended the call, she said to him, 'Sorry, my love. There's a dead body in a shelter on the seafront. Duty calls.'

He nodded.

She kissed him. 'I'll be as quick as I can. See you in bed. Don't die on me.'

'I'll try to stay alive.'

'Just one part of you anyway. The bit that matters to me!' She touched him gently, just below his belt.

'Slapper!'

'Horny bastard!'

Then she put a printout in front of him. 'Have a read – make any amendments you want.'

He glanced at the paper.

Mr and Mrs Charles Morey
request the pleasure of your company
at the marriage of their daughter
Cleo Suzanne
to Roy Jack Grace
at All Saints' Church, Little Bookham

'Don't forget to let Humphrey out for a pee and a dump before you go up!' she said.

Then she was gone.

Moments after she closed the door, his own phone rang. He pulled it from his pocket and checked the display. The number was withheld, which meant almost certainly it was someone calling from work.

It was.

And it was not good news.

49

In another part of the city, just a couple of miles away in a quiet, residential Kemp Town street, another couple were also discussing their wedding plans.

Jessie Sheldon and Benedict Greene were ensconced opposite each other in Sam's restaurant, sharing a dessert.

Anyone looking at them would have seen two attractive people, both in their mid-twenties, clearly in love. It was evident from their body language. They sat oblivious of their surroundings, and anyone else, their foreheads almost touching over the tall glass dish, each taking it in turn to dig a long spoon in and feed the other tenderly and sensually.

Neither was dressed up, even though it was Saturday night. Jessie, who had come straight from a kick-boxing class at the gym, wore a grey tracksuit with a large Nike tick across it. Her shoulder-length bleached hair was scooped up into a ponytail, with a few loose strands hanging down. She had a pretty face and, if it weren't for her nose, she would be almost classically beautiful.

Jessie had had a complex about her nose throughout her childhood. In her view, it wasn't so much a nose as a *beak*. In her teens she was forever glancing sideways to catch her reflection in mirrors or shop windows. She had been determined that one day she would have a nose job.

But that was then, in her life before Benedict. Now, at twenty-five, she didn't care about it any more. Benedict told her he loved her nose, that he would not hear of her changing it and that he hoped their children would inherit that same shape. She was less happy about that thought, about putting them through the same years of misery she had been through.

They would have nose jobs, she promised herself silently.

The irony was that neither of her parents had that nose, nor did her grandparents. It was her great-grandfather's, she had been told by her mother, who had a framed and fading sepia photograph of him. The damned hooked-nose gene had managed to vault two generations and fetch up in her DNA strand.

Thanks a lot, great-grandpa!

'You know something, I love your nose more every day,' Benedict said, holding up the spoon she had just licked clean and handing it to her.

'Is it *just* my nose?' she teased.

He shrugged and looked pensive for a moment. 'Other bits too, I suppose!'

She gave him a playful kick under the table. 'Which other bits?'

Benedict had a serious, studious face and neat brown hair. When she had first met him, he had reminded her of those clean-cut, almost impossibly perfect-looking boy-next-door actors who seemed to star in every US television mini series. She felt so good with him. He made her feel safe and secure, and she missed him every single second that they were apart. She looked forward with intense happiness to a life with him.

But there was an elephant in the room.

It stood beside their table now. Casting its own massive shadow over them.

'So, did you tell them, last night?' he asked.

Friday night. The Shabbat. The ritual Friday night with her mother and father, her brother, her sister-in-law, her grandmother, that she never missed. The prayers and the meal. The gefilte fish that her mother's appalling cooking made taste like cat food. The cremated chicken and shrivelled sweetcorn. The candles. The grim wine her father bought that tasted like boiled tarmac – as if drinking alcohol on a Friday night was a mortal sin, so he had to ensure that the stuff tasted like a penance.

Her brother, Marcus, was the big success of the family. He was a lawyer, married to a good Jewish girl, Rochelle, who was now irritatingly pregnant, and they were both irritatingly smug about that.

She had fully intended breaking the news, the same way she had intended breaking it for the past four Friday nights. That she was in love with and intended to marry a *goy*. And a *poor goy* to boot. But she had funked it yet again.

She shrugged. 'I'm sorry, I – I was going to – but – it just wasn't the right moment. I think they should meet you first. Then they'll see what a lovely person you are.'

He frowned.

She put down the spoon, reached across the table and took his hand. 'I've told you – they're not easy people.'

He put his free hand over hers and stared into her eyes. 'Does that mean you're having doubts?'

She shook her head vigorously. 'None. Absolutely none. I love you, Benedict, and I want to spend the rest of my life with you. I don't have one shred of doubt.'

And she didn't.

But she had a problem. Not only was Benedict not Jewish or wealthy, but he wasn't ambitious in the sense that her parents could – or would ever – understand: the *monetary* sense. He did have big ambitions in a different direction. He worked for a local charity, helping homeless people. He wanted to improve the plight of underprivileged people throughout his city. He dreamed of the day when no one would ever have to sleep on the streets of this rich city again. She loved and admired him for that.

Her mother had dreamed of her becoming a doctor, which had once been Jessie's dream too. When, with lower sights, she'd opted instead to go for a nursing degree at Southampton University, her parents had accepted it, her mother with less good grace than her father. But when she graduated she decided that she wanted to do something to help the underprivileged, and she got a job that was low-paid but she loved, as a nurse/counsellor at a drug addict drop-in centre at the Old Steine in central Brighton.

A job with no prospects. Not something either of her parents could easily get their heads around. But they admired her dedication, no question of that. They were proud of her. And they were looking forward to a son-in-law, one day, they would be equally proud of. It was a natural assumption that he would be a big earner, a provider, to keep Jessie in the manner to which she was accustomed.

Which was a problem with Benedict.

'I'm happy to meet them any time. You know that.'

She nodded and gripped his hand. 'You're going to meet them next week at the ball. You'll charm them then, I'm sure.'

Her father was chair of a large local charity that raised money for Jewish causes around the world. He had booked a table at a fund-raising ball at the Metropole Hotel to which she had been invited to bring a friend.

She'd already bought her outfit and what she needed now was a pair of shoes to go with it. All she had to do was ask her father for the money, which she knew would please him no end. But she just could not bring herself to do that. She'd spotted some Anya Hindmarch shoes earlier today, in the January sale at a local store, Marielle Shoes. They were dead sexy but classy at the same time. Black patent leather, five-inch heels, ankle straps and open toe. But at £250 they were still a lot of money. She hoped that perhaps, if she waited, there might be a further reduction on them. If someone else bought them in the interim, well, too bad. She'd find something else. Brighton had no shortage of shoe shops. She'd find something!

The Shoe Man agreed with her.

He'd stood right behind her at the counter of Deja Shoes in Kensington Gardens earlier today. He'd listened to her telling the shop assistant that she wanted something classy and sexy to wear for her fiancé at an important function next week. Then he'd stood behind her at Marielle Shoes, just along the road.

And he had to admit she looked really sexy in those strapped black patent shoes she had tried on but not bought. So very sexy.

Much too sexy for them to be wasted on her fiancé.

He sincerely hoped she would return and buy them.

Then she could wear them for him!

50

Saturday 10 January

The words on the data unit's screen in Yac's taxi read:

China Garden rest. Preston St. 2 Pass. Starling. Dest.
Roedean Cresc.

It was 11.20 p.m. He had been parked up for some minutes now and had started the meter running. The man who owned the taxi said he should only wait for five minutes and then start the meter. Yac wasn't sure how accurate his watch was and he wanted to be fair to his passengers. So he always allowed twenty seconds' grace.

Starling. Roedean Crescent.

He had picked these people up before. He never forgot a passenger and especially not these people. The address: 67 Roedean Crescent. He had memorized that. She wore Shalimar perfume. The same perfume as his mother. He had memorized that too. She had been wearing Bruno Magli shoes. Size four. His mother's size.

He wondered what shoes she would be wearing tonight.

Excitement rose inside him as the restaurant door opened and he saw the couple emerge. The man was holding on to the woman and looked unsteady. She helped him negotiate the step down to the pavement, then he still clung to her as they walked the short distance, through the blustery wind, over to Yac.

But Yac wasn't looking at him. He was looking at the woman's shoes. They were nice. Tall heels. Straps. His kind of shoes.

Mr Starling peered in through the window, which Yac had opened.

'Taaxish for Roedean Chresshent? Shtarling?'

He sounded as drunk as he looked.

The man who owned the taxi said he did not have to take drunk passengers, especially ones who might be likely to throw up. It cost a lot of money to clear vomit out of the taxi, because it went everywhere, into the vents, down the windows into the electric motors, into the cracks down the sides of the seats. People didn't like getting into a taxi that smelt of stale sick. It wasn't nice to drive one either.

But it had been a quiet night. The man who owned the taxi would be angry with the poor takings. He had already complained about how little Yac had taken since New Year and he'd told Yac that he'd never known any taxi driver take so little on New Year's Eve itself.

He needed all the fares he could get, because he didn't want to risk the man who owned the taxi firing him and having someone else drive. So he decided to take a risk.

And he wanted to smell her perfume. Wanted those shoes in the taxi with him!

The Starlings climbed into the back and he drove off. He adjusted the mirror so he could see Mrs Starling's face, then he said, 'Nice shoes! Alberta Ferretti, I'll bet those are!'

'You a fucking pervert or shomething?' she said,

sounding almost as sloshed as her husband. 'I think you drove us before, didn't you, quite recently? Last week? Yesh?'

'You were wearing Bruno Maglis.'

'You're too fucking pershonal! None of your damned fucking business what shoes I'm wearing.'

'Into shoes, are you?' Yac asked.

'Yesh, she is into fucking shoes,' Garry Starling butted in. 'Spends all my money on them. Every penny I make ends up on her sodding feet!'

'That's because, my darling, you can only get it up when – ouch!' she cried out loudly.

Yac looked at her again in the mirror. Her face was contorted in pain. She'd been rude to him last time she had been in his taxi.

He liked seeing that pain.

1998

51

He'd spent the whole of the past few days thinking about Rachael Ryan lying in his chest freezer in his lock-up. It was hard to avoid her. Her face stared out at him from every damned newspaper. Her tearful parents spoke to him personally, and to him alone, from every damned television news broadcast.

'Please, whoever you are, if you have taken our daughter, give her back to us. She's a sweet, innocent girl and we love her. Please don't harm her.'

'It was your daughter's damned fault!' he whispered back at them. 'If she hadn't taken my mask off she'd be fine. Fine and dandy! She'd still be your loving daughter and not my damned problem.'

Slowly, steadily, the idea he had last night took hold more and more inside him. It could just be the perfect solution! He risk-assessed it over and over again. It stood up to each problem he tested it against. It would be riskier to delay than to act.

In almost every paper the white van was mentioned. It was referred to in big headlines on the front page of the *Argus*: DID ANYONE SEE THIS VAN? The caption beneath read: *Similar to the one seen in Eastern Terrace.*

The police said they had been overwhelmed with calls. How many of those calls were about white vans?

About his white van?

White Transit vans were a dime a dozen. But the police were not stupid. It was only a matter of time before a phone call led them to his lock-up. He had to get the girl out of there. And he had to do something about the van – they were getting smart with forensics these days. But deal with one problem at a time.

Outside, the rain was torrenting down. It was now 11 p.m. on Saturday. Party night in this city. But not so many people as usual would be out and about in this dreadful weather.

He made his decision and left the house, hurrying out to his old Ford Sierra runabout.

Ten minutes later, he pulled down the garage door behind the dripping-wet car, closing it with a quiet metallic clang, then switched on his torch, not wanting to risk putting on the overhead lights.

Inside the freezer, the young woman was completely frosted over, her face translucent in the harsh beam of light.

'We're going to take a little drive, Rachael. Hope you're cool with that?'

Then he smirked at his joke. Yeah. *Cool.* He felt OK. This was going to work. He just had to stay cool too. How did that saying go that he had read somewhere: *If you can keep your head while all about you are losing theirs . . .*

He pulled out his packet of cigarettes and tried to light one. But his damned hand was shaking so much, first he couldn't strike the wheel of the lighter, then he couldn't get the flame near the tip of the cigarette. Cold sweat was pouring down his neck as if it was coming from a busted tap.

*

At a few minutes to midnight, with his toolkit clipped to his belt, he drove around the Lewes Road gyratory system, past the entrance to the Brighton and Hove Borough Mortuary, wipers clunk-clunking away the rain, and then turned left on to the hard driveway of his destination, J. Bund and Sons, funeral directors.

He was shaking, all knotted up inside and perspiring heavily. *Stupid woman, stupid bloody Rachael, why the hell did you have to take my mask off?*

Up on the wall, above the curtained shop window of the premises, he clocked the burglar alarm box. Sussex Security Systems. Not a problem, he thought, pulling up in front of the padlocked steel gates. The lock was also not a problem.

Directly across the road was a closed estate agent's, with flats on the two storeys above. There was a light on in one of them. But they would be used to seeing vehicles come and go at a funeral parlour around the clock.

He switched the lights off, then climbed out of the Sierra into the rain to deal with the padlock. A trickle of cars and taxis drove past along the road. One of them was a police patrol car, its blue lights flashing and siren wailing. He held his breath, but its crew paid him no attention, just swishing straight past to some emergency or other. Moments later he drove through into the rear yard and parked between two hearses and a van. Then he hurried back through the rain and closed the gates, pulling the chain around them, but leaving the padlock dangling open. So long as no one came, all would be fine.

It took him less than a minute to pick the Chubb on the double rear receiving doors, then he entered the dark entrance hallway, wrinkling his nose at the smells of embalming fluid and disinfectant. The alarm was beeping.

Just the internal warning signal. He had sixty precious seconds before the external bells would kick off. It took him less than thirty to remove the front casing of the alarm panel. Another fifteen and it fell silent.

Too silent.

He closed the door behind him. And now it was even more silent. The faint click-whirr of a fridge. A steady tick-tick-tick of a clock or a meter.

These places gave him the creeps. He remembered the last time he had been in here; he had been alone then, and shit-scared. They were dead, all of the people in here, dead like Rachael Ryan. They couldn't hurt you, or tell tales on you.

Couldn't leap out at you.

But that didn't make it any better.

He flashed his torch beam along the corridor ahead, trying to orient himself. He saw a row of framed Health and Safety notices, a fire extinguisher and a drinking-water dispenser.

Then he took a few steps forward, his trainers silent on the tiled floor, listening intently for any new sounds inside or out. There was a staircase up to his right. He remembered it led to the individual rooms – or Chapels of Rest – where friends and relatives could visit and mourn their loved ones in privacy. Each room contained a body laid out on a bed, men in pyjamas, women in nightgowns, their heads poking out from beneath the sheets, hair tidy, faces all rosy from embalming fluid. They looked like they were checked into some tacky hotel for the night.

But for sure they wouldn't be doing a runner without paying their bills in the morning, he thought, and grinned despite his unease.

Then, flashing his torch through an open doorway to his left, he saw a prostrate white marble statue. Except, as he took a closer look, he saw it wasn't a statue. It was a dead man on a slab. Two handwritten tags hung from his right foot. An old man, he lay with his mouth open like a landed fish, embalming-fluid lines cannu-lated into his body, his penis lying uselessly against his thigh.

Close to him was a row of coffins, open and empty, just one of them with its lid closed. There was a brass plaque on the lid, engraved with the name of its occupant.

He stopped for a moment, listening. But all he could hear was the thudding of his own heart and the blood coursing through his veins louder than the roar of a river in flood. He could not hear the traffic outside. All that entered here from the world beyond the walls was a faint, eerie orange glow leaking in from a street light on the pavement.

'Hi, everyone!' he said, feeling very uncomfortable as he swung the beam around until it struck what he was looking for. The row of duplicated white A4 forms hanging on hooks from the wall.

Eagerly, he walked over to them. These were the registration forms for each of the bodies in here. All the information was on them: name, date of death, place of death, funeral instructions, and a whole row of optional disbursement boxes to be ticked – organist's fee, cemetery fee, churchyard burial fee, clergy's fee, church fee, doc-tor's fee, removal of pacemaker fee, cremation fee, grave-digger's fee, printed service sheets fees, flowers, memorial cards, obituary notices, coffin, casket for remains.

He read quickly through the first sheet. No good: the *Embalming* box had been ticked. The same applied to the next four. His heart began to sink. They were embalmed and their funerals were not until later in the week.

But on the fifth it looked like he might have struck gold:

Mrs Molly Winifred Glossop

D. 2 January 1998. Aged 81.

And further down:

Funeral on: 12 January 1998, 11 a.m.

Monday morning!

His eyes raced down the form to the words *Committal.* Not so good. He would have preferred a cremation. Done and dusted. Safer.

He turned to the remaining six forms. But none of them was any good at all. They were all funerals to be held later in the week – too risky, in case the family came to view. And all but one had requested embalming.

No one had requested that Molly Winifred Glossop be embalmed.

Not having her embalmed meant her family was probably too mean. Which might be an indication that they weren't going to care too much about her body. So hopefully no distraught relative was going to rush in tonight or first thing in the morning, wanting to have one last peep at her.

He shone his beam down on the plaque on the one closed coffin, trying hard to ignore the corpse lying just a few feet away.

Molly Winifred Glossop, it confirmed. *Died 2 January 1998, aged 81.*

The fact that it was closed, with the lid screwed down,

was a good indicator that no one was coming along tomorrow to see her.

Unclipping a screwdriver from his belt, he removed the shiny brass screws holding down the lid, lifted it away and peered inside, breathing in a cocktail of freshly sawn wood, glue and new fabric and disinfectant.

The dead woman nestled in the cream satin lining of the coffin, her head poking out of the white shroud that wrapped the rest of her. She did not look real; she looked like some kind of weird *granny* doll, that was his first reaction. Her face was emaciated and bony, all wrinkles and angles, the colour of a tortoise. Her mouth was sewn shut; he could see the threads through her lips. Her hair was a tidy bob of white curls.

He felt a lump in his throat as a memory came back to him. And another lump, this time of fear. He slipped his hands down either side of her and began to lift. He was startled by how light she was. He could feel the weightlessness of her frame in his arms. There was nothing on her, no flesh at all. She must have been a cancer victim, he decided, laying her down on the floor. Shit, she was a lot lighter than Rachael Ryan. Several stones lighter. But hopefully the pall-bearers would never realize.

He hurried back outside, popped open the boot of the Sierra and removed Rachael Ryan's body, which he had wrapped in two layers of heavy-duty plastic sheeting to prevent any water leaking out as she thawed.

*

Ten minutes later, with the alarm casing replaced, the system reset and the padlock again locked shut on the chain around the gate, he pulled the Ford Sierra out into the busy Saturday-night traffic on the rain-lashed road. A whole weight was gone from his mind. He accelerated recklessly, swinging out across the lanes, halting at a red light on the far side of the road.

He needed to keep calm, did not want to risk attracting the attention of the police, not with Molly Winifred Glossop lying in the boot of his car. He switched on the radio and heard the sound of the Beatles: 'We Can Work It Out'.

He thumped the steering wheel, almost elated with relief. *Yes! Yes! Yes! We* can *work it out!*

Oh yes!

Stage one had gone to plan. Now he just had stage two to worry about. It was a big worry; there were unknown factors. But it was the best of his limited options. And, in his view, quite cunning.

NOW

52

St Patrick's night shelter relaxed the rules on Sundays that
it applied for the rest of the week. Although the residents
still had to vacate the premises by 8.30 a.m., they could
return at 5 p.m.

Even so, Darren Spicer thought that was a bit harsh,
since it was a church and all that, and wasn't a church
supposed to give you sanctuary at any time? Especially
when the weather was crap. But he wasn't going to argue,
as he didn't want to blot his copybook here. He wanted
one of the MiPods. Ten weeks of personal space and you
could come and go as you pleased. Yeah, that would be
good. That would enable him to get his life together –
though not in the kind of way the people who ran this
place had in mind.

It was pissing down outside. And sodding freezing.
But he did not want to stay in all day. He'd showered and
eaten a bowl of cereal and some toast. The television was
on and a couple of the residents were watching a replay
of a football match on its slightly fuzzy screen.

Football, yeah. Brighton and Hove Albion was his
home team. He remembered that magical day, when he
was a teenager, they'd played at Wembley in the FA Cup
Final and drawn. Half the home-owners of Brighton and
Hove had gone up there to watch the game, while the

other half were in their sitting rooms, glued to their tellies. It had been one of the best day's burgling of his whole career.

Yesterday he'd actually been along to the Withdean Sports Stadium for a game. He liked football, not that he was much of an Albion supporter. He preferred Manchester United and Chelsea, but he had his reasons yesterday. He needed to score some charlie – as cocaine was known on the street – and the best way was to show his face. His dealer was there, in his usual seat. Nothing had changed there, apart from the price, which had gone up, and the quality, which had gone down.

After the game he'd acquired himself an eight ball for £140, dipping deep into his meagre savings. He'd washed down two of the three and a half grams with a couple of pints and a few whisky chasers almost straight away. The last gram and a half he'd saved to see himself through the tedium of today.

He pulled his donkey jacket on and his baseball cap. Most of the rest of his fellow residents were lazing around, talking in groups or lost in their thoughts or watching the TV. Like himself, none of them had anywhere to go, particularly on a Sunday, when the libraries were shut – the only warm places where they could hang out for hours for free without being hassled. But he had plans.

The round clock on the wall above the now closed food hatch said 8.23. Seven minutes to go.

It was at times like this that he missed being in prison. Life was easy in there. You were warm and dry. You had routine and companionship. You had no worries. But you had dreams.

He reminded himself of that now. His dreams. The

promise he had made himself. To make himself some kind of a future. Get a stash and then go straight.

Lingering in the dry for those last few minutes, Spicer read some of the posters stuck to the walls:

MOVING ON?

FREE CONFIDENCE BUILDING COURSE FOR MEN

FREE FOOD SAFETY COURSE

FREE NEW COURSE –
FEELING SAFER AT HOME AND IN THE COMMUNITY

INJECTING INTO MUSCLE? PLEASE BE AWARE

DO YOU THINK YOU MIGHT HAVE A PROBLEM
WITH COCAINE OR OTHER DRUGS?

He sniffed. Yeah, he did have a problem with cocaine. Not enough of it, that was the problem right now. He didn't have cash spare for any more and that was going to be a real problem. That's what he needed, he realized. Yeah. The coke he'd scored yesterday had made him fly, had put him in a great mood, made him horny, dangerously so. But what the hell?

Now he was down with a bang this morning. A deep trough. He'd get himself a few drinks, take the rest of his charlie and then he wouldn't care about the crap weather – he'd set off around a few parts of the city he'd decided to target.

Sunday was a dangerous day to break into houses. Too many people were at home. Even if someone was out, their neighbours might not be. He would spend today on research, casing. He had a list of properties from contacts in insurance companies that he'd been steadily building up while in prison so as not to squander his precious time there. A whole list of houses and flats where the owners had quality jewellery and silverware. In some cases, he had the complete list of their valuables. Some very rich pickings to be had. If he was careful, enough to set him up for his new life.

'Darren?'

He turned, startled to hear his name. It was one of the volunteer workers here, a man of about thirty in a blue shirt and jeans, with short hair and long sideburns. His name was Simon.

Spicer looked at him, wondering what was wrong. Had someone reported him last night? Seen his enlarged pupils? If they caught you taking drugs or you were even just high on them in here, you could be thrown straight out.

'There are two gentlemen to see you outside.'

The words were like a sudden sideways pull of gravity deep inside him. As if all his innards had turned to jelly. It was the same feeling he always had when he realized the game was up and he was being arrested.

'Oh, right,' he said, trying to sound nonchalant and uninterested.

Two gentlemen could only mean one thing.

He followed the young man out into the corridor, his stomach really churning now. His brain was racing. Wondering which of the things he had done in the past few days they had come to get him for.

It felt more like a church out here. A long corridor with a pointed arch at the end. The reception office was next to it, glassed in. Outside it stood two men. From the way they were suited and booted, they could only be coppers.

One of them was thin and tall as a beanpole, with short, spiky hair that was a mess; he looked like he hadn't had a decent night's sleep in many months. The other was black, with his head shaven as bald as a meteorite. Spicer vaguely recognized him.

'Darren Spicer?' the black one said.

'Yeah.'

The man held up a warrant card, which Spicer barely bothered to glance at.

'DS Branson, Sussex CID, and this is my colleague, DC Nicholl. Wonder if we could have a chat.'

'I got a pretty busy schedule,' Spicer said. 'But s'pose I could fit you in.'

'Very accommodating of you.'

'Yeah, well, I like to be accommodating, with the police and all that.' He nodded. 'Yeah.' He sniffed.

The volunteer worker opened a door and indicated for them to walk through.

Spicer entered a small meeting room containing a table and six chairs, with a large stained-glass window on the far wall. He sat down and the two detectives sat opposite him.

'We've met before, haven't we, Darren?' DS Branson said.

Spicer frowned. 'Yeah, maybe. You look familiar. Trying to think where.'

'I interviewed you about three years ago, when you were in custody – about some house break-ins. You'd just been arrested for burglary and indecent assault. Remember now?'

'Oh yeah, rings a bell.'

He grinned at each of the detectives, but neither of

them smiled back. The mobile phone of the one with ragged hair rang suddenly. He checked the number, then answered it quietly.

'I'm tied up. I'll call you back,' he murmured, before sticking the phone back into his pocket.

Branson pulled out a notebook and flipped it open. He studied it for a moment.

'You were released from prison on 28 December, correct?'

'Yeah, that's right.'

'We'd like to talk to you about your movements since then.'

Spicer sniffed. 'Well, the thing is, I don't keep a diary, you see. Got no secretary.'

'That's all right,' the spiky-haired one said, pulling out a small black book. 'I've got one here. This one is for last year and I've got another for this year. We can help you on dates.'

'Very obliging of you,' Spicer replied.

'That's what we're here for,' Nick Nicholl said. 'To be obliging.'

'Let's start with Christmas Eve,' Branson said. 'I understand you were on day release at Ford Open Prison, working in the maintenance department of the Metropole Hotel up until your release on licence. Is that correct?'

'Yeah.'

'When was the last time you were at the hotel?'

Spicer thought for a moment. 'Christmas Eve,' he said.

'What about New Year's Eve, Darren?' Glenn Branson went on. 'Where were you then?'

Spicer scratched his nose, then sniffed again.

'Well, I had been invited to spend it up at Sandringham with the royals, but then I thought, nah, can't be spending all my time with toffs—'

'Cut it out,' Branson said sharply. 'Remember you're out on licence. We can do this chat the easy way or the hard way. The easy way is here, now. Or we can bang you back up and do it there. It's no sweat to us either way.'

'We'll do it here,' Spicer said hastily, sniffing again.

'Got a cold, have you?' Nick Nicholl asked.

He shook his head.

The two detectives caught each other's eye, then Branson said, 'Right, New Year's Eve. Where were you?'

Spicer laid his hands on the table and stared down at his fingers. All his nails were badly bitten, as was the skin around them.

'Drinking up at the Neville.'

'The Neville pub?' Nick Nicholl asked. 'The one near the greyhound stadium?'

'Yeah, that's right, by the dogs.'

'Can anyone vouch for you?' Branson queried.

'I was with a few – you know – acquaintances – yeah. Can give you some names.'

Nick Nicholl turned to his colleague. 'Might be able to verify that on CCTV if they've got it in there. I seem to remember they have, from a past inquiry.'

Branson made a note. 'If they haven't wiped it – a lot of them only keep seven-day records.' Then he looked at Spicer. 'What time did you leave the pub?'

Spicer shrugged. 'I don't remember. I was shit-faced. One, one-thirty maybe.'

'Where were you staying then?' Nick Nicholl asked.

'The Kemp Town hostel.'

'Would anyone remember you coming home?'

'That lot? Nah. They're not capable of remembering nothing.'

'How did you get home?' Branson asked.

'Had the chauffeur pick me up in the Roller, didn't I?'

He said it so innocently that Glenn had to struggle to stop himself from grinning. 'So your chauffeur can vouch for you?'

Spicer shook his head. 'I walked, didn't I? Shanks's pony.'

Branson flipped a few pages back in his notebook. 'Let's move on to this past week. Can you tell us where you were between 6 p.m. and midnight on Thursday 8 January?'

Spicer answered quickly, as if he had already known what the question would be. 'Yeah, I went to the dogs. Ladies' night. Stayed there till about 7.30 and then came back here.'

'The greyhound stadium? Your local pub, then, is that the Neville?'

'One of 'em, yeah.'

Branson made a mental note that the greyhound stadium was less than fifteen minutes' walk from Drove-way Avenue, where Roxy Pearce was raped on Thursday night.

'Do you have anything to prove you were there? Betting stubs? Anyone with you?'

'There was a bird I picked up.' He stopped.

'What was her name?' Branson asked.

'Yeah, well, that's the thing. She's married. Her husband was away for the night. I don't think she'd be too happy, you know, having the Old Bill asking questions.'

'Gone all moral, have we, Darren?' Branson asked. 'Suddenly developed a conscience?'

He was thinking, but did not say, that it was rather a strange coincidence that Roxy Pearce's husband had been away that night too.

'Not moral, but I don't want to give you her name.'

'Then you'd better deliver us some other proof that you were at the dogs, and during that time period.'

Spicer looked at them. He needed a smoke badly.

'Do you mind telling me what this is about?

'A series of sexual assaults have been committed in this city. We're looking to eliminate people from our enquiries.'

'So I'm a suspect?'

Branson shook his head. 'No, but your release date on licence makes you a possible Person of Interest.'

He did not reveal to Spicer that his records had been checked for 1997–8, and they showed he had been released from prison just six days before the Shoe Man's first suspected attack back then.

'Let's move on to yesterday. Can you account for where you were between 5 p.m. and 9 p.m.?'

Spicer was sure his face was burning. He felt boxed in, didn't like the way these questions kept on coming. Questions he couldn't answer. Yes, he could say exactly where he was at 5 p.m. yesterday. He was in a copse behind a house in Woodland Drive, Brighton's so-called Millionaire's Row, buying charlie from one of its residents. He doubted he'd live to see his next birthday if he so much as mentioned the address.

'I was at the Albion game. Went for some drinks with a mate afterwards. Until curfew here, right? Came back and had me dinner, then went to bed.'

'Crap game, wasn't it?' Nick Nicholl said.

'Yeah, that second goal, like . . .' Spicer raised his hands in despair and sniffed again.

'Your mate got a name?' Glenn Branson asked.

'Nah. You know, that's a funny thing. See him about, known him for years – yet I still don't know his name. Not the sort of thing you can ask someone after you've been drinking with them on and off for ten years, is it?'

'Why not?' Nicholl asked.

Spicer shrugged.

There was a long silence.

Branson flipped his notebook over a page. 'Lock-up here is 8.30 p.m. I'm told you arrived back at 8.45 p.m., your voice was slurred and your pupils dilated. You were lucky they let you back in. Residents are forbidden to take drugs.'

'I don't take no drugs, Detective, sir.' He sniffed again.

'I'll bet you don't. You've just got a bad head cold, right?'

'Right. Must be what it is. Exactly right. A bad head cold!'

Branson nodded. 'I'll bet you still believe in Father Christmas, don't you?'

Spicer gave him a sly grin, unsure quite where this was going. 'Father Christmas? Yeah. Yeah, why not?'

'Next year write and ask him for a sodding hand-kerchief.'

53

Sunday 11 January

Yac did not drive the taxi on Sundays because he was *otherwise engaged*.

He had heard people use that expression and he liked it. *Otherwise engaged*. It had a nice ring to it. He liked, sometimes, to say things that had a nice ring to them.

'Why don't you ever take the cab out on Sunday nights?' the man who owned the taxi had asked him recently.

'Because I'm otherwise engaged,' Yac replied importantly.

And he was. He had important business that filled his Sundays from the moment he got up until late into the night.

It was late at night now.

His first duty every Sunday morning was to check the houseboat for leaks, both from below the waterline and from the roof. Then he cleaned the houseboat. It was the cleanest floating home in all of Shoreham. Then he fastidiously cleaned himself. He was the cleanest, best-shaven taxi driver in the whole of Brighton and Hove.

When the owners of *Tom Newbound* finally came back from living in India, Yac hoped they would be proud of him. Maybe they would continue to let him live here with them, if he agreed to clean the boat every Sunday morning.

He so much hoped that. And he had nowhere else to go.

One of his neighbours told Yac the boat was so clean he could eat off the deck, if he wanted to. Yac didn't understand that. Why would he want to? If he put food on the deck, gulls would come and eat it. Then he'd have the mess of food and gulls on the deck, and he'd have to clean all that up as well. So he ignored that suggestion.

He had learned over the years that it was wise to ignore suggestions. Most suggestions came from idiots. Intelligent people kept their thoughts to themselves.

His next task, in between making his hourly cups of tea and eating his Sunday dinner – always the same meal, microwaved lasagne – was removing his childhood collection of high-flush toilet chains from their hiding place in the bilges. *Tom Newbound*, he had discovered, provided him with several good hiding places. His collection of shoes was in some of them.

He liked to take his time laying the chains out on the floor of the saloon. First, he would count them to make sure that no one had been on the boat when he was out and stolen any of them. Then he would inspect them, to check there were no rust spots. Then he would clean them, lovingly rubbing each of the chain links with metal polish.

After he had put the chains carefully away, Yac would go on the Internet. He would spend the rest of the afternoon on Google Earth, checking for changes from his maps. That was something he had realized. Maps changed, just like everything else. You couldn't depend on them. You couldn't depend on anything. The past was shifting sand. Stuff that you read and learned and stored away in your head could – and did – get changed. Just because you knew something once did not mean it was still true today. Like with maps. You couldn't be a good taxi driver just from relying on maps. You had to keep up to date, up to the minute!

It was the same with technology.

Things you knew five or ten or fifteen years ago weren't always any good today. Technology changed. He had a whole filing cabinet on the boat filled with wiring diagrams of burglar alarm systems. He liked to work them out. He liked to find the flaws in them. A long time ago he had figured out that if a human being designed something, there would be a flaw in it somewhere. He liked to store those flaws away in his head. Information was knowledge and knowledge was power!

Power over all those people who thought he was no good. Who sneered or laughed at him. He could tell, sometimes, that people in his cab were laughing at him. He could see them in the mirror, sitting on the back seat smirking and whispering to each other about him. They thought he was a bit soft in the head. Potty. Doolally. Oh yes.

Uh-huh.

The way his mother did.

She made the same mistake. She thought he was stupid. She did not know that some days, or nights, when she was home, he watched her. She was unaware that he had made a small hole in the ceiling of her bedroom. He used to lie silently in the loft above her, watching her hurting a man with her shoes. He would watch her screwing her stiletto heels into the naked men's backs.

Other times she would lock Yac in his bedroom with a tray of food and a bucket, leaving him alone in the house for the night. He would hear the thunk of the lock, then he would hear her footsteps, her heels clicking on the floorboards, getting fainter and fainter.

She never knew that he understood locks. That he had read and memorized every specialist magazine and every instruction manual he could lay his hands on in the reference library. He knew just about everything there was to know about bored cylindrical locks, tumbler locks, lever locks. There wasn't a lock or alarm system on the planet, Yac reckoned, that could defeat him. Not that he had tried all of them. He thought that would be hard work and would take too long.

When she went out, leaving him alone, with the *clack-clack-clack* of her shoes fading into silence, he would pick the lock of his bedroom door and go into her room. He liked to lie naked on her bed, breathing in the heady, musky smells of her Shalimar perfume, and the air that still smelt of her cigarette smoke, holding one of her shoes in his left hand, safe from her, and then relieve himself with his right hand.

It was the way he liked to end each of his Sunday evenings now.

But tonight was better than ever! He had newspaper articles on the Shoe Man. He had read and re-read them, and not just the *Argus*, but other papers too. Sunday papers. The Shoe Man raped his victims and took their shoes.

Uh-huh.

He sprayed Shalimar around the interior of his room in the houseboat, short bursts into each corner, then a longer one towards the ceiling, directly above his head, so that tiny, invisible droplets of the fragrance would fall all around him.

He then stood, aroused, starting to shake. In moments he became drenched in perspiration, breathing with his eyes closed, as the smell brought back so many memories. Then he lit a Dunhill International cigarette and inhaled the sweet smoke deeply, holding it in his lungs for some moments before jetting it out through his nostrils, the way his mother did.

It was smelling like her room in here now. Yes.

In between puffs, getting more and more deeply aroused, he began unbuttoning his trousers. Then, lying back on his bunk, he touched himself and whispered, *Oh, Mummy! Oh, Mummy! Oh yes, Mummy, I'm such a bad boy!*

And all the time he was thinking of the really bad thing he had just done. Which aroused him even more.

54

Roy Grace was in a sombre mood at 7.30 a.m. The New Year was not even a fortnight old and he now had three violent stranger rapes on his hands.

He was seated in the office that always made him feel uncomfortable, even though its previous incumbent, the sometimes tyrannical Alison Vosper, was no longer there. Replacing her behind the large rosewood desk, which was now a lot more cluttered, was Assistant Chief Constable Peter Rigg, starting his second week here. And for the first time ever, Grace had actually been offered a drink in this office. He was now gratefully sipping strong coffee from an elegant china cup.

The ACC was a dapper, rather distinguished-looking man, with a healthy complexion, fair hair neatly and conservatively cut, and a sharp, posh voice. Although several inches shorter than Grace, he had fine posture, giving him a military bearing which made him seem taller than his actual height. He was dressed in a navy suit with discreet pinstripes, an elegant white shirt and a loud tie. From a row of photographs on his desk, and new pictures now hanging on the walls, the man was evidently keen on motor racing, which pleased Grace because that was something they would have in common, although he'd not had a chance to bring this up yet.

'I've had the new Chief Executive of the City Corporation on the phone,' said Rigg – his manner pleasant but no-nonsense. 'This was before the ghost train attack. Stranger rape is a very emotive subject. Brighton's already lost the Labour Party Conference for many years to come – not that that's connected to these rapes in any way – and he feels it would greatly help the future chances of this city to attract top-end conference trade if we can show how safe it is to come here. Fear of crime seems to have become a major issue in the competitive conference business.'

'Yes, sir, I appreciate that.'

'Our New Year's resolution should be to focus on the crimes that cause fear in the community – fear among ordinary decent people. That's where I think we should be maximizing our resources. Our subliminal message should be that people are as safe anywhere in Brighton and Hove as they are in their own homes. What do you think?'

Grace nodded his agreement, but privately he was concerned. The ACC's intentions were right, but his timing was not great. Roxy Pearce had clearly not been safe in her own home. Also, what he had just said wasn't new. He was merely reinforcing what, in Grace's view, had always been the police force's main role. Certainly, at any rate, his own main goal.

When he had first been promoted to the rank of detective superintendent, his immediate boss, the then head of CID, Gary Weston, had explained his philosophy to him very succinctly: 'Roy, I try as a boss to think what it is the public expect from me and would like me to do. What does my wife want? My elderly mum? They want to feel safe, they want to go about their lawful business unhindered, and they want me to lock up all the bad guys.'

Grace had used that as a mantra ever since.

Rigg held up a typewritten document, six sheets of paper clipped together, and Grace knew immediately what it was.

'This is the twenty-four-hour review from the Crime Policy and Review Branch on *Operation Swordfish*,' the ACC said. 'I had it dropped round last night.' He gave the Detective Superintendent a slightly worried smile. 'It's positive. You've ticked all the boxes – something I would have expected, from all the good things I've heard about you, Roy.'

'Thank you, sir!' Grace said, pleasantly surprised. Clearly the man hadn't spoken too much to the now departed Alison Vosper, his big fan – not.

'I think the political ride's going to get a lot rougher when the news on this third rape gets out. And, of course, we don't know how many more our offender might commit before we lock him up.'

'Or before he disappears again,' Grace replied.

The ACC looked as if he had just bitten a red-hot chilli.

55

Sussex Security Systems and Sussex Remote Monitoring Services were housed in a large 1980s building on an industrial estate in Lewes, seven miles from Brighton.

As the business which Garry Starling had started in a small shop in Hove fifteen years earlier expanded into two separate fields, he knew he would have to move into bigger premises. The perfect opportunity presented itself when the building in Lewes became vacant following a bankruptcy, with the receiver keen to do a deal.

But what attracted him even more than the favourable terms was the location itself, less than a quarter of a mile from Malling House, the headquarters of Sussex Police. He'd already secured two contracts with them, installing and maintaining alarms in a couple of small-town police stations that were closed at night, and he was sure that being so close to the hub of the whole force could do no harm.

He had been right. A combination of knocking on doors, schmoozing on the golf course and some very competitive pricing had brought a lot more work his way, and when, just over a decade ago, the CID moved into their new headquarters, Sussex House, it had been SSS that had secured the contract for the internal security system.

Despite his success, Garry Starling was not into flash,

339

expensive cars. He never drove them because in his view all you did was draw attention to yourself – and the flashier your wheels, the more your customers would think you were overcharging. Success to him meant freedom. The ability to hire people to do the stuff you didn't want to be stuck in the office doing. The freedom to be out on the golf course when you wanted. And to do other things you wanted too. He left it to Denise to be the spender. She could spend for England.

When they'd first met she'd been sex on legs. She liked everything that turned him on and she was randy as hell, with few limits. Now she just sat on her fat arse, letting it get fatter by the hour, and she didn't want to know about sex – at least, not any of the things that he enjoyed.

He drove his small grey Volvo along the industrial estate, passing a Land Rover dealer, the entrance to Tesco and then Homebase. He made a right, then a left and ahead, at the end of the cul-de-sac, he saw his twin single-storey building and a row of nine white vans, each bearing the company logo, outside.

Ever mindful about costs, the vans were plain white and the company name was on magnetic panels stuck to their sides. It meant he didn't have to pay sign-writing costs each time he purchased a new van; he could simply pull the panels off and use them again.

It was 9 a.m. and he wasn't happy to see so many vans still parked up. They should have been out doing installations or making service calls on customers. That was thanks to the recession.

Not many things made him happy these days.

*

Dunstan Christmas's butt was itching, but he did not dare scratch it. If he took his weight off this chair for more than two seconds during his shift, without first properly logging off, the alarm would sound and his supervisor would come running in.

You had to hand it to the guy who had thought of this, Christmas grudgingly admitted to himself, it was a damned good system. Foolproof, just about.

Which of course it needed to be, because that was what the customers of Sussex Remote Monitoring Services paid for: trained CCTV operators like himself to sit, in a uniform, and watch the images of their homes and business premises, in real time, around the clock. Christmas was thirty-six years old and weighed twenty stones. Sitting on his butt suited him well.

He couldn't much see the point of the uniform, as he never left the room, but the Big Cheese, Mr Starling, had everyone on the premises, even the receptionists, wear uniform. It gave people a sense of pride and purpose, Mr Starling said, and it impressed visitors. Everyone did what Mr Starling said.

Alongside the camera selection button on the panel in front of him was a microphone. Even though some of the houses and business premises on the twenty screens in front of him were many miles away, one click of the microphone button and he could scare the shit out of any intruder by talking straight to them. He liked that part of the job. Didn't happen too often, but when it did, boy, was it fun to see them jump! That was a perk.

Christmas worked an eight-hour shift, alternating between day, evening and night, and he was happy enough with the pay he got, but the job itself, Jesus, sometimes, particularly during the night, it could be mind-numbingly boring. Twenty different programmes on television and nothing happening on any of them! Just a picture of a factory gate on one. A domestic driveway on another. The rear of a big Dyke Road Avenue mansion on another. Occasionally a cat would slink across, or an urban fox, or a badger, or a scurrying rodent.

Screen no. 17 was one he had a bit of an emotional connection with. It showed images of the old Shoreham cement works that had been shut down for the past nineteen years. Twenty-six CCTV cameras were sited around the vast premises, one for the front entrance, the rest covering all key internal access points. At the moment the image was of the front, a high steel fence topped with razor wire, and chained gates.

His dad used to work there, as a cement tanker driver, and sometimes Dunstan would ride up front in the cab when his dad was making a collection. He loved the place. He always thought it was like being on the set of a Bond film, with its huge cement clinker kilns, grinding mills and storage silos, the bulldozers, dumptrucks and diggers, and activity around the clock.

The cement works sat in a huge quarried bowl in isolated countryside, a few miles inland and just to the north-west of Shoreham. The site covered several hundred acres and was now full of vast, derelict buildings. Rumour had it there were plans to reactivate it all, but since the last lorry had driven out of there, nearly two decades ago, it had lain derelict, a grey ghost village of mostly windowless structures, rusting components, old vehicles and weed-strewn tracks. The only visitors were the occasional vandals and thieves who had systematically stolen some of the electric motors, cables and lead piping, which was why the elaborate security system had been put in place.

But this particular Monday morning was more interesting than usual. Certainly on one particular screen, no. 11.

Each of the screens had feeds to ten different properties. Motion-sensor software would instantly bring a property up if there was any movement, such as a vehicle arriving or leaving, someone walking, or even a fox or large dog prowling. There had been constant activity on screen no. 11 since he had come on shift at 7 a.m. That was the front view of the Pearce house. He could see the crime scene tape, a Police Community Support Officer scene guard. A POLSA and three Police Search Officers in protective blue oversuits and rubber gloves, on their hands and knees, were searching inch by inch for any clues left behind by the intruder who had assaulted Mrs Pearce inside the house last Thursday night, and sticking small numbered markers here and there in the ground.

He dug his hand into the large packet of Kettle crisps beside the control panel on his workstation, shovelled the crisps into his mouth, then washed them down with a swig of Coke. He needed to pee, but decided to hang on for a while. He could log off the system to take a comfort break, as they were called, but it would be noted. An hour and a half was too soon after starting his shift; he needed to give it a bit longer, as he wanted to impress his boss.

The voice right behind him startled him.

'I'm glad to see the feed to Droveway Avenue has been fixed.'

Dunstan Christmas turned to see his boss, Garry Starling, the owner of this company, looking over his shoulder.

Starling had a habit of doing this. He was always snooping on his employees. Creeping silently up behind them, sometimes in working clothes of a white shirt, jeans and trainers, sometimes in a neat business suit. But always stealthily, silently, on rubber-soled shoes like some weirdo stalker. His big, owl-like eyes were peering at the bank of screens.

'Yes, Mr Starling. It was working when I came on shift.'

'Do we know what the problem was yet?'

'I haven't spoken to Tony.'

Tony was the chief engineer of the company.

Starling watched the activity at the Pearce house for some moments, nodding.

'Not good, is it, sir?' Christmas said.

'It's incredible,' Garry Starling said. 'The worst thing that's ever happened on any of the properties we monitor and the fucking system wasn't working. Incredible!'

'Bad timing.'

'You could say that.'

Christmas moved a toggle switch on the panel and zoomed in on one SOCO, who was bagging something of interest that was too small for them to see.

'Kind of interesting, watching how thorough these guys are,' he said.

There was no reply from his boss.

'Like something out of *CSI*.'

Again there was no reply.

He turned his head and discovered, to his astonishment, that Garry Starling had left the room.

56

Wearing expensive high heels makes you feel sexy, doesn't it? You think spending money on these things is an investment, don't you? All part of your trap. Do you know what you are like? All of you? Venus fly traps! That's what you are like.

Have you ever looked closely at the leaves of a Venus fly trap? They are all pink inside. Do they remind you of something? I'll tell you what they remind me of: vaginas with teeth. Which is of course exactly what they are. Nasty incisors all the way around, like prison cell bars.

The moment an insect enters and touches one of the tiny hairs in those inviting, sensual pink lips, the trap snaps shut. It seals out all the air. Just like you all do. Then the digestive juices set to work, slowly killing the prey if it hasn't been lucky enough to have suffocated first. Just like you all do! The soft, inner parts of the insect are dissolved, but not the tough outer part, the exoskeleton. At the end of the digestive process, after several days, sometimes a couple of weeks, the trap reabsorbs the digestive fluid and then reopens. The remains of the insect are blown away in the wind or washed away by the rain.

That's why you put those shoes on, isn't it? To trap us, suck all the fluids out of us, then excrete our remains.

Well, I've got news for you.

57

MIR-1 was capable of housing up to three Major Incident investigations at the same time. But with Roy Grace's rapidly expanding team, *Operation Swordfish* needed the entire room. Fortunately he'd always kept on the right side of the Senior Support Officer, Tony Case, who controlled all four Major Incident Suites in the county.

Case obligingly moved the only other major investigation currently taking place in Sussex House at the moment – the late-night street murder of an as yet unidentified man – to the smaller MIR-2 along the corridor.

Although Grace had held two briefings yesterday, several of his team had been absent on outside inquiries, for a number of important reasons. He had ordered full attendance this morning.

He sat down at a free space at one of the workstations, placing his agenda and Policy Book in front of him. Beside them sat his third coffee of the day, so far. Cleo was constantly reproaching him for the amount he consumed, but after his early pleasant but testy meeting with ACC Rigg, he felt in need of another strong caffeine hit.

Although MIR-1 had not been redecorated or refurbished for some years, the room always had a sterile, faintly anodyne modern-office smell. A big contrast to police offices before the smoking ban had been imposed, he thought. Almost all of them reeked of tobacco and had a permanently fuggy haze. But it gave them atmosphere and in some ways he missed that. Everything in life was becoming too sterile.

He nodded greetings to various members of his team as they filed into the room, most of them, including Glenn Branson, who appeared to be having yet another of his endless arguments with his wife, talking on their phones.

'Morning, old-timer,' Branson greeted him when he ended his call. He pocketed his phone, then tapped the top of his own shaven dome and frowned.

Grace frowned back. 'What?'

'No gel. Did you forget?'

'I was seeing the new ACC first thing, so thought I ought to be a little conservative.'

Branson, who had given Roy Grace a major fashion makeover some months ago, shook his head. 'You know what? Sometimes you're just plain sad. If I was the new ACC, I'd want officers with a bit of zing – not ones who looked like my grandfather.'

'Sod you!' Grace said with a grin. Then he yawned.

'See!' Branson said gleefully. 'It's your age. You can't take the pace.'

'Very funny. Look, I have to concentrate for a few minutes, OK?'

'You know who you remind me of?' Branson said, ignoring him.

'George Clooney? Daniel Craig?'

'Nah. Brad Pitt.'

For a moment Grace looked quite pleased. Then the Detective Sergeant added, 'Yeah, in *Benjamin Button* –

like at the point where he looks a hundred and hasn't started getting younger yet.'

Grace shook his head, stifling a grin, then another yawn. Monday was a day most normal people dreaded. But most *normal* people at least started the week feeling rested and fresh. He had spent the whole of his Sunday at work, first going to the pier, to the maintenance room of the ghost train, where Mandy Thorpe had been raped and seriously injured, and then visiting her at the Royal Sussex County Hospital, where she was under police guard. Despite a bad head injury, the young woman had managed to give a detailed initial statement to the SOLO allocated to her, who had in turn relayed this information to him.

Quite apart from the trauma to these poor victims, Roy Grace was feeling a different kind of trauma of his own, from the pressure to solve this and make an arrest. To compound matters, the head crime reporter of the *Argus*, Kevin Spinella, had now left three messages on his mobile phone asking him to call back urgently. Grace knew if he wanted the cooperation of his main local paper in this inquiry, rather than just a sensational headline in tomorrow's edition, he was going to have to manage Spinella carefully. That would mean giving him an exclusive extra titbit to the information he would release at the midday press conference – and at the moment he didn't have anything for the man. At least, nothing he wanted the public to know.

He gave the reporter a quick call back and got connected straight through to his voicemail. He left Spinella a message asking him to come to his office ten minutes before the press conference. He'd think of something for him.

And one day soon he was going to think of a suitable trap. Someone inside the police regularly leaked information to Spinella. The same person, Grace was sure, who had leaked every major crime story this past year to the sharp young crime reporter within minutes of the police being called to the scene. It had to be someone in either the Call Handling Centre or the IT department who had access to the minute-by-minute updated serials. It could be a detective, but he doubted that, because the leaked information was on *every* serious crime, and no one detective got early information on anything other than his own cases.

The only positive was that Kevin Spinella was savvy, a newspaper reporter with whom the police could do business. So far they had been lucky, but one day he might not be there, and a lot of damage could be done by someone less cooperative in his shoes.

'Bloody Albion – what is going on with them?' Michael Foreman strutted in, smartly suited as ever, with gleaming black Oxford shoes.

In the early stages of an inquiry, most detectives wore suits because they never knew when they might have to rush out to interview someone – particularly close relatives of a major crime victim, to whom they needed to show respect. Some, like Foreman, dressed sharply all the time.

'That second goal!' DC Nick Nicholl, who was normally quietly spoken, was talking animatedly, shaking his balled fists in the air. 'Like, what was all that about? Hello!'

'Yeah, well, Chelsea's my team,' said the HOLMES analyst, John Black. 'Gave up on the Albion a long time ago. The day they left the Goldstone Ground.'

'But when they move – the new stadium – that'll be something, right!' Michael Foreman said. 'Give them a chance to settle into that – they'll get their pride back.'

'Gay Pride, that's all they're good for,' grumbled Norman Potting, who shambled in last, shaking his head, reeking of pipe smoke.

He sat down heavily in a chair opposite Grace. 'Sorry I'm late, Roy. Women! I tell you, I've had it. I'm not getting married again. That's it. Four and out!'

'Half the female population of the UK will be very relieved to hear that,' Bella Moy murmured, loudly enough for everyone to hear.

Ignoring her, Potting stared gloomily at Grace. 'You know that chat we had before Christmas, Roy?'

Grace nodded, not wanting to be distracted by the latest in the long saga of disasters of the Detective Sergeant's love life.

'I'd appreciate a bit more of your wisdom – some time over the next week or so, if that's all right with you, Roy. When you've got a minute.'

When I've got a minute I want to spend it sleeping, Grace thought wearily. But he nodded at Potting and said, 'Sure, Norman.' Despite the fact that the DS frequently irritated him, he felt sorry for the man. Potting had remained in the force long past the age when he could have taken his pension, because, Grace suspected, his work was all he had in life that gave him purpose.

The last to enter the room was Dr Julius Proudfoot, a tan-leather man bag slung from his shoulder. The forensic psychologist – as behavioural analysts were now called – had worked on a large number of high-profile cases during the past two decades, including the original Shoe Man case. For the past decade he had been enjoying minor media celebrity status, and the spoils of a lucrative publishing deal. His four autobiographical books, charting his career to date, boasted of his achievements in playing a crucial role in bringing many of the UK's worst criminals to justice.

A number of senior police officers had privately said the books should be on the fiction rather than non-fiction shelves in the bookshops. They believed he had wrongly taken the credit in several cases where he had actually only played a bit part – and then not always successfully.

Grace did not disagree, but felt that because of Proudfoot's earlier involvement in the Shoe Man case, *Operation Houdini*, the man could bring something to the table on *Operation Swordfish*. The psychologist had aged in the twelve years since they had last met, and put on a considerable amount of weight, he thought, as he introduced him to his team members. Then he turned to his agenda.

'First, I want to thank you all for giving up your weekends. Second, I'm pleased to report that we have no issues from the Crime Policy and Review Branch. They are satisfied to date with all aspects of our investigation.' He looked down quickly at his agenda. 'OK, it is 8.30 a.m., Monday 12 January. This is our sixth briefing of *Operation Swordfish*, the investigation into the stranger rape of two persons, Mrs Nicola Taylor and Mrs Roxy Pearce, and maybe now a third victim, Miss Mandy Thorpe.'

He pointed to one of the whiteboards, on which were stuck detailed descriptions of the three women. To protect their privacy, Grace chose not to display their photographs openly, which he felt would be disrespectful. Instead he said, 'Victim photographs are available for who those who need them.'

Proudfoot raised a hand and wiggled his pudgy fingers. 'Excuse me, Roy, why do you say *maybe* now a third victim? I don't think there's much doubt about Mandy Thorpe, from what I have on this.'

Grace looked across to the workstation where Proudfoot was seated.

'The MO is significantly different,' Roy Grace replied. 'But I'll come on to that a bit later, if that's OK – it's on the agenda.'

Proudfoot opened and closed his tiny rosebud lips a couple of times, fixing his beady eyes on the Detective Superintendent and looking disgruntled at being put back in his box.

Grace continued. 'First, I want to review our progress to date into the rape of Nicola Taylor on New Year's Eve, and of Roxy Pearce, last Thursday. We have six hundred and nineteen possible suspects at this moment. That number is made up of the staff of the Metropole Hotel and guests staying there that night, plus partygoers at the hotel on New Year's Eve, including, as we know, several senior police officers. We also have names phoned in by the public, some directly to us, some through *Crimestoppers*. The suspects for the moment include all registered sex offenders in the Brighton and Hove area. And two different perverts who have been making nuisance calls to Brighton shoe shops, who have now been identified through phone records by the Outside Inquiry Team.'

He sipped some coffee.

'One suspect on this list is particularly interesting. A local repeat burglar and small-time drugs dealer, Darren Spicer. I should think he's known to a number of you here.'

'That piece of shit!' Norman Potting said. 'I nicked

him twenty years ago. Did a series of burglaries around Shirley Drive and Woodland Drive.'

'He has one hundred and seventy-three previous,' the Analyst, Ellen Zoratti, said. 'A regular charmer. He's out on licence after indecently assaulting a woman in a house in Hill Brow that he broke into. He tried to snog her.'

'Which is unfortunately a regular pattern,' Grace said, looking at Proudfoot. 'Burglars turning into rapists.'

'Exactly,' Proudfoot said, seizing his cue. 'You see, they start off penetrating houses, then they graduate to penetrating any woman they happen to find in the house.'

Grace clocked the frowns on the faces of several of his colleagues, who clearly thought this was mere psycho-babble. But he knew that, sadly, it was true.

'Spicer was released from Ford Open Prison on licence, on 28 December. DS Branson and DC Nicholl interviewed him yesterday morning.'

He nodded at Glenn.

'That's right, boss,' Branson replied. 'We didn't get much – just a lot of lip, really. He's a wily old trout. Claims he's got alibis for the times all three offences were committed, but I'm not convinced. We told him we want them substantiated. He was apparently seeing a married woman last Thursday night, and refuses to give us her name.'

'Has Spicer got any form for sex offences, apart from the last one?' DS Bella Moy asked. 'Or domestic violence, or fetishes?'

'No,' replied the Analyst.

'Wouldn't our offender be likely to have some *previous* as a pervert, Dr Proudfoot, on the assumption that rapists taking shoes is not a regular occurrence?' Bella Moy asked.

'Taking trophies of some kind is not uncommon for serial offenders,' Proudfoot said. 'But you are right, it is very unlikely these are the only offences he's committed.'

'There's something that could be very significant regarding Spicer,' Ellen Zoratti said. 'Last night I studied the victim statement – the one given by the woman Spicer indecently assaulted in her home just over three years ago – Ms Marcie Kallestad.' She looked at Roy Grace. 'I don't understand why no one's made the connection, sir.'

'Connection?'

'I think you'd better have a read of it. After Marcie Kallestad fought Spicer off, he knocked her to the floor, grabbed the shoes from her feet – and ran off with them. They were high-heeled Roberto Cavallis which had cost her three hundred and fifty quid. She'd only bought them that day, from a shop in Brighton.'

58

There was a palpable change of mood in the briefing room. Roy Grace could sense the sudden, intangible buzz of excitement. It happened every time there was a possible breakthrough in an inquiry. Yet he was the least excited member of his team at this moment.

'Shame we didn't know about this yesterday,' Glenn Branson said. 'We could have potted Spicer then.'

Nick Nicholl nodded in agreement.

'We've got enough to arrest him now, boss, haven't we?' said Michael Foreman.

Grace looked at Ellen. 'Do we know whether the shoes were recovered subsequently?'

'No, I'm afraid not,' she replied. 'I don't have that information.'

'Would they have had a cash value for him?' Nick Nicholl asked.

'Absolutely,' Bella Moy said. 'Brand-new Roberto Cavalli shoes like that – there are loads of second-hand clothes shops in the city that would buy them – at a knockdown price. I buy things from some of them. You can get brilliant bargains.'

Grace looked at Bella for a moment. In her early thirties, single and living at home, caring for her aged mother, he felt a little sorry for her, because she was not an unattractive woman but appeared to have no real life beyond her work.

'Ten per cent of their cost, Bella?' he asked.

'I don't know – but they wouldn't pay much. Twenty quid, perhaps, max.'

Grace thought hard. This new information was certainly enough to justify arresting Darren Spicer. And yet . . . it didn't feel right. Spicer seemed almost too obvious to him. Sure, the villain was conveniently out of prison in time to have committed the first rape, on New Year's Day. Even more conveniently, he had been working at the Metropole Hotel, where it occurred. And now they had just learned that he'd taken his last burglary victim's shoes. But, Grace fretted, could the man really be so stupid?

More significantly, Spicer's past form was as a career burglar and drugs dealer. He made his living, such as it was, breaking into properties and into safes inside them, taking jewellery, watches, silverware, cash. Neither Nicola Taylor nor Roxy Pearce had, so far, reported any property stolen other than their shoes and, in Nicola's case, her clothes as well. It was the same with Mandy Thorpe on Saturday night. Just her shoes were gone. Unless Spicer had come out of prison a changed man – which, with his history, he doubted – this did not seem like Spicer's MO.

On the other hand, how could he be sure that Spicer had not committed other sexual offences for which he had not been caught? Could he possibly be the Shoe Man? The records produced by Ellen showed that he had been out of jail at the time of the Shoe Man offences. But the Shoe Man raped and assaulted his victims in vile ways. He didn't just try to kiss them, as Spicer had done. Again, the MO did not match.

Yes, they could bring him into custody. It would please the brass to get such a quick arrest, but that pleasure could be short-lived. Where would he go from there with Spicer? How would he get the proof needed for a conviction? The offender wore a mask and barely spoke, so there was no facial description or voice to go on. They hadn't even got an estimate of the offender's height that they were happy with. Medium seemed to be the best guess. Slight build. Few bodily hairs.

The forensic examination results showed that the offender had left no semen in any of the three victims. So far there were no DNA hits on any hairs or fibres or nail scrapings taken – although it was very early days. It would be a couple of weeks before everything taken was examined, and they couldn't hold Spicer for that length of time without charging him. For certain the Crown Prosecution Service would not consider there was enough to bring any charge on what they had.

They could question him about why he had taken Marcie Kallestad's shoes, but if he really was the Shoe Man that would alert him. Just as getting a search warrant for his locker at the night shelter would. From what Glenn and Nick had reported, Spicer thought he'd been clever and answered their questions to their satisfaction. Now he might not be worried about offending again. If they showed too much interest in him, it could drive him to ground – or out of the city. And what Grace needed more than anything was a result – not another twelve years of silence.

He thought for another moment, then said to Glenn Branson, 'Does Spicer have a car, or access to one?'

'I didn't get the impression he's got anything. I doubt it, boss, no.'

'He said he walks everywhere to save the bus fares, chief,' Nick Nicholl added.

'He can probably get one when he needs it,' Ellen Zoratti said. 'He's got a couple of previous convictions for vehicle theft – one for a van and one for a private car.'

That was good he had no transport, Grace thought. It would make the task of keeping him under observation much simpler.

'I think we'll get more chance of a result by watching him than pulling him, at the moment. We know where he is between 8.30 p.m. and 8.30 a.m., thanks to the curfew at the night shelter. He's got his retraining job at the Grand Hotel, so we'll know where he is during the day on weekdays. I'm going to get Surveillance to watch him when he leaves work and to see he doesn't leave the shelter at night.'

'If he's a real *Person of Interest*, Roy, which seems to be the case,' said Proudfoot, 'then I think you'd better move quickly on this.'

'I hope to get them started today,' Grace replied. 'This would be a good point to tell us your thoughts.'

The forensic psychologist stood up and walked over to a whiteboard on which there was a wide sheet of graph paper. Several spiking lines had been drawn on it in different-coloured inks. He took his time before speaking, as if to demonstrate he was so important he didn't need to hurry.

'The offender matrix of the Shoe Man and your current offender are very similar,' he said. 'This graph shows the linking factors to date between the two. Each colour is a different aspect: the geography, time of day, his approach to his victims, the form of his attack, appearance of the offender.'

He pointed each out, then stepped aside and continued: 'There are a number of characteristics of the Shoe Man offences that were never made public, but which nonetheless are apparent in your current offender's MO. This leads me to say with some certainty that there are sufficient linking factors for us to be able to assume at this stage we are dealing with the same person. One of the most significant is that the same name, Marsha Morris, was used in the hotel register both at the Grand in 1997 and at the Metropole on this past New Year's Eve – and this name was never made public knowledge.'

He now moved over to a blank whiteboard.

'I am also fairly certain that the offender is a local man, or at least a man with good local knowledge who has lived here in the past.'

He quickly drew some small squares in the top half of the whiteboard in black ink and numbered them 1 to 5, talking as he drew.

'The Shoe Man's first reported sexual assault was a botched one on 15 October 1997. I'm going to discount that for our purposes and just concentrate on the successful ones. His first successful one was at the Grand Hotel, in the early hours of 1 November 1997.' He wrote GH above the first square. 'His second was in a private house in Hove Park Road two weeks later.' He wrote HPR above the second square. 'The third was beneath the Palace Pier a further two weeks later.' He wrote PP over the third square. 'The fourth was in the Churchill Square car park another two weeks later.' He wrote CS above that one. 'A possible fifth attack was on Christmas morning, again two weeks later, in Eastern Terrace – although unconfirmed.' He wrote ET above the fifth box. Then he turned back to face the team, but fixed his gaze on Roy Grace.

'We know that all five of these women had bought an expensive pair of shoes at one of Brighton's shoe shops immediately prior to the attacks. I think it is likely the offender was familiar with these locations. It could have been a stranger coming into town, of course, but I really don't think so. Historically, strangers don't stick around. They attack, then move on.'

Grace turned to Michael Foreman, who was heading the Outside Inquiry Team. 'Michael, have you been on to the shoe shops where our current victims bought their shoes, to find out if they have CCTV?'

'It's being covered, boss.'

Julius Proudfoot then drew a circle around all five boxes. 'It is worth noting the relatively small geographical area within the city where these attacks took place. Now we come to the current series of attacks.'

Changing to a red pen, he drew three boxes on the lower half of the whiteboard, numbering them 1 to 3. He turned briefly to his audience, then back to the board.

'The first attack took place in the Metropole Hotel, which, as you know, is next door to the Grand.' He wrote MH above the first box. 'The second attack, approximately one week later, occurred in a private residence in a smart residential street, Droveway Avenue.' He wrote TD above the second box. 'The third attack – and I accept there are differences in the MO – took place just two days later on the Palace Pier – or *Brighton* Pier, as I understand it now calls itself.' He wrote BP above the third box, then turned back to face the team again.

'The Droveway is the next street along from Hove Park Road. I don't think any of us need a degree in rocket science to see the geographical similarities in these attacks.'

DC Foreman raised a hand. 'Dr Proudfoot, this is a very smart observation. What can you tell us about the offender himself, from your very considerable experience?'

Proudfoot smiled, the flattery hitting his ego's G-spot. 'Well,' he said, flapping his arms expansively, 'he will almost certainly have had a dysfunctional childhood. Very likely a single-parent child, or possibly a repressively religious upbringing. He may have been subjected to childhood sexual abuse from one or more parent or a close relative. He will probably have been involved in low-level crime in the past, starting with cruelty to animals in childhood and perhaps minor thieving from classmates at school. He will definitely have been a loner with few if any childhood friends.'

He paused for a moment and cleared his throat before continuing: 'From early adolescence, he is likely to have been obsessed with violent pornography, and probably committed a range of minor sexual offences – exposure, indecent assaults, that sort of thing. He will have graduated to using prostitutes and quite likely become involved with those offering sadomasochistic services. And he's very likely to be a drug user – probably cocaine.'

He paused for a moment. 'His use of female clothing as a disguise is indicative to me of both a fantasy world he inhabits and the fact that he is intelligent, and he may have a perverse sense of humour which might be significant – in his choice of locations in 1997 and now and in his timings. The fact that he is so forensically aware is another indication that he is clever – and has knowledge or direct experience of police methodology.'

DC Emma-Jane Boutwood raised her hand. 'Are you able to suggest any theories, if he is the Shoe Man, why he might have stopped for twelve years, then restarted?'

'It's not uncommon. There was a sexual serial killer named Dennis Rader in the US who stopped offending for twelve years after getting married and starting a family. He was on the brink of starting again when he tired of the relationship, but fortunately he was caught before that happened. This could be the scenario for our offender. But it is equally possible that he moved elsewhere in the country, or even went overseas and continued offending there, and now has returned.'

*

When the briefing ended, Grace asked the forensic psychologist to come to his office for a few minutes. Grace closed the door. It was a stormy day and rain rattled against the windows as he sat behind his desk.

'I didn't want to have an argument with you in front of the team, Dr Proudfoot,' he said firmly, 'but I'm really concerned about the third attack, on the ghost train. Everything about the MO is different.'

Proudfoot nodded, with a smug smile, like a parent humouring a child.

'Tell me what you think the key differences are, Detective Superintendent.'

Grace found his tone patronizing and irritating, but tried not to rise to it. Instead, raising a finger, he said, 'First, unlike all the other victims, Mandy Thorpe had not recently bought the shoes that were used in the assault on her – and I'm including Rachael Ryan, about whom we still have an open mind. All five of those women back then had bought a brand-new pair of expensive designer shoes in the hours or days before they were attacked. As did the first two of our current victims, Nicola Taylor and

Roxy Pearce. Mandy Thorpe was different. She'd bought them months ago on holiday in Thailand.'

He raised another finger. 'Second, and I think this could be significant, unlike all the others, Mandy Thorpe was wearing fake designer shoes – copies of Jimmy Choos.'

'With respect, I'm no expert in these matters, but I thought the whole point about fakes was that people couldn't tell the difference.'

Grace shook his head. 'It's not about telling the difference. It's in shoe shops where he finds his victims. Third, and very importantly, he did not make Mandy Thorpe abuse herself with her shoes. That's how he gets his kicks, through his power over his victims.'

Proudfoot gave a shrug that indicated he might or might not agree with Grace. 'The young woman was unconscious, so we don't really know what he did.'

'Vaginal swabs taken show she was penetrated by someone wearing a condom. There was no indication vaginally or anally of penetration with part of a shoe.'

'He might have been disturbed and left hurriedly,' Proudfoot replied.

Grace raised another finger and continued. 'Perhaps. Fourth, Mandy Thorpe is plump – fat to be blunt. Obese. All the previous victims have been slim.'

The psychologist shook his head. 'Her figure isn't the significant factor. He's on the hunt. What is significant is the time frame. Previously with the Shoe Man it was two-week gaps. This new spate started off as one week, now it is down to two days. Neither of us knows what he was up to in the intervening twelve years, but his appetite could have become stronger – either from being bottled up if he repressed it for that length of time, or from confidence if he's continued to offend and got away with it. One thing I am certain about, the more an offender like this gets away with things, the more invincible he feels – and the more he's going to want.'

'I have a press conference at midday, Dr Proudfoot. What I say then could come home to roost. I want to put out accurate information that will help us catch our man, and give the public some degree of assurance. Presumably for your reputation, you want me putting the most accurate information out there too – you don't want to be shown up for getting something wrong.'

Proudfoot shook his head. 'I'm seldom mistaken, Detective Superintendent. You won't go far wrong if you listen to me.'

'I'm comforted to hear that,' Grace said coolly.

'You're an old pro, like me,' Proudfoot continued. 'You've got all kinds of political and commercial pressures on you – I know you have, every SIO I've ever worked with has. Here's the thing: which is worse for public consumption? For them to believe there's one violent sexual offender out there, preying on your women, or that there are two?' The psychologist stared hard at Grace and raised his eyebrows. 'I know which I'd go for if I was trying to protect the reputation of my city.'

'I'm not going to be driven by politics into making the wrong decision,' Grace replied.

'Roy – if I can call you that?'

Grace nodded.

'You're not dealing with Mr Norman Normal here, Roy. This is a clever guy. He's hunting victims. Something in his head is driving him to do the same as he did before, but he knows, because he's not stupid, that he needs to vary his routine or his methods. He'd be having a laugh if he could hear this conversation between us now. It's not just power over women that he enjoys; it's power over the police too. All part of his sick game.'

Grace thought for some moments. His training as an SIO told him to listen to experts, but not to be influenced by them, and always to form his own opinions.

'I hear what you are saying,' he said.

'I hope it's loud and clear, Roy. Just look at my past record if you've any doubts. I'm going to put a marker down about this offender. He's someone who needs a comfort zone, a bit of routine. He's sticking to the same pattern that he had before. That's his comfort zone. He'll take his victims from the same, or at least similar, places. Someone is going to be seized and raped in a car park in the centre of this city before the end of this week and their shoes will be taken. You can tell them that at your press conference from me.'

The smugness of the man was beginning to irritate Grace beyond belief. But he needed him. He needed every straw he could grasp at this moment.

'I can't stake out the whole damned city centre – we just don't have the surveillance resources. If we cover the city centre with uniform it won't help us catch him. It will just drive him somewhere else.'

'I think your man is smart enough and bold enough to do it right under your nose. He might even get a kick from that. You can cover the city wall to wall in police and he'll still get his victim.'

'Very reassuring,' Grace said. 'So what do you suggest?'

'You're going to have to make some guesses – and hope you get lucky. Or . . .' He fell silent for a moment, thinking. 'The case of Dennis Rader in the US – a particularly nasty individual who styled himself BTK – initials that stood for Bind, Torture, Kill. He was caught after twelve years of silence when the local paper wrote something about him that he didn't like. It was just a speculation . . .'

'What kind of thing?' Grace said, very curious suddenly.

'I think it was questioning the perpetrator's manhood. Something along those lines. You can be sure of one thing: that your current offender is going to be keeping a hawk-eye on the media, reading every word your local paper prints. The ego goes with the territory.'

'You don't think inflaming him will provoke him into offending even more?'

'No, I don't. He got away with those attacks twelve years ago. God knows what he's got away with since then. And now these new attacks. I imagine he thinks he's invincible – all-clever, all-powerful. That's how the press coverage to date has made him seem. Create a demon of our Shoe Man, make him the Monster of Brighton and Hove, and, *bingo*, newspaper sales shoot up across the nation, and so do news audience ratings. And all the time in reality we're dealing with a nasty, warped misfit with a screw loose.'

'So we get the local paper to say something demeaning about his manhood? That he's got a tiny dick or something?'

'Or how about the truth, that he can't get it up – or keep it up? No man's going to like reading that.'

'Dangerous,' Grace said. 'It could send him on a rampage.'

'He's dangerous enough already, Roy. But at the

moment he's clever, calculating, taking his time, not making any mistakes. Put him in a rage, provoke him into losing his cool – that way he'll make a mistake. And then you'll get him.'

'Or *them*.'

59

Sussex Square was one of the jewels in Brighton's architectural crown. Comprising one straight row and two magnificent crescents of Regency houses, each with views across five acres of private gardens and the English Channel beyond, the square had originally been built to provide weekend seaside homes for fashionable, rich Londoners. Now most of the buildings were divided up into apartments, but none of their grandeur had been lost in the process.

He drove the van slowly, passing the tall, imposing façades that were all painted a uniform white, checking out the numbers. Looking for no. 53.

He knew that it was still a single-dwelling home on five floors, with servants' quarters at the top. A fine residence, he thought, to reflect the status of a man like Rudy Burchmore, the Vice-President, Europe, of American & Oriental Banking, and of his socialite wife, Dee. A perfect home for entertaining in style. For impressing people. For wearing expensive shoes in.

He drove around the square again, quivering and clammy with excitement, and this time stopped short of the house, pulling into a gap on the garden side of the road. This was a good place to stop. He could see her car and he could see her front door, but she wouldn't notice him, regardless of whether she was looking out of her window or coming out of her front door.

He was invisible!

He had learned that certain things were invisible to the inhabitants of the affluent world. There were invisible people, like road sweepers and office cleaners and navvies. And there were invisible vehicles, like milk floats and white vans and taxis. Drug dealers used taxis a lot, because they never aroused suspicion driving around late at night. But the van suited his purposes better than a taxi at the moment.

He smiled, increasingly aroused, his breathing quickening. He could still smell her Armani Code fragrance. He could smell it so strongly, as if his whole van was filled with it now.

Oh yes, you bitch! he thought. *Oh yes! Oh yes! Oh yes!*

He would enjoy breathing that in while he made her do things to herself with those shoes, and then when he did things to her too. Fear would make her perspire and her perspiration would make the scent even stronger.

He could imagine her coming out of her front door wearing those blue Manolos and smelling of Armani Code. He could imagine her sliding into the driving seat of her car. Then parking somewhere safe, like she had done on Saturday, in an underground car park.

He knew exactly when she would be wearing those shoes. He'd heard her in the shop on Saturday when she bought them. *For an important speech*, she'd told the assistant. The *after-lunch thing* for which she had bought *a divine blue dress* and now had the shoes to match.

It would be nice if Dee Burchmore came out of her front door now, he thought, except she would not be wearing those new blue Manolos today.

Very conveniently, she had a section on her website for all her social engagements. In addition, she had a Facebook site where she announced them. And she told the world her movements, sometimes hour by hour, on Twitter. She was so helpful to him!

She had confirmed on her website and on Facebook that her next big social engagement was on Thursday, when she was giving a speech at a luncheon in aid of the local hospice, the Martlets. She had already started Tweeting it. The great and the good of the city of Brighton and Hove's female society would be attending. One of the guests of honour would be the wife of the current Lord Lieutenant of Sussex.

The luncheon was being held at the Grand Hotel, which had a big car park behind it.

That really could not be more convenient!

60

There was an insolence about the way Kevin Spinella entered Roy Grace's office, shortly before ten minutes to midday, pulled up a chair, uninvited, and sat down. Spinella always irked him and yet at the same time there were qualities about the young, ambitious reporter that Grace couldn't help, privately, liking.

Spinella lounged nonchalantly back in his chair on the other side of Grace's desk, hands in the pockets of his raincoat. Beneath it he wore a suit, with a slack, clumsily knotted tie. A slight, thin-faced man, Spinella was in his mid-twenties, with alert eyes and thin black hair gelled into tiny spikes. His sharp incisors, as always, were busily working on a piece of gum.

'So, what do you have for me, Detective Superintendent?'

'You're the man in the know,' Grace replied, testing him. 'What do you have for me?'

The reporter cocked his head to one side. 'I hear that the Shoe Man's back.'

'Tell me, Kevin, what's your source?'

The reporter smiled and tapped the side of his nose.

'I will find out. You know that, don't you?' Grace said, his tone serious.

'I thought you asked me to come and see you because you want to do business.'

'I do.'

'So?'

Grace held his cool with difficulty and decided to let the subject of the leaks drop for the moment. Changing tack, he said, 'I want your help. If I tell you something off the record, can I have your word you'll keep it that way until I tell you otherwise? I need to trust you absolutely on this.'

'Can't you always?'

No, not always, actually, Grace recalled. Although, he had to admit, Spinella had been good as gold during this past year.

'Usually,' he conceded.

'What's in it for the *Argus*?'

'Possibly a credit for helping us to catch the offender. I'd certainly give an interview on that.'

'Just one offender, is there?' Spinella asked pointedly.

Shit, Grace thought, wondering where the hell he had got *that* from. Who had speculated about that outside of the briefing meeting earlier this morning? Was it one of his team members? Just where had that come from? Anger rose inside him. But it was clear from Spinella's expression he would get nothing from him. For the moment he had to park it.

'At this stage we believe there is one offender responsible for all the attacks.'

Spinella's shifty eyes said he did not believe him.

Grace ignored that and went on: 'OK, here's the deal.' He hesitated for an instant, knowing he was taking a massive gamble. 'I have two exclusives for you. The first I don't want you to print until I tell you, the second I'd like you to print right away. I'm not giving either of these to the press conference.'

There was a brief silence as the two men stared at each other. For a moment Spinella stopped chewing.

'Deal?' Grace asked.

Spinella shrugged. 'Deal.'

'OK. The first, not for you to print, is that we think there could be another attack this week. It's likely to be somewhere in the town centre, possibly in a car park.'

'Hardly rocket science if there have been three in the past two weeks already,' Spinella retorted sarcastically.

'No, I agree with you.'

'Not much of an exclusive. I could have predicted that off my own bat.'

'It'll make you look good if it does happen – you can write one of those *A senior detective had forewarned the* Argus *this attack was likely* kind of pieces that you've been good at inventing in the past.'

Spinella had the decency to blush. Then he shrugged. 'Car park? So you think he's mirroring the same sequence as before?'

'The forensic psychologist does.'

'Dr Proudfoot's got a bit of a reputation as a tosser, hasn't he?'

'You said that, not me.' Grace's eyes twinkled.

'So what are you doing to prevent the next attack?'

'All we can, short of closing down the centre of Brighton to the public. We're going to throw as much resourcing as we can behind it – but invisible. We want to catch him, not drive him away and lose him.'

'How are you going to warn the public?'

'I hope we can get the support of the press and media at the conference we're about to have – and warn them in a general but not specific way.'

Spinella nodded, then pulled out his notebook. 'Now tell me the one I can print.'

Grace smiled, then said, 'The offender has a small dick.'

The reporter waited, but Grace said nothing more.

'That's it?' Spinella asked.

'That's it.'

'You're joking?'

The Detective Superintendent shook his head.

'That's my exclusive? That the offender has a small dick?'

'Hope I'm not touching a nerve,' Grace replied.

1998

61

The old lady sat in the driver's seat of the stolen van, at the start of the steep hill, with her seat belt on as tight as it would go. Her hands rested on the steering wheel, with the engine idling, but the lights switched off.

He stood beside her, holding the driver's door open, nervous as hell. It was a black night, the sky densely lagged with clouds. He could have used some moonlight, but there was nothing to be done about that.

His eyes scanned the darkness. It was 2 a.m. and the country road, a few hundred yards to the north of the entrance to the Waterhall Golf Club, two miles from the outskirts of Brighton, was deserted. There was a half-mile steep descent, with a sharp left-hander at the bottom, the road winding on through the valley between the hills of the South Downs. The beauty of this location, he figured, was that he could see from the headlights if anything was coming, for over a mile in either direction. It was all clear for the moment.

Time to rock and roll!

He reached across her lap, released the handbrake, then jumped clear as the van immediately rolled forward, picking up speed rapidly, the driver's door swinging shut with a dull clang. The van veered worryingly into the oncoming lane, and stayed there, as it continued to pick up speed.

It was just as well no vehicle was coming up the hill towards the van, because the old lady would have been incapable of taking any avoiding action, or reacting in any way at all, on account of the fact that she had been dead for ten days.

He jumped on his bike and, with the boost of additional weight from his backpack, pedalled, then free-wheeled down the hill after her, rapidly picking up speed.

Ahead of him he saw the silhouette of the van, which he had stolen from a construction site, veering towards the offside verge and, for one heart-in-his-mouth moment, he was sure it was going to crash into the thick gorse hedge, which might have stopped it. But then, miraculously, it veered briefly left, made a slight correction and careered on down the hill on a dead straight path, as if she really was steering it. As if she was having the ride of her life. Or rather, he thought, of her death!

'Go, baby, go! Go for it, Molly!' he urged. 'Enjoy!'

The van, which had the name *Bryan Barker Builders* emblazoned all over it, was continuing to pick up speed. Going so fast now he was feeling dangerously out of control, he touched the brakes of the mountain bike and slowed a little, letting the van pull away. It was hard to gauge distances. The hedgerows flashed by. Something flapped close to his face. What the fuck was it? A bat? An owl?

The cold, damp wind was streaming into his eyes, making them water, half-blinding him.

He braked harder. They were coming towards the bottom, approaching the left-hander. The van went straight on. He heard the crunching, tearing, screeching of barbed wire against paintwork as it ploughed through the hedge and the farmer's fence. He brought the bike to a skidding halt, his trainers bouncing along on the tarmac for several yards, narrowly avoiding going head over heels.

Through his watering eyes, more accustomed to the darkness now, he saw a massive black shape disappear. Then he heard a dull, rumbling metallic booming sound.

He leapt off his bike, tossing it into the hedge, pulled out his torch and switched it on, then scrambled through the hole in the hedge. The beam found its mark.

'Perfect! Oh yes, perfect! Sweet! Oh yes, baby, yes! Molly, you doll! You did it, Molly! You did it!'

The van was lying on its roof, all four of its wheels spinning.

He ran up to it, then stopped, switched the torch off and looked in every direction. Still no sign of any head-lights. Then he shone the beam inside. Molly Glossop lay upside down, suspended from her lap-strap, her mouth still closed from the stitches through her lips, her hair hanging untidily down in short grey clumps.

'Thanks!' he whispered, as if his voice might travel ten miles. 'Well driven!'

He shrugged his backpack off and clumsily fumbled the buckles open with his trembling, gloved fingers. Then he lifted out the plastic five-litre container of petrol, hurried through the sodden winter wheat and the sticky mud up to the driver's door and tried to open it.

It would not budge.

Cursing, he put down the container and pulled the handle with both hands, with all his strength, but it only yielded a couple of inches, the buckled metal shrieking in protest.

It didn't matter because the window was open; that

would do. He shot another nervous glance in both directions. Still no sign of any vehicle.

He unscrewed the cap of the container, which came away with a hiss, and poured the contents in through the window, shaking as much of the petrol over the old lady's head and body as he could.

When it was empty he replaced the lid and returned the container to his backpack, retied the buckles and put it over his shoulders.

Next, he stepped several yards away from the upturned van, pulled out a packet of cigarettes, removed one and stuck it in his mouth. His hands were shaking so much he found it hard to flick the lighter wheel. Finally a flame erupted, briefly, then the wind blew it out.

'Shit! Fuck! Don't do this!'

He tried again, shielding it with his palm, and finally got the cigarette alight. He took two long drags on it and once more checked for headlights.

Shit.

A vehicle was coming down the hill.

Don't see us. Please don't see us.

He flattened himself in the wheat. Heard the roar of the engine. Felt the glare of the headlights wash over him, then darkness returned.

The roar of the engine was fading.

He stood up. Red tail lights were briefly visible, then vanished. He saw them again a few seconds later. Then they were gone for good.

He waited a few more seconds before walking towards the van, then tossed the cigarette in through the open window of the driver's door, turned and ran for several yards. He stopped and looked back.

Nothing happened. No flicker of a flame. Nothing at all.

He waited for what felt like an eternity. Still nothing happened.

Don't do this to me!

Headlights were coming from the other direction now.

Don't let this be the vehicle that passed, now turned round to come and look through the hole in the hedge!

To his relief, it wasn't. It was a car, sounding like it wasn't firing on all cylinders, blat-blatting its way up the hill. Its weak tail lights told him it was an old banger of some kind, its electrical system not liking the damp.

He waited another full minute, breathing in the increasingly strong reek of petrol in the air, but still nothing happened. Then he lit a second cigarette, stepped cautiously across and tossed that in. The result was the same. Nothing.

Panic started to grip him. Was the petrol dud?

A third vehicle came down the hill and passed by.

He pulled his handkerchief out, stepped cautiously up to the van, shone his flashlight in and saw both cigarettes, soggy and extinguished, lying in the pool of petrol on the cab roof. What the fuck was this? Cigarettes always lit petrol tanks in movies! He dabbed the handkerchief into the pool of petrol on the roof of the van, then stepped back and lit it.

There was such a violent explosion of flame that he dropped it, from shock, on to the ground. The handkerchief burned so intensely that all he could do was watch the flames consume it.

Now another bloody vehicle was coming down the

hill! He hastily stamped on the burning handkerchief, stamping again and again, extinguishing it. His heart thumping, he waited for the sweep of lights to pass and the roar of the engine to fade.

He removed the backpack, took his anorak off, squashed it into a ball, leaned in through the window and dunked it into the pool of petrol for a couple of seconds. Then he stepped back, holding it at arm's length, and shook it open. He clicked the lighter and there was a massive WHUMPH.

Flames leapt at him fiercely, searing his face. Ignoring the pain, he hurled the blazing anorak through the window, and this time the result was instant.

The whole interior of the van lit up like a furnace. He could see Molly Glossop clearly for some seconds before her hair disappeared and her colour darkened. He stood mesmerized, watching the flames, watching her get darker and darker still. Then, suddenly, what he had hoped for happened. The fuel tank exploded, turning the entire van into a blazing inferno.

Grabbing his backpack, he stumbled back to where he had flung his bike, mounted it and pedalled away from the scene as fast as he could, in the beautifully cool, silent air, taking his planned, circuitous route back to Brighton.

No vehicles passed him all the way back to the main road. He listened intently for the wail of a siren. But heard nothing.

NOW

62

Billy No Mates was seated in a window table of the café, digging her fork into a mountainous veggie salad, with watercress and frisée lettuce overflowing all around the rim of the bowl. It looked like she was eating a hairdo.

She chewed pensively, picking up her iPhone and staring at something on the screen in between mouthfuls. Her shoulder-length bleached hair was scooped up into a ponytail, with a few loose strands hanging down, just the way it had been the last time he had seen her, in Marielle Shoes, on Saturday.

She had a pretty face, despite her curiously hooked nose, and was dressed casually, almost sloppily, in a shapeless, sleeveless grey tunic over a black roll neck, jeans and sparkly trainers. He would have to get her to change out of those! Trainers on women just did not do it for him.

Clearly Jessie Sheldon didn't bother with her appearance for work, or maybe her look was deliberate. Her albums on Facebook showed she could look very pretty with her hair down and in nice clothes. Beautiful in some. Stunning. A very sexy lady indeed!

And she wasn't really Billy No Mates at all, although she did look like that at this moment, just sitting there all on her own. She actually had 251 friends, as of earlier today, when he'd last checked out her Facebook site. And one of them, Benedict Greene, was her fiancé – well, as good as, although they were not formally engaged, yet, she'd explained on the site. *Sssshh! Don't tell my parents!*

She was a good networker. She kept all her friends updated daily on her activities. Everyone knew what she would be doing in three hours' time, in six hours' time, in twenty-four hours' time, and for the next several weeks. And just like Dee Burchmore, she Tweeted. Mostly, at the moment, about her diet. *Jessie is thinking of eating a KitKat . . . Jessie resisted the KitKat . . . Lost a pound today! . . . Rats, put on a pound today! Only eating vegetarian for rest of this week!*

She was a good girl, so helpful to him! She Tweeted far more than Dee Burchmore. Her latest was sent just an hour ago: *Keeping to diet! Lunching vegetarian today at Lydia, my current fave!*

She was tapping away on the iPhone now. Maybe she was Tweeting again?

He liked to keep an eye on his women. This morning, Dee Burchmore was at the spa at the Metropole Hotel, having a Thalgo Indocéane Complete Body Ritual. He wondered whether to have one too. But thought better of it. He had things to do today; in fact he should not be here at all. But it felt so good! How could he resist?

Billy No Mates had Tweeted earlier: *Going to look at those shoes again at lunchtime – hope they'll still be there!*

They were! He'd watched her take a photo of them with her iPhone, then tell the assistant she was going to have a think about them over lunch. She asked the shop assistant if she would keep them aside for her until 2 p.m. The assistant said she would.

They were dead sexy! The black ones, with the ankle

straps and the five-inch steel-coloured heels. The ones she wanted to wear, she had told the assistant, when she went to a function with her boyfriend, who would be meeting her parents for the first time.

Billy No Mates tapped out something on the keyboard, then raised the phone to her ear. Moments later her face lit up, animated. 'Hi, Roz! I just sent you a photo of the shoes! Have you got it? Yeah! What do you think? You do? Really? OK! I'm going to get them! I'll bring them over and show them to you tonight, after my squash game! What film are we going to see? You got *The Final Destination*? Great!'

He smiled. She liked horror movies. Maybe she might even enjoy the little show he had planned for her! Although it was not his intention to give pleasure.

'No, the car's fine now, all fixed. I'll pick up the takeaway. I'll tell him not to charge us for the seaweed. He forgot it last week,' she continued. 'Yeah, OK, soy sauce. I'll make sure he puts extra in.'

His own mobile rang. He looked at the display. Work. He pressed the red button, sending it to voicemail.

Then he looked down at the copy of the *Argus* he had just bought. The front page headline shouted:

POLICE STEP UP VIGILANCE AFTER THIRD CITY RAPE

He frowned, then began to read. The third attack, over the weekend, was in the ghost train on the pier. There was hot speculation that the so-called Shoe Man, who in 1997–8 had committed four and perhaps five rapes – and possibly many more that had never been reported – was back. Detective Superintendent Roy Grace, the Senior Investigating Officer, stated it was too soon for such speculation. They were pursuing a number of lines of enquiry, he said, and gave assurances that every possible resource Sussex Police had at their disposal was being harnessed. The safety of the city's women was their number-one priority.

Then the next paragraph hit him with a jolt.

> In an exclusive interview with the *Argus*, Detective Superintendent Grace stated that the offender had a physical sexual deformity. He declined to be specific, but told this reporter that it included an exceptionally diminutive manhood. He added that any woman who had had previous relations with him would remember this feature. A psycho-sexual therapist said that such an inadequacy could lead a person to attempt to compensate via violent means. Anyone who believed they might know such a person was urged either to phone 0845 6070999 and ask for the *Operation Swordfish* Incident Room or to call the Crimestoppers number anonymously.

His phone beeped twice with a voicemail message. He ignored it, glaring down at the print with rising fury. *Sexual deformity?* Was that what everyone was thinking of him? Well, maybe Detective Superintendent Grace was not very well endowed in another department, his brain. The detective hadn't caught him twelve years ago and he was not going to catch him now.

Little dick, big brain, Mr Grace.

He read the article again, every word of it, word by word. Then again. Then again.

A friendly female voice with a South African accent startled him. 'Are you ready to order, madam?'

He looked up at the young waitress's face. Then across to the table next to him by the window.

Billy No Mates had left.

It didn't matter. He knew where to find her later. In the car park at Withdean Sports Stadium after her game of squash this evening. It was a good car park, open air and large. It should be quiet at that time of day and pitch dark. With luck he'd be able to park right alongside the bitch's little black Ka.

He looked up at the waitress. 'Yes, I'll have a rump steak and chips, bloody.'

'I'm afraid this is a vegetarian restaurant.'

'Then what the fuck am I doing here?' he said, totally forgetting his ladylike voice.

He got up and flounced out.

63

At the end of Kensington Place he turned left and walked down Trafalgar Street, looking for a payphone. He found one at the bottom and went in. Several cards featuring half-naked ladies offering *French Lessons*, *Oriental Massage*, *Discipline Classes* were stuck in the window frames. 'Bitches,' he said, casting his eye across them. It took him a moment to work out what he had to do to make a call. Then he dug in his pocket for a coin and shoved the only thing he had, a pound, into the slot. Then, still shaking with rage, he looked at the first number in the *Argus* article and dialled it.

When it was answered, he asked to be put through to the Incident Room for *Operation Swordfish*, then waited.

After three rings, a male voice answered. 'Incident Room, Detective Constable Nicholl.'

'I want you to give a message to Detective Superintendent Grace.'

'Yes, sir. May I say who's calling?'

He waited for a moment, as a police car raced past, its siren wailing, then he left his message, hung up and hurried away from the booth.

64

All the team at the 6.30 p.m. briefing of *Operation Sword-fish*, gathered in MIR-1, were silent as Roy Grace switched on the recorder. The tape that had been sent over from the Call Handling Centre began to play.

There was a background rumble of traffic, then a man's voice, quiet, as if he had been making an effort to stay calm. The roar of traffic made it hard to hear him distinctly.

'I want you to give a message to Detective Superintendent Grace,' the man said.

Then they could hear Nick Nicholl's voice replying. *'Yes, sir. May I say who's calling?'*

Nothing for some moments, except the almost deafening wail of a passing siren, then the man's voice again, this time louder: *'Tell him it's not small, actually.'*

It was followed by a loud clattering sound, a sharp click and the line went dead.

No one smiled.

'Is this real or a hoax?' Norman Potting asked.

After a few moments Dr Julius Proudfoot said, 'I'd put my money on that being real, from the way he spoke.'

'Can we hear it again, boss?' Michael Foreman asked.

Grace replayed the tape. When it finished, he turned to Proudfoot. 'Anything you can tell us from that?'

The forensic psychologist nodded. 'Well, yes, quite a bit. The first thing, assuming it is him, is that you've clearly succeeded in rattling his cage. That's why I think it's real, not a hoax. There's genuine anger in the voice. Full of emotion.'

'That was my intention, to rattle his cage.'

'You can hear it in his voice, in the way the cadence rises,' the forensic psychologist went on. 'He's all bottled up with anger. And the fact that it sounded like he fumbled replacing the receiver – probably shaking so much with rage. I can tell also that he's nervous, feeling under pressure – and that you've struck a chord. Is that information about him true? Something that's been obtained from statements by the victims?'

'Not in so many words, but yes, reading between the lines of the witness statements from back in 1997 and now.'

'What's your reasoning for giving that to the *Argus*, Roy?' Emma-Jane Boutwood asked.

'Because I suspect this creep thinks he's very clever. He got away with his attacks before and now he's confident he's going to get away with these new ones too. If Dr Proudfoot is right and he committed the ghost train rape as well, then he's clearly stepping up both the speed and the brazenness of his attacks. I wanted to lance his ego a little and hopefully get him into a strop. People who are angry are more likely to make mistakes.'

'Or be more brutal to their victims,' Bella Moy said. 'Isn't that a risk?'

'If he killed last time, Bella, which I think is likely,' Grace replied, 'there's a high risk he'll kill again, strop or no strop. When someone has taken a life once, they've crossed a personal Rubicon. It's far easier the second time. Particularly if they found they enjoyed it the first time. We're dealing with a nasty, warped freak here – and someone who's not stupid. We need to find ways to trip him up. I don't just want him not being more brutal to a victim – I want him not to have another victim, full stop. We have to catch him before he attacks again.'

'Anyone figure out his accent?' Nick Nicholl asked.

'Sounds local to me,' DC Foreman said, 'but difficult with that background noise. Can we get the recording enhanced?'

'That's being worked on now,' Grace replied. Then he turned to Proudfoot. 'Can you estimate the man's age from this?'

'That's a hard one – anywhere between thirty and fifty, I'd guess,' he said. 'I think you need to run this through a lab, somewhere like J. P. French, which specializes in speaker profiling. There's quite a bit of information they could get us from a call like this. Probably the man's regional and ethnic background, for a start.'

Grace nodded. He'd used the specialist firm before and the results had been helpful. He could also get a voiceprint from the lab that would be as unique as a fingerprint or DNA. But could they do it in the short amount of time he believed he had?

'There have been mass DNA screenings in communities,' Bella Moy said. 'What about trying something like that in Brighton with the voiceprint?'

'So all we'd have to do, Bella,' Norman Potting said, 'is get every bloke in Brighton and Hove to say the same words. There's only a hundred and forty thousand or so males in the city. Shouldn't take us more than about ten years.'

'Could you play it again, boss, please,' said Glenn

Branson, who'd been very quiet. 'Wasn't it that movie, *The Conversation*, with Gene Hackman, where they worked out where someone was from the traffic noise in the background on the tape?'

He played the tape again.

'Have we been able to trace the call, sir?' Ellen Zoratti asked.

'The number was withheld. But it's being worked on. It's a big task with the amount coming through the Call Centre every hour.' Grace played the tape again.

When it finished, Glenn Branson said, 'Sounds like somewhere in the centre of Brighton. If they can't trace the number we've still got the siren and the time of day – that vehicle sounds like it went right past very close to him. We need to check what emergency vehicle was on its blues and twos at exactly 1.55 p.m., and we'll get its route and know he was somewhere along it. A CCTV might have picked up someone on their mobile – and possibly bingo.'

'Good thinking,' Grace said. 'Although it sounded more like a landline than a mobile from the way he hung up.'

'Yes,' Michael Foreman said. 'That clunking sound – that's like an old-fashioned handset being replaced.'

'He might have just dropped his phone, if he was as nervous as Dr Proudfoot suggests,' said DC Boutwood. 'I don't think we should rule out a mobile.'

'Or it could be a public phone booth,' Foreman said. 'In which case there may be fingerprints.'

'If he's angry,' Proudfoot said, 'then I think it's even more likely he'll strike again quickly. And a racing certainty is that he'll copy his pattern from last time. He'll know that worked. He'll be fine if he sticks to the same again. Which means he's going to strike in a car park next – as I've said before.'

Grace walked over to a map of central Brighton and stared at it, looking at each of the main car parks. The station, London Road, New Road, Churchill Square, North Road. There were dozens of them, big and small, some run by the council, some by NCP, some part of supermarkets or hotels. He turned back to Proudfoot.

'It would be impossible to cover every damned car park in the city – and even more impossible to cover every level of every multi-storey,' he said. 'We just don't have the number of patrols. And we can hardly close them down.'

He was feeling anxious suddenly. Maybe it had been a mistake telling Spinella that yesterday. What if it pushed the Shoe Man over the edge into killing again? It would be his own stupid fault.

'The best thing we can do is get plain-clothes officers into the CCTV control rooms of those car parks that have it, step up patrols and have as many undercover vehicles drive around the car parks as we can,' Grace said.

'The one thing I'd tell your team to watch out for, Detective Superintendent, is someone on edge tonight. Someone driving erratically on the streets. I think our man is going to be in a highly wired state.'

65

You think you've been clever, don't you, Detective Superintendent Roy Grace? You think you're going to make me angry by insulting me, don't you? I can see through all that shit.

You should accept you are just a lame duck. Your colleagues didn't catch me before and you won't catch me now. I'm so much smarter than you could ever dream of being. You see, you don't realize I'm doing you a favour!

I'm getting rid of the poison in your manor! I'm your new best friend! One day you'll come to realize that! One day you and I will walk along under the cliffs at Rottingdean and talk about all of this. That walk you like to take with your beloved Cleo on Sundays! She likes shoes too. I've seen her in some of the shops I go in. She's quite into shoes, isn't she? You are going to need saving from her, but you don't realize that yet. You will do one day.

They're all poison, you see. All women. They seduce you with their Venus fly trap vaginas. You can't bear to be apart from them. You phone them and text them every few minutes of your waking day, because you need to know how much they still love you.

Let me tell you a secret.

No woman ever loves you. All she wants to do is control you. You might sneer at me. You might question the size of my manhood. But I will tell you something, Detective Superintendent. You'll be grateful to me, one day. You'll walk with me arm in arm along the Undercliff Walk at Rottingdean and thank me for saving you from yourself.

66

DEAD LIKE YOU

Tuesday 13 January

Jessie felt a deep and constant yearning all the time she was away from Benedict. It must be an hour now since she had texted him, she thought. Tuesdays were their one night apart. She played squash with a recently married friend, Jax, then after would pick up a takeaway Chinese and go round to Roz's and watch a DVD – something they had done almost every Tuesday night for as long as she could remember. Benedict, who liked to compose guitar music, had a similar long-standing Tuesday evening commitment – working late into the night with his co-writing partner, coming up with new songs. At the moment they were putting together an album they hoped might be their breakthrough.

Some weekends Benedict played gigs in a band in a variety of Sussex pubs. She loved watching him on stage. He was like a drug she just could not get enough of. Still, after eight months of dating, she could make love to him virtually all day and all night – on the rare opportunities they had such a length of time together. He was the best kisser, the best lover by a million, million miles – not that she'd had that many for comparison. Four, to be precise, and none of them memorable.

Benedict was kind, thoughtful, considerate, generous, and he made her laugh. She loved his humour. She loved the smell of his skin, his hair, his breath and his perspiration. But the thing she loved most of all about him was his mind.

And of course she loved that he really, truly, genuinely did seem to like her nose.

'You don't really like it, do you?' she'd asked him in bed, a few months ago.

'I do!'

'You can't!'

'I think you're beautiful.'

'I'm not. I've got a hooter like Concorde.'

'You're beautiful to me.'

'Have you been to an optician lately?'

'Do you want to hear something I read that made me think of you?' he asked.

'OK, tell me.'

'It's beauty that captures your attention, personality that captures your heart.'

She smiled now at the memory as she sat in the traffic jam in the sodium-lit darkness, the heater of her little Ford Ka whirring noisily, toasting her feet. She was half listening to the news on the radio, tuned to Radio 4, Gordon Brown being harangued over Afghanistan. She didn't like him, even though she was a Labour supporter, and she switched over to Juice. Air were playing, 'Sexy Boy'.

'Yayyyy!' She grinned, nodding her head and drumming the steering wheel for a few moments, in tune to the music. *Sexy Boy, that's what you are, my gorgeous!*

She loved him with all her heart and soul, of that she was sure. She wanted to spend the rest of her life with him – she had never ever been so certain of anything. It was going to hurt her parents that she wasn't marrying a

Jewish boy, but she couldn't help that. She respected her family's traditions, but she was not a believer in any religion. She believed in making the world a better place for everyone who lived in it, and she hadn't yet come across a religion that seemed capable of or interested in doing that.

Her iPhone, lying beside her on the passenger seat, pinged with an incoming text. She smiled.

The rush-hour gridlock up the London Road was being made worse than usual by new roadworks. The traffic light ahead had gone from green to red, to green to red again now, and they hadn't moved in inch. She was still alongside the brightly lit window display of British Bookshops. She had time to look at her phone safely, she decided.

Hope you win! XXXXXXXXXXXXXX

She smiled. The engine idled and the wipers alternated between a scraping and a screeching sound, flattening the droplets of rain that landed on the windscreen into an opaque smear. Benedict told her she needed new wiper blades and was going to get her some. She could have done with them now, she thought.

She looked at her watch: 5.50. *Shit.* Normally, the half an hour she allowed to get from the charity's offices in the Old Steine, where she had a free parking space, to the Withdean Sports Stadium was more than adequate. But this evening she had not moved an inch for over five minutes. She was due on court at 6 p.m. Hopefully it would be better once she was past the roadworks.

Jessie wasn't the only person being made anxious by the bad traffic. Someone waiting for her at the Withdean Sports Stadium, someone who was not her squash partner, was in a very bad mood. And it was worsening by the second.

67

It was meant to be dark here! It had been dark when he'd checked it out last night. It was less than a month since the longest night of the year – only 13 January, for Christ's sake! At 6 p.m. it should be totally dark. But the sodding car park of Withdean Sports Stadium was lit up like a sodding Christmas Tree. Why did they have to pick tonight to have bloody outdoor athletics practice? Hadn't anyone told the stadium about global warming?

And where the fuck was she?

The car park was a lot fuller than he had expected. He'd already driven around it three times, checking that he had not missed the little black Ka. It definitely wasn't here.

She distinctly said on Facebook that she would meet Jax here at 5.45. The court was booked for 6 p.m. *As usual.*

He'd looked up pictures of Roz on Facebook, too. *View photos of Roz (121). Send Roz a message. Poke Roz. Roz and Jessie are friends.* Roz was quite a sexy vixen, he thought. She rocked! There were some photos of her all dressed up for a prom night.

He focused on the task in hand as his eyes hunted through the windscreen. Two men hurried across in front of him, each carrying sports bags, heads ducked low against the rain, going into the main building. They didn't see him. White vans were always invisible! He was tempted to follow them inside, to check in case somehow he had missed Jessie Sheldon and she was already on court. She'd said something about her car, that it had been fixed. What if something had gone wrong with it again and she'd got a lift from someone instead, or taken a bus or a taxi?

He stopped the van alongside a row of parked vehicles, in a position that gave him a clear view of the entrance ramp to the car park, switched the engine off and killed the lights. It was a God-awful cold, rainy night, which was perfect. No one was going to take any notice of the van, floodlights or no sodding floodlights. Everyone had their heads down, dashing for the cover of the buildings or their cars. All except the stupid athletes on the track.

He was prepared. He was already wearing his latex gloves. The chloroform pad was in a sealed container in his anorak pocket. He slipped his hand inside, to check again. His hood was in another pocket. He checked that again too. Just one thing concerned him: he hoped that Jessie would have a shower after her game, because he didn't like sweaty women. He didn't like some of the unwashed smells women had. She must shower, surely, because she was going straight on to pick up a Chinese takeaway and then to watch a horror film with Roz.

Headlights approached up the ramp. He stiffened. Was this her? He switched on the ignition to sweep the wipers over the rain-spattered screen.

It was a Range Rover. Its headlights momentarily blinded him, then he heard it roar past. He kept the wipers going. The heater pumped in welcoming warm air.

A guy in baggy shorts and a baseball cap was trudging

across the car park, with a sports bag slung over his shoulders, engrossed in a conversation on his mobile. He heard a faint beep-beep and saw lights wink on a dark-coloured Porsche, then the man opened the door.

Wanker, he thought.

He stared again at the ramp. Looked at his watch: 6.05 p.m. *Shit.* He pounded the wheel with his fists. Heard a faint, high-pitched whistling sound in his ears. He got that sometimes when he was all tensed up. He pinched the end of his nose shut and blew hard, but it had no effect and the whistling grew louder.

'Stop it! Fuck off! Stop it!'

It grew louder still.

Exceptionally diminutive manhood!

Jessie would be the judge of that.

He looked at his watch again: 6.10 p.m.

The whistling was now as loud as a football referee's whistle.

'Shut up!' he shouted, feeling all shaky, his eyes blurring with anger.

Then he heard voices, suddenly, and the scrunch of shoes.

'I told her he's an absolute waste of space.'

'She said she loves him! I told her, like, I mean, what??????'

There was a sharp double beep. He saw a flash of orange over to his left. Then he heard car doors click open and, a few moments later, slam shut. The brief whir of a starter motor, then the rattle of a diesel. The interior of the van suddenly stank of diesel exhaust. He heard the blast of a horn.

'Sod off,' he said.

The horn blasted again, twice, to his left.

'Sod off! Screw you! Fuck you! Fuck off!'

There was a mist in front of his eyes, inside his head. The wipers screeched, clearing the rain. More came. They cleared that too. More came.

Then the horn blasted again.

He turned in fury and saw reversing lights on. And then realized. A big, ugly people carrier was trying to reverse and he was parked right in front of it, blocking it.

'Fuck you! Screw you!' He started the van, crunched it into gear, jerked forward a few inches and stalled. His head was shaking, the whistling even louder, slicing his brain to bits like a cheese-wire. He started the van again. Someone knocked on the passenger door window. 'Fuck you!' He rammed the gear lever into first and shot forward. He carried on, almost blind with fury now, and hurtled down the ramp.

In his haze of fury he was utterly oblivious of the headlights of the little black Ford Ka racing up the ramp, in the opposite direction, and passing him.

1998

68

'I'm sorry I'm late, my darling,' Roy Grace said, coming through the front door.

'If I had a pound for every time you've said that, I'd be a millionaire!' Sandy gave him a resigned smile, then kissed him.

There was a warm smell of scented candles in the house. Sandy lit them most evenings, but there seemed more than usual tonight, to mark the special occasion.

'God, you look beautiful,' he said.

She did. She'd been to the hairdresser's and her long fair hair was in ringlets. She was wearing a short black dress that showed every curve of her body and she had sprayed on his favourite perfume, Poison. She raised her wrist to show him the slim silver bracelet he'd bought her from a modern jeweller in the Lanes.

'It looks great!' he said.

'It does!' She admired it in the mirror on the Victorian coat-stand in the hall. 'I love it. You have great taste, Detective Sergeant Grace!'

He held her in his arms and nuzzled her bare neck. 'I could make love to you right now, here on the hall floor.'

'Then you'd better be quick. There's a taxi coming in thirty minutes!'

'Taxi? We don't need a taxi. I'll drive.'

'You're not going to drink on my birthday?'

She helped him out of his coat, slung it on a hook on the stand and led him by the hand into the sitting room. The juke box they'd bought a couple of years earlier in the Saturday morning Kensington Gardens market, and had restored, was playing one of his favourite Rolling Stones tracks, their version of 'Under the Boardwalk'. The lights were dimmed and candles were burning all around. On the coffee table sat an open bottle of champagne, two glasses and a bowl of olives.

'I had thought we might have a drink before we went out,' she said wistfully. 'But it's OK. I'll put it in the fridge and we can have it when we get back! You could drink it off my naked body.'

'Mmmm,' he said. 'It's a lovely idea. But I'm on duty, darling, so I can't drink.'

'Roy, it's my *birthday*!'

He kissed her again, but she pulled away from him. 'You're not on duty on my birthday. You were on duty all over Christmas. You've been at work all day today since very early. Now you're switching off!'

'Tell Popeye that.'

Popeye was his immediate boss, Detective Chief Inspector Jim 'Popeye' Doyle. The DCI had been appointed the Senior Investigating Officer on *Operation Sundown*, the investigation into the disappearance of Rachael Ryan, which was currently consuming all Grace's working hours – and keeping him awake every night, his brain racing.

'Give me his number and I will!'

Grace shook his head. 'My darling, all leave has been cancelled. We're on this case around the clock. I'm sorry.

But if you were Rachael Ryan's parents, that's what you'd expect of us.'

'You're not telling me you can't have a drink on my birthday?'

'Let me nip up and change.'

'You're not going anywhere until you promise me you're going to drink with me tonight!'

'Sandy, if I get called out and someone smells alcohol on my breath, I could lose my job and get kicked off the force. Please understand.'

'*Please understand!*' she mimicked. 'If I had a pound for every time you said that as well, I'd be a *multi-millionaire*!'

'Cancel the cab. I'm going to drive.'

'You are not bloody driving!'

'I thought we were trying to save money for the mortgage and for all the work on the house.'

'I don't think one taxi's going to make much bloody difference!'

'It's two taxis actually – one there and one back.'

'So?' She placed her hands on her hips defiantly.

At that moment, his radio phone crackled into life with an incoming call. He tugged it from his pocket and answered.

'Roy Grace.'

She looked at him, giving him a *Don't you dare, whatever it is*, glare.

It was his DCI.

'Good evening, sir,' he said.

The reception was poor, Jim Doyle's voice crackly.

'Roy, there's a burnt-out van just been found in a field by a farmer out lamping for rabbits. The index shows it was stolen yesterday afternoon. There's a body in it which he thinks is female – he was in the Tank Corps of the army out in Iraq and knows a bit about these things apparently. Sounds possible it could be our missing Rachael Ryan – we need to secure the vehicle immediately. It's off the Saddlescombe Road, half a mile south of the Waterhall Golf Club. I'm on my way over now. Can you meet me there? How long would it take you?'

Grace's heart sank. 'You mean *now*, sir?'

'What do you think? Three weeks' time?'

'No, sir – it's just – it's my wife's birthday.'

'Wish her Happy Birthday from me.'

NOW

69

Norman Potting entered MIR-1 carrying a coffee he had just made in the kitchenette along the corridor. He was stooping, holding the steaming mug out at arm's length, as if mistrustful of it. He grunted a couple of times as he crossed the room, seeming to be about to say something, then changing his mind.

Like most of the team, Potting had been at his desk since before 7 a.m. It was now coming up to 8.30 a.m., and the morning briefing. Temporarily absent from the room was Roy Grace, who had an early appointment with the ACC, Peter Rigg, and Julius Proudfoot, who was due at any moment.

A phone rang, loudly, to the sound of a trumpet fanfare. Everyone looked around. Embarrassed, Nick Nicholl plucked his offending machine out and silenced it.

As Roy Grace entered the room another phone went off. The ring tone was the *Indiana Jones* theme. Potting had the decency to blush. It was his.

Mouthing an apology to Roy Grace, he yanked it out of his pocket and checked the display. Then he raised a finger. 'I'll just take this quickly . . . Someone who may have a lead.'

Another phone rang. It was Julius Proudfoot's. The

forensic psychologist entered the room, extricating his mobile from his man bag as he walked, answered it and sat down, holding it to his ear.

The last to arrive was the Sexual Offences Liaison Officer, Claire Westmore, who had been interviewing and spending time with each of the three rape victims. This was the first of the briefings she had attended.

Potting, wedging his phone to his ear with his shoulder, was writing on his notepad. 'Thank you. That's very helpful. Thank you.'

He replaced his phone and turned to Roy, looking pleased with himself. 'We have another suspect, chief!'

'Tell me?'

'It's from a bloke I know, one of my *contacts*.' Potting tapped the side of his nose. 'Drives for Streamline Taxis. Told me there's a bloke – he's a bit of a joke among the other cabbies apparently – name of John Kerridge. But he calls himself by a funny nickname: Yac. Well, apparently this Yac fellow drives a journeyman night shift and is always going on about strange stuff – ladies' shoes is one of his things.'

Now he had the full attention of the room.

'There have been a few complaints about him by passengers – he gets a bit too personal about things, in particular the toilets in their homes and their footwear. I've spoken to the Hackney Carriage officer in the council. He tells me this driver hasn't actually propositioned anyone, but he's a bit more personal than some of his passengers like. The council want people – particularly women – to feel safe in licensed taxis, not vulnerable. He says he's planning to have a word with him.'

'Do you have an address for Kerridge?' Grace asked.

Potting nodded. 'Lives on a houseboat at Shoreham.'

'Good work,' Grace said. 'I've got *Suspects* on the agenda, so we'll add him to the list when we get to it.' He put his briefing notes down on the work surface in front of him, along with his Policy Book. 'OK, it is 8.30 a.m., Wednesday 14 January. This is our tenth briefing of *Operation Swordfish*, the investigation into the stranger rape of three persons, Mrs Nicola Taylor, Mrs Roxy Pearce and Miss Mandy Thorpe. I've asked the SOLO, Claire Westmore, to attend in order to update us on her interviews with the victims.'

He nodded at her.

'All three of them are, as you would expect, deeply traumatized by what they have been through – the assaults, and the intrusive procedures afterwards,' the SOLO said in her soft Scouse accent. 'I'll start with the first victim, Nicola Taylor, who still has only very limited recall of the attack at the Metropole. Her trauma has deepened since the original interview with her, part of which you and DS Branson witnessed. At the moment she is under sedation at her home in Brighton, being cared for around the clock by a female friend, and has attempted twice to self-harm. She may have to be taken into psychiatric care for a while before we can start a full interview process.'

She paused to look at her notes. 'I think we are making some progress with Mrs Roxanna Pearce, who was attacked in her home in Droveway Avenue last Thursday night. What is interesting in her situation is that when the offender struck, she was in the process of getting dressed up – while her husband was away on a business trip in Scandinavia. SOCO found evidence in her kitchen that she was expecting a guest.'

There were a few raised eyebrows. Then Bella said,

'She could simply have invited a girlfriend round. Why the innuendo?'

'Well,' Claire Westmore said, 'I don't think the signs indicate an *innocent* evening with a mate. There were Italian hors d'oeuvres in a carrier bag on the kitchen table. Two steaks on plates. An open bottle of a very expensive wine and another bottle in the fridge. I've asked her who she was going to be cooking these steaks for and she goes very defensive. She keeps repeating that she'd bought them to give her husband a treat when he came home. But he wasn't due home until the next day.'

'You don't let a wine breathe that long. It would be kaput,' Michael Foreman said. 'It's one of my interests. Doesn't matter what the quality, an hour or two perhaps. But that long? Never. I've had a look at the report. That opened bottle would cost over a hundred quid. That's not plonk you drink over a casual supper.'

'Yep, well, I don't know much about wine,' Westmore said, 'but I would have to agree with you. I think she was expecting someone.'

'You mean a lover?' Nick Nicholl asked.

'You don't open a bottle of wine for someone who's going to rape you,' Emma-Jane Boutwood said.

'Maybe she was planning a kinky sex session,' Norman Potting interjected.

'In your dreams,' Bella Moy retorted.

'She's obviously not going to tell you the truth if she was up to something while her husband was away,' Potting went on. 'And she's not going to want him finding out now, is she?'

'Could we be looking at a kinky sex game gone wrong?' Proudfoot asked.

'I don't think so,' Claire Westmore said. 'Not from the way I'm reading her.'

'So who was her mystery dinner guest?' Nick Nicholl asked.

'She's denying there was one.'

Glenn Branson spoke. 'The Mercedes car that was seen leaving her house at around the time of the attack, for which we only have two digits and one letter of the alphabet. We've now narrowed that down to eighty-three vehicles registered in the Brighton and Hove area. All the registered keepers are being contacted and interviewed. Of course, we've no way of being sure this was a local car, but it seems probable.'

'How many have been eliminated so far?' Roy Grace asked.

'Seventy-one, sir,' said a young DC, Alan Ramsay. 'We should have the rest covered in the next twenty-four hours.'

'So it could be the offender – or her dinner guest,' Grace said.

'If it was her guest, why did he drive away, do you think, boss?' Michael Foreman asked.

'Sounds like, if Claire is right, we might get a chance to ask him that directly.' Grace looked at her. 'Any more on the third victim?'

'Mandy Thorpe is still in hospital, under observation for her head injury, but she's improving – physically if not mentally, sir,' the SOLO said. 'But she's responding well to questioning.'

'Anything new from her?'

'No, sir.'

'I'm still not happy about the link with the first two

and her. I'm just not convinced it is the same offender.' Grace looked at Proudfoot, who said nothing. 'OK, let's move on to the suspect list. First, can I have an update on where we are with Darren Spicer?'

Glenn Branson spoke again. 'Me and DC Nicholl interviewed him again last night at the St Patrick's shelter – we checked first he had been at work all that day at the Grand Hotel, just to see if he was keeping his word about wanting to go straight. We asked him why he'd taken the shoes of his last victim – Marcie Kallestad – after sexually assaulting her.'

'And?'

'He said it was to stop her chasing him.'

There was a titter of laughter.

'Did you believe him?' Grace asked.

'Not as far as I could throw him. He'll tell you whatever he wants you to hear. But I didn't get the impression he took them for any kinky reason.'

He turned towards Nick Nicholl, who shook his head and said, 'I agree.'

'Did he say what he did with them?'

Nicholl nodded. 'He said he flogged them to a shop down Church Street.'

'Is it still there?' Grace asked. 'Could we get them to verify that?'

'Think they're going to remember a pair of shoes that long ago, sir?'

Grace nodded. 'Good point. OK. Norman, what can you tell us about this taxi driver, Johnny Kerridge – Yac?'

'He's a piece of work, from what I've gathered. I'm planning to go and have a chat with him this morning.'

'Good. If you have enough for an arrest, bring him in.

The ACC's blowing smoke up my backside. But only if you really feel you have enough, understand?'

'Yes, chief.'

'What about a search warrant? Take him by surprise and stop him getting rid of any evidence.'

'I don't know if we have enough, chief,' Potting said.

'From what I've heard we've enough to justify. We're going in hard on all suspects now, so that's your next action, Norman.' Grace looked down at his notes. 'OK, where are we with other sex offenders on the register? Has anyone moved up the offender status?'

'No, sir,' Ellen Zoratti said. 'We're working through the list. I've got a possible in Shrewsbury four years ago – very similar MO and no suspect ever apprehended, and another in Birmingham six years ago. I'm waiting for more details.'

Grace nodded. 'One important question, Ellen, is have we captured all offences so far in our territory? Are we sure we haven't missed any? We know for a fact that only 6 per cent of rapes get reported. How are we going to get crucial information from the other 94 per cent? We've talked so far to our neighbouring forces, Kent, Surrey, Hampshire and the Met as well. That hasn't yielded anything.' He thought for a moment. 'You've been trawling SCAS for stranger rapes – any joy there?'

SCAS was the Serious Crime Analysis Section, which covered every county in the UK except for the London Metropolitan Police, who were not linked in on it.

'Nothing so far, sir,' she said, 'but I'm waiting on several forces to get back to me.'

'Let me know as soon as you have anything.'

Proudfoot coughed and then spoke. 'As I said, I'd be

very surprised if our man hasn't offended elsewhere in these past twelve years. Very surprised indeed. You can take it as a given that he has.'

'Offended as in *rape*?' Emma-Jane Boutwood asked.

'Urges don't just go away,' Proudfoot said. 'He'll have needed outlets for his urges.' His phone rang again. After a quick look at the display, he silenced it. 'I presume you're in contact with *Crimewatch*, Roy? They could be helpful here.'

'We have an excellent relationship with them, Julius,' Grace replied. 'Unfortunately, it's two weeks until they are on air again. I want to have our offender potted long before then.'

He could have added, but did not, that so did the ACC, Peter Rigg, the Chief Constable, Tom Martinson, and the Chief Executive of Brighton and Hove Corporation.

Suddenly, his own phone rang.

It was his former boss from 1997, Jim Doyle, who was now part of the recently formed Cold Case Team.

'Roy,' he said. 'Those missing pages from the Rachael Ryan cold-case file – about the white van seen near her flat on Christmas morning, 1997?'

'Yes?'

'We've found out who last signed that file out. I think you're going to like this rather a lot.'

70

'I'm all ears,' Roy Grace said.

The next words from Jim Doyle stunned him. Totally stunned him. After they had fully sunk in, he said, 'You're not serious, Jim.'

'Absolutely I am.'

In his nineteen years in the police force to date, Roy Grace had found his fellow officers tended to be good, decent people and, for the most part, people whose company he enjoyed both at work and socially. Sure there were a few prats: some, like Norman Potting, who at least had the redeeming feature of being a good detective, and others, very occasionally, who were a total waste of space. But there were only two people he could really genuinely say that he did not like.

The first was his acerbic former ACC, Alison Vosper, who seemed to have made her mind up from the start that she and Grace were not going to get on; the second was a London Metropolitan Police detective who'd had a brief sojourn here last year, and had tried very hard to stick the boot into him. His name was Cassian Pewe.

Grace excused himself and stepped out of the room, closing the door behind him.

'Cassian Pewe? Are you serious, Jim? You're saying

that Cassian Pewe was the last person to sign that file out?'

'*Detective Superintendent* Cassian Pewe. He was working here in the autumn, wasn't he?' Doyle said. 'Hadn't he moved here from the Met, to help you out on cold cases?'

'Not to help me out, Jim, to take over from me – and not just on cold cases, but on everything. That was his plan, courtesy of Alison Vosper! He was out to eat my sodding lunch!'

'I heard there was a bit of friction.'

'You could call it that.'

Grace had first met Pewe a few years ago, when the man was a detective inspector. The Met had sent in re-inforcements to help police Brighton during the Labour Party Conference, Pewe being one of them. Grace had had a big run-in with him and found him supremely arrogant. Then, to his utter dismay, last year Pewe had moved down to Sussex CID with the rank of detective superintendent, and Alison Vosper had given him Grace's cold-case work-load – plus the clear signal that the former Met officer would be taking over more and more of Grace's duties.

Cassian Pewe fancied himself as a ladies' man. He had golden hair, angelic blue eyes and a permanent tan. He preened and strutted, exuding a natural air of author-ity, always acting as if he was in charge, even when he wasn't. Working secretly, behind Grace's back, Pewe had taken it upon himself to ruin Grace's career by trying to reopen investigations into Sandy's disappearance – and point suspicion at him. Returning from a trip to New York last October, Grace found, to his utter incredulity, that Pewe had assembled a Police Search Unit team to scan and dig up his garden for Sandy's suspected remains.

Fortunately, that had proved a step too far. Pewe left Sussex CID and returned to the Met not long after, with his tail between his legs.

After a few more questions to Jim Doyle, Grace hung up and then stood thinking for some moments. There was no way, at this stage, he could mention anything openly to his team. Questioning another officer as high-ranking as Pewe as a suspect would have to be done discreetly, regardless of his personal feelings towards the man.

He would do this himself and it would be a pleasure.

71

twitter
jessiesheldonuk

Working late today. Audit review – soooo boring!
But Benedict taking me out after for sushi meal
at Moshi Moshi. Yayyyy!

He read the text which had just Tweeted through on his phone. *Sushi*, he thought disdainfully. He didn't understand that stuff. What was the point of going to a restaurant to eat uncooked fish? Seemed like easy money for the chef. He'd read somewhere that in Japan there were restaurants where you could eat sushi off the naked bodies of women. He could think of much better things to do with naked women.

He was looking forward to doing those things with Jessie Sheldon.

Too bad Jessie was going to be busy tonight. But it didn't matter. Dee Burchmore was making her speech at the Martlets lunch tomorrow. She would be wearing her blue satin Manolo Blahniks with the diamanté buckles. He knew where she was going to park and the place was perfect. He was going to enjoy her.

Meantime, Jessie Sheldon would be keeping in touch. She had 322 followers on Twitter. It was so thoughtful of her to let him know all her movements.

72

Back in his office after the morning briefing, Roy Grace was deep in thought. Was it possible that a serving police officer could be the Shoe Man?

There had been bad apples in the Sussex Police, as in all other forces around the country in the past, at some time or other. Murderers, rapists, thieves, porn merchants, drug dealers and fraudsters hiding behind one of the ultimate façades of respectability and trust. It was rare, but with a team of over 5,000 people in Sussex alone, it could never be ruled out.

And it fitted. The inside information that had been fed to the press on the Shoe Man back in 1997, and now on the current investigation, could have been supplied by anyone with the access codes to the Sussex Police computer network. Cassian Pewe had access to them back in October last year. Who knew what he could have copied or taken then?

He dialled the central internal number for the London Metropolitan Police, his thoughts on what he planned to say crystal clear.

After two minutes of being shunted around various extensions, he heard Detective Superintendent Pewe's voice, as sharp and invasive as a dentist's drill, and as charming as a pipette full of sulphuric acid.

'Roy! How good to hear from you! Need me back, do you?'

Cutting to the chase, he said, 'No, I need some information from you. When you were with us, you logged out a cold-case file from the storeroom. You are the last signature on the form. It's regarding a missing person, Rachael Ryan, who disappeared on Christmas morning, 1997. Ring a bell?'

'I looked at a lot of files in the brief time I was with you, Roy.' His voice sounded pained.

'Well, there are two pages missing from this one, Cassian. Just wondering if by any chance you had given them to anyone else? A researcher perhaps?'

'Let me think. No, absolutely not. No way! I wanted to review everything myself.'

'Did you read that particular file?'

'I honestly can't remember.'

'Try harder.'

Pewe sounded uneasy suddenly. 'What is this, Roy?'

'I'm asking you a question. Did you read that file? It's only a few months ago.'

'It rings a faint bell,' he said defensively.

'Would you have noticed if the last two pages were missing?'

'Well, yes, of course I would.'

'So they weren't missing when you read them?'

'I don't think so.'

'Do you remember what they said?'

'No – no, I don't.'

'I need you to remember what they said, because they may now be crucial to a current investigation.'

'Roy!' He sounded pained. 'Come on. Do you remember stuff you read three months ago?'

'Yes, actually, I do. I have a good memory. Isn't that what detectives are supposed to have?'

'Roy, I'm sorry. I'm really busy at the moment on a report I need to have finished by midday.'

'Would it help to refresh your memory if I had you arrested and brought you back down here?'

Grace heard a sound like the blade of a lawnmower striking a half-buried flint. 'Ha-ha! You are joking, aren't you?'

On an operation last October, Roy Grace had saved Cassian Pewe's life – at considerable risk to himself. Yet Pewe had barely thanked him. It was hard to imagine that he could ever feel more contempt for any human than he felt for this man. Grace hoped it wasn't clouding his judgement, although at this moment he didn't really care that much if it was.

'Cassian, Tony Case, our Senior Support Officer, whom you will remember from when you were with us, has informed me that since Sussex House became operational, back in 1996, all cold-case files have been kept down in a secure storeroom in the basement. Access is strictly controlled, for chain-of-evidence purposes. A digital alarm protects it and anyone entering needs access codes, which are registered. He has a log, signed by you, showing that you returned the Shoe Man's file to one of his assistants last October. No one has looked at that file subsequently, until the Cold Case Team this week. OK?'

He was greeted with silence.

'You were in Brighton during the Labour Party Conference of 1997, weren't you? On secondment from the Met when you were working for Special Branch. You then continued working in Brighton straight after that, on an inquiry into a series of armed jewellery raids in London that were linked with Brighton. You bought a flat, with a view to living here. Correct?'

'Yes. So?'

'The dates you were in this city coincide exactly with the dates that the Shoe Man committed his offences. You spent Christmas Eve, 1997, in Brighton, didn't you?'

'I can't remember without checking my diary.'

'One of my staff can verify that, Cassian. Bella Moy? Remember her?'

'Should I?'

'You tried to shag her in the back of your car at about midnight, after a boozy night out with a bunch of local officers. You drove her home, then tried to stop her getting out of your car. Remember now?'

'No.'

'Probably a good thing. She remembers it well. You're lucky she didn't press charges for sexual harassment.'

'Roy, are you trying to tell me you've never snogged a girl pissed?'

Ignoring him, Grace said, 'I want to know what you did after you left Bella outside her mother's house. Those hours between midnight and Christmas morning? I want to know what you did on Halloween, 1997. I have more dates for you. I want to know where you were a fortnight ago on New Year's Eve. Where were you last Thursday evening, 8 January? Where were you last Saturday evening, 10 January? I hope you are writing all those down, Cassian.'

'You're wasting police time, Roy!' He tried to sound good-humoured. 'Come on. Do you really expect me to be able to tell you where I was at any given moment twelve years ago? Could you tell me where you were?'

'I could, Cassian. I could tell you exactly. So tell me, this past New Year's Eve – where did you spend it?'

There was a long silence. Then Pewe said reluctantly, 'In Brighton, actually.'

'Can someone vouch for you?'

There was another long silence before Pewe said, 'I'm sorry, Roy, I'm not prepared to continue this conversation. I don't like your tone. I don't like your questions.'

'And I don't like your answers,' Grace replied.

73

Wednesday 14 January

Yac was tired. At 3 a.m. the city had been quiet. The second Tuesday in January and people were staying home. He'd cruised around because the man who owned the taxi got angry if he stopped too early, but he'd only had two fares since midnight – barely enough to cover the cost of the fuel. He'd been about to head home when a call had come in to take two people up to Luton Airport. He'd only got back to the boat just before 7 a.m. Exhausted, he'd fed the cat and crashed out in his berth.

Footsteps woke him. A steady *clump, clump, clump* on the deck above his head. He sat up and looked at the clock. It showed 2 p.m.

Tea! was his first thought. His second was, *Who the hell is up there?*

He never had visitors. Ever. Apart from the postman and delivery men. But he was not expecting any deliveries.

It sounded like a whole group of people up there. Was it kids? Kids had been on the boat a few times, jeering and shouting at him, before he'd chased them off.

'Go away!' he shouted at the ceiling. 'Piss off! Sod off! Screw off! Fuck off! Take a hike! Get lost, kids!' He liked using words he heard in the taxi.

Then he heard knocking. A sharp, insistent *rap, rap, rap*.

Angrily, he swung his legs out of his bunk and staggered into the saloon, padding across the wooden floor, partially covered with rugs, in his underpants and T-shirt.

Rap, rap, rap.

'Go to hell!' he shouted. 'Who are you? Didn't you hear me? What do you want? Are you deaf? Go away! I'm asleep!'

Rap, rap, rap!

He climbed up the wooden steps, into the sun lounge at the top. It had glass patio doors and a big brown sofa, and windows all around with views out on the grey afternoon across the mudflats. It was low tide.

A man in his fifties, balding, with a comb-over, wearing a shabby tweed jacket, grey flannel trousers and scuffed brown brogues, was standing outside. He held up a small black leather wallet and mouthed something at him that Yac did not understand. Behind him stood a whole group of people wearing blue jackets with POLICE written on them, and helmets with visors. One of them was lugging a big yellow cylinder that looked like a fire extinguisher.

'Go away!' Yac shouted. 'I'm sleeping!'

Then he turned and started walking back down the stairs. As he did so he heard the *rap, rap, rap* again. It was starting to annoy him. *They should not be on his boat. This was private property!*

The sound of splintering glass stopped him in his tracks just as he stepped on to the saloon floor. Anger surged inside him. That idiot. That stupid idiot had knocked too hard! Well, he would go and teach him a lesson!

But as he turned, he heard a cacophony of leather and rubber-soled footsteps.

A voice shouted out, 'POLICE! DON'T MOVE! POLICE!'

The man with the comb-over was clattering down the steps, followed by several police officers in their yellow vests. The man was still holding up the wallet. Inside it was a badge of some kind and writing.

'John Kerridge?' the man asked him.

'I'm Yac,' he replied. 'My name is Yac. I'm a taxi driver.'

'I'm Detective Sergeant Potting, Sussex CID.' The man was now holding up a sheet of paper. 'I have a warrant to search these premises.'

'You'll have to speak to the owners. I'm just looking after it for them. I have to feed the cat. I'm late doing that, because I slept in today.'

'I'd like to have a few words with you, Yac. Perhaps we can sit down somewhere?'

'Actually I have to go back to bed now, because I need my sleep. It's quite important for my night shift, you see.' Yac looked around at the police officers standing in the saloon beside him and behind him. 'I'm sorry,' he said. 'I have to speak to the owners before I allow you on this boat. You will have to wait outside. It might be difficult getting hold of them because they are in Goa.'

'Yac,' Norman Potting said, 'there's an easy way to do this and a hard way. Either you cooperate and help us, or I arrest you. Simple as that.'

Yac cocked his head. 'Simple as what?'

Potting looked at him dubiously, wondering if all the man's lights were fully switched on. 'The choice is yours. Do you want to spend tonight sleeping in your bed, or in a cell at our custody unit?'

'I have to work tonight,' he said. 'The man who owns the taxi will be very angry if I don't.'

'OK, sunshine, then you'd better cooperate.'

Yac looked at him. 'I don't think the sun is always shining.'

Potting frowned, ignoring the comment. 'Bit of a fisherman, are you?'

'I'm a taxi driver.'

Potting jerked a thumb up at the deck. 'You've got fishing lines out.'

Yac nodded.

'What do you catch here? Mostly crabs?'

'Plaice,' Yac replied. 'Flounder. Sometimes Dover soles.'

'Good fishing, is it? I'm a bit of a fisherman myself. Never fished up this far.'

'You broke my patio doors. You'd better fix those. They will be very angry with you. I'm not allowed to break anything.'

'To tell you the truth, Yashmak, I don't give a toss about your patio doors. I don't actually give much of a toss about you either, and I don't like your taste in underpants, but don't let's get personal. Either you're going to cooperate or I'm going to arrest you, then take this floating skip apart, plank by plank.'

'If you do that it will sink,' Yac said. 'You need some of the planks. Unless you're a good swimmer.'

'A comedian, are you?' Potting said.

'No, I'm a taxi driver. I do night shifts.'

Potting held his temper with some difficulty. 'I'm looking for something on this boat, Yashmak. Anything you've got here you'd like to tell me about – and show me?'

'I have my high-flush toilet chains, but they're private. You can't see those – except the ones I have in my berth. I can show you those.' Yac perked up suddenly. 'There's a really good high-flush toilet near Worthing Pier – I could take you over there and show you them if you like?'

'I'll flush you down your own sodding toilet if you don't shut it,' Potting said.

Yac stared back at him, then grinned. 'I wouldn't fit,' he said. 'The diaphragm's too small!'

'Not by the time I finished with you, it wouldn't be.'

'I – I'll bet you!'

'And I'll bet you, sunshine. I'll bet you we find something here, all right? So why don't you save us all lot of time and show us where the ladies' shoes are?'

He saw the flicker in the strange man's face and instantly he knew he had hit the mark.

'I don't have any shoes. Not ladies' shoes.'

'Are you sure?'

Yac eyeballed him for a moment, then looked down. 'I don't have any ladies' shoes.'

'That's good to hear, Yashmak. I'll get my team to verify that and then we'll be off.'

'Yes,' Yac said. 'But they can't touch my toilet chains.'

'I'll let them know that.'

Yac nodded, perspiration running down him. 'I've been collecting them a long time, you see.'

'Toilet chains?' Norman Potting said.

Yac nodded.

The Detective Sergeant stared at him for some moments. 'Tell you what, Yashmak, how about I flush you down the sodding toilet now?'

1998

74

Roy Grace hated coming to this place. He got the heebie-jeebies every time he drove in through the wrought-iron gates. The gold lettering made them seem like the entrance to some grand house, until you took a closer look at the wording: BRIGHTON AND HOVE MORTUARY.

Not even the Rod Stewart cassette playing on his car's stereo, which he'd put on to try to cheer himself up, was having any effect on his gloomy mood. There was a line of cars occupying all the spaces close to the entrance, so he had to drive to the far end and park beside the exit doors to the covered receiving bay. As if to make it even worse, the rain started coming down harder – solid, pelting stair-rods. He switched the engine off and 'Maggie May' died with it. The wipers scratched to a halt across the screen. Then he touched the door handle and hesitated.

He was really not looking forward to this. His stomach felt as though it had curdled.

Because of the heat of the burning van in the field and the difficulty of getting any fire hoses down to it, it had been midday yesterday before the vehicle had cooled enough to allow an inspection, and for it to be identified as stolen. The stench of scorched grass, burnt rubber, paint, fuel, plastic and seared human flesh had made him retch several times. Some smells you never ever got used to, no matter how often you'd experienced them before. And some sights too. The van's unfortunate occupant had not been a pretty one.

Nor had Sandy's expression been when he'd arrived home, at 4 a.m. on Wednesday, to get his head down for a few hours before returning to the scene.

She had said nothing – she was in one of her silent moods. It was what she always did when she was really angry, just went silent on him, sending him to Coventry, shutting him out, sometimes for days. Not even the massive bunch of flowers he'd bought her had thawed her.

He had not been able to sleep, but it wasn't because of Sandy. She'd get over it eventually, she always did, and then it would be forgotten. All night he'd just lain in bed thinking one thought, over and over. Was the body in the van the missing Rachael Ryan?

Charred human corpses were the worst thing of all, so far as he was concerned. As a rookie PC, he'd had to help recover the remains of two children, aged five and seven, from a burnt-out house in Portslade after an arson attack; the horror had been made ten times worse because it was children. It had given him nightmares for months.

He knew what he was about to see in the mortuary would have a similar effect and would be staying with him for a long time. But he had no choice.

Already late because his SIO, Jim Doyle, had called an early briefing which had overrun, he climbed out of the car, locked it, then hurried to the front door of the mortuary, holding the collar of his mackintosh tight around his neck.

The briefing had been attended by a sergeant from

the Accident Investigation Unit, the team which forensically examined all vehicles involved in serious crashes. It was early days with the van, the sergeant had told them, but on first impressions the fire was extremely unlikely to have been caused by the accident.

He rang the bell and moments later the door was opened by the Senior Mortician herself, Elsie Sweetman, wearing a green apron over blue surgical scrubs that were tucked into long white wellington boots.

In her late forties, with a bob of curly hair, Elsie had a kind face and a remarkably cheery demeanour, considering the horrific things she had to deal with on a daily – and nightly – basis. Roy Grace always remembered she'd been kind to him when he had nearly keeled over at the first post-mortem he'd attended. She had led him into her sitting room and made him a cup of tea, telling him not to worry, that half the coppers on the force had done the same thing.

He stepped in through the door, which was like the front door of any suburban bungalow, into the narrow entrance hallway, and there the similarities ended, starting with the pervading reek of Jeyes Fluid and Trigene disinfectant. Today his nostrils detected something else, and the curdling in his stomach worsened.

In the small changing room he wrestled a green apron over his head and tied the tapes, then put on a face mask, tied that securely too, and slipped his feet into a pair of short white rubber boots that were too big. He clumped out along the corridor and turned right, passing the sealed, glassed-in room where corpses that had died of suspected contagious diseases were examined, then walked into the main post-mortem room, trying to breathe in through his mouth only.

There were three stainless-steel tables on wheels, two of which were pushed to one side against a cupboard. The third was in the centre of the room, its occupant, lying on her back, surrounded by people similarly clad to himself.

Grace swallowed. The sight of her made him shiver. She didn't look human, her blackened remains like some terrible monster created by the special effects team on a horror or sci-fi movie.

Is this you, Rachael? What happened? If it is you, how did you come to be in this stolen van?

Leaning over her, with a surgical probe in one gloved hand and tweezers in the other, was the Home Office pathologist, Dr Frazer Theobald, a man Grace always thought was a dead ringer for Groucho Marx.

Theobald was flanked by a fifty-year-old retired police officer, Donald Whitely, now a Coroner's Officer, Elsie Sweetman, her assistant mortician, Arthur Trumble, a drily humorous man in his late forties, with Dickensian mutton chops, and a SOCO photographer, James Gartrell, who was intently focusing his lens on a section of the woman's left leg that had a measuring rule lying across it.

Almost all of the dead woman's hair was gone and her face was like melted black wax. It was difficult to make out her features. Grace's stomach was feeling worse. Despite breathing through his mouth, and the mask over his nose, he could not avoid the smell. The Sunday lunchtime smell of his childhood, of roast pork and burnt crackling.

It was obscene to think that, he knew. But the smell was sending confused signals to his brain and his stomach. It was making him feel increasingly queasy and he was beginning to perspire. He looked at her again, then away, breathing deeply through his mouth. He glanced at the others in the room. They were all smelling the same thing, with the same associations too; he knew that, they'd talked about this before, yet none of them seemed affected by it the way he was. Were they all so used to it?

'Here's something interesting,' the pathologist announced nonchalantly, holding up an oval object, about an inch wide, in his tweezers.

It was translucent, scorched and partially melted.

'See this, Detective Sergeant Grace?' Theobald seemed to be addressing him specifically.

Reluctantly, he moved closer to the corpse. It looked like it might be a contact lens of some kind.

'This is most curious,' the pathologist said. 'Not what I would have expected to find in someone driving a motor vehicle.'

'What is it?' Grace asked.

'An eye shield.'

'Eye shield?'

Theobald nodded. 'They're used in mortuaries. The eyes start to sink quite quickly post-mortem, so morticians pop them in between the eyelids and the globes – makes them look nicer for viewing.' He gave a wry smile. 'As I said, not what I'd expect the driver of a motor vehicle to be wearing.'

Grace frowned. 'Why might this woman have been wearing it?'

'I suppose possibly if she had a false eye, or had had some kind of reconstructive surgery, it could be there for cosmetic purposes. But not in both eyes.'

'Are you suggesting she was blind, Dr Theobald?' Arthur Trumble said, with a mischievous twinkle.

'A bit more than that, I'm afraid,' he replied. 'She

was dead quite a long time before she was put into this vehicle.'

There was a long silence.

'Are you absolutely certain?' the Coroner's Officer asked him.

'There's a small amount of lung tissue that's survived, which I'll need to take and examine in the lab, but from what I can see with my naked eye there is no sign of smoke or flame inhalation – which, to put it bluntly, means she wasn't breathing when the fire started.'

'You're saying she was dead before the accident happened?'

'Yes, I am,' he said. 'I'm certain she was.'

Trying to make sense of this in his mind, Grace asked, 'Are you able to estimate her age, Dr Theobald?'

'I would say she's quite old – late seventies, eighties. I can't be specific without tests, but certainly she's no younger than mid-fifties. I can get you a more accurate estimate in a couple of days.'

'But definitely no younger than mid-fifties?'

Theobald nodded. 'Absolutely not.'

'What about dental records?' Grace asked.

The pathologist pointed his probe at her jaw. 'I'm afraid one of the effects of intense heat is to cause the crowns to explode. There's nothing I can see remaining that would get you anywhere with dental records. I think DNA's going to be your best chance.'

Grace stared back down at the corpse again. His revulsion was fading just a fraction, as he got more accustomed to the sight of her.

If you're not Rachael Ryan, who are you? What were you doing in this van? Who put you there?

And why?

NOW

75

Roy Grace followed Tony Case down the back stone staircase into the basement of the CID headquarters. No one could accuse Sussex Police of squandering money on the decor here, he observed wryly, walking past cracked walls with chunks of plaster missing.

Then the Senior Support Officer led him along the familiar, gloomily lit corridor that felt like it was leading to a dungeon. Case stopped in front of a closed door and pointed at the digi-alarm pad on the wall, then raised his index finger.

'OK, first thing, Roy. Anyone wanting access would need the code for this – only a handful of people, such as your good self, have it – and I've given it to them personally.'

Case was a solidly built man in his mid-fifties, with close-cropped hair and tough good looks, dressed in a fawn suit, shirt and tie. A former police officer himself, he had rejoined the force as a civilian after retirement. With a small team, he ran the CID headquarters and was responsible for all the equipment here, as well as in the three other Major Crime Suites in the county. He could be an invaluable aide to those officers he respected and a total pain in the butt to those he didn't, and his judgement was usually right. Fortunately for Roy Grace, they got on well.

Tony Case then raised a second finger. 'Anyone who comes down here – workmen, cleaners, anyone like that – is escorted all the time.'

'OK, but there must be some occasions when they would be left alone – and could rummage through files.'

Case looked dubious. 'Not in a place as sensitive as this evidence store, no.'

Grace nodded. He used to know his way around here blindfolded, but the new team had rearranged the filing. Case opened the door and they went in. Wall-to-ceiling red-painted cages, all with padlocks, stretched into the distance. On the shelves behind them were red and green crates stacked with files, and sealed evidence bags.

'Anything in particular you want to see?'

'Yes, the files on the Shoe Man.' Although Grace had summary files in his office, all the actual evidence was kept securely in here.

Case walked along several yards, then stopped, selected a key from a bunch dangling from his belt and opened a padlock. Then he pulled open the cage door.

'I know this one,' he said, 'because it's currently being accessed by your team.'

Grace nodded. 'Do you remember Detective Super-intendent Cassian Pewe, who was here last autumn?'

Case gave him a bemused look. 'Yeah, don't think I'll forget him in a hurry. Treated me like his personal lackey. Tried to get me hanging pictures in his office for him. Nothing bad happened to him, I hope. Like he didn't fall off another cliff and this time didn't have you around to save him.'

Grace grinned. Saving Pewe's life had turned out to be the least popular thing he'd ever done.

'Unfortunately not.'

'Can't understand why you didn't get a bravery medal for what you did, Roy.'

'I can.' Grace smiled. 'I'd only have got it if I'd let him fall.'

'Don't worry. He's a shit. Know what they say about shit?'

'No.'

'Shit always falls, eventually, from its own weight.'

76

Thirty minutes later, Grace sat down in front of ACC Peter Rigg's vast desk at Malling House, the Sussex Police headquarters. It was 4 p.m.

'So, Roy, you wanted to see me. Do you have some good news on the Shoe Man?'

'Possibly, sir.' Grace gave him a general update and told him he hoped to have more for him after the evening briefing at 6.30 p.m. Then he went on: 'I have a rather delicate situation that I want to run by you.'

'Go ahead.'

Grace gave him the background on Cassian Pewe and what had happened during the brief time he had been with Sussex CID. Then he went on to outline his current concerns about the man.

Rigg listened intently, making occasional notes. When Grace had finished he said, 'So, let me get this clear. Detective Superintendent Pewe was in the right places to be a potential suspect during the Shoe Man's original attacks back in 1997?'

'It would appear so, sir.'

'And again, during these past two weeks, his movements might fit with the current attacks?'

'I've asked him to account for his whereabouts at the times of these three recent attacks, yes, sir.'

'And you think Detective Superintendent Pewe could be the person who took the pages from the file that could contain crucial evidence?'

'Pewe was one of only a handful of people with access to that file.'

'Could he be responsible for these past and present leaks to the press, in your view?'

'It's quite possible,' Grace said.

'Why? What's in it for him to do that?'

'To embarrass us? Perhaps me in particular?'

'But why?'

'I can see it quite clearly now, sir. If he could make me look incompetent by undermining me in various ways, he might get me transferred out of CID HQ – and safely away from the cold-case files which could incriminate him.'

'Is that just theory, or do you have anything concrete?'

'At the moment it's just theory. But it fits.' He shrugged. 'I just hope I'm not letting the past history cloud my judgement.'

The ACC looked at him. He had a wise face. Then he gave Roy a kindly smile. 'You mustn't let this get personal, you know.'

'I want to avoid that at all costs, sir.'

'I know your experiences with him were less than satisfactory – and that you put yourself at enormous personal risk in saving him, which has been noted – but he is a very widely respected officer. It's never good to make enemies. Know that old proverb?'

Grace thought he seemed to he hearing rather a lot of expressions this afternoon. 'No?'

'One thousand friends are too few; one enemy is too many.'

Grace smiled. 'So I should let it drop with Pewe, even if I suspect he may be our man?'

'No, not at all. I want to start our working relationship on a footing of mutual trust. If you genuinely think he might be our offender, then you should arrest him and I'll stand by you. But this is a politically sensitive issue and it won't be too clever if we screw up.'

'You mean if *I* screw up?'

Rigg smiled. 'You'll be including myself and the Chief Constable in the screw-up, by association. That's all I'm saying. Make very sure of your facts. There'll be an awful lot of egg on our faces if you're wrong.'

'But even more if I'm right and another woman is attacked and we did nothing.'

'Just make sure your evidence against him is as watertight as your logic.'

77

Roy Grace's rapidly expanding team on *Operation Sword-fish* was now too big to fit comfortably into MIR-1, so he held the 6.30 p.m. briefing in the Conference Room in the Major Incident Suite.

The room could hold twenty-five people seated on the red chairs around the open-centred rectangular table and another thirty standing. One of its uses was for Major Crime briefings for press conferences, and it was to provide a visual backdrop for these that there stood, at the far end opposite the video screen, a concave, two-tone blue board, six feet high and ten feet wide, boldly carrying the Sussex Police website address and the *Crimestoppers* legend and phone number.

The Detective Superintendent sat with his back to this, facing the door, as his team filed in, half of them on their phones. One of the last to enter was Norman Potting, who strutted in, looking very pleased with himself.

At 6.30 sharp, Roy Grace opened the meeting by announcing, 'Team, before I start on the agenda, DS Potting has some news for us.' He gestured to him to begin.

Potting coughed, then said, 'I'm pleased to report I've arrested a suspect.'

'Brilliant!' Michael Foreman said.

'He's in custody now while we continue a search of his home, a houseboat moored on the Adur at Shoreham Beach.'

'Who is he, Norman?' Nick Nicholl asked.

'John Kerridge, the man I mentioned at this morning's briefing. A local taxi driver. Calls himself by a nickname, Yac. We conducted a search of his premises and discovered a cache of eighty-seven pairs of ladies' high-heeled shoes concealed in bags in the bilges.'

'Eighty-seven pairs?' Emma-Jane Boutwood said, astonished.

'There may be more. The search is continuing,' he said. 'I suspect we're going to find the ones taken from our first two victims – and past ones.'

'You don't have those yet?' Nick Nicholl asked.

'No, but we'll find 'em. He's got a whole stack of current newspaper cuttings about the Shoe Man that we've seized, as well as a wodge of printouts from the Internet on the Shoe Man back in 1997.'

'He lives alone?' Bella Moy asked.

'Yes.'

'Any wife? Separated? Girlfriend, or boyfriend?'

'Doesn't sound like it.'

'What reason did he give for having these cuttings – and the shoes?' she asked.

'He didn't. When I asked him that question he went into a sulk and refused to speak. We also found a large number of toilet chains concealed, as well as the shoes, which he got extremely agitated about.'

Branson frowned, then made a flushing movement with his arm. 'Toilet chains? You mean as in *bog* chains, right?'

Potting nodded.

'Why?' Branson continued.

Potting looked around, a little hesitantly, and then stared at Roy Grace. 'Dunno if it's politically correct to say it – um – chief.'

'The suspense is killing us,' Grace replied, with good humour.

Potting tapped the side of his head. 'He's not got all his lights on.'

There was a titter of laughter. Potting smiled proudly. Grace watched him, glad for this man to have shown his value to the team. But at the same time, he was thinking hard about Pewe, privately concerned that while this current suspect under arrest ticked a lot of boxes, he left one big unanswered question.

He turned his attention back to DS Potting's prisoner in custody. Great they had an arrest, and here was a story the *Argus* would lead with in the morning. But he was experienced enough to know there was a big gap between arresting a suspect and establishing he was the offender.

'How is he reacting, Norman?' he asked.

'He's angry, chief,' Potting said. 'And we could have a problem. His brief's Ken Acott.'

'Shit,' Nick Nicholl said.

There were a number of Legal Aid solicitors available to suspects, and their abilities and attitudes varied widely. Ken Acott was the smartest of all of them, and the bane of any arresting officer's life.

'What's he saying?' Grace asked.

'He's requesting a medical examination of his client before he speaks any further to us,' the Detective Sergeant replied. 'I'm arranging that. Meantime I'm holding Kerridge in custody overnight. Hopefully the search team will find further evidence.'

'Perhaps we'll get a DNA match,' DC Foreman said.

'So far the Shoe Man has shown himself very forensically aware,' Grace said. 'It's one of the big problems that we've never obtained anything from him. Not one damned hair or fibre.' He looked at his notes. 'OK, excellent work, Norman. Let's move on for a moment. Glenn, you have something to report on another possible suspect.'

'Yes, boss. I'm pleased to say we've identified the driver of the Mercedes E Class saloon. The one that was seen driving at speed away from the Pearces' house in Droveway Avenue around the time of the attack on Mrs Roxanna Pearce, and we've now interviewed him. It explains the romantic dinner for two she was preparing, but it's not helpful news, I'm afraid.' Branson shrugged, then went on. 'His name's Iannis Stephanos, a local restaurateur. He owns Timon's down in Preston Street, and Thessalonica.'

'I know that!' DC Foreman said. 'Took my wife there for our anniversary last week!'

'Yeah, well, me and E-J went and spoke to Stephanos this afternoon. He admitted with some embarrassment that he and Mrs Pearce were having an affair. She's subsequently confirmed this. She'd invited him over because her husband was away on a business trip – which we know to be the case. He'd gone to the house but not been able to gain access. He said he'd hung around outside, ringing the doorbell and phoning. He was sure she was in because he'd seen shadows move behind the curtains. In the end, he wasn't sure what she was playing at – then had a sudden fit of panic that perhaps the husband had returned home early, which was why he left at speed.'

'Do you believe him?' Grace looked first at him, then at Emma-Jane Boutwood.

Both of them nodded.

'Doesn't make any sense that he should have raped her if he'd been invited over.'

'Can you be sure she didn't cry *rape* because her husband returned and she felt guilty?' Michael Foreman asked.

'Her husband didn't return until we contacted him the next day,' Branson replied.

'Does he know about the affair?' Grace asked Glenn.

'I've tried to be discreet,' he said. 'I think we'd best keep that to ourselves, for the moment.'

'I've had Mr Pearce on the phone several times, asking about our progress,' Grace said. He looked at the SOLO, Claire Westmore. 'Are you happy for us to try to keep it quiet?'

'I don't see any value in making things worse than they already are for Mrs Pearce, at this stage, sir,' she replied.

*

After the meeting, Grace asked DC Foreman to come to his office, and there he briefed him, in confidence, about his suspicions concerning Detective Superintendent Pewe.

Foreman had not been around during the time Cassian Pewe was with Sussex CID, so no one would be able to accuse him of being biased against the man. He was the perfect choice.

'Michael, I want you to check all Detective Superintendent Cassian Pewe's alibis back in 1997 and now. I have concerns about him, because so much fits. But if we arrest him, it has to be on watertight evidence. We don't have that yet. See what you can come up with. And remember, you're going to be dealing with a very devious and manipulative person.'

'I'm sure I'm his match, boss.'

Grace smiled. 'That's why I've chosen you.'

1998

78

The lab tests confirmed the age of the woman who had been partially incinerated in the van as being between eighty and eighty-five.

Whoever she was – or rather had been – she was not the missing Rachael Ryan. Which now left Detective Sergeant Roy Grace with a second problem. Who was she, who had put her in the van, and why?

Three big unticked boxes.

So far no undertakers had reported a missing body, but Grace could not get the image of the woman out of his mind. During the past couple of days some of her details had been filled in for him. She was five feet, four inches tall. White. Lab tests carried out by Dr Frazer Theobald on her lung tissue and on the small amount of flesh intact on her back confirmed that she had been dead for some considerable time before the van caught fire – several days before. She had died from cancer secondaries.

But, it seemed, the county of Sussex was knee deep in little old ladies who were terminally ill. Some of its towns, like Worthing, Eastbourne and Bexhill, with their high elderly populations, were jokily known as God's waiting rooms. To contact every undertaker and every mortuary was a massive task. Because of the pathologist's findings, the case was regarded as bizarre rather than as a major crime, so resources allocated to it were limited. It was virtually down to Roy Grace alone.

She had been someone's child, he thought. Someone's daughter. She'd had children herself, so she had been someone's wife or lover. Someone's mother. Probably someone's grandmother. Probably a caring, loving, decent person.

So how come her last journey had been buckled into the driver's seat of a stolen van?

Was it a sick prank by a bunch of youths?

But if so, where had they taken her from? If an undertaker's premises had been broken into and a corpse stolen, surely it would have been reported as a matter of urgency? But there was nothing on the serials. He'd checked them all, for three weeks back.

It just did not make sense.

He expanded his enquiries to undertakers and mortuaries beyond Sussex and into all the bordering counties, without success. The woman must have had family. Perhaps they were all dead, but he hoped not. The thought made him sad. It also saddened him to think that no undertaker had noticed her absence.

The indignity of what had happened to her made matters worse too.

If she wasn't the helpless victim in some sick prank, was there something he was missing?

He replayed the scenario over and over in his mind. For what possible reason would someone steal a van and then put a dead old lady into it?

How stupid would you have to be not to know there were tests that would prove the old woman had not been driving, and that her age would be worked out?

A prank was the most likely. But where had they got the body from? Every day he was broadening his search of undertakers and mortuaries. There had to be one, somewhere in this country, that had a body that was missing. Surely?

It was a mystery that was to remain with him for the next twelve years.

NOW

79

Norman Potting sat on the green chair in the interview room in the Custody Suite adjoining the CID head-quarters. There was a window, high up, a CCTV camera and a microphone. The heavy green door, with its small viewing window, was closed and locked.

Opposite the DS, across a small table the colour of granite, sat John Kerridge, dressed in a regulation-issue, ill-fitting blue paper jump suit and plimsolls. Beside him sat a Legal Aid solicitor who had been allocated to him, Ken Acott.

Unlike many of his duty solicitor colleagues, who tended not to fuss too much about their clothing as they weren't needing to impress their clients, Acott, who was forty-four, was always impeccably dressed. Today he wore a well-cut navy suit, with a freshly laundered white shirt and a sharp tie. With his short, dark hair and genial good looks, he reminded many people of the actor Dustin Hoffman, and he had plenty of the theatrical about him, whether protesting his client's rights in an interview room or addressing the bench in a courtroom. Of all the criminal practice solicitors in the city, Ken Acott was the one that arresting officers disliked coming up against the most.

Kerridge seemed to be having problems sitting still. A

465

man of about forty, with short hair brushed forward, he was squirming, writhing, as if attempting to free himself from imaginary bonds, and repeatedly looking at his watch.

'They haven't brought my tea,' he said anxiously.

'It's on its way,' Potting assured him.

'Yes, but it's ten past,' Yac said nervously.

On the table sat a tape recorder with slots for three cassettes, one for the police, one for the defence and one file copy. Potting inserted a cassette into each slot. He was about to press the Play button when the solicitor spoke.

'DS Potting, before you waste too much of my client's time, and my own, I think you should take a look at these, which were recovered from my client's home on the *Tom Newbound* houseboat during the night.'

He pushed a large brown envelope across the table to the Detective Sergeant.

Hesitantly, Potting opened it and pulled out the contents.

'Take your time,' Acott said with an assurance that made Potting feel uneasy.

The first item was an A4 printout, which he stared at. It was a receipt from an eBay transaction for a pair of Gucci high-heeled shoes.

During the next twenty minutes, Norman Potting read, with increasing gloom, the receipts from second-hand clothes shops and eBay auctions for eighty-three of the eighty-seven pairs of shoes they had seized from the houseboat.

'Can your client account for the last four pairs?' Potting asked, sensing he was clutching at straws.

'I am told that they were left in his taxi,' Ken Acott

said. 'But as none of these, or any of the others, fit the descriptions of the ones in the recent series of attacks, I would respectfully ask that my client be released from custody immediately, so he does not suffer further loss of earnings.'

Potting insisted on proceeding with the interview. But Acott made his client reply *No comment* to every question. After an hour and a half, Potting left to speak to Roy Grace. Then he returned and conceded defeat.

'I'll accept bailing him 47(3), to come back in two months while our enquiries are continuing,' Potting suggested as a compromise.

'He also wants his property returned to him,' Ken Acott said. 'Any reason why he shouldn't have back the shoes and newspaper cuttings that were seized, his computer and his mobile phone?'

Despite a tantrum from Kerridge, Potting insisted on retaining the shoes and the cuttings. The phone and the laptop were not a problem, as the High-Tech Crime Unit had extracted all they needed from the phone, and they had cloned the hard drive of the computer, which they would continue to analyse.

Acott gave in on the shoes and cuttings, and twenty minutes later Yac was released. The solicitor drove him home with his computer and phone.

80

Thursday 15 January

It was a rush to get here and he had misjudged how heavy the seafront traffic would be. Unless he was imagining it, there seemed to be more police out than usual.

He drove into the car park behind the Grand Hotel shortly after 3 p.m., worried she might have already left. In her new blue satin Manolos. Then, to his relief, he saw her black VW Touareg.

It was in such a good place for his purposes. She could not have picked a better bay. Bless. It was one of the few areas on this level that was out of sight of any of the CCTV cameras in here.

Even better, the space beside her was empty.

And he had her car keys in his pocket. The spare set that he had found where he hoped he would, in a drawer in her hall table.

Reversing the van in, he left enough space behind him to be able to open the rear doors. Then he hurriedly climbed out to check, aware he did not have much time, then looked around carefully. The car park was deserted.

Dee Burchmore would be coming soon from her ladies' luncheon, because she had to get home – she was hosting a meeting of the West Pier Trust there at 4 p.m. Then she was due back into the city centre for drinks in the Mayor's Parlour at Brighton Town Hall at 7 p.m., where she was attending a *Crimestoppers* fund-raising event at the Police Museum. She was a model citizen, supporting lots of different causes in Brighton. And its shops.

And she was such a good girl, posting all her schedules up on Facebook.

He hoped she had not changed her mind and that she was wearing those blue satin Manolo Blahniks with the diamanté buckles. Women had a habit of changing their minds, which was one of the many things he did not like about them. He'd be very angry if she had different shoes on and would have to teach her a lesson about not disappointing people.

Of course, he would punish her even more if she *was* wearing them.

He pressed the door unlock button on the key fob. The indicators flashed and there was a quiet *clunk*. Then the interior light came on.

He pulled the solid-feeling driver's door open and climbed in, noticing the rich smell of the car's leather upholstery and traces of her perfume, Armani Code.

Glancing through the windscreen to ensure that all was clear, he checked the buttons for the interior lights, until he found the one that kept them switched off, and pressed it.

All set.

So much to think about. In particular all those CCTV cameras everywhere. It wasn't enough just to put fake number plates on the van. Many police cars drove around with onboard ANPR. These could read a number plate and in a split second get all the details of the vehicle from the licensing department in Swansea. If the registration did not match the vehicle, they would know instantly. So the registration plates he had on this van were a copy of those on an identical van to this – one he'd seen parked in a street in Shoreham.

Just to make sure that the van in Shoreham didn't go anywhere for a day or two, in case by chance they should both be spotted by the same police patrol, he'd emptied a couple of bags of sugar into its petrol tank. He liked to think he had covered every eventuality. That was how you stayed free. Always cover your tracks. Always have an explanation for everything.

He climbed across on to the back seat, then pulled the black hood over his head, adjusting it until the slits were aligned with his eyes and mouth. Then he squeezed himself down on to the floor, between the front and rear seats, out of sight to anyone peering in the window – not that they would see much through the tinted privacy glass anyway. He took a deep breath and pressed the button on the key fob to lock the doors.

Soon now.

81

Dee Burchmore had a golden rule, never to drink before she gave a talk. But afterwards, boy, did she need one! It didn't matter how many times she had done it before, standing up and speaking in public always made her nervous; and today for some reason, she didn't know why – perhaps because this was a particularly big and prestigious event – she had been even more nervous than usual giving her fund-raising speech for the Martlets hospice.

So afterwards, although she had been anxious to get home in good time to greet her guests for her 4 p.m. meeting, she'd stayed chatting to friends. Before she knew it, she'd drunk three large glasses of Sauvignon Blanc. Not smart, as she'd barely eaten one mouthful of her food.

Now, entering the car park, she felt decidedly unsteady on her legs and was having trouble focusing. She should leave the car, she realized, and take a taxi, or walk – it wasn't that far. But it had just started to rain and she did not want to get her brand-new Manolos sodden.

Even so, it was not a good idea to drive. Quite apart from the danger, she was thinking about the embarrassment it would cause to her husband if she was stopped for it. She stepped up to the pay machine, then fumbled in her bag for the ticket. As she pulled it out, it fell from her fingers.

Cursing, she knelt down, then had problems picking it up.

I'm smashed!

She tried to remember if she had an umbrella in the car. She was sure she did. And of course her flat driving shoes were in there too! Brilliant! She would put them on and walk home – and that would be the best way to sober up.

She put the ticket back in her bag, then staggered on up to Level 2.

82

He heard the echoing *clack-clack-clack* of her heels on the concrete floor. Getting closer. Walking fast.

He liked the sound of heels getting closer. He'd always liked that sound. So much better than the sound of them receding into the distance. Yet, at the same time, they had frightened him as a child. The sound of heels fading meant his mother was going out. The sound getting louder meant she was returning.

Which meant she was probably going to punish him. Or make him do things to her.

His heart thudded. He could feel the adrenalin rush, like the hit of a drug. He held his breath. She was coming nearer.

This had to be her. *Please be wearing the blue satin Manolos.*

CLUNK.

The noise startled him. It was like five simultaneous gunshots all around him, as all five door locks of the car released together. He nearly cried out.

Then another sound.

Clack-clack-clack.

Footsteps walking to the rear of the car. Followed by the hiss of the gas struts of the tailgate rising. What was she putting in there? Shopping? More shoes?

Almost silently, with a practised hand, he popped off the lid of the plastic travelling soap dish in his pocket and eased the chloroform pad out with his gloved hand. Then braced himself. In a moment she would get into the car, close the door and put her seat belt on. That was the moment he would strike.

To his total surprise, instead of the driver's door, she pulled the rear door open. He stared up at her startled face. Then she backed away in shock as she saw him.

An instant later, she screamed.

He levered himself up, made a lunge at her face with the pad, but misjudged the height of the car above the ground, stumbled and fell on his face. As he scrambled to his feet, she stepped back, screaming again, then again, then turned, running, screaming, her shoes *clack-clack-clacking*.

Shit, shit, shit, shit, shit.

He watched her, crouched in the space between the Touareg and his van for some moments, debating whether to run after her. She would be in full view of the cameras now. Someone was going to hear her screams.

Shit, shit, shit, shit, shit.

He was trying to think clearly but he couldn't. His brain was a muzz of stuff.

Got to get out, away from here.

He ran around the rear of the van, climbed in through the doors and pulled them shut, then stumbled forward, climbed over the seat-back, eased himself behind the steering wheel and started the engine. Then he shot forward out of the bay and turned left, accelerating hard, following the arrows to the down ramp and the exit.

As he turned left, he saw her halfway down the ramp, stumbling on her heels, waving her arms hysterically. All he needed to do was to accelerate and he'd wipe her out. The idea flashed through his mind. But that would bring more complications than it would solve.

She turned at the sound of his engine and waved her arms even more frantically.

'Help me! Please help me!' she screamed, stepping into his path.

He had to brake sharply to avoid hitting her.

Then, as she peered through the windscreen, her eyes widened in terror.

It was his hood, he realized. He'd forgotten he still had it on.

She backed away almost in slow motion, then turned and ran, as fast as she could again, tripping, stumbling, screaming, her shoes falling off, first the left one, then the right one.

Suddenly a fire exit door to his right opened and a uniformed police officer came running out.

He floored the accelerator, screeching the van around and down the next ramp, then raced towards the twin exit barriers.

And suddenly realized he hadn't paid his ticket.

There was no one in the booth, but in any case he didn't have time. He kept on accelerating, bracing himself for the impact. But there was no impact. The barrier flew off as if it was made of cardboard and he sped on, up into the street, and kept going, dog-legging left, then right around the rear of the hotel, until he reached the traffic lights at the seafront.

Then he remembered his hood. Hastily he tugged it off and shoved it in his pocket. Someone behind him hooted angrily. The light had turned green.

'OK, OK, OK!'

He accelerated and stalled the van. The vehicle behind hooted again.

'Fuck you!'

He started the van, jerked forward, turned right and headed west along the seafront towards Hove. He was breathing in short, sharp gulps. Disaster. This was a disaster. Had to get away from here as quickly as he could. Had to get the van off the road.

The traffic lights ahead were turning red. The drizzle had transformed his windscreen to frosted glass. For an instant he debated whether to run the lights, but a long, articulated lorry had already started moving across. He halted, nervously pounding the steering wheel with the palms of his hand, then flicked on the wipers to clear the screen.

The lorry was taking forever to move across. It was towing a bloody trailer!

Out of the corner of his eye he saw something. Someone to his right was waving at him. He turned his head and his blood froze.

It was a police car.

He was boxed in. That damned lorry towing the trailer belonged to a circus or something and was moving at the speed of a snail. Another great big artic was right behind him.

Should he get out and run?

The officer in the passenger seat continued waving at him, and pointing, with a smile. The officer pointed at his own shoulder, then at him, then back at his own shoulder again.

He frowned. What the hell was his game?

Then he realized.

The officer was telling him to put on his seat belt!

He waved back and pulled it on quickly. *Clunk-click.*

The officer gave him a thumbs-up. He returned it. All smiles.

Finally, the lorry was gone and the lights turned green. He drove on steadily, keeping strictly to the limit, until, to his relief, the police car turned off into a side street. Then he upped his speed, as fast as he dared.

One mile to go. One mile and he would be safe.

But that bitch would not be.

83

Thursday 15 January

Glenn Branson's driving had always reduced Roy Grace to a state of silent terror, but even more so since he had got his green pursuit ticket. He just hoped never to have the misfortune to be in a car when his colleague used it in earnest.

But this Thursday afternoon, as the Detective Sergeant bullied the unmarked silver Ford Focus through the Brighton rush-hour traffic, Grace was silent for a different reason. He was immersed in thought. He didn't even react as he saw the old lady step out from behind the bus and hastily jump back as they drove past well over the speed limit.

'It's OK, old-timer, I saw her!' Glenn said.

Grace did not reply. Norman Potting's suspect had been released at midday, and now this afternoon, in exactly the place the profiler, Dr Julius Proudfoot, had predicted, an attempted attack had taken place.

Of course, it might not be connected to the Shoe Man, but from the limited amount he had heard so far, it had all the hallmarks. Just how good was it going to look if the man they had released was the man who had now done this?

Glenn switched on the blues and twos to help them through the snarled-up traffic at the roundabout in front

478

of the Pier, reaching to the panel and altering the tones of the sirens every few seconds. Half the drivers in the city were either too dim-witted to be behind a steering wheel, or deaf, or blind – and some were all three, Grace thought. They passed the Old Ship Hotel, then staying on King's Road, Glenn took the traffic island at the junction with West Street on the wrong side, swerving almost suicidally across the path of an oncoming lorry.

Probably not a good idea to be driven by someone whose marriage was on the rocks and didn't think he had anything to live for any more, Grace thought suddenly. But fortunately they were approaching their destination. The odds on stepping out of the car intact, rather than being cut out of it by a fire engine rescue crew, were improving.

Moments later they turned up the road beside the Grand Hotel and stopped as they reached what looked like a full-scale siege. There were too many police cars and vans clustered around the entrance to the car park behind it to count, all with their blue-light spinners rotating.

Grace was out of the car almost before the wheels had stopped. A cluster of uniformed officers, some in high-visibility jackets and some in stab vests stood around, in front of a blue-and-white chequered crime scene tape, along with several onlookers.

The only person who seemed to be missing was reporter Kevin Spinella from the *Argus*.

One of the officers, the Duty Inspector, Roy Apps, was waiting for him.

'Second floor, chief. I'll take you up there.'

With Glenn Branson, on his phone, striding behind, they ducked under the tape and hurried into the car park.

It smelt of engine oil and dry dust. Apps updated him as they walked.

'We're lucky,' he said. 'A particularly bright young PC, Alec Davies, who was in the car park's CCTV room with the attendant, thought there might be more to this and got it all sealed off before we arrived.'

'Have you found anything?'

'Yes. Something that may be interesting. I'll show you.'

'What about the van?'

'The CCTV room at Brighton nick picked it up travelling west along Kingsway towards Hove. The last sighting was of it turning right up Queen Victoria Avenue. We dispatched all available patrols and a Road Policing Unit car to try to intercept, but so far no contact.'

'We have the index?'

'Yes. It's registered to a decorator who lives in Moulsecoomb. I've got a unit watching his house. I've also got RPU cars covering all exits from the city in the direction he was travelling, and we've got Hotel 900 up.'

Hotel 900 was the police helicopter.

They reached the second level, which was sealed off by a second crime scene tape. A tall, young uniformed constable stood in front of it with a clipboard.

'This is the lad,' Roy Apps said.

'PC Davies?' Grace said.

'Yes, sir.'

'Good work.'

'Thank you, sir.'

'Can you show me the vehicle?'

The PC looked hesitant. 'SOCO are on their way here, sir.'

'This is Detective Superintendent Grace. He's the SIO on *Operation Swordfish*,' Apps reassured him.

'Ah. OK, right. Sorry, sir. This way.'

They ducked under the tape and Grace followed him across to a row of empty parking bays, at the end of which was a shiny black Volkswagen Touareg with its rear door open.

PC Davies put out a cautionary hand as they approached, then pointed at an object on the ground, just beneath the doorsill. It looked like a wad of cotton wool. Pulling out his torch, the constable directed the beam on to it.

'What is it?' Grace asked.

'It's got a strange smell, sir,' the Constable said. 'Being so close to the scene of the attack, I thought it might have some relevance, so I didn't touch it, in case it's got fingerprints or DNA on it.'

Grace looked at the serious face of the young man and smiled. 'You've got the makings of a good detective, son.'

'That's what I'd like to do, sir, after my two years in uniform.'

'Don't wait until then. If you've done twelve months, I might be able to fast-track you into CID.'

The PC's eyes lit up. 'Thank you, sir. Thank you very much!'

Roy Grace knelt down and put his nose close to the wad. It gave off a smell that was both sweet and astringent at the same time. And almost instantly he became very slightly dizzy. He stood up and felt a little unsteady for some seconds. He was pretty sure he knew that smell, from a course in toxicology he had attended some years back.

The reports from Nicola Taylor and Roxy Pearce were remarkably similar. They tallied with statements from some of the victims of the Shoe Man in 1997. It was the same smell they had described when something had been pressed against each of their faces.

Chloroform.

84

You don't know who I am or where I am, do you, Detective Superintendent Roy Grace? Not a clue! One arrest. Then you had to let him go for lack of evidence. You're panicking.

And I'm not.

Bit of a screw-up this afternoon, I've got to admit that. But I've recovered from far worse. I've been off the radar for twelve years and now I'm back. I might go again, but rest assured, hasta la vista, baby! I'll be right back! Maybe next week, maybe next month, or next year, or next decade! When I do come back, you'll be very sorry you said that small dick thing about me.

But I'm not gone just yet. I don't want to leave with unfinished business.

I don't want to leave without giving you something to really panic about. Something that's going to make you look stupid to your new ACC boss. What's that word you used in the Argus this evening? Hunting! You said that the Shoe Man is hunting.

Well, you're right, I am! I'm hunting! Stalking!

I didn't get her at the Withdean Sports Stadium, but I'll get her tomorrow night.

I know her movements.

85

Roy Grace was not often in a bad mood, but at this Friday morning briefing he was in a truly vile one, not helped by having had a virtually sleepless night. He'd stayed in MIR-1 with some of his team until past 1 a.m., going through everything they had on the Shoe Man past and present. Then he'd gone to Cleo's house, but she had been called out within minutes of his arrival to recover a body found in a churchyard.

He'd sat up for an hour, drinking whisky and smoking one cigarette after another, thinking, thinking, thinking about what he might be missing, while Humphrey snored loudly beside him. Then he re-read a lengthy report he'd brought home, from the High-Tech Crime Unit. Their Covert Internet Investigator had come up with a whole raft of foot- and shoe-fetish websites, chat-room forums and social-networking presences. There were hundreds of them. In the past six days he'd only managed to cover a small percentage of the total. So far with nothing conclusive.

Grace put down the report with some astonishment, deciding that perhaps he'd led too sheltered a life, but not sure he would want to share any fetish he developed with a bunch of total strangers. Then he'd gone to bed and tried to sleep. But his brain was on warp drive. Cleo had come back at about 4.30 a.m., showered, then climbed into bed and fallen asleep. It always amazed him how she could deal with any kind of corpse, no matter how horrific the condition or the circumstances of the death, then come home and fall asleep in moments. Perhaps it was her ability to switch off that enabled her to cope with the stuff her job entailed.

After lying restlessly for another half-hour, totally wired, he decided to get up and go for a run down to the seafront, to try to clear his head and freshen himself up for the day ahead.

And now, at 8.30 a.m., he had a blinding headache and was shaky from a caffeine overdose; but that did not stop him from cradling yet another mug of strong black instant as he sat in the packed briefing room, his inquiry team now extended to over fifty officers and support staff.

A copy of the morning's *Argus* lay in front of him, next to a pile of documents, on the top of which was one from the Crime Policy and Review Branch. It was their '7-Day Review' of *Operation Swordfish*, which had just come in, somewhat delayed.

The *Argus* featured a photograph of a white Ford Transit on the front page, with the caption: *Similar to the one used by the suspect.*

Inset separately, and with good dramatic effect, the paper reproduced the cloned registration plate, with a request for anyone who saw this vehicle between 2 p.m. and 5 p.m. yesterday to phone the Police Incident Room or *Crimestoppers*, urgently.

The owner of the van whose registration had been cloned was not a happy bunny. He was a decorator who had been unable to leave the site where he was working to buy some materials he urgently needed because the van would not start. But at least he had the perfect alibi. From 2 p.m. to 5 p.m. yesterday, he had been at the roadside, accompanied by an RAC patrolman who had drained his van's petrol tank, and cleaned out the carburettor. In the patrolman's view, someone had very kindly emptied a bag of sugar into the tank.

Was this another of the Shoe Man's touches, Grace wondered?

The only good news so far today was that the '7-Day Review' was at least positive. It agreed with all he had done in the running of this case – at least in its first seven days. But now they were another nine days on. The next review would be at twenty-eight days. Hopefully the Shoe Man would be getting a taste of prison-issue footwear long before then.

He sipped some more coffee, then, because of the large number of people in the room for the briefing, he stood up to address them.

'So,' he said, skipping his normal introduction, 'how sodding great is this? We release our suspect at midday and in the afternoon the next offence happens. I'm not very happy about it. What's going on? Is this John Kerridge – Yac – character having a laugh on us? The bloody *Argus* certainly is!'

He held the paper aloft. The front page splash read:

SHOE MAN FOURTH VICTIM'S LUCKY ESCAPE?

There was little doubt in anyone's mind that the man who had been waiting in Dee Burchmore's car yesterday was the Shoe Man. The location and the confirmation from an emergency analysis by the path lab that the substance on the cotton wool was chloroform both pointed to it. The car was now in the SOCO workshop, where it would remain for several days, being examined for clothing fibres, hairs, skin cells or any other telltale sign the offender might have left behind, however microscopic.

The timeline, established by Norman Potting, cleared John Kerridge from involvement. The taxi driver's solicitor, Ken Acott, had driven him home to his houseboat. A neighbour had confirmed his alibi, that he was on the boat until 5.30 p.m. yesterday, when he had left to start his evening driving shift.

But there was something else, something personal, that was helping to fuel Roy Grace's mood. DC Michael Foreman had reported back that Pewe was being completely unhelpful. So far he had made no progress at all with the Detective Superintendent.

The temptation to arrest Pewe was so strong. But the words of his new ACC were even stronger.

'You mustn't let this get personal, you know.'

He had to admit to himself that to arrest Pewe now, on the flimsy evidence he had to date, would smack of being *personal*. And to arrest and then have to release a second suspect without charge would look like he was clutching at straws. Instead, reluctantly, he told Foreman to keep working on it.

To rub the final salt into the wound, Nick Nicholl had reported that he'd viewed CCTV footage from the Neville pub. The image was poor and he was having it enhanced, but it showed someone who *might* be Darren Spicer drinking there until past 1.30 a.m. on New Year's Day. If it did turn out to be him, that would clear the serial burglar of involvement in the attack on Nicola Taylor. However, the man had no corroboration for his alibi as to where he was at the time of the attack on Roxy

Pearce, other than restating he was at the greyhound stadium – a mere fifteen minutes' walk from her house. Nor did he have any corroboration for his alibi for last Saturday night, at the time when Mandy Thorpe was attacked on the ghost train at Brighton Pier.

That timeline was interesting to Roy Grace. She was attacked at around 7.30 p.m. – one hour before the curfew at St Patrick's night shelter, where Spicer was staying. He *could* have committed the attack and still been back at the shelter in time.

But the evidence at this moment was too circumstantial to warrant arresting the man. A smart brief like Ken Acott would rip them to shreds. They needed a lot more, and at this stage they did not have it.

'Right,' Grace said. 'I want to review all the facts that we have so far. Fact one: our Analysts have established that back in 1997 all five of the Shoe Man's known victims, as well as the sixth possible victim, Rachael Ryan, who disappeared never to be found, were known to have bought a new and expensive pair of designer shoes from shops in Brighton within seven days of being attacked.'

There were several nods of confirmation.

'Fact two: three of our four victims and potential victims, in the past sixteen days – including Mrs Dee Burchmore – have done the same. The exception is Mandy Thorpe. I'm including her for the present moment in our enquiries, although I personally suspect that her attacker was not the Shoe Man. But I won't go there right now.'

He looked at Julius Proudfoot. The forensic psychologist gave him a faintly hostile glare back.

'Fact three: the location of yesterday's attack fits

exactly the prediction made by our forensic psychologist. Julius, perhaps you'd like to come in at this juncture.'

Proudfoot puffed his chest out importantly. 'Yes, well, the thing is, you see, I think there's a lot more than we realize. We have a lot of imponderables, but we know a few important things about the Shoe Man. For a start, he's a very damaged man. I suspect that now he's very angry because he's been rebuffed. If, as I believe, we're dealing with someone damaged by his mother, he could be feeling hurt in a sort of *mummy's rejected me* way. A child would react by sulking, but an adult in quite a different way. It's my guess he's now in a very dangerous and violent frame of mind. He didn't get his way yesterday, but he's damned well going to soon.'

'With the same victim?' Michael Foreman asked.

'No, I think he'll move on to another one. He may return to this victim, Dee Burchmore, at some future point, but not immediately. I think he'll go for a softer target.'

'Do we know how Mrs Burchmore is?' Bella Moy asked.

Claire Westmore, the Sexual Offences Liaison Officer, replied, 'She's very traumatized, as you might expect. There's also an issue on how the offender got into her car – a Volkswagen Touareg with all the latest security bells and whistles. The spare keys are apparently missing.'

'In my experience, women are always losing keys,' Norman Potting said.

'Oh, and never men?' retorted Bella Moy.

'The Burchmores kept them in a drawer in their house,' Claire Westmore went on, ignoring both of them. 'Which raises the question whether the offender might have entered the house and stolen them at some point. They are both extremely distressed about this possibility.'

'*Penetrating* the victim's home!' Proudfoot announced, with a triumphant smile. 'The Shoe Man would enjoy that. It's all part of his gratification.'

'We know he's got breaking and entering skills,' Bella Moy said. 'His attack on Roxy Pearce and his previous attack in the private house in 1997 show that.'

'Darren Spicer's speciality,' Glenn Branson said. 'Right? This fits with him.'

'There's something else which might be significant,' Proudfoot said. 'In 1997 all five of the Shoe Man's attacks occurred late at night. This new spate, apart from New Year's Eve, have taken place mid-afternoon or early evening. This indicates to me the possibility that he might have married, which would explain why he stopped offending. Something is now wrong in the marriage, which is why he has started again.'

DS Bella Moy raised her hand. 'I'm sorry, I don't understand your reasoning – about why he would be attacking earlier just because he's married.'

'Because he needs to be home at night to avoid arousing suspicion,' Proudfoot replied.

'Or be back in time for evening lock-in at St Patrick's night shelter?' Bella responded.

'Possibly so, indeed,' Proudfoot conceded. 'Yes, that too.'

'So how would he have got away with it on New Year's Eve if he was married?' Michael Foreman asked. 'Has anyone checked the meter in this man Kerridge's taxi? Would that not show what he was doing at the time of the Metropole attack on Nicola Taylor?'

'I've spoken to the owner of the taxi he drives and

requested the full log since 31 December,' Potting answered. 'At this stage we just don't have enough evidence to justify impounding the taxi and having the meter analysed.'

'What do we need, in your view, Norman?' Roy Grace asked.

'The shoes of the victims, boss. Or forensic evidence linking Kerridge with them. We don't have it, not yet. Not without rearresting him. He gives the impression of being a harmless nutter who likes shoes. The brief tells me he has mental health issues. He's on the autism spectrum.'

'Does that give him some kind of exemption from prosecution for rape?' Glenn Branson asked.

'It makes the interrogation process a lot harder,' Grace said. 'We'd have to have him assessed, go through all that procedure. DS Potting's right. We don't have enough on him.' He sipped some coffee. 'Were you able to ascertain, Norman, if Kerridge has carried any of the victims in his taxi, as passengers?'

'I showed him all their photos,' he said. 'He claims not to recognize any of them.'

Grace turned to DC Nicholl. 'How soon will you have the enhancement of the CCTV images from the Neville pub?'

'Later today, I hope, sir.'

Proudfoot went on. 'I've been doing some more geographic profiling, which I think we're going to find helpful.'

He turned and pointed at a large map of the central area of the city attached to the whiteboard on the wall behind him. Five red circles were drawn on it.

'I talked you through the offender matrix of the Shoe Man back in 1997 and the current attacks. After his botched attack, the Shoe Man's first reported rape in 1997 was at the Grand Hotel. His first reported attack this year was at the Metropole Hotel – which is almost next door. His second reported attack in 1997 was in a house in Hove Park Road and his second reported attack this year was in a house in Droveway Avenue, one street north. His third attack then was under the pier – then known as the Palace Pier. His third attack now was on the ghost train of this same pier. His fourth attack then was in the Churchill Square car park. Now we have yesterday's attack, in the car park behind the Grand Hotel. A few hundred yards south.'

He paused to let the significance sink in. 'The fifth attack, if Detective Superintendent Grace is correct, occurred in Eastern Terrace, just off Paston Place and St James's Street.' He turned back to the map and pointed at the fifth circle. 'In the absence of anything better to go on, I'm going to predict that the Shoe Man's next attack will take place in a location close to this. He's wounded by his last failure. He's angry. He's likely to default to his comfort zone.' Proudfoot pointed to the street above and the street below St James's. 'Eastern Road and Marine Parade. Now, Marine Parade has only buildings on one side – it has the promenade on the other. Eastern Road is the one that is most similar to St James's. There's a warren of streets running off it and that's where I think he is most likely to strike again, either tonight or tomorrow. My guess is tomorrow is more likely, because the streets will be a bit busier, giving him more cover.'

'Eastern Road is a long road,' DC Foreman said.

'If I had a crystal ball, I'd give you a house number,' Proudfoot said, with a smug grin. 'But if I was running this operation, that's where I would concentrate.'

'Do you think he has selected his next victim already?' Grace asked.

'I may have something interesting on that,' the Analyst, Ellen Zoratti, cut in. 'Something I'd like you to see.'

86

Ellen Zoratti picked up a remote control and pressed a button. A white screen lowered, covering Julius Proud-foot's map.

'We know that the room where the first victim of the Shoe Man was raped, in the Grand Hotel in 1997, was booked in the name of Marsha Morris,' she said. 'We also know that the room where Nicola Taylor was raped in the Metropole on New Year's morning was also booked in this same name. I've now got the CCTV footage from the front desk at the Metropole and I'd like you to see it. Unfortunately they don't have sound.'

Ellen pressed the remote again. A time-delay sequence of grainy black-and-white images appeared. They showed several people with luggage queuing at the front desk of the hotel. She put down the remote, picked up a laser pointer and shone the red dot on the head of a female figure standing in the queue. She had bouffant, shoulder-length blonde hair, huge dark glasses masking much of the top half of her face and a shawl wound around her neck that concealed most of her mouth and chin.

'I believe this is *Marsha Morris*, checking in at the Metropole at 3 p.m. on New Year's Eve, just over two weeks ago. Now, look very closely at her hair, OK?'

She pressed the remote and the scene changed to a time-delay sequence of CCTV images from one of Brighton's premier shopping areas, East Street.

'I came across this in a trawl of CCTV images from all cameras in close proximity to shoe shops in the city. There are several within a couple of hundred yards of this particular camera. They include Last, L. K. Bennett, Russell and Bromley, and Jones. Now take a look at this footage.'

In the next sequence of frames an elegantly dressed woman in her forties, with flyaway blonde hair, wearing a long dark coat and high-heeled boots, strode confidently along towards the camera, then passed it.

'That's Dee Burchmore, who was attacked yesterday,' Ellen Zoratti said. 'This footage was recorded last Saturday, 10 January. Keep watching!'

Moments later a slim woman with light, bouffant hair, wearing a long camel coat, a shawl around her neck, a shoulder bag and shiny wet-look boots, strode into view. She had a determined air, as if on a mission.

An instant later she collided with a man walking in the opposite direction and fell sprawling to the ground. The bouffant hair, which was a wig, rolled on to the pavement. A pedestrian stopped, blocking their view of the man's exposed head.

Within seconds she – or, as looked more likely, he – had grabbed the wig and jammed it, slightly crookedly, back on to her head. Then she scrambled to her feet, checked her handbag and an instant later hurried out of frame, hands up, adjusting the wig.

It was impossible, from the angle of the camera and the poor quality of the image, to make out the person's features. Other than that they were distinctly masculine.

'Marsha Morris?' said Michael Foreman.

'You can always tell them shemale poofs by their Adam's apples,' Potting said. 'That's the giveaway.'

'Actually, Norman,' said Bella Moy, 'I've read that they can have them surgically removed now – or at least reduced. And I'm not quite sure why you're calling them *poofs*?'

'This person was wearing a roll neck,' Nick Nicholl said, ignoring them. 'Whether he – or she – had an Adam's apple or not, it couldn't be seen.'

'Is that the enhanced image, Ellen?' Grace said.

'I'm afraid so, sir,' she replied. 'It's the clearest I could get from the lab. Not great, but it tells us a couple of important things. The first is that the Shoe Man might stalk his victims in drag. The second is that Mrs Burchmore bought an expensive pair of shoes that day. Take a look at this next sequence. I'm afraid the image quality is also poor, it was taken from the shop's own CCTV.'

She pressed the remote control and on the screen appeared the interior of a shoe shop, again in a sequence of frames from a static camera.

'This is one of the Profile shops in Duke's Lane,' Ellen said.

A blonde woman was sitting on a chair, hunched over what looked like her iPhone or BlackBerry, pecking at the keys. Ellen pointed the red laser dot on her face.

'This is Dee Burchmore, five minutes on from the footage you just saw in East Street.'

An assistant jerked into frame, holding a pair of high-heeled shoes.

In the background, the camera showed a woman with bouffant hair, in a long coat, dark glasses and a shawl covering much of the lower part of her face, entering the shop. It was the same person they had just seen fall over.

Ellen pointed the laser dot on her.

'It's good old Marsha Morris again!' DC Foreman said. 'With her wig back on the right way around!'

They watched the transvestite jerk left and right across the frame in the background, while Dee Burchmore purchased her shoes. She then appeared to chat to the assistant at the counter as the young woman entered details on her computer keypad. Marsha Morris stood close by, appearing to examine some shoes, but clearly listening.

Then Dee Burchmore left with her purchase in a carrier bag.

After only a few seconds, Marsha Morris also left. Then Ellen halted the tape.

'Do we know,' asked Norman Potting, 'if the person who attacked Dee Burchmore yesterday was in drag?'

'He was wearing a dark hood with eye slits,' Claire Westmore said. 'It's the only description she's been able to give so far. But historically the only two attacks in which the Shoe Man wore drag were at the Grand Hotel, in 1997, and early on New Year's Day, at the Metropole. None of the subsequent victims has mentioned drag.'

'I think he's wearing it as a disguise,' Proudfoot said. 'Not for sexual gratification. It's gets him into ladies' shoe shops without suspicion and it's a good disguise at the hotels.'

Grace nodded in agreement.

Proudfoot went on: 'Looking at the case file from 1997, the victim who was attacked in the Churchill Square car park was a creature of habit. She always parked in the same car park, on the top floor, because it was the emptiest. There's a parallel with Dee Burchmore, who always parked on Level 2 of the car park behind the Grand Hotel. They both made it very easy for someone stalking them.'

The SOLO added, 'Dee has told me that she regularly posts her movements on the social networking sites Facebook and Twitter. I've had a look at some of her posts over this past week and it wouldn't have taken a rocket scientist to plot her whereabouts on an almost hourly basis. All three previous victims have had a Facebook presence for a while also, and Mandy Thorpe Tweeted regularly as well.'

'So,' Nick Nicholl said, 'we've narrowed the Shoe Man's next victim down to someone who's bought an expensive pair of shoes in the past week and has a presence on either Facebook or Twitter, or both.' He grinned.

'We might be able to be more specific than that,' Ellen Zoratti said. 'The age of the victims could be significant. Nicola Taylor is thirty-eight, Roxy Pearce is thirty-six, Mandy Thorpe is twenty, and Dee Burchmore is forty-two. These four ages correspond closely to the age range of the Shoe Man's victims back in 1997.'

The Crime Analyst paused to let this sink in, then went on: 'If Detective Superintendent Grace is correct that Rachael Ryan was the Shoe Man's fifth victim back in 1997, maybe it can help us narrow down who his next will be now – assuming there will be another one.'

'There will be,' Proudfoot said confidently.

'Rachael Ryan was twenty-two years old,' Ellen said. She turned to the forensic psychologist. 'Dr Proudfoot, you've already told us you think the Shoe Man could be repeating his pattern because that's his comfort zone. Might that comfort zone extend to the age of his next victim? Someone of corresponding age to his fifth victim in 1997? A twenty-two-year-old?'

Proudfoot nodded pensively. 'We can't be sure about Rachael Ryan, of course,' he said pompously, and gave Roy Grace a pointed look. 'But if we assume for the moment that Mandy Thorpe was a victim of the Shoe Man and that Roy is right about Rachael Ryan, then yes, Ellen, your assumption is one we shouldn't rule out. It's very possible he'll go for someone of that age. If he attacked poor Rachael Ryan, and she's never been found, and he's never been caught for whatever he did to her, then it's quite likely, after yesterday's shock, that he'll go for the familiar. Someone more vulnerable than an experienced middle-aged woman. Someone who'll be a soft touch. Yes, I think that's who we should be focusing on. Young women in high heels and with a Facebook presence.'

'Which means just about every young woman in Brighton and Hove. And everywhere else in this country,' E-J said.

'There can't be that many who can afford the prices of the shoes that attract the Shoe Man,' Bella Moy said. 'I would think we could get a list of recent customers in that age bracket from the local shops.'

'Good thinking, Bella, but we haven't got the time,' Grace said.

'It could be narrowed down, sir,' Ellen Zoratti said. 'The connection could be this person in the bouffant wig. If we could find footage of a woman in her early twenties in a shop and footage of this person close to her, we might have something.'

'We've had the Outside Inquiry team viewing all the footage they can from cameras inside shoe shops, but it's a nightmare, because of the January sales,' Bella Moy said. 'I've been in the CCTV room at Brighton nick, looking at footage from cameras close to some of the city's shoe shops. There are hundreds of people of that age out and about shopping. And the problem is there's hundreds and hundreds of hours of CCTV footage.'

Grace nodded.

'Sir,' Claire Westmore said, 'a lot of shoe shops these days take down customer details for their mailing lists. The chances are that the shop that has sold – or has yet to sell – the shoes of the next potential victim will have her name and address on its system.'

Grace considered this. 'Yes, worth a try. We have a list of all the shops in the city that sell expensive designer shoes.' He looked down at his notes. 'Twenty-one of them. The victim is likely to have bought her shoes within the past week – if she has bought them yet. We could try a trawl of all the shops, and get the names and addresses of all the customers who fit this profile who've bought shoes, but with the resources we have this is going to take days. Our problem is we don't have the luxury of that time.'

'How about putting out some decoys, sir?' DC Boutwood said.

'Decoys?'

'Send some of us out shopping.'

'You mean send you out to buy expensive shoes?'

She nodded, beaming. 'I'd volunteer!'

Grace grimaced. 'Women and nice shoes in the January sales. It's like looking for a bloody needle in a haystack! We'd need dozens of decoys to hit the right shops at the right times. Dr Proudfoot thinks the Shoe Man will attack again tonight or tomorrow.' He shook his head. 'It's an interesting idea, E-J, but it's too much of a long shot – and we just don't have the time. We need to get the Eastern Road area under observation by 3 p.m. today.'

He looked at his watch. It was coming up to 9 a.m. He had just six hours.

The CCTV surveillance camera was a clever invention, Roy Grace thought. But there was a big issue with them. There were currently hundreds of cameras running 24/7 in this city. But there simply wasn't the manpower to physically examine all the footage – and half of it was crap quality anyway. He needed some kind of super computer program to check it automatically – and he didn't have one. All he had was a limited number of human beings with limited concentration spans.

'Sir, you were involved yourself with the Rachael Ryan disappearance, weren't you?' Ellen Zoratti said.

Grace smiled. 'I still am. The file's still open. But yes, I was, very involved. I interviewed the two friends she had been out with on that Christmas Eve several times. Rachael was into shoes, big time, which was why I've always suspected the Shoe Man's involvement. She'd bought a very expensive pair of shoes a week before, from Russell and Bromley in East Street, I think.' He shrugged. 'That's another reason I'm not sure we'd gain anything by sending people out shopping today. I think he plans ahead.'

'Unless he's feeling frustrated by yesterday, chief,' Glenn Branson said. 'And just decides to go for someone at random.'

'Our best hope at the moment,' Proudfoot said, 'is that after yesterday afternoon he's feeling rattled, and that maybe he'll rush into something unprepared. Perhaps you succeeded in rattling his cage by insulting his manhood in the *Argus* – which is how he came to make his mistake.'

'Then I think we'd better find a way of rattling his cage again, and this time even harder,' Grace said.

87

The job at the Grand Hotel was not working out the way Darren Spicer had hoped. There were security systems in place to prevent him creating his own room keys on the system, and a supervisor who kept watch on him and his co-workers from the minute he started in the morning to the minute he signed off each evening.

Sure, he was getting paid for his work, renovating the hotel's antiquated electrical system, replacing miles of wiring along its labyrinth of basement corridors, where the laundry, kitchens, boilers, emergency generators and stores were housed. But in taking this particular job, he'd had hopes of being able to do a little more than spend his days unspooling lengths of new electric cables from huge reels and hunt for wires chewed by mice.

He'd imagined he would be getting access to the 201 bedrooms, and the contents left in their safes by their well-off occupants, but so far this first week he had not found a way. He needed to be patient, he knew. He could do patience all right. He was very patient when he fished, or when he waited outside a house he planned to burgle for the occupants to go out.

But there was such temptation here, he was keen to get started.

Because 201 bedrooms meant 201 bedroom safes!

And the hotel was busy, 80 per cent occupancy all year round.

A mate in prison had told him the way to do hotel safes. Not how to break into them – he didn't need that, he had all the kit he needed for the safes in the Grand. No, this was how to steal from safes without getting found out.

It was simple: you stole only a little. You mustn't get greedy. If someone left 200 quid in cash or some foreign currency, you took just a small amount. Always cash, never jewellery; people missed jewellery, but they weren't going to miss twenty quid out of 200. Do that ten times a day and you were on to a nice little earner. A grand a week. Fifty Gs in a year. Yeah. Nice.

He had made his decision that he was going to keep out this time. Stay free. Sure, Lewes Prison had more comforts than St Patrick's night shelter, but soon he'd get his MiPod, then hopefully, a couple of months after he'd have enough cash together for a deposit on his own place. Something modest to start with. Then find himself a woman. Save, maybe get enough cash together to rent a flat. And maybe one day buy one. Ha! That was his dream.

But at this moment, trudging back along Western Road towards St Patrick's, at 6.30 on this freezing, dry Friday night, shoulders stooped, hands in the pockets of his donkey jacket, the dream was a long way off.

He stopped in a pub, the Norfolk Arms by Norfolk Square, and had a pint with a whisky chaser. Both tasted good. This was something he missed when doing bird. The freedom to have a drink in a pub. Simple things like that. Life's little pleasures. He bought a second pint, took it on to the pavement and smoked a cigarette. An old man, who was also holding a pint and was puffing on a pipe, tried to strike up a conversation, but Spicer ignored him. He was thinking. He couldn't just rely on the hotel, he was going to have to do other stuff. Emboldened by his drinks, he was thinking, *Why not start now?*

Between 4 and 5 on winter afternoons was a good time for burgling homes. It was dark but people were still out at work. Now was a bad time, for homes. But there was a place he'd seen on his walk around his neighbourhood in Hove last Sunday, when he'd been looking for opportunities. A place that, around 6.30 on a Friday evening, was almost certain to be unoccupied. A place that had intrigued him.

A place, he was sure, that had possibilities.

He finished his drink and his cigarette without hurrying. He had plenty of time to go to St Patrick's and get the bag containing all the specialist kit he'd acquired or made himself over the years. He could do this job and still be back at the night shelter by lock-in time. Yeah, for sure.

Lock-in, he thought, the drink definitely getting to him a little. *Lock-in, lock-up.*

That made him grin.

'Want to share the joke?' the old man with the pipe said.

Spicer shook his head. 'Not really,' he said. 'Nah.'

88

At 6.45 p.m., Roy Grace, running on adrenalin and caffeine, sat in a small office at the end of the Ops Room, on the third floor of Brighton Central police station. The John Street location of the huge, six-storey building, right on the edge of Kemp Town and just a couple of hundred yards from Edward Street – part of the area where Julius Proudfoot was predicting the Shoe Man's next attack would take place – made it ideal for this current operation.

In the short space of time since this morning's briefing, with the aid of some helpful pressure in the right places from ACC Rigg, the Detective Superintendent had assembled a Covert Team of twenty officers, and was busily working on increasing that to his target of thirty-five for tomorrow.

He currently had a surveillance team of eight out on the streets, on foot and in vehicles, and another twelve, including some members of his own inquiry team, together with several constables, Specials and PCSOs he had commandeered, who were located in buildings at strategic intervals along Edward Street and Eastern Road – as it became – and some of the nearby side streets. Most of them, as was common in surveillance, were in upstairs rooms of private houses or flats, with the consent of their owners.

A bank of CCTV monitors covered most of the wall in

front of his desk. Grace could instantly call up on them views from any of the 350 cameras situated around the city's downtown area, as well as zooming, panning and tilting them. The room was used for the officer in charge, the Gold Commander, at all major public order events, such as party political conferences or for monitoring major demonstrations, and for major operations in the city, as this had now become.

His number two on this, his Silver Commander, was the Crime and Ops Superintendent at John Street, who was currently in the Ops Room, liaising by secure radio with the two Bronze commanders. One, a female detective inspector who ran the Force Surveillance Teams from CID headquarters, was out in an unmarked car, coordinating the street surveillance team. The other, Roy Apps, a senior uniform inspector at John Street, was running the static team, who radioed in anything of potential interest from their observation points.

So far all had been quiet. To Grace's relief it was not raining – many police officers jokingly referred to foul weather as *policeman rain*. Crime levels always dropped during heavy rain. It seemed that villains didn't like getting wet any more than anyone else did. Although the Shoe Man appeared, on past form, to have a penchant for light drizzle.

The rush hour was drawing to an end and Eastern Road was quietening down. Grace flicked through all the screens showing views close to his observation points. He stopped as he saw one unmarked surveillance car slow down and park.

Taking a quick break, he phoned Cleo, telling her he was likely to be late and not to wait up. She was exhausted after last night, she said, and was going to bed early.

'I'll try not to wake you,' he said.

'I *want* you to wake me,' she replied. 'I want to know you're home safe.'

He blew her a kiss and turned back to his task.

Suddenly his internal command phone rang. It was the Silver Commander.

'Boss,' he said. 'Just had an alert from an RPU car – it's picked up the index of the taxi driven by John Kerridge on its ANPR and just clocked it turning left into Old Steine from the seafront.'

Grace tensed, feeling the hollow sensation he often got in the pit of his stomach when things were starting.

'OK, alert the Bronzes.'

'I'm on to it.'

Grace switched his radio to pick up all comms from the Bronzes to any members of their team. He was just in time to hear the excited voice of one of the surveillance team, through a radio crackling with interference, 'Target turning right-right, into Edward Street!'

Moments later there was a response from an observation post just to the east of John Street. 'Target passing, continuing east-east. Hang on – he's stopping. Picking up one male passenger.'

Bugger! Grace thought. *Bugger! Bugger!*

If Kerridge stopped for a passenger, that meant he wasn't hunting. Yet it seemed curious that he had turned into the very area where they suspected the next attack would take place.

Coincidence?

He wasn't so sure. Something about this John Kerridge character bothered him. From his years of experience, offenders like the Shoe Man often turned out to be oddball loners and Kerridge ticked that box. They might have had to let him go because of lack of evidence at this moment, but that did not mean he wasn't their man.

If I was driving a cab, plying for fares, why would I drive along almost deserted Eastern Road at this time on a Friday night? Why not along St James's Street, one street to the south, which was always teeming with people? Or North Street, or London Road, or Western Road?

He phoned Streamline Taxis, stated who he was and asked if John Kerridge had been sent to Eastern Road to do a pick-up. The controller confirmed back to him that he had.

Grace thanked her. So there was an innocent explanation for the taxi driver's presence here.

But he still had a bad feeling about him.

89

Spicer was perspiring, despite the cold. The innocuous-looking Tesco supermarket carrier bag, filled with his tools, weighed a ton, and the walk from St Patrick's to the junction with The Drive and Davigdor Road seemed much further tonight than it had on Sunday. The two pints of beer and the whisky chaser, which an hour ago had fuelled his courage, were now sapping his energy.

The old apartment block loomed on his left. The traffic on the road was light and he had passed few pedestrians on his way here. Half a dozen vehicles on his right, travelling north up The Drive, were waiting for the red light to change. Spicer slowed his pace, also waiting for it to change, not wanting to risk anyone noticing him, just in case. You never knew . . .

Finally the cars moved off. Hurriedly, he turned left, down the steep driveway beside the apartment block, crossed the car park at the front and walked around the side of the building, towards the row of lock-up garages around the corner at the rear that were in almost total darkness, lit only by the glow of lights from some of the apartment windows above.

He walked along to the one at the far left end, the one that had interested him so much on his recce on

Sunday. All of the others had just a single, basic lock inset into their door handles. But this one had four heavy-duty deadlocks, two on each side. You didn't put locks like that on a garage unless you had something of serious value inside.

Of course, it could just be a vintage car, but even then he knew a dealer who would pay good money for instruments from vintage cars; steering wheels, gear levers, badges, bonnet mascots and anything else that could be removed. But, if he was lucky, he might find a stash of valuables of some kind. He knew from his years of experience that burglars like himself favoured anonymous lock-up garages as storage depots. He'd used one himself for many years. They were good places to keep valuables that could be easily identified by their owners until things had quietened down and he could then fence them, maybe a year or so later.

He stood still in the darkness, looking up at the apartment building, checking for shadows at the window that might signal someone looking out. But he could see no one.

Quickly, he delved into his bag and set to work on the first of the locks. It yielded after less than a minute. The others followed suit, equally easily.

He stepped back into the shadows and again checked all around him and above. No sign of anyone.

He pulled open the up-and-over door, then stood still in astonishment, for some moments, absorbing what he was looking at. This was not what he had expected at all.

He stepped inside nervously, yanked the door down behind him, pulled his torch out of his carrier and switched it on.

'Oh shit,' he said, as the beam of light confirmed it for him.

Scared as hell, he backed out, his thoughts in a whirl. With trembling hands he locked it up again, not wanting to leave any tracks. Then he hurried away into the night.

90

Saturday 17 January

Facebook

Jessie Sheldon

View photos of me (128)

Jessie now has 253 friends on Facebook

Benedict's meeting my parents tonight at
charity ball for first time. I'm nervous!!! Got my
early-evening kick-boxing class first, so if there
are any issues and they start being horrible to
him, they'd better watch out. And . . . will be
wearing my new Anya Hindmarch shoes with
five-inch stilettos!!!!

He read Jessie's latest Facebook entry with a thin smile.
*You are so good to me, Jessie. You let me down at the
Withdean Sports Stadium, but you won't let me down
tonight, will you? You will finish your kick-boxing at the
usual time, then walk back the half-mile to your Sudeley
Place flat and change into your beautiful dress and your
new shoes – dressed to kill. Then you will step out into
Benedict's car, which will be waiting outside. That's your
plan, isn't it?*

Sorry to be a party pooper . . .

91

Because of the surveillance operation, Roy Grace had cancelled yesterday's evening briefing. Now, at the 8.30 a.m. Saturday briefing, there was a whole twenty-four hours of activity for the team to catch up on.

Plenty of activity but little progress.

Ellen Zoratti and her colleague analyst still had no results in their nationwide trawl of sexual offences that could be linked to the Shoe Man and the High-Tech Crime Unit still had no potential leads for them.

The Outside Inquiry Team's questioning of the managers and working girls at all thirty-two of the city's known brothels was now complete and had produced nothing tangible so far. Several of their regular punters had shoe or feet fetishes, but as none of the managers kept names and addresses of their clientele, all they could do was promise to phone when any of them next made an appointment.

It was looking more and more as if whatever the Shoe Man might have been up to during these past twelve years, he'd done a damned good job of keeping it quiet.

Last night had also been quiet. The whole city had felt like a graveyard. Having partied hard over the Christmas holidays, it seemed that now its inhabitants, last night at least, were well and truly homebodies in recovery mode and feeling the bite of the recession. And despite his team's long vigil, there had been no further sighting of taxi driver John Kerridge – Yac – since his earlier, brief appearance in the area.

One positive was that Grace now had the full surveillance complement of thirty-five officers he needed to blanket cover the Eastern Road vicinity tonight. If the Shoe Man showed up, his team was going to be ready for him.

Dr Julius Proudfoot remained confident that he would.

As the meeting ended, an internal phone began ringing. Glenn Branson made his way towards the exit of the packed Conference Room to call Ari – he'd blocked one from her during the briefing. He knew why she was calling, which was to ask him to take the kids today. No chance, he thought sadly. Much though he would have given anything to have been able to.

But just as he stepped out through the doorway, Michael Foreman called out to him, 'Glenn! For you!'

He squeezed back through the crowd of people leaving and picked up the receiver, which Foreman had laid on the table.

'DS Branson,' he answered.

'Oh, yeah. Er, hello, Sergeant Branson.'

He frowned as he recognized the rough-sounding voice.

'It's *Detective* Sergeant Branson,' he corrected.

'Darren Spicer here. We met, at the—'

'I know who you are.'

'Look, I have – er – what you might call a delicate situation here.'

'Lucky you.'

Branson was anxious to get him off the line and call
Ari. She always hated it when he killed her incoming
calls. He'd also found another unwelcome letter from her
solicitor awaiting him at Roy Grace's house, when he'd
finally got home last night, or rather earlier this morning,
and he wanted to talk to her about it.

Spicer gave him a half-hearted, uncertain laugh.
'Yeah, well, I've got a problem. I need to ask you a
question.'

'Fine, ask it.'

'Yeah, well, you see – I got this problem.'

'You just told me that. What's your question?'

'Well, it's like – if I said to you that I was, like – like,
I saw something, right? Like – someone I know saw
something, like, when they were somewhere that they
shouldn't ought to be? Yeah? If they, like, gave you information that you really needed, would you still prosecute
them because they were somewhere they shouldn't have
been?'

'Are you trying to tell me you were somewhere you
shouldn't have been and saw something?'

'It wasn't like I breached my licence restrictions or
anything. It wasn't like that.'

'Do you want to come to the point?'

Spicer was silent for a moment, then said, 'If I saw
something that might help you catch your Shoe Man,
would that give me immunity? You know, from
prosecution.'

'I haven't got that power. Calling to collect the
reward, are you?'

There was a sudden silence at the other end, then
Spicer said, '*Reward?*'

'That's what I said.'

'Reward for what?'

'The reward for information leading to the arrest of the man who attacked Mrs Dee Burchmore on Thursday afternoon. It's been put up by her husband. Fifty thousand pounds.'

Another silence, then, 'I didn't know about that.'

'No one does yet, he only informed us this morning. We're about to pass it on to the local media, so you've got a head start. So, anything you'd like to tell me?'

'I don't want to go back inside. I want to stay out, you know, try to make a go of it,' Spicer said.

'If you've got information, you could call *Crimestoppers* anonymously and give it to them. They'll pass it on to us.'

'I wouldn't get the reward then, would I, if it was anonymous?'

'Actually, I believe you might. But you're aware that withholding information's an offence, aren't you?' Branson said.

Instantly he detected the panic rising in the old lag's voice.

'Yeah, but wait a minute. I'm phoning you, to be helpful, like.'

'Very altruistic of you.'

'Very what?'

'I think you'd better tell me what you know.'

'What about if I just give you an address? Would that qualify me for the reward if you find something there?'

'Why don't you stop fucking about and tell me what you have?'

92

Shortly after 2 p.m. Roy Grace drove in through the front entrance of a large, tired-looking apartment block, Mandalay Court, then down an incline at the side, as he had been directed. He was curious to see what Darren Spicer's tip-off revealed.

As he headed around the rear of the building, his wipers clearing away a few tiny spots of drizzle, he saw a long row of shabby lock-up garages that did not look like they had been used for years. At the far end were three vehicles: Glenn Branson's unmarked silver Ford Focus, identical to the one Grace had come in; the little blue van, which he presumed belonged to the locksmith; and the white police van, containing two members of the Local Support Team, who had been requested in case they had to break their way in, and had brought a battering ram with them as backup. Not that there were many doors, in Grace's experience, that could defeat ever-cheery Jack Tunks, whose day job was maintaining the locks at Lewes Prison.

Tunks, in heavy-duty blue overalls, a grimy bag of tools on the ground beside him, was busy inspecting the locks.

Grace climbed out of the car, holding his torch, and greeted his colleague, then nodded towards the last of the garages in the row. 'This the one?'

'Yep. No. 17, not very clearly marked.' Branson double-checked the search warrant that had been signed half an hour ago by a local magistrate. 'Yep.'

'Blimey,' Tunks said. 'What's he got in there? The blooming crown jewels?'

'Does seem a lot of locks,' Grace agreed.

'Whoever's had these put on isn't messing about. I'll guarantee the door's reinforced behind too.'

Grace detected a degree of grudging respect in his voice. The recognition of one professional's work by another.

While Tunks applied himself to his task, Grace stood rubbing his hands against the cold. 'What do we know about the owner of this garage?' he asked Branson.

'I'm on to it. Got two PCSOs going round the apartment block now so see if anyone knows who the owner is, or at least one of the tenants. Otherwise I'll see what we can get from the Land Registry online.'

Grace nodded, dabbed a drip from his nose with his handkerchief, then sniffed. He hoped he didn't have a cold coming – he especially didn't want to give any infection to Cleo while she was pregnant.

'You've checked this is the only way in?'

The Detective Sergeant, who was wearing a long, cream, belted mackintosh, with epaulettes, and shiny brown leather gloves, made a *duh!* motion with his head, rocking it from side to side. 'I know I'm not always the sharpest tack in the box, old-timer, but yeah, I did check.'

Grace grinned, then took a walk around the side to check for himself. It was a long garage, but there was no window or rear door. Returning to Branson, he said, 'So, what news on the Ari front?'

'Ever see that film *War of the Roses*?'

He thought for a moment. 'Michael Douglas?'

'You got it. And Kathleen Turner and Danny DeVito. Everything gets smashed up. We're about there – only worse.'

'Wish I could give you some advice, mate,' Grace said.

'I can give you some,' Glenn replied. 'Don't bother getting married. Just find a woman who hates you and give her your house, your kids and half your income.'

The locksmith announced he was done, and pulled the door back and up a few inches, to show it was now free. 'Would one of you like to do the honours?' he said, and stepped away, a tad warily, as if worried a monster was going to leap out.

Branson took a deep breath and pulled the door up. It was much heavier than he had imagined. Tunks was right, it had been reinforced with steel plating.

As the door clanged home on its rollers, sliding parallel with the roof, all of them stared into the interior.

It was empty.

In the shadows they could make out an uneven dark stain towards the far end, which looked like it had been made by a parked vehicle dripping oil. Roy Grace detected a faint, car-park smell of warm vehicle. On the right-hand side of the far end wall was floor-to-ceiling wooden shelving. An old, bald-looking vehicle tyre was propped against the left-hand side. A couple of spanners and an old claw hammer hung from hooks on the wall to their left. But nothing else.

Glenn stared gloomily into the void. 'Having a laugh on us, is he?'

Grace said nothing as he shone his torch around the walls, then the ceiling.

'I'll tear fucking Spicer's head off!' Glenn said.

Then they both saw it at the same time, as the beam fell on the two plain, flat strips of plastic on the floor. They strode forward. Grace snapped on a pair of latex gloves, then knelt and picked the up first strip.

It was a vehicle front registration plate, black lettering on a reflective white surface.

He recognized the index instantly. It was the cloned registration on the van which had shot away from the Grand Hotel car park on Thursday afternoon, almost certainly driven by the Shoe Man.

The second plastic strip was the rear plate.

Had they found the Shoe Man's lair?

Grace walked across to the end wall. On one shelf was a row of grey duct-tape rolls. The rest of the shelves were bare.

Glenn Branson started walking across to the left wall. Grace stopped him. 'Don't trample everywhere, mate. Let's try to retrace our steps, leave it as clean as we can for SOCO – I want to get them in here right away.'

He looked around carefully, thinking. 'Do you think that's what Spicer saw? These licence plates?'

'I don't think he's smart enough to have put two and two together from just licence plates. I think he saw something else.'

'Such as?'

'He won't talk unless we give him immunity. I have to say, at least he was smart relocking the door.'

'I'll speak to the ACC,' Grace said, stepping as lightly as he could on the way back out. 'We need to know what he saw in here. We need to know what might have been here that isn't here now.'

'You mean he could have nicked something?'

'No,' he replied. 'I don't think Spicer nicked what was

in here. I think what he probably saw in here was a white van. An engine's been running in here within the last few hours. If the van's gone, then where the hell is it? And, more to the point, *why's* it gone? Go and talk to him. Twist his arm. Tell him if he wants a crack at that reward, he has to tell us what he saw, otherwise no deal.'

'He's scared he'll get banged up again for breaking and entering.'

Grace looked at his mate. 'Tell him to lie, to say that the door was open, unlocked. I'm not interested in nicking him for breaking and entering.'

Branson nodded. 'OK, I'll go and talk to him. Just had a thought – if you put SOCO in and the Shoe Man returns and sees them, he'll do a runner. Aren't we smarter having someone covert watching it? Get Tunks to lock it up again so he doesn't know we've been here?'

'Assuming he's not watching us now,' Grace said.

Branson glanced around, then up, warily. 'Yeah, assuming that.'

*

Grace's first action when he arrived at the Ops Control Room at John Street, twenty minutes later, was to inform his Silver and Bronze Commanders that any white Ford Transit van sighted in the vicinity of Eastern Road, for the rest of the day and night, was to be kept under close observation. Then he put out a broader request to all patrols in the city to keep a vigilant eye on all current model white Ford Transit vans.

Twelve years ago, if he was right, the Shoe Man had used a white van in his attack. It would fit Proudfoot's theory on his symmetry if he did the same thing again tonight.

Was that the reason those particular pages had been taken from the file, he wondered? The ones relating to an eyewitness report about a woman abducted in a white van? Did they contain vital clues about his behaviour? His MO? The identity of the van?

Something that had been bothering him about the lock-up garage was bothering him even more now. If the Shoe Man had driven the van out of the garage, why had he bothered to lock all four locks? There was nothing in there to steal except two useless licence plates.

That really did not make sense to him.

93

The only passengers Yac disliked more than drunks were the ones who were high on drugs. This girl on the back seat was almost bouncing off the roof.

She talked and she talked and she talked. She had spewed words non-stop since he had collected her from an address close to the beach in Lancing. Her hair was long and spiky, the colour of tomato ketchup and pea soup. She talked rubbish and she was wearing rubbish shoes. She reeked of cigarettes and Dolce & Gabbana Femme, and she was a mess. She looked like a Barbie doll that had been retrieved from a dustbin.

She was so out of it, he doubted she would notice if he drove her to the moon, except he didn't know how to get to the moon. He hadn't worked that one out yet.

'Thing is, you see,' she went on, 'there's a lot of people going to rip you off in this city. You want quality stuff. You tell them you want brown and they just give you shit, yep, shit. You had that problem?'

Yac wasn't sure whether she was talking into her mobile phone, which she had been for much of the journey, or to him. So he continued driving in silence and looking at the clock and fretting. After he dropped her off in Kemp Town he would park up and ignore any calls on his data unit from the dispatcher, wait for 7 p.m. and then drink his tea.

'Have you?' she asked more loudly. 'Have you?'

He felt a prod in his back. He didn't like that. He did not like passengers touching him. Last week he had a drunk man who kept laughing and thumping him on the shoulder. He had begun to find himself wondering what the man's reaction would be if he hit him in the face with the heavy, four-way steel brace for removing wheel nuts that was stored in the boot.

He was starting to wonder how this girl would react if he did that now. He could easily stop and get it out of the boot. She'd probably still be sitting in the back, talking away, even after he had hit her. He'd seen someone do that in a film on television.

She prodded him again. 'Hey? So? Have you?'

'Have I what?'

'Oh shit, you weren't listening. Like, right, OK. Shit. Haven't you got any music in this thing?'

'Size four?' he asked.

'Size *four*? Size *four* what?'

'Shoes. That's what you are.'

'You a shoemaker when you're not driving or something?'

Her shoes were really horrible. Fake leopard skin, flat and all frayed around the edges. He could kill this woman, he decided. He could. It would be easy. He had lots of passengers he did not like. But this was the first one he actually thought he might like to kill.

But it was probably better not to. You could get into trouble for killing people if you got caught. He watched *CSI* and *Waking the Dead* and other shows about forensic scientists. You could learn a lot from those. You could learn to kill a stupid person like this woman, with her stupid hair and her stupid black nail paint and her breasts almost popping free of their scarlet cups.

As he turned left at the roundabout in front of Brighton Pier and headed up around the Old Steine, she suddenly fell silent.

He wondered if she could read his mind.

94

Roy Grace, seated in the office at the end of the Ops Room, was working his way through a horrible slimy and almost stone-cold mound of chicken and shrimp chow mein that some well-meaning officer had brought him. If he hadn't been ravenous, he would have binned it. But he'd eaten nothing since an early-morning bowl of cereal and needed the fuel.

All had been quiet at the garage behind Mandalay Court. But the number and quality of the locks on the door continued to bother him. ACC Rigg had agreed readily to allowing Darren Spicer to tell them what he saw without incriminating himself, but as yet Glenn had been unable to find him. Grace hoped the serial villain wasn't playing a macabre game with them.

He dug the plastic fork into the foil dish, while staring at the gridded image on the computer screen on the desk in front of him. All the cars and the thirty-five officers on his operation were equipped with transponders which gave him their exact position to within a few feet. He checked the location of each in turn, then the images of the city streets on the CCTV cameras. The images on the screens on the wall showed their night-vision sight as clear as daylight. The city was definitely busier today. People might have stayed home yesterday evening, but

Saturday was starting to look like it might be something of a party night.

Just as he munched on a desiccated shrimp, his radio phone crackled into life and an excited voice said, 'Target One sighted! Turning right-right into Edward Street!'

Target One was the code designated to John Kerridge – Yac. *Target Two*, and further numbers, would be applied to any white van or pedestrian arousing suspicion.

Instantly, Grace put down the foil dish and tapped the command to bring up, on one of the wall-mounted monitors, the CCTV camera trained on the junction of Edward Street and Old Steine. He saw a Peugeot estate taxi, in the turquoise and white Brighton livery, accelerate out of the camera's view along the road.

'One female passenger. He is proceeding east-east!' he heard.

Moments later Grace saw a small Peugeot heading in the same direction. The transponder showed on the grid this was one of his covert cars, no. 4.

He called up the next image in sequence on the CCTV screens and saw the taxi crossing the intersection with Egremont Place, where Edward Street became Eastern Road.

Almost exactly the same pattern as last night, Grace thought. But this time, although he could not have explained why, he sensed there was a difference. At the same time, he was still worried about the amount of faith he had put in Proudfoot's judgement.

He spoke on the internal phone to his Silver. 'Have we found out his destination from the taxi company?'

'No, chief, didn't want to alert them, in case the operator says anything to the driver. We've enough cover to keep him in view if he stays in the area.'

'OK.'

Another excited voice crackled on the radio phone. 'He's turning right – right into – what's that street – Montague, I think. Yes, Montague! He's stopping! Rear door opening! She's out of the car! Oh, my God, she's running!'

95

Saturday 17 January

He had come early in the afternoon, to ensure he got a parking space in one of the pay-and-display bays close to her flat. One that she would have to walk past on her way back from her kick-boxing class.

But every damned one of them was taken when he arrived. So he had waited, at the end of the road, on a yellow line.

This area to the south of Eastern Road was a warren of narrow streets of two- and three-storey Victorian terraced houses, popular with students and singles, and in the heart of the gay community. There were several estate agent's hoardings, advertising properties for sale or to let. Cars, mostly small and grimy, and a few vans were parked along both sides.

He'd had to wait over an hour, to almost 3.30 p.m. before, to his relief, a rusty old Land Cruiser had driven off, leaving behind a space big enough for him. It was just thirty feet from the front door of the pale blue house, with bay windows, where Jessie Sheldon had the upstairs flat. The gods were smiling on him!

It was perfect. He had put sufficient coins in to cover him until 6.30 p.m., when the parking restrictions expired. It was now just past that time.

An hour and ten minutes ago, Jessie had come out of

her front door in her tracksuit and trainers, and walked straight past him on her way to her kick-boxing class – the one she attended every Saturday afternoon, and which she had chattered about on Facebook. He could have taken her then, but it wasn't quite dark enough, and there had been people around.

But now it was dark and, for the moment, the street was deserted.

She would have to hurry home, he knew. She had informed the world that she was going to have to rush in order to get changed into her finery, to take Benedict to meet her parents for the first time.

I am soooooooooo nervous about that meeting! she had put on Facebook.

What if they don't like him?

She added that she was *soooooooooo* excited about the Anya Hindmarch shoes she had bought!

He was *soooooooooo* excited about the pair of Anya Hindmarch shoes he had bought too. They were lying on the floor right behind him, waiting for her! And he was *soooooooooooo* nervous also. But nervous in a nice, excited, tingly-all-over way.

Where are you tonight, Detective Superintendent Big-Swinging-Dick Detective Superintendent Roy Grace?

Not here, are you? You haven't a clue! Again!

He had parked so that he could watch her approaching through the crack in the rear window curtains, although these were hardly necessary. He'd applied dense black-out privacy film to all the rear and side windows. It was impossible to see in from outside, even in broad daylight. Of course, he knew, aficionados of these classic VW camper vans would frown at such a thing as darkened windows. Fuck them.

He checked his watch, pulled on his latex gloves, then his baseball cap, and raised his night-vision binoculars to his eyes. Any minute now she would appear around the corner, either walking or perhaps running. It was 200 yards from that street corner to her front door. If she was running he would have twenty seconds; if she was walking, a little longer.

All that mattered was that she was alone, and that the street was still deserted.

If not, then he'd have to switch to his alternative plan, to take her inside her house. But that would make it harder for him to then get her outside again and into the camper van undetected. Harder, but not impossible; he had that worked out too.

He was shaking with excitement as he once again went through his checklist. His heart was thudding. He opened the sliding door, grabbed the fake fridge he had made from plywood and moved it closer to the door. Then he took his baseball cap off, pulled his hood on and tugged his baseball cap down again, to disguise the hood as much as possible. Then he looked at the shoes on the floor. Identical to the ones she had bought.

He was ready. After the mess-up on Thursday, he had planned today much more carefully, the way he normally did. He had everything covered, he was quite confident of that.

96

'Hey!' Yac shouted in fury. 'Hey! Hey!'

He couldn't believe it. She was doing a runner on him! He'd driven her all the way from Lancing, a £24 fare, and as he pulled over at the address she'd given him, she opened the rear door and legged it.

Well, he wasn't having it!

He yanked off his seat belt, hurled open the door and stumbled out on to the pavement, shaking with anger. Without even switching off the engine or shutting the door, he began sprinting after the fast-disappearing figure.

She raced along the pavement, downhill, then turned left into the busy thoroughfare of St George's Road, which was more brightly lit, with shops and restaurants on both sides. Dodging past several people, he was gaining on her. She glanced over her shoulder, then suddenly darted into the road, right across the path of a bus, which blared its horn at her. Yac didn't care, he followed her, running between the rear of the bus and a car that was following, hearing the scream of brakes.

He was gaining!

He wished he had the wheel brace to hit her with, that would bring her down!

He was only yards behind her now.

At one of the schools he had attended, they'd made him play rugby, which he hated. But he was good at tackling. He had been so good at tackling they'd stopped him from playing any more rugby, because they said he hurt the other boys and frightened them.

She threw another glance at him, her face lit up in the glare of a street light. He saw fear.

They were heading down another dark, residential street, towards the bright lights of the main seafront road, Marine Parade. He never heard the footsteps closing behind him. Never saw the two men in jeans and anoraks who appeared in front of her at the end of the street. He was utterly focused on his fare.

On his £24.

She was not getting away with it.

Closing the gap!

Closing!

He reached out and clamped a hand on her shoulder. Heard her squeal in fear.

Then, suddenly, arms like steel pincers were around his waist. He smacked, face first, on to the pavement, all the air shot out of him by a crashing weight on his spine.

Then his arms were jerked harshly back. He felt cold sharp steel on his wrists. Heard a snap, then another.

He was hauled, harshly, to his feet. His face was stinging and his body hurt.

Three men in casual clothing stood around him, all panting, breathless. One of them held his arm painfully hard.

'John Kerridge,' he said, 'I'm arresting you on suspicion of sexual assault and rape. You do not have to say anything, but it may harm your defence if you do not mention when questioned something which you later rely on in court. Anything you do say may be given in evidence. Is that clear?'

97

Suddenly, he could see her. She was coming around the corner at a steady jog, a slender green figure against the grey tones of the darkness, through his night vision binocular lenses.

He turned, all panicky now it was happening, shooting a quick glance up and down the street. Apart from Jessie, who was fast closing on him, it was deserted.

He slid open the side door, grabbed the fake fridge with both arms and staggered one step back on to the kerb, then screamed with pain. 'Oh, my back, my back! Oh, God, help me!'

Jessie stopped in her tracks as she saw the back of a clumsy-looking figure in an anorak, jeans and baseball cap holding a fridge half in and half out of the Volkswagen camper van.

'Oh, God!' he screamed again.

'Can I help you?' she asked.

'Oh, please, quick. I can't hold it!'

She hurried over to assist him, but when she touched the fridge it felt strange, not like a fridge at all.

A hand grabbed the back of her neck, hurling her forward into the van. She slithered across the floor, cracking her head against something hard and unyielding. Before she had time to recover her senses, a heavy weight on her back pinned her down, crushing her, then something sickly sweet and damp was pressed over her face, stinging her nose and throat and blinding her with tears.

Terror seized her.

She tried to remember her moves. Still early days, she was just a novice, but she had learned one basic. *Bend before kicking.* You didn't get enough power if you just kicked. You brought your knees towards you, then launched your legs. Coughing, spluttering, trying not to breathe the noxious stinging air, but already feeling muzzy, she clenched her elbows hard into her ribs and rolled sideways, her vision just a blur, trying to break free, bending her knees, then kicking out hard.

She felt them strike something. She heard a grunt of pain. Heard something clattering across the floor, kicked again, shook her head free, twisted, feeling dizzy now and weaker. The sickly sweet wetness pressed against her face again, stinging her eyes. She rolled sideways, breaking free of it, kicking hard with both feet together, feeling even dizzier now.

The weight lifted from her back. She heard sliding, then the slam of the door. She tried to get up. A hooded face was staring down at her, eyes peering through the slits. She attempted to scream, but her brain was working in slow motion now and disconnected from her mouth. No sound came out. She stared at the black hood, which was all blurry. Her brain was trying to make some sense of what was happening, but the inside of her head was swirling. She felt a deep, nauseous giddiness.

Then the sickly, stinging wetness again.

She went limp. Engulfed in a vortex of blackness. Falling deeper into it. Hurtling down a helter-skelter in a void.

98

There was an almost celebratory mood in the Ops Room at Brighton Central. Roy Grace ordered the surveillance team to stand down; they were free to go home. But he was in no mood to share any of their elation and it was going to be a while yet before he got to head home.

This John Kerridge – Yac – character had bugged him all along. They'd released him too damned easily, without thorough enough questioning and investigation. He just thanked his lucky stars that the creep had been caught before harming another victim, which would have made them all look like even bigger idiots.

As it was, difficult questions were going to be asked, to which he was going to have to provide some damned good answers.

He was cursing himself for having allowed Norman Potting to run the initial interview, and for so readily agreeing with Potting's decision that Kerridge should be released. He intended to be fully involved in planning the interview strategy and in the whole interview process of this suspect from now on.

Thinking hard, he left Brighton police station and drove back towards the Custody Centre, behind Sussex House, where Kerridge had been taken. He was fully expecting a phone call at any moment from Kevin Spinella at the *Argus*.

It was shortly after 7 p.m. when he pulled the Ford Focus estate into the bay in the front of the long, two-storey CID HQ building. He phoned Cleo to tell her that, with luck, he might be home earlier than he had thought, before midnight at any rate, then climbed out of the car. As he did so, his phone rang. But it wasn't Spinella.

It was Inspector Rob Leet, the Golf 99 – the Duty Inspector in charge of all critical incidents in the city. Leet was a calm, extremely capable officer.

'Sir, in case this is connected, I've just had a report from East Sector – a unit is attending a van on fire in remote farmland north of Patcham.'

Grace frowned. 'What information do you have on it?'

'It seems to have been on fire for some time – it's pretty well burnt out. The fire brigade's on its way. But this is why I thought it might be of interest. It's a current model Ford Transit – sounds similar to the one you have an alert out on.'

The news made Grace uneasy. 'Any casualties?'

'It appears to be empty.'

'No one seen running away from it?'

'No.'

'Anything from its registration?'

'The licence plates are burned beyond recognition, I'm told, sir.'

'OK, thanks,' he said. 'We have our man in custody. It may not be connected. But keep me updated.'

'I will, sir.'

Grace ended the call and entered the front door of Sussex House, nodding a greeting to the night security man.

'Hi, Duncan. How's the running?'

The tall, athletic forty-year-old smiled at him proudly. 'Completed a half-marathon last weekend. Came fifteenth out of seven hundred.'

'Brilliant!'

'Working up for the London marathon this year. Hope I can touch you for some sponsorship – for St Wilfred's Hospice?'

'Absolutely!'

Grace walked through to the rear of the building and out of the door, crossing the courtyard. He passed the wheelie bins and the SOCO vehicles which were permanently housed there, then went up the steep incline towards the custody block. As he pressed his key card against the security panel to unlock the door, his phone rang again.

It was Inspector Rob Leet once more.

'Roy, I thought I'd better call you right away. I know you have the Shoe Man in custody, but we've got a unit on site in Sudeley Place, Kemp Town, attending a Grade One.'

This was the highest category of emergency call, requiring immediate attendance. Grace knew Sudeley Place. It was just south of Eastern Road. The tone of Leet's voice worried him. What the Duty Inspector had to say fuelled that worry further.

'Apparently a local resident happened to be looking out of her window and saw a woman having a fight with a man over a fridge.'

'A fridge?'

'He was in some sort of van – a camper of some kind – she's not very good on vehicles, couldn't give us the make. She reckons he hit her, then drove off at high speed.'

'With her on board?'

'Yes.'

'When was this?'

'About thirty-five minutes ago – just after 6.30 p.m.'

'He could be anywhere by now. Did she get the registration?'

'No. But I'm treating this as a possible abduction and I've cordoned off that section of pavement. I've asked Road Policing to check all camper vans on the move in the vicinity of the city. We're going to see if we can get anything from CCTV.'

'OK. Look, I'm not quite sure why you're telling me this. We have our Shoe Man suspect in custody. I'm about to go and see him.'

'There's a reason why I think it could be significant for you, sir.' Leet hesitated. 'My officers attending have found a woman's shoe on the pavement.

'What kind of a shoe?'

'Very new, apparently. Black patent leather, with a high heel. The witness saw it fall out of the camper.'

Grace felt a falling sensation deep in the pit of his stomach. His mind was whirling. They had the Shoe Man. At this very moment they were booking John Kerridge into custody.

But he did not like the sound of the burning van.

And he liked the sound of this new incident even less.

99

In the CCTV room of Sussex Remote Monitoring Services, Dunstan Christmas shifted his twenty-stone bulk on the chair, careful not to lift his weight off altogether and trigger the alarm sensor. It was only 7.30 p.m. Shit. Another hour and a half to wait before he would be relieved for a five-minute comfort break.

He was not due on nights for another two weeks, but he'd agreed to cover for someone who was sick because he needed the overtime pay. Time wasn't even crawling by; it felt like it had stopped altogether. Maybe it was even going backwards, like in a sci-fi movie he'd watched recently on Sky. It was going to be a long night.

But thinking about the money he was making cheered him. Mr Starling might be a strange boss, but he paid well. The money here was good; much better than in his previous job, watching X-rayed luggage at Gatwick Airport.

He reached forward, pulled a handful of Doritos out of the giant-size packet in front of him, munched them and washed them down with a swig of Coca-Cola from the two-litre bottle, then belched. As he routinely ran his eyes over all twenty screens, his hand close to the microphone button in case he should happen to spot any intruder, he noticed that No. 20, which had been dead when he had started his shift, was still not showing any images. It was the old Shoreham cement works, where his dad had been a driver.

He pressed the control toggle to change the image on the screen, in case it was just one of the twenty-six CCTV cameras that was on the blink. But the screen remained blank. He picked up the phone and dialled the night engineer.

'Hi, Ray. It's Dunstan in Monitor Room 2. I've not had any image on screen 17 since I started my shift.'

'Mr Starling's instruction,' the engineer replied. 'The client hasn't paid his bill. Over four months now apparently. Mr Starling's suspended the service. Don't worry about it.'

'Right, thanks,' Dunstan Christmas said. 'I won't.'

He ate some more Doritos.

100

A terrible pain, like a vice crushing her head, woke Jessie. For an instant, utterly disoriented, she had no idea where she was.

In Benedict's room?

She felt all muzzy and queasy. What had happened last night? What had happened at the dinner dance? Had she got drunk?

She felt a crashing jolt. There was a constant whooshing sound beneath her. She could hear the steady blatter of an engine. Was she in a plane?

Her queasiness deepened. She was close to throwing up.

Another jolt, then another. There was a banging sound like a loose door. Fear squirmed through her. Something felt very wrong; something terrible had happened. As she became more conscious, her memory trickled back, reluctantly, as if something was trying to hold it at bay.

She couldn't move her arms or her legs. Her fear deepened. She was lying face down on something hard and constantly jolting. Her nose was bunged up and she was finding it harder and harder to breathe. She tried, desperately, to breathe in though her mouth, but something was clamped over it and no air would come through. She couldn't breathe through her nose now either. She tried to cry out but just heard a dull moan and felt her mouth reverberating.

Panicking, juddering, fighting for breath, she sniffed harder. She could not get enough air in through her nose to fill her lungs. She squirmed, moaned, twisted on to her side, then on to her back, sniffing, sniffing, sniffing, fighting for air, close to blacking out. Then, after a few moments of lying on her back, the blockage freed a little and more air came in. Her panic subsided a little. She took several long, deep breaths, calming a fraction, then tried to call out again. But the sounds stayed trapped in her mouth and gullet.

Bright lights lit up the darkness for an instant and she could see above her the roof of the vehicle. Then darkness again.

Another bright light and she saw a hunched figure in the driver's seat, just shoulders and the back of a baseball cap. The light passed and was instantly replaced by another. Headlights of oncoming cars, she realized.

Suddenly there were bright lights to her right, as a vehicle overtook them. For a fleeting instant she saw part of his face reflected in the interior mirror. She froze in terror. It was still masked by the black hood.

His eyes were on her.

'Just lie back and enjoy the ride!' he said in a bland, small voice.

She tried to speak again, struggling once more to move her arms. They were behind her back, her wrists clamped together. There was no slack, nothing to get a purchase on. She tried to move her legs, but they felt as if they had been welded together at the ankles and knees.

What time was it? How long had she been here? How long since . . .

She should be at the dinner dance. Benedict was going to meet her parents. He was coming round to pick her up. What was he thinking now? Doing now? Was he standing outside her flat ringing the bell? Phoning her? As headlights again brightened the interior, she looked around. Saw what seemed to be a small kitchen unit; one cupboard door was swinging, banging but not closing. Now they were slowing down. She heard him change gear, heard an indicator click-clicking.

Her fear deepened even more. Where were they going?

Then she heard a siren wailing, faintly at first, then louder. It was behind them. Now louder still! And suddenly her spirits soared. Yes! Benedict had come round to collect her and called the police when he realized she wasn't there. They were coming! She was safe. Oh, thank God! Thank God!

Shards of blue light, as if from a shattered chandelier, flooded the interior of the van and the air filled with the scream of the siren. Then, in an instant, the blue lights were gone. Jessie heard the siren recede into the distance.

No, you idiots, no, no no no, no. Please. Come back! Please come back!

She slithered across the floor to her left, as the van made a sharp right. Two hard, jarring jolts and it pulled up. She heard the ratchet of the handbrake. *Please come back!* Then a torch beam flashed into her eyes, momentarily dazzling her.

'Nearly there!' he said.

All she could see when he moved the beam away from her face were his eyes through the slits in the hood.

She tried to speak to him. 'Please, who are you? What do you want? Where have you taken me?' But all that came out was the reverberating moan, like a muffled foghorn.

She heard the driver's door open. The engine ticked over with a steady clatter. Then she heard metal clanking – it sounded like a chain. It was followed by the creaking sound of rusty hinges. A gate being opened?

Then she heard a familiar sound. A soft, rasping buzzing. Hope suddenly sprang up inside her. It was her mobile phone! She'd switched it to silent, vibrate, for her kick-boxing class. It sounded as if it was coming from somewhere up front. Was it on the passenger seat?

Oh, God, who was it? Benedict? Wondering where she was? It stopped after four rings, going automatically to voicemail.

Moments later he jumped back in, drove forward a short distance, then jumped out again, once more leaving the engine ticking over. She heard the same creaking sound, then the same metal clanking of a chain again. Wherever they were, they were now on the far side of locked gates, she realized, her terror deepening even more. Somewhere private. Somewhere that police patrols would not drive by. Her mouth was dry and she felt as if she was going to throw up, bile rising in her throat, sharp and bitter. She swallowed it.

The van lurched, then lurched again – speed humps, she thought – dipped down an incline, sending her sliding forward, her shoulder bashing painfully into something, then rose up, so that she slid back again, helplessly. Then they were driving along a smooth surface, with a steady bump-bump every few moments, like joins in concrete. It was pitch dark in here and he seemed to be driving without lights on.

For an instant her terror turned to anger, then to wild, feral fury. *Let me out! Let me out! Untie me! You have no fucking right to do this!* She struggled against her bonds, pulling her wrists, her arms, with all her strength, shaking, thrashing. But whatever was binding them did not budge.

She lay limp and sniffing air, her eyes filled with tears. She should be at the dinner dance tonight. In her beautiful dress and her new shoes, holding Benedict's arm as he chatted wittily to her parents, winning them over, as she was sure he would. Benedict had been nervous as hell. She had tried to reassure him that they would be charmed by him. Her mother would adore him and her father, well, he seemed a tough guy when you first met him, but underneath he was a big softie. They would adore him, she had promised him.

Yeah, right, until they find out I'm not Jewish.

The van continued its journey. They were turning left now. The headlights came on for a brief second and she saw what looked like the wall of a tall, derelict, slab-like structure with panes of broken glass. The sight sent a vortex of icy air corkscrewing through her. It was like one of the buildings the film *Hostel* was set in. The building where innocent people who had been captured were taken and tortured by wealthy sadists who paid for the privilege.

Her imagination was in freefall. She'd always been a horror movie fan. Now she was thinking about all the deranged killers in movies she had seen, who kidnapped their victims, then tortured and killed them at their leisure. Like in *Silence of the Lambs*, *The Texas Chainsaw Massacre*, *The Hills Have Eyes*.

Her brain was shorting out in terror. She was breathing in short, sharp, panicky bursts, her chest thudding, thudding, thudding, and she was so angry inside.

The van stopped. He got out again. She heard the rumbling of a metal door, then a terrible grinding of metal against some other hard surface. He climbed back in, slammed his door shut and drove forward, putting his lights on again.

Have to talk to him, somehow.

Now she could see through the windscreen that they were inside some vast, disused industrial building, the height of an aircraft hangar, or several aircraft hangars. The headlights briefly showed a railed steel walkway going around the walls high up and a network of what looked like giant, dusty Apollo rocket fuel cylinders stretching into the distance, supported by massive steel and concrete cradles. As they turned, she saw rail tracks disappearing into dust and rubble, and a rusted open goods carriage, covered in graffiti, which did not look like it had moved in decades.

The van halted.

She was shaking so much in terror she could not think straight.

The man got out and switched the engine off. She heard him walking away, then the groaning noise of metal, a loud, echoing clang, following by the clanking of what sounded like a chain. She heard him walking back towards the camper.

Moments later she heard the door slide open and now he was inside the rear with her. He shone the torch down at her, first at her face, then at her body. She stared up at his hooded face, shaking in terror.

She could kick him, she thought wildly. Although her legs were strapped together, she could bend her knees, then lash out at him, but unless she could free her arms, what good would that achieve? Other than to anger him.

She needed to speak to him. She was remembering tips from all she had read in newspapers about hostages who had survived capture. You needed to try to bond with your captors. It was harder for them to harm you if you established a rapport. Somehow she had to get him to free her mouth so she could talk to him. Reason with him. Find out what he wanted.

'You shouldn't have kicked me,' he said suddenly. 'I bought you nice new shoes, the same as the ones you were going to wear tonight to take Benedict to meet your parents. You're all the same, you women. You think your-selves so powerful. You put on all these sexy things to snare your man, then ten years later, you're all fat and horrible, with cellulite and a slack belly. Somebody has to teach you a lesson, even if I have to do it with only one shoe.'

She tried to speak again.

He leaned down and, in a sudden movement that took her by surprise, flipped her over on to her stomach, then sat on her legs, pinioning them to the floor, crushing them painfully with his weight. She felt something being wound around her ankles and knotted tight. He stood up and suddenly her legs were being pulled over to the left. Then, after some moments, she felt them being pulled to the right. She tried to move them, but couldn't.

Then she heard the clank of metal and an instant later felt something cold and hard being wound around her neck and pulled tight. There was a sharp snap that sound liked a lock closing. Suddenly her head was jerked forward, then to the right. She heard another snap, like another lock. Then her head was being pulled to the left. Another snap.

She was stretched out as if she was on some medieval rack. She could not move her head or her legs or her arms. She tried to breathe. Her nose was blocking up again. She shimmied in growing panic.

'I have to go now. I'm expected for dinner,' he said. 'I'll see you tomorrow. *Hasta la vista!*'

She moaned in terror, trying to plead with him. *No, please! No, please don't leave me face down. I can't breathe. Please, I'm claustrophobic. Please—*

She heard the door sliding shut.

Footsteps. A distant rending and echoing bang of metal.

Then the sound of a motorcycle engine starting up, revving and fading into the distance, roaring away, fading rapidly into silence. As she listened, quaking in terror, fighting for air she felt a sudden, unpleasant warm sensation spreading around her groin and along her thighs.

101

Roy Grace sat in the small interview room in the Custody Centre, alongside DC Michael Foreman, who, like himself, was a trained Witness and Suspect Cognitive Interviewer. But at this moment, none of that past training was doing them any good. John Kerridge had gone *no comment* on them. Thanks but no thanks to his smart-alec lawyer, Ken Acott.

The tape recorder with three blank cassettes sat on the table. High up on the walls, two CCTV camera lenses peered down at them like mildly inquisitive birds. There was a tense atmosphere. Grace was feeling murderous. At this moment he could have happily reached across the narrow interview table, grabbed John Kerridge by the neck and strangled the truth out of the little shit, disability or no disability.

His client was on the autism spectrum, Ken Acott had informed them. John Kerridge, who kept insisting he be called Yac, suffered from Asperger's syndrome. His client had informed him that he was in pursuit of a passenger who had run off without paying. It was patently obvious that it was his client's passenger who should have been apprehended, not his client. His client was being discriminated against and victimized because of his disability.

552

Kerridge would make no comment without a specialist medical expert present.

Grace decided he would like to strangle Ken sodding Acott too at this moment. He stared at the smooth solicitor in his elegantly tailored suit, his shirt and tie, and could even smell his cologne. In contrast his client, also in a suit, shirt and tie, cut a pathetic figure. Kerridge had short dark hair brushed forward, and a strangely haunted face that might have been quite handsome, were his eyes not a little too close together. He was thin, with rounded shoulders, and seemed unable to keep totally still. He fidgeted like a bored schoolboy.

'It's nine o'clock,' Acott said. 'My client needs a cup of tea. He has to have one every hour, on the hour. It's his ritual.'

'I've got news for your client,' Grace said, staring pointedly at Kerridge. 'This is not a Ritz-Carlton hotel. He'll get tea outside of the normal times that tea is provided here if and when I decide he can have it. Now, if your client would care to be more helpful – or perhaps if his solicitor would care to be more helpful – then I'm sure something could be done to improve the quality of our room service.'

'I've told you, my client is not making any comment.'

'I have to have my tea,' Yac said suddenly.

Grace looked at him. 'You'll have it when I decide.'

'I have to have it at nine o'clock.'

Grace stared at him. There was a brief silence, then Yac eyeballed Grace back and said, 'Do you have a high-flush or low-flush toilet in your home?'

There was a vulnerability in the taxi driver's voice, something that touched a chord in Grace. Since the news of the reported abduction in Kemp Town two hours ago, and the discovery of a shoe on the pavement where it had allegedly taken place, there had been a development. A young man had arrived to collect his fiancée for an evening out at a black-tie function, thirty minutes after the time of the abduction and she had not answered the door. There was no response from her mobile phone, which rang unanswered, then went to voicemail.

It had already been established that the last person to have seen her was her kick-boxing instructor, at a local gym. She'd been in high spirits, looking forward to her evening out, although, the instructor had said, she was nervous at the prospect of introducing her fiancé to her parents for the first time.

So she could have funked out, Grace considered. But she didn't sound the type of girl to stand up her boyfriend and let down her family. The more he heard, the less he liked the way the whole scenario was developing. Which made him even angrier here.

Angry at the smugness of Ken Acott.

Angry at this creepy suspect hiding behind *no comment* and behind his condition. Grace knew a child with Asperger's. A police officer colleague and his wife, with whom he and Sandy had been friends, had a teenage son with the condition. He was a strange but very sweet boy who was obsessed with batteries. A boy who was not good at reading people, lacking normal social skills. A boy who had difficulty distinguishing between right and wrong in certain aspects of behaviour. But someone, in his view, who was capable of understanding the line between right and wrong when it came to things as major as rape or murder.

'Why are you interested in toilets?' Grace asked Kerridge.

'Toilet chains! I have a collection. I could show you them some time.'

'Yes, I'd be very interested.'

Acott was glaring daggers at him.

'You didn't tell me,' Kerridge went on. 'Do you have high flush or low flush in your home?'

Grace thought for a moment. 'Low flush.'

'Why?'

'Why do you like ladies' shoes, John?' he replied suddenly.

'I'm sorry,' Acott said, his voice tight with anger. 'I'm not having any questioning.'

Ignoring him, Grace persisted. 'Do you find them sexy?'

'Sexy people are bad,' Yac replied.

102

Saturday 17 January

Roy Grace left the interview room feeling even more uneasy than when he had gone in. John Kerridge was a strange man and he sensed a violent streak in him. Yet he did not feel Kerridge possessed the cunning or sophistication that the Shoe Man would have needed to get away undetected with his crimes of twelve years ago and those in the past few weeks.

Of particular concern to him at the moment was the latest news of the possible abduction of Jessie Sheldon this evening. It was the shoe on the pavement that really worried him. Jessie Sheldon had been in her tracksuit and trainers. So whose was the shoe? A brand-new ladies' shoe with a high heel. The Shoe Man's kind of shoe.

But there was something else gnawing at him even more than John Kerridge and Jessie Sheldon at this moment. He couldn't remember exactly when the thought had first struck him – some time between leaving the garage behind Mandalay Court this afternoon and arriving at the Ops Room at the police station. It was bugging him even more now.

He walked out of Sussex House and over to his car. The drizzle had almost stopped and now the wind was getting up. He climbed in and started the engine. As he did so, his radio crackled. It was an update from one of the officers attending the burning van at the farm north of Patcham. The vehicle was still too hot to enter and search.

A short while later, coming up to 10.15 p.m., he parked the unmarked Ford Focus in the main road, The Drive, some way south of his destination. Then, with his torch jammed out of sight into his mackintosh pocket, he walked a couple of hundred yards up to Mandalay Court, trying to look like a casual evening stroller, not wanting to risk putting off the Shoe Man, or whoever used the garage, should he decide to return.

He'd already spoken to the on-site surveillance officer, to warn him he was coming, and the tall figure of DC Jon Exton, from the Covert Team, stepped out of the shadows to greet Grace as he walked down the ramp.

'All quiet, sir,' Exton reported.

Grace told him to stay on lookout and to radio him if he saw anyone approaching, then walked around the rear of the block of flats and along past the lock-ups to the one at the far end, no. 17.

Using his torch now, he strode along the length of it, counting his paces. The garage was approximately twenty-eight feet long. He double-checked as he retraced his steps, then walked back around to the front and pulled on a pair of latex gloves.

Jack Tunks, the locksmith, had left the garage unlocked for them. Grace lifted the up-and-over door, closed it behind him and shone his torch beam around the inside. Then he counted his paces to the end wall.

Twenty feet.

His pulse quickened.

Eight feet difference.

He rapped on the wall with his knuckles. It sounded

hollow. False. He turned to the floor-to-ceiling wooden shelves on the right-hand side of the wall. The finishing on them was poor and uneven, as if they were home-made. Then he looked at the row of rolls of grey duct tape. The stuff was a favoured tool of kidnappers. Then, in the beam of the torch, he saw something he had not noticed on his visit here earlier today. The shelves had a wooden backing to them, bringing them out a good inch from the wall.

Grace had never been into DIY, but he knew enough to question why the lousy handyman who had made these shelves had put a backing on them. Surely you only put a backing to shelves to hide an ugly wall behind them? Why would someone bother in a crappy old garage?

Holding the torch in his mouth, he gripped one of the shelves and pulled hard, testing it. Nothing happened. He pulled even harder, still nothing. Then he gripped the next shelf up and instantly noticed some play in it. He jiggled it and suddenly it slid free. He pulled it out and saw, recessed into the groove where the shelf should have fitted, a sliding door bolt. He propped the shelf against the wall and unlatched the bolt. Then he tried first pulling, then pushing the shelving unit. It would not budge.

He checked each of the remaining shelves and found that the bottom one was loose too. He slid that out and discovered a second bolt, also recessed into the grove. He slid that open, then stood up, gripped two of the shelves that were still in place and pushed. Nothing happened.

Then he pulled, and nearly fell over backwards as the entire shelving unit swung backwards.

It was a door.

He grabbed the torch and shone the beam into the void behind. And his heart stopped in his chest.

His blood froze.

Icy fingers crawled down his spine as he stared around him.

There was a tea chest on the floor. Almost every inch of the walls was covered in old, yellowing newspaper cuttings. Most of them were from the *Argus*, but some were from national papers. He stepped forward and read the headlines of one. It was dated 14 December 1997:

SHOE MAN'S LATEST VICTIM CONFIRMED BY POLICE

Everywhere that he pointed his torch, more headlines shouted out at him from the walls. More articles, some showing photographs of the victims. There were photographs of Jack Skerritt, the Senior Investigating Officer. And then, prominently displayed, a large photograph of Rachael Ryan stared out from beneath a front-page headline from the *Argus* from January 1998:

IS MISSING RACHAEL SHOE MAN'S VICTIM NO. 6?

Grace stared at the photograph, then at the headline. He could remember when he had first seen this page of the paper. This chilling headline. It had been the shoutline on every news-stand in the city.

He tested the lid of the tea chest. It was loose. He lifted it up and stood, his eyes boggling, at what was inside.

It was crammed with women's high-heeled shoes, each wrapped and sealed in cellophane. He rummaged through them. Some packages contained a single shoe and a pair of panties. Others, a pair of shoes. All of the shoes looked as if they'd barely been worn.

Shaking with excitement, he needed to know how many. Mindful of not wanting to damage any forensic evidence, he counted them out and laid them on the floor in their wrapping. Twenty-two packages.

Also bundled together in one taped-up sheet of cellophane were a woman's dress, tights, panties and bra. The Shoe Man's drag gear, maybe. He wondered. Or were these the clothes taken from Nicola Taylor at the Metropole?

He knelt, staring at the shoes for some moments. Then he returned to the cuttings on the wall, wanting to ensure he did not miss anything significant that might lead him to his quarry.

He looked at each one in turn, focusing on the ones on Rachael Ryan, big and small, which covered a large section of one wall. Then his eyes fell on an A4 sheet of paper that was different. This wasn't a newspaper cutting; it was a printed form, partly filled out in ballpoint pen. It was headed:

J. BUND & SONS, FUNERAL DIRECTORS

He walked across so that he could read the small printing on it. Beneath the name it said:

Registration Form

Ref. D5678

Mrs Molly Winifred Glossop

D. 2 January 1998. Aged 81.

He read every word of the form. It was a detailed list:

- ☑ Church fee
- ☑ Doctor's fee
- ☐ Removal of pacemaker fee

☐ Cremation fee

☑ Gravedigger's fee

☑ Printed service sheets fees

☑ Flowers

☑ Memorial cards

☑ Obituary notices

☑ Coffin

☐ Casket for remains

☐ Organist's fee

☑ Cemetery fee

☐ Churchyard burial fee

☑ Clergy's fee

☑ Church fee

Funeral on: 12 January 1998, 11 a.m.
Lawn Memorial Cemetery, Woodingdean.

He read the sheet again. Then again, transfixed.

His mind was racing back to twelve years ago. To a charred body on a post-mortem table at Brighton and Hove Borough Mortuary. A little old lady, whose remains had been found, incinerated, in the burnt-out shell of a Ford Transit van, and who had never been identified. As was customary, she had been kept for two years and then buried in Woodvale cemetery, her funeral paid for out of public funds.

During his career with the police to date, he'd seen many horrendous sights, but most of them he had been able to put out of his mind. There were just a few, and he could count them on the fingers of one hand, that he knew he would carry to his grave. This old lady, and the mystery accompanying her, he had long thought would be one of them.

But now, standing in the back of this shabby old lock-up garage, something was starting, finally, to make sense.

He had a growing certainty that he now knew who she was.

Molly Winifred Glossop.

But then who had been buried at 11 a.m. on Monday 12 January 1998 in the Lawn Memorial Cemetery in Woodingdean?

He was pretty damned sure he knew the answer.

103

Jessie heard the vibrating sound of her phone, yet again, in the half-darkness. She was parched. Once in a while she drifted into a fitful doze, then woke again in stark panic, unable to breathe through her bunged-up nose and fighting for air.

She had agonizing pains in her shoulders, from her arms being stretched out in front of her. There were noises all around her: clankings, creakings, bangings, grindings. With every new sound, she was terrified that the man was returning, that he might be creeping up behind her at this very moment. Her mind swirled in a constant vortex of fear and confused thoughts. Who was he? Why had he brought her here, wherever it was? What was he planning to do? What did he want?

She couldn't stop thinking about all the horror films that had most scared her. She tried to shut them out, to think of happy times. Like her last holiday with Benedict on the Greek island of Naxos. The wedding they had been discussing, their life ahead.

Where are you now, darling Benedict?

The vibrating sound continued. Four rings, then it stopped once more. Did that mean there was a message? Was it Benedict? Her parents? She tried again and again, desperately, to free herself. Shaking and tossing, struggling to loosen the bonds on her wrists, to work one of her hands free. But all that happened was that she bounced around, painfully, her shoulders almost wrenched out of their sockets, her body crashing down against the hard floor, then up again, until she was exhausted.

Then all she could do was lie here in utter frustration, the damp patch around her groin and thighs no longer warm and starting to itch. She had an itch on her cheek too that she desperately wanted to scratch. And all the time she was fighting constantly to swallow back the bile that kept rising in her throat, which could choke her, she knew, if she allowed herself to vomit with her mouth still clamped shut.

She cried again, her eyes raw with the salt from her tears.

Please help me, somebody, please.

For a moment she wondered whether she should just let herself vomit, choke on it and die. End it all before the man came back to do whatever terrible things he had in mind. To at least deprive him of that satisfaction.

Instead, putting a faltering half-trust in the man she loved, she closed her eyes and prayed for the first time in as long as she could remember. It took her a while before she could properly remember the words.

No sooner had she finished than her phone rang again. The usual four rings, then it stopped. Then she heard a different sound.

A sound she recognized.

A sound that froze her.

The roar of a motorbike engine.

104

The Coroner for the city of Brighton and Hove was a doughty lady. When she was in a bad mood, her demeanour was capable of scaring quite a few of her staff, as well as many hardened police officers. But, Grace knew, she possessed a great deal of common sense and compassion, and he'd never personally had a problem with her, until now.

Perhaps it was because he'd just called her at home after midnight and woken her – from the sleepy sound of her voice. As she became more awake, she grew increasingly imperious. But she was professional enough to listen intently, only interrupting him when she wanted clarification.

'This is a big thing you're asking, Detective Superintendent,' she said, when he had finished, distinctly school-marmy now.

'I know.'

'We've only ever had two of these in Sussex. It's not something that can be granted lightly. You're asking a lot.'

'It's not normally a life or death situation, madam,' Grace said, deciding to address her formally, 'but I really believe it is here.'

'Solely on the evidence of the missing girl's friend?'

'In our search for Jessie Sheldon, we contacted a

number of her friends, from a list given to us by her fiancé. The one who is apparently her best friend received a text from Jessie last Tuesday, with a photograph of a pair of shoes she had bought specifically for this evening. The shoes in that photograph are identical to the one shoe found on the pavement outside her flat, exactly where her reported abduction took place.'

'You're certain her fiancé is not involved in any way?'

'Yes, he's eliminated as a suspect. And all three of our current prime suspects for the Shoe Man are eliminated from being involved.'

Cassian Pewe was confirmed as being at a residential course at the Police Training Centre at Bramshill. Darren Spicer had returned to St Patrick's night shelter at 7.30 p.m., which did not work with the timeline of the abduction, and John Kerridge was already in custody.

After a few moments, the Coroner said, 'These are always carried out early in the morning, usually at dawn, to avoid distress to the public. That would mean Monday morning at the very earliest.'

'That's too long to wait. It would mean a whole thirty hours before we could even begin to start searching for any forensic evidence that might help us. We'd be looking at the middle of this coming week, at the very earliest, on any possible matches. I think every hour could be crucial. We can't leave it that long. This really could be the difference between life and death.'

There was a long silence. Grace knew he was asking for a massive leap of faith. He was taking a huge personal gamble in making this request. It still was not 100 per cent certain that Jessie Sheldon had been abducted. The likelihood was that, after twelve years, there would be no forensic evidence that could help his inquiry anyway. But he'd spoken to Joan Major, the forensic archaeologist that Sussex CID regularly consulted, who told him that it would at least be worth a try.

With the pressures on him at this moment, he was willing to clutch at any straw. But he believed what he was requesting now was much more than that.

Her voice becoming even more imperious, the Coroner said, 'You want to do this in a public cemetery, in broad daylight, on a Sunday, Detective Superintendent? Just how do you think any bereaved people, visiting the graves of their loved ones on the holy day, might feel about this?'

'I'm sure they'd be very distressed,' he replied. 'But not half as distressed as this young woman, Jessie Sheldon, who is missing. I believe the Shoe Man may have taken her. I could be wrong. We could be too late already. But if there's a chance of saving her life, that's more important than temporarily hurting the feelings of a few bereaved people who'll probably leave the cemetery and head off to do their shopping in ASDA or Tesco, or wherever else they shop on the *holy* day,' he said, making his point.

'OK,' she said. 'I'll sign the order. Just be as discreet as you can. I'm sure you will.'

'Of course.'

'I'll meet you at my office in thirty minutes. I take it you've never been involved in one of these before?'

'No, I haven't.'

'You won't believe the bureaucracy that's involved.'

Grace could believe it. But at this moment he was more interested in saving Jessie Sheldon than in worrying about pleasing a bunch of pen-pushers. But he didn't want to risk saying anything inflammatory. He thanked the Coroner and told her that he would be there in thirty minutes.

105

Jessie heard the familiar grating clatter of the side door of the camper van opening. Then the vehicle rocked slightly and she was aware of footsteps right beside her. She was quaking in terror.

An instant later, she was dazzled by the beam of a torch straight in her face.

He sounded furious. 'You stink,' he said. 'You stink of urine. You've wet yourself. You filthy cow.'

The beam moved away from her face. Blinking, she looked up. He was now directing the beam on to his own hooded face deliberately, so she could see him.

'I don't like dirty women,' he said. 'That's your problem, isn't it? You're all dirty. How do you expect to pleasure me when you stink like you do?'

She pleaded with her eyes. *Please untie me. Please free my mouth. I'll do anything. I won't fight. I'll do anything. Please. I'll do what you want, then let me go, OK? Deal? Do we have a deal?*

She was suddenly desperate to pee again, even though she had drunk nothing for what seemed an eternity and her mouth was all furred. What time was it? It was morning, she guessed, from the light that had momentarily filled the interior of the van a few minutes ago.

'I have a Sunday lunch engagement,' he said. 'I don't have time to sort you out and get you cleaned up, I'll have to come back later. Too bad I can't invite you. Are you hungry?'

He shone the torch back on her face.

She pleaded with her eyes for water. Tried to form the word inside her clamped mouth, inside her gullet, but all that came out was an undulating moan.

She was desperate for water. And shaking, trying to keep control of her bladder.

'Can't quite understand what you're saying – are you wishing me bon appétit?'

'Grnnnnmmmmmooooowhhh.'

'That's so sweet of you!' he said.

She pleaded with her eyes again. *Water. Water.*

'You probably want water. I'll bet that's what you're saying. The problem is, if I bring you some, you're just going to wet yourself again, aren't you?'

She shook her head.

'No? Well, we'll see then. If you promise to be a very good girl, then maybe I'll bring you some.'

She continued trying desperately to control her bladder. But even as she heard the sound of the sliding door closing, she felt a steady warm trickle again spreading around her groin.

106

Sunday 18 January

The Lawn Memorial Cemetery at Woodingdean was located high up, on the eastern perimeter of Brighton, with a fine view out across the English Channel. Not that the residents of this cemetery were likely to be able to appreciate it, Roy Grace thought grimly, as he stepped out from the long, blue, caterpillar-shaped tent into the blustery wind, and crossed over to the smaller changing room and refreshments tent, his hooded blue paper suit zipped to the neck.

The Coroner had not been wrong when she had talked about the bureaucracy involved in an exhumation. The granting and signing of the order were the easy parts. Much harder, early on a Sunday morning, was to assemble the team that was required.

There was a commercial firm that specialized in exhumations, its main business being the removal of mass graves to new sites for construction companies, or for churches that had been deconsecrated. But they would not be able to start until tomorrow morning without punitive overtime charges.

Grace was not prepared to wait. He called his ACC and Rigg agreed to sanction the costs.

*

The team assembled for the briefing he'd held at John Street an hour ago was substantial. A Coroner's Officer, two SOCOs, including one forensic photographer, five employees of the specialist exhumation company, a woman from the Department of the Environment, who made it clear she resented giving up her Sunday, a now mandatory Health and Safety Officer and, because it was consecrated ground, a clergyman. He'd also had present Joan Major, the forensic archaeologist, as well as Glenn Branson, whom he had put in charge of crowd control, and Michael Foreman, whom he had made an official observer.

Cleo, Darren Wallace – her number two at the mortuary – and Walter Hordern, who was in charge of the city's cemeteries, and drove the Coroner's discreet dark green van to body recoveries, were also present. He only needed two of them, but because none of the mortuary trio had been to an exhumation before, they were keen to attend. Clearly, Grace thought, none of them could get enough of dead bodies. What did that say, he sometimes wondered, about Cleo's love for him?

It wasn't only the mortuary staff who had been curious. He had received phone calls throughout the morning from other members of the CID as word had spread, asking if there was any chance of attending. For many of them, it would be a once-in-a-career opportunity, but he'd had to say no to all of them on the grounds of lack of space, and, in his tired and increasingly tetchy state, he had nearly added that it wasn't a bloody circus.

It was 4 p.m. and absolutely freezing. He stepped back out of the tent, cradling a mug of tea. The daylight was fading rapidly, and the glare of the mobile lights, situated around the cemetery, illuminating the vehicle path to the tent covering Molly Glossop's grave, and several around it, was getting brighter.

The site was ring-fenced by a double police cordon. All entrances to the cemetery were sealed off by a police guard and so far the public reaction had been more one of curiosity than anger. Then there was a second line of police tape directly around the two tents. No press had been allowed closer than the street.

The team inside the main tent were getting close to the bottom of the grave. Grace hadn't needed anyone to tell him, they all knew from the worsening stench. The smell of death was the worst smell in the world, he always thought, and he was catching whiffs of it now, as he stood out in the open air. It was the reek of a long-blocked drain suddenly being cleared, of the rotten meat in a fridge after a two-week power cut in the summer's heat, a heavy, leaden smell that seemed to suck your own spirits into it as it sank to the ground.

None of the experts had been able to predict what condition the body in this coffin would be in, as there were too many variables. They did not know what body – if any – was in here, or how long it had been dead before being buried. The humidity of any burial ground would be a major factor. But with this one being on chalky soil, on high ground, it was hopefully above the water table and would be relatively dry. Judging by the worsening smell, they would find out in a few minutes now.

He finished his tea and was about to go back inside when his phone rang. It was Kevin Spinella.

'Has the *Argus* hot-shot been having a Sunday lie-in?' Grace said, by way of a greeting.

There was a lot of wind roar, and the rumble of the huge portable generator, close by.

'Sorry!' the reporter shouted. 'Couldn't hear you!'

Grace repeated what he had said.

'Actually I've been doing a tour of local cemeteries, trying to find you, Detective Superintendent. Any chance I could come in?'

'Sure, book a plot here, then go and get hit by a bus.'

'Ha-ha! I mean now.'

'I'm sorry, no.'

'OK. So what do you have for me?'

'Not much more than you can see from the perimeter at the moment. Bell me back in an hour, I might have more then.'

'Excuse me, but I thought you were hunting for a young lady who disappeared last night, Jessie Sheldon? What are you doing here digging up an eighty-year-old lady?'

'You do your work by digging stuff up, sometimes I do mine that way too,' Grace replied, wondering how, yet again, the reporter had such an inside track.

Joan Major suddenly emerged from the entrance to the main tent, waving at him. 'Roy!' she called out.

He hung up.

'They've reached the coffin! Good news. It's intact! And the plaque on it reads *Molly Winifred Glossop*, so we have the right one!'

Grace followed her back in. The stench was horrific now and as the flap closed behind him he tried to breathe in only through his mouth. The crowded interior of the tent felt like a film set, with the battery of intense bright lights on stands all focused around the grave and the mound of earth at the far end, and several fixed video cameras recording all that was happening.

Most of the people in here were having problems

with the stench too, with the exception of the four officers
from the Specialist Search Unit. They were wearing white
bio-chemical protective suits with breathing apparatus.
Two of them were kneeling on the roof of the coffin,
screwing heavy-duty hooks into the sides, ready to attach
cables to block and tackle lifting gear once the sides of
the coffin had been cleared, which the other two were
now manoeuvring into position, a good yard above the
top of the grave.

Joan Major took over the excavation work, for the
next hour painstakingly excavating down the sides, and
under the base at each end of the coffin, for lifting straps
to be placed there. As she worked she carefully bagged
soil samples from above, the side and beneath the coffin
for later examination of any possible leaked fluids from
the contents of the coffin.

When she was finished, two of the exhumation
specialists then clipped ropes to each of the four hooks,
and to the underneath of the coffin front and back, and
clambered out of the grave.

'OK,' one said, moving clear. 'Ready.'

Everyone moved back.

The police chaplain stepped forward, holding a
prayer book. He asked for silence, then, standing over the
grave, read out a short, non-denominational prayer, welcoming back to earth whoever it might be that was in the
coffin.

Grace found the prayer strangely touching, as if they
were greeting some long-lost returning traveller.

The other members of the exhumation team began
heaving on a sturdy rope. There was a brief, anxious
moment when nothing happened. Then a strange sucking
noise that was more like a sigh, as if the earth was only

very reluctantly yielding something it had claimed for its own. And suddenly the coffin was steadily rising.

It came up, swinging, scraping against the sides, the pulley creaking, all the way until the bottom of the coffin was several inches clear of the grave. It swayed. Everyone in the tent watched for some moments in silent awe. A few clumps of earth tumbled and fell back into the grave.

Grace stared at the light-coloured wood. It did look remarkably well preserved, as if it had been down there for only a few days, rather than twelve years. *So, what secrets do you contain? Please God, something that will connect us to the Shoe Man.*

The Home Office pathologist, Nadiuska De Sancha, had already been contacted, and would head straight to the mortuary as soon as the body was loaded into the Coroner's van.

Suddenly there was a deafening crack, like a clap of thunder. Everyone in the tent jumped.

Something that was the shape and size of a human body, shrouded in black plastic wrapping and duct tape, plunged through the bottom of the coffin and disappeared into the grave.

107

Jessie was fighting for breath again. Panicking, she thrashed about, frantically trying to turn her head sideways to clear her nose a little. *Benedict, Ben, Ben, please come. Please help me. Please don't let me die here. Please don't.*

It hurt like hell, every muscle in her neck feeling as if it was being torn free from her shoulders. But at least now she could get some air. Still not enough, but her panic momentarily subsided. She was desperate for water. Her eyes were raw from crying. The tears trickled down her cheeks, tantalizing her, but she couldn't taste them with her mouth clamped tightly shut.

She prayed again. *Please God, I've just found such incredible happiness. Ben is such a lovely man. Please don't take me away from him, not now. Please help me.*

Through her living hell, she tried to focus her mind, to think clearly. Some time, she did not know when, but some time, probably soon, her captor was going to return.

If he was going to bring her the water he had talked about, unless he was just taunting her, he would have to untie her – at least enough so she could sit up and drink. If she was going to have a chance, it would be then.

Just one chance.

Even though every muscle in her body hurt, even

though she felt exhausted, she still had her strength. She tried to think of different scenarios. How clever was he? What game could she play to fool him? Play dead? Pretend to have a fit? There must be something, something she had not thought of.

That he had not thought of.

What time was it? In this long, dark void in which she was suspended, she suddenly felt a burning need to measure time. To figure out what time it was, how long she had been here.

Sunday. That was all she knew for sure. The lunch he had talked about must be Sunday lunch. Was it an hour since he had gone? Thirty minutes? Two hours? Four? There had been faint grey light but that had gone now. She was in pitch darkness.

Maybe there was a clue in the sounds she could hear. The endless, mostly faint clangings, clatterings, squeakings and bangings of loose windows, doors, panels of corrugated iron, sheet metal or whatever it was outside the building. There was just one that seemed to have a rhythm to it, she noticed. One of the banging sounds that reverberated. She heard it again now and counted.

One thousand and one, one thousand and two, one thousand and three, one thousand and four. Bang. One thousand and one, one thousand and two, one thousand and three, one thousand and four. Bang.

Her father was a keen photographer. She remembered as a small child, before digital photography had taken over, her father had a darkroom where he developed films himself. She liked to stand in the darkness with him, either the total darkness, or in the glow of the weak red light bulb. When he opened a film roll, they would stand in total darkness and her father would get her to count the seconds, the way he had taught her. If you said, *One thousand and one* slowly, that equalled, quite accurately, one second. It worked the same for all numbers.

So now she was able to calculate that the banging occurred every four seconds. Fifteen times a minute.

She counted out one minute. Then five. Ten. Twenty minutes. Half an hour. Then a surge of anger ripped through her at the futility of what she was doing. *Why me, God, if you bloody exist? Why do you want to destroy the love between Benedict and me? Because he's not Jewish, is that what this is about? Boy, are you one sick God! Benedict's a good man. He's dedicated his life to helping people less well off than himself. That's what I try to do also, in case you hadn't sodding noticed.*

Then she began sobbing again.

And counting automatically, like the banging was a metronome. Four seconds. Bang. Four seconds. Bang. Four seconds. Bang.

Then a loud, sliding clang.

The vehicle rocked.

Footsteps.

108

The Brighton and Hove mortuary had recently undergone substantial building works. The reason for this was that more people were eating themselves to death and then were too fat to fit into the fridges. So now new super-sized fridges had been installed to accommodate them.

Not that it required an extra-wide fridge to accommodate the desiccated remains of the woman who lay on the stainless-steel table, in the centre of the newly refurbished main post-mortem room, at 5.30 p.m. this Sunday afternoon.

Even after half an hour in here, Grace had not got used to the horrendous smell and breathing though his mouth only helped a little. He could understand why almost all pathologists used to smoke and carry out their work on corpses with a cigarette between their lips. Those who didn't put a blob of Vicks just above their upper lips. But that tradition appeared to have stopped along with the smoking ban a few years back. He could have sure done with something now.

Was he the only one in here who was affected?

Present in the room, and all gowned, masked and rubber-booted, were the Coroner's Officer, the forensic archaeologist, Joan Major, the SOCO photographer, James

Gartrell, who was busy alternately videoing and photographing every stage of the examination, Cleo and her assistant, Darren Wallace, and, centre stage, Nadiuska De Sancha. Spanish born and of Russian descent, the Home Office pathologist was a statuesque beauty almost every male police officer in Sussex lusted after – and liked to work with, as she was fast and good-humoured.

Also present was Glenn Branson – not that it was necessary for him to be here, but, Grace had decided, it was better to keep him occupied, rather than leaving him on his own to mope about his calamitous separation.

It was always strange attending a post-mortem when Cleo was at work. She was almost a stranger to him, bustling around, efficient and impersonal. Apart from the occasional smiling glance at him.

Since the start of the post-mortem, Nadiuska had painstakingly taped every inch of the dead woman's skin, bagging each strip of tape separately, in the hope that it might contain an errant skin or semen cell invisible to the naked eye, or a hair or clothing fibre.

Grace stared down at the body, mesmerized. The skin was almost black from desiccation, in a virtual mummified state. Her long brown hair was well preserved. Her breasts, although shrunken, were still clearly visible, as were her pubic hairs and her pelvis.

There was an indent in the rear of her skull, consistent with a heavy blow or fall. Before going into a detailed examination, just from what she could see, Nadiuska said that would be enough, in that part of the skull, to kill a normal person.

Joan said that her teeth indicated the woman was between late teens and mid-twenties.

Rachael Ryan's age.

Is that how Rachael Ryan would look now?
Dead like you? If you are not her.

In an attempt to ascertain her age more accurately, Nadiuska was now removing some of the skin around the corpse's neck to expose her collar bone. As she did so, Joan Major watched intently.

The forensic archaeologist suddenly became increasingly animated.

'Yes, look! Look at the clavicle, see? There's no sign of fusion on the medial clavicle, or even the beginning of it. That normally occurs around the age of thirty. So we can say pretty much for certain she was well below thirty – in her early twenties, I would estimate. I'll be able to get a more accurate age estimate when we've exposed more of the skeleton.'

Grace stared at the dead woman's face, feeling desperately sad for her.

Rachael Ryan, is that who you are?

He was feeling increasingly certain that it was.

He remembered so vividly talking to her distraught parents on those terrible days following her disappearance at Christmas 1997. He could recall her face, every detail of it, despite all that had happened in the intervening years. That smiling, happy, pretty face; such a young face, so full of life.

Have I found you at last, Rachael? Too late, I know. I'm sorry it's much too late. I apologize. I tried my best.

A DNA test would tell him if he was right and there was going to be no problem getting a good sample. Both the pathologist and the forensic archaeologist were profoundly impressed with the condition of the corpse. Nadiuska declared that it was better preserved than some bodies that were only weeks old, and attributed it to the fact that she had been wrapped in the two layers of plastic sheeting, and buried in a dry place.

At this moment, Nadiuska was conducting vaginal scrapings, carefully bagging and tagging each separate sample as she worked her way deeper up inside it.

Grace continued to stare at the body, the twelve years slipping away. And suddenly he wondered if, one day, he'd be in a mortuary, somewhere, looking at a body and nodding his head that it was Sandy.

'It is quite remarkable!' Nadiuska announced. 'The vagina is absolutely intact!'

Grace could not take his eyes from the body. The long brown hair looked in almost obscenely fresh condition, compared to the wizened scalp it sprouted from. There was a myth that hair and nails kept growing long after death. The prosaic truth was that skin contracted – that was all. Everything stopped at death, except for the parasitic cells inside you, which revelled in the fact that your brain no longer launched the antibodies to destroy them. So as your skin slowly shrank, shrivelling, being eaten away from inside, so more of your hair and nails became exposed.

'Oh, my God!' Nadiuska suddenly exclaimed. 'Look what we have here!'

Grace turned towards her, startled. She was holding up, in her gloved hand, a small metal object with a thin handle. Something dangled on the end of it. At first he thought it was a piece of torn flesh.

Then, looking more closely, he realized what it actually was.

A condom.

109

Sunday 18 January

He ripped away the duct tape covering Jessie's mouth, and as he pulled off the last layer, tearing it from her skin and lips and hair, she croaked in pain, then moments later, almost oblivious of the stinging pain, began gulping down air. Momentary relief that she was able to breathe normally flooded through her.

'Nice to meet you properly,' he said through the mouth slit in his hood, in his small voice.

He put the interior light in the van on and for the first time she could get a proper look at him. Sitting on a seat, staring down at her, he didn't appear particularly big or strong, even dressed in his macho head-to-toe motor-cycling leathers. But the hood chilled her. She saw his helmet lying on the floor, with heavy gauntlets folded into it. On his hands now he just wore surgical gloves.

'Thirsty?'

He had moved her on the floor, propped her back against the wall, but leaving her trussed up. She looked in desperation at the open water bottle he held out to her and nodded. 'Please.' It was hard to speak, her mouth was so dry and gummed up. Then her eyes darted to the ser-rated hunting knife he held in the other gloved hand. Not that he needed it; her arms were pinioned behind her back and her legs were still bound at the knees and the ankles.

She could kick him, she knew. She could bend her knees and kick out and really hurt him. But what use would that be? Just enrage him further, and make him do something worse to her than he already had in mind?

It was vital to keep her powder dry. She knew from her nursing days where the vulnerable points were; and from her kick-boxing training, where to land a venomous kick, one that, if she struck the right place, would disable him for a few seconds at the very least, and if she was lucky, longer.

If she got the chance.

She would have only one chance. It was absolutely crucial she didn't blow it.

She swigged down the water greedily, gulping, gulping, until she couldn't swallow fast enough and it overflowed down her chin. She choked, coughing hard. When she had finished coughing, she drank some more, still parched, then thanked him, smiling, looking straight at him pleasantly, as if he was her new best friend, knowing that somehow she had to establish a rapport with him.

'Please don't hurt me,' she croaked. 'I'll do whatever you want.'

'Yes,' he answered. 'I know you will.' He leaned forward and held up the knife in front of her face. 'It's sharp,' he said. 'Do you want to know how sharp?' He pressed the flat of the cold steel blade against her cheek. 'It's so sharp, you could shave with it. You could shave off all your disgusting bodily hairs – especially your pubes, all soaked in urine. Do you know what else I could do with it?'

He kept the flat of the blade to her face as she replied, shaking in terror, almost in a whisper. 'No.'

'I could circumcise you.'

He let the words sink in.

She said nothing. Her brain was kicking off in every direction. *Rapport. Must establish a rapport.*

'Why?' she said, trying to sound calm, but it came out as a gasp. 'I mean – why would you want to do that?'

'Isn't that what happens to all Jewish boys?'

She nodded, feeling the blade starting to bite into her skin, just beneath her right eye.

'Tradition,' she said.

'But not girls?'

'No. Some cultures, but not Jewish.'

'Is that right?'

The blade was pressing so hard she daren't move her head any more. 'Yes.' She only mouthed the word; the sound was trapped, by terror, in her throat.

'Circumcising a woman stops her from getting sexual pleasure. A circumcised woman can't have an orgasm, so after a short while she doesn't bother to try. Which means she doesn't bother being unfaithful to her husband, there's no point. Did you know that?'

Again her reply would not leave her throat. 'No,' she mouthed.

'I know how to do it,' he said. 'I've studied it. You wouldn't like me to circumcise you, would you?'

'No.' This time it came out as a faint whisper. She was quaking, trying to breathe steadily, to calm herself down. To think straight. 'You don't need to do that to me,' she said, her voice a fraction louder now. 'I'll be a good girl to you, I promise.'

'Will you wash yourself for me?'

'Yes.'

'Everywhere?'

'Yes.'

'Will you shave your pubes off for me?'

'Yes.'

Still keeping the knife to her cheek he said, 'I've got water in this van – warm running water. Soap. A sponge. A towel. A razor. I'm going to let you take all your clothes off so you can clean yourself up. Then we're going to play with that shoe.' He pointed at the floor with the water bottle. 'Recognize it? Identical to the pair you bought on Tuesday in Marielle Shoes in Brighton. It's a shame you kicked one out of the van or we could have played with a pair. But we'll have fun with just one, won't we?'

'Yes,' she said. Then, trying to sound bright, she added, 'I like shoes. Do you?'

'Oh, very much. I like the ones with high heels. Ones that women can use like a dildo.'

'Like a dildo? You mean use on themselves?'

'That's what I mean.'

'Is that what you'd like to do?'

'I'll tell you what you're going to do when I'm ready,' he snapped suddenly, anger flaring from nowhere. Then he pulled the knife away from her cheek and began to cut free the duct tape binding her knees together.

'I'm going to give you one word of warning, Jessie,' he said, his tone all friendly again. 'I don't want anything to spoil our fun, yeah? Our little session that we're going to have, OK?'

She pursed her lips and nodded her agreement, giving him all she could manage of a smile.

Then he raised the knife blade so that it was right in front of her nose. 'If you try anything, if you try to hurt me or escape, then what I'm going to do is tie you up again, but without any tracksuit bottoms or panties, yeah? Then I'm going to circumcise you. Just think about that when you're on your honeymoon with Benedict. And every time your husband makes love to you, for the rest of your life. Just think what you'll be missing. Do we understand each other?'

'Yes,' she mouthed.

But she was thinking.

He wasn't big. He was a bully.

She had been bullied at school. Bullied for her hooked nose, bullied for being the rich kid whose parents collected her in flash cars. But she'd learned how to deal with them. Bullies expected to get their own way. They weren't prepared for people to stand up to them. She once whacked her school's biggest bully, Karen Waldergrave, on the knee with a hockey stick during a game. Hit her so hard she'd shattered the bone, and she had to have an artificial kneecap made. Of course, it was an accident. One of those unfortunate things that happen in sport – at least, that was how it seemed to the teachers. No one ever bullied her again.

The instant she had her chance, this man wasn't going to bully her again either.

He cut free the tape securing her ankles. As she gratefully began moving her legs, to get the circulation back, he went to the sink and ran a tap. 'Get it nice and warm for you!' He turned back and looked hard at her. 'I'm going to free your hands now, so you can wash and shave for me. Remember what I've told you?'

She nodded.

'Say it out aloud.'

'I remember what you've told me.'

He cut the bonds joining her wrists, then told her to remove the duct tape.

She shook her hands for some seconds to get them working again, then picked at the strands of tape, getting purchase and ripping them free. He held the knife up, all the time, stroking the flat of the blade with his opaque, gloved finger.

'The floor is fine,' he said, as he noticed her wondering what to do with the curled strips.

Then he reached down, picked up the leather shoe from the floor and handed it to Jessie. 'Smell it!' he said.

She frowned.

'Hold it to your nose. Savour the smell!'

She sniffed the strong smell of fresh leather.

'Good, isn't it?'

His eyes, for an instant, were on the shoe and not her. She saw a glint in them. He was distracted. The shoe was at this moment the focus of his attention, not her. She held it up beneath her nose again, pretending to savour it, and surreptitiously changed her grip on it, so she was holding it by the toe. At the same time, on the pretext of working circulation back into her legs, she began to bend her knees.

'Are you the one they talked about in the papers, with the little winkie?' she asked suddenly.

He jerked towards her at the insult. As he did so, she arched her back and straightened her knees, springing both her legs up as hard as she could, striking him beneath the chin with the toes of her trainers, physically lifting him up, and slamming his head into the ceiling of the camper van. He fell, dazed, to the floor, the knife clattering away from him.

Before he had a chance to recover his wits, she was up on her feet, tearing the hood from his head. He looked almost pathetic without it, like a little startled mole. Then she slammed the shoe, stiletto heel first, as hard as she could into his right eye.

He screamed. A terrible howl of pain and shock and fury. Blood sprayed from his face. Then, grabbing the knife from the floor, she jerked open the sliding door and stumbled out, almost tumbling head first into pitch darkness. Behind her she heard the terrible howl of pain of a maddened, wounded beast.

She ran and crashed into something solid and unyielding. Then streaks of bright light darted around her.

Shit, shit, shit.

How could she have been so stupid? She should have taken the bloody torch!

In the beam, she momentarily saw the disused goods carriage on the dusted-over tracks. A gantry. Part of the steel walkway halfway up the walls. What looked like massive suspended turbines.

Where was the door?

She heard a shuffle. He was screaming out, in pain and fury. 'YOU THINK YOU'RE GOING TO GET AWAY – YOU ARE NOT, YOU BITCH.'

She gripped the knife. The beam shone straight in her face, dazzling her. She turned. Saw huge double doors, over the railway tracks. For the carriages to come in and out through. She sprinted towards them, the beam guiding her all the way there.

All the way to the padlocked chain between them.

110

Jessie turned and stared straight into the beam, her brain racing. He didn't have a gun, she was pretty sure of that, otherwise he'd have pulled that on her, not the knife. He was wounded. He was not big. She had the knife. She knew some self-defence. But he still frightened her.

There must be another exit.

Then the torch went off.

She blinked at the darkness, as if that might make it go away, or somehow lighten it. She was shaking. She could hear herself panting. She struggled to quieten her breathing down.

Now they were equal, but he had an advantage. He presumably knew the layout in here.

Was he creeping up on her now?

In the torch beam, she'd seen to her left a vast space with what looked like some kind of silo at the end of it. She took a few steps and almost instantly stumbled. There was a loud metal *pingggggg* as something rolled away from under her feet and fell with a swoosh, splashing into water below seconds later.

Shit.

She stood still. Then she remembered her phone!

If she could get back to the van, she could call for help. Then with panic rising, she thought again, *Call who?*

Where was she? Trapped inside some fucking great disused factory building somewhere. How great would that sound if she told the 999 operator?

*

He was already back at the camper van. His face was throbbing in agony and he couldn't see out of his right eye, but he didn't care, not at this moment. He did not care about anything except getting that bitch. She'd seen his face.

He had to find her. Had to stop her getting away.

Had to, because she could bring him down.

And he knew how.

He did not want to reveal his position by switching on the torch, so he moved as slowly as he could, feeling his way around the interior of the van until he found what he was looking for. His night-vision binoculars.

It took him only seconds to spot her. A green figure through the night-vision lens, moving slowly, inching her way left, walking like someone in slow motion.

Think you are so smart, don't you?

He looked around for an implement. Something heavy and solid that would bring her down. He opened the cupboard beneath the sink, but it was too dark to see in, even with his night-vision. So he briefly switched on the torch. The night-vision flared, shooting searing light into his right eye, startling him so much he dropped the torch and stumbled back, falling over.

*

Jessie heard the crash. She looked over in its direction and instantly saw light inside the camper. She hurried further away towards the silo she had seen, fumbling her way, tripping over something, then banging her head into a sharp protruding object. She stifled a groan. Then carried on, feeling with her hands in the darkness until they reached an upright steel stanchion.

One of the pillars supporting the silo?

She crept forward, feeling the downward curve of the base of the silo, and crawled under it, then, still inching her way with her hands, she stood up, breathing in a dry dusty smell. Then she touched something that felt like the rung of a ladder.

*

He carried on searching with the torch, frantically opening each of the drawers. In the last one he found a bunch of tools. Among them was a big, heavy spanner. He picked it up, feeling the pain in his eye worsening with every second, feeling the blood streaming down his face. He retrieved the binoculars and moved to the door, staring out through them.

The bitch had vanished.

He didn't care. He would find her. He knew the whole of this cement works like the back of his hand. He'd supervised the installation of all the surveillance cameras in here. This building housed the giant kilns that heated the combined limestone, clay, sand and bottom ash to 1,500 degrees Celsius, then fed it into twin giant cooling turbines, forward to the grinding mills and, when processed, into a series of storage silos to feed into waiting empty goods trucks. If the bitch wanted to hide, there were plenty of places.

But there was only one exit.

And he had the keys to the padlock in his pocket.

111

Roy Grace delayed the Sunday evening briefing to 7.30 p.m., to give him time to report on the findings from the exhumation.

He left Glenn Branson in the mortuary, to cover any new developments that might occur, as the post-mortem was still not completed and was not likely to be for some while yet. The corpse had a broken jawbone and fractured skull, and it was the blow to the skull that had almost certainly killed her.

His best hopes, both of identifying the dead woman and of achieving his aim in having this exhumation, lay in the hair follicles and skin samples taken from the corpse, along with the condom which contained, in the views of Nadiuska De Sancha and Joan Major, what might be intact traces of semen. The forensic archaeologist thought that although it was twelve years old there was a good chance of DNA being extracted intact from that.

These items had been couriered in an icebox to the DNA laboratory he favoured for fast turnarounds and with whom he had a good working relationship, Orchid Cellmark Forensics. They had promised to start work the moment the items arrived. But there was a slow sequencing process and even if the lab worked around the clock, the earliest they could expect any results would be mid-afternoon tomorrow, Monday. Grace was assured he would be notified instantly by phone.

He took his place and addressed his team, bringing them up to date, then asked for progress reports.

Bella Moy went first, handing out photographs of a young woman with wild hair. 'Sir, this is a photograph up in Brighton nick of one of the wanted persons in the city. Her current name – she's used several aliases – is Donna Aspinall. She's a known user, with a string of previous for fare dodging, both on trains and in taxis. She's got an ASBO and she's currently wanted on three separate counts of violent assault, GBH and actual assault. She's been identified by two covert officers in the operation last night – one of whom she bit on the arm – as the person John Kerridge, the taxi driver, was chasing.'

Grace stared at the photograph, realizing the implication. 'You're saying that Kerridge is telling the truth?'

'This would imply that he might be telling the truth about this passenger, sir.'

He thought for a moment. Kerridge had now been held for twenty-four hours. The maximum period for detaining a suspect without charge and without obtaining a court extension was thirty-six hours. They would have to release the taxi driver at 9.30 tomorrow, unless they had enough reason to convince a magistrate to hold him longer. They didn't yet have evidence that Jessie Sheldon's disappearance was the work of the Shoe Man. But if Kerridge's solicitor, Acott, got hold of this – and he undoubtedly would and probably already had – they'd have a fight on their hands to get an extension. He needed to think about this, and getting an emergency magistrates' court appearance tonight to request a further extension.

'OK, thanks. Good work, Bella.'

Then Norman Potting raised his hand. 'Boss, I've had a lot of help today from the mobile phone company, O₂. I spoke to Jessie Sheldon's fiancé early this morning, who told me that's the supplier her iPhone's registered with. They provided me half an hour ago with the tracking report on her phone. We may have a result here.'

'Go on,' Grace said.

'The last call she made on it was logged at 6.32 p.m. last night, to a number I've identified as belonging to her fiancé, Benedict Greene. He confirms he received a call from her at approximately that time, telling him she was heading home from her kick-boxing lesson. He told her to hurry, because he was picking her up at 7.15 p.m. The phone then remained in standby mode. No further calls were made, but it was plotted, from contact with base stations in the city, moving steadily west from approximately 6.45 p.m. – the time of the abduction. At 7.15 p.m. it stopped moving and has remained static since then.'

'Where?' Grace asked.

'Well,' the DS said, 'let me show you.'

He stood up and pointed to an Ordnance Survey map stuck to a whiteboard on the wall. A squiggly blue line ran the entire length of it. There was a red oval drawn on the map, with two red Xs at the top and bottom.

'The two crosses mark the O2 base stations that Jessie Sheldon's phone is currently communicating with,' Potting said. 'It's a pretty big area and unfortunately there's no third base station within range to give us the triangulation which would enable us to pinpoint her position more accurately.'

He pointed at the squiggly blue line. 'This is the River Adur, which runs up from Shoreham.'

'Shoreham's where John Kerridge lives,' Bella Moy said.

'Yes, but that's not helpful to us, since he's in custody,' Potting replied in a patronizing tone. Then he continued: 'There's open countryside on both sides of the river and Coombes Road, a busy main road which runs between these two base stations. There are a few detached private houses, a row of cottages that used to belong to the old cement works, and the cement works itself. It would seem that Jessie Sheldon, or at least her mobile phone, is somewhere inside this circle. But it's a big area.'

'We can rule out the cement works,' said DC Nick Nicholl. 'I attended there a couple of years ago when I was on Response. It's got extremely high security – round-the-clock monitoring. If a bird shits, it pings an alarm.'

'Excellent, Nick,' Grace said. 'Thank you. OK. Immediate action. We need to get a ground search of the entire area at first light. A POLSA and as many Uniform, Specials and PCSOs as we can muster. I want the river searched – we'll put the Specialist Search Unit in there. And we'll get the helicopter up right away. They can do a floodlight search.'

Grace made some notes, then looked up at his team.

'According to the Land Registry records, the lock-up is owned by a property company, sir,' Emma-Jane Boutwood said. 'I'll go to their offices first thing in the morning.'

He nodded. Despite round-the-clock surveillance, no one had shown up there. He was not hopeful that anyone would now.

He wasn't sure what to think.

He turned to the forensic psychologist. 'Julius, anything?'

Proudfoot nodded. 'The man who has taken Jessie Sheldon, he's your man,' he said emphatically. 'Not the chap you have in custody.'

'You sound very certain.'

'Mark my words. The right location, the right time, the right person,' he said, so smugly that Grace wished desperately, for an instant, that he could prove the man wrong.

*

When he returned to his office after the briefing had ended, Grace found a small FedEx package awaiting him.

Curious, he sat down and tore it open. And his evening just got a whole lot worse.

There was a handwritten note inside, on Police Training College, Bramshill headed paper, and attached to it was a photocopy of an email dated October last year.

The email was addressed to him, from Detective Superintendent Cassian Pewe. It informed him that there were some pages missing from the file on the Shoe Man that Grace had asked him to look through. The same crucial pages on the witness who had seen the van in which Rachael Ryan might have been abducted back in 1997.

The handwritten note said breezily. *Found this in my Sent box, Roy! Hope it's helpful. Perhaps your memory's not what it was – but hey, don't worry – happens to all of us! Cheers. Cassian.*

After ten minutes of searching through his email system, Grace found the original sitting among hundreds of others that were unread. It had been chaos around that time and Pewe seemed to have taken delight in bombarding him with dozens of e-missives daily. If he had read them all, he'd never have got anything done.

Nonetheless, it was going to leave him with a red face, and one less suspect.

112

Jessie had always been petrified of heights and for that reason at least she was grateful for the darkness. She had no idea where she was, but she had just climbed, one rung at a time, what she figured might be an inspection ladder inside the silo chute.

She had climbed for so long it felt like the ladder reached up to the skies, and she was glad she could not see down. She looked, every few rungs, scared he might already be climbing up after her, but there was no sign – or sound – of him.

Finally at the top she'd felt a railing and a gridded metal floor, and had hauled herself up on to this. Then she had gone head first into a stack of what felt and smelt like old cement bags, and had crawled on top of them. It was where she crouched now, peering into the blackness all around her and listening, trying to keep still to stop the bags rustling.

But she could hear nothing beyond the regular sounds of her prison. The regular clangings, clatterings, squeakings and bangings that were all much louder up here than they'd been when she was in the van, as the wind battered broken metal sheeting all around her.

She was thinking hard. What was his plan? Why wasn't he using the torch?

Was there another way up here?

The only thing that she could see was the luminous dial of her watch. It was just coming up to 9.30 p.m. Sunday night, she figured, it had to be. Over twenty-four hours since she'd been kidnapped. What was happening at home and with Benedict? He'd be isolated from her parents, she thought, wishing desperately now she had introduced them sooner, so they could all be doing something together.

Were the police involved? They must be. She knew her father. He would get every emergency service in the country involved.

How were they? What was her mother thinking? Her father? Benedict?

She heard the distant clatter of a helicopter. That was the second time in the past half-hour she had heard one.

Maybe it was looking for her.

*

He heard the sound of the helicopter again too. A powerful machine, not one of the smaller training ones from the school at nearby Shoreham Airport. And not many helicopters flew at night either. Mainly military, rescue services, air ambulances – and police.

The Sussex Police helicopter was based at Shoreham. If it was theirs that he was hearing, there was no reason to panic. It could be up for all kinds of reasons. The clatter was fading now; it was heading away to the east.

Then he heard a new sound that worried him much more.

A sharp, insistent buzzing. It was coming from the front of the camper. He lowered the binoculars and saw a weak, pulsing light that was also coming from the same place.

'Oh, shit. No, no, no!'

It was the bitch's mobile phone, which he had taken from her pocket. He thought he had switched the fucking thing off.

He stumbled up to the front, able to see the light from the phone's flashing display, seized it, then threw it on the floor in fury and stamped on it, crushing it like a massive beetle.

He stamped on it again. Then again. Then again.

Maddened with pain from his eye, anger at the bitch and anger at himself, he stood shaking. *Christ! Oh, Christ! Oh, Christ!* How could he have been so stupid?

Mobile phones gave away your location, even when they were only on standby. It would be one of the first things any intelligent police officer would be looking for.

Perhaps the phone companies were not able to access detailed stuff like that on Sundays?

But he knew he could not take the risk. He had to move Jessie Sheldon away from here as quickly as possible. Tonight. During darkness.

Which made it even more imperative to find her and quickly.

She'd made no sound for over an hour. Playing some clever hiding game. She might think she was clever that she had the knife. But he had two far more valuable tools at this moment. The torch and the binoculars.

He'd never had much truck with literature and shit. But there was one line he remembered from somewhere, through his pain: *In the land of the blind, the one-eyed man is king.*

That's what he was now.

He stepped down out of the van on to the concrete floor and raised his binoculars to his face. Hunting.

113

The evening was passing slowly for Roy Grace. He sat in his office, looking at Jessie Sheldon's family tree, which had been assembled by one of his team members. Her computer and mobile phone records were currently being examined by two members of the overloaded and under-manned High-Tech Crime Unit, who had given up their Sundays for the task.

The only report he'd received so far was that Jessie was very active on social networking sites – something she had in common with the woman who had nearly become a victim of the Shoe Man on Thursday afternoon, Dee Burchmore.

Was that how he followed his victims?

Mandy Thorpe had been active on Facebook and on two other sites as well. But neither Nicola Taylor, who had been raped in the Metropole Hotel, early on New Year's Day, nor Roxy Pearce, who had been raped in her home in Droveway Avenue, had presences on any social networking sites, nor did they Tweet.

It came back to the same thing linking each of these women. They had all recently bought expensive shoes from shops in Brighton. All except Mandy Thorpe.

Despite Dr Proudfoot's insistence to the contrary, the Detective Superintendent continued to believe that

Mandy Thorpe had not been raped by the Shoe Man but by someone else. Perhaps by a copycat. Or possibly the timing was coincidental.

His phone rang. It was DC Michael Foreman from MIR-1.

'Just had a report in from Hotel 900, who are going down to refuel, sir. So far they have nothing to report, except for two possible anomalies in the old cement works.'

'*Anomalies*?' Grace queried, wondering what the police helicopter crew meant by that.

He knew they had thermal-imaging equipment on board, which could detect humans in pitch darkness or dense fog just from the body heat they gave off. Unfortunately, while good for following villains who were fleeing from a stolen car and trying to hide in woods, or in alleys, it was easily fooled by animals or by anything that retained warmth.

'Yes, sir. They can't be sure they're human – could be foxes or badgers or stray cats or dogs.'

'OK, get a response unit down there to check it out. Keep me posted.'

*

Half an hour later, DC Foreman rang Grace back. A patrol car had attended the entrance to the old cement works and reported that the place was secure. There were ten-foot-high locked gates, topped with razor wire, and extensive surveillance.

'What kind of surveillance?' Grace asked.

'Remote monitoring. A Brighton firm with a good reputation, Sussex Remote Monitoring Services. If there was anything going on in there it would have been picked up by now by them, sir.'

'I know the name,' Grace said.

'The police use them. I think the Sussex House door pads were all installed by them.'

'Right. OK.' Like everyone in the city, he knew the cement works. It was one of the big landmarks, heading west, and there were rumours that at some point it was going to be reactivated after nearly two decades in mothballs. It was a vast place, situated in a chalk quarry hewn out of the Downs, comprising a group of buildings, each of them bigger than a football pitch. He wasn't even sure who the current owners were, but no doubt there would be a sign on the front.

To do a search he'd either have to get their consent or obtain a search warrant. And for an effective search, he'd have to put a big team in there. It would need to be done in daylight.

He made a note on his pad for the morning.

114

'Jessie!' he shouted. 'Phone call for you.'

He sounded so plausible, she almost believed him.

'Jessie! It's Benedict! He wants to do a deal with me to let you go! But first he needs to know you are OK. He wants to speak to you!'

She remained silent, trying to think this through. Had Benedict rung, which was highly probable, and the creep answered?

Was this about a ransom?

Benedict didn't have any money. What kind of deal could he do? And anyhow, this creep was a pervert, the Shoe Man, or whoever he was. He wanted her to masturbate with her shoe. What deal was he talking about? It didn't make sense.

And she knew, if she shouted, she would give her location away.

Lying on the old cement sacks, aching with cramp and craving water, she realized, for the moment anyway, that despite everything she was safe up here. She'd heard him creeping around the place for nearly two hours, downstairs first, then up on the floor above her, then clambering on to another level that did not sound far below her. At one point he had been so close she could hear him breathing. But mostly he had been silent, just every now and then giving away his position by kicking something, or crunching something underfoot, or with a ping of metal on metal. But he had not switched on his torch.

For a while she'd wondered if he had broken it, or if the battery had run out. But then she'd seen something that chilled her.

A very faint red glow.

It was not an area of technology on which she was clued up, but she remembered a movie in which a character had used night-vision equipment and that had given off a barely detectable red glow. Was that what he was using in here, she wondered?

Something through which he would watch her, without being seen?

So why hadn't he already sneaked up on her? There had to be only one reason: he had not been able to find her.

That's what this pretend call from Benedict was all about.

*

He knew one thing for certain. He'd searched every inch of this floor and she wasn't down here. She had to have climbed up, but where? There were two vast upstairs areas housing the long cooling pipes and the kilns that blasted the hot cement clinker into them. Any number of hiding places, but he thought he had searched them all.

She was clever, this bitch. Maybe she kept moving. He was getting more anxious and desperate with every passing minute. He had to get her away from here and somehow secure her in another place. And he had to be at work tomorrow. It was a very important day. A major new client and a key meeting with the bank about his expansion plans. He was going to have to get some sleep before then.

And his eye needed to be looked at. The pain was worsening all the time.

'Jessie!' he called out again, all friendly. 'It's for yoooooooooouuuu!'

Then, after a few moments silence, he said, 'I know where you are, Jessie! I can see you up there! If Mohammed won't come to the mountain, then the mountain's coming to Mohammed!'

Silence greeting him. Then the bang of a metal flap. Four seconds later, it banged again.

'You're only making this worse for yourself, Jessie. I'm not going to be happy when I find you. I'm really not!'

*

Jessie did not make a sound. She realized one thing. All the time it was dark, this creep had the advantage. But the moment dawn broke and some light started seeping in here, however little, all that changed. He frightened her and she did not know what he was capable of. But she was sure she had hurt his eye badly. And she still had the knife, on the floor, right by her hand.

It was midnight. Dawn would be some time around seven o'clock. Somehow she had to find the strength to forget her raging thirst and her tiredness. Sleep was not an option.

Tomorrow maybe there'd be a chink of light coming through a wall. This place was derelict. In semi ruins. There had to be a hole somewhere that she could crawl through. Even if it was on to the roof.

115

Despite the vigorous protests of the taxi driver's solicitor, Ken Acott, Grace had refused to allow John Kerridge – Yac – to be freed, and insisted on applying to the magistrates' court for a further thirty-six-hour extension. It had been granted readily, since, after the solicitor's insistence on having a specialist medic present, they had not yet been able to start interviewing Kerridge.

Grace was still not happy with this suspect, although he had to admit the evidence against Kerridge did not look strong, so far. The man's mobile phone had yielded nothing. He only had five numbers stored on it. One belonged to the owner of his taxi, one was for the taxi company, two were for the owners of the boat he lived on, who were in Goa – a mobile and a landline – and one for a therapist he had not seen in over a year.

The taxi driver's computer had not revealed anything of interest. Just endless visits to sites involving ladies' shoes – mostly on the fashion rather than fetish side – visits to eBay, as well as countless visits to perfume sites, sites concerned with Victorian period toilets and mapping sites.

A medical expert, a psychologist of some sort who was trained in Asperger's syndrome patients was on her way down. When she arrived, if she assessed Kerridge favourably, Acott said he would allow his client to be interviewed. Hopefully they'd find out more then.

Just as he returned to his office from the morning briefing, his mobile phone rang.

'Roy Grace,' he answered.

It was a technician he knew at the forensic laboratories and she was sounding very pleased with herself. 'Roy, I've got DNA results for you!'

'On what we sent you last night?' he replied, astonished.

'It's a new bit of kit – it's still undergoing trials and it's not reliable enough for court work. But we had such good DNA from both of those samples, we took some to experiment with, knowing the urgency.'

'So, tell me?'

'We have two hits – one for each sample. One is complete, a 100 per cent match, the other is partial, a familial match. The complete match is on DNA from a hair follicle from the corpse. Her name is Rachael Ryan. She disappeared in 1997. Any help?'

'You're certain?'

'The *machine* is certain. We're still running conventionally with the rest of her DNA, so we'll have that result later today. But I'm pretty sure.'

He allowed himself only a couple of seconds for this to sink in. It was what he was expecting, but even so it was a shock. A confirmation of his failure to save this young woman's life. He made a mental note to contact her parents, hoping they were both still alive and still together. At least now they would have closure, if nothing else.

'And the familial match?' he asked.

Familial, Grace knew, meant a near match, but not an exact match. It was normally a match between siblings or a parent and child.

'That's from the semen inside the condom that was found inside the corpse – Rachael Ryan as we now know. It's a woman called Mrs Elizabeth Wyman-Bentham.'

Grace wrote the name down, checking the spelling with her, so excited his hand was shaking. Then the technician gave him her address.

'Do we know why she's on the database?'

'Drink-driving.'

He thanked her, and as soon as he had terminated the call, he dialled Directory Enquiries, gave the name of Elizabeth Wyman-Bentham and her address.

Moments later, he had the number and dialled it.

It went straight to voicemail. He left a message with his name and rank, asking her to call him back urgently on his mobile number. Then he sat down and Googled her name to see if he could find out anything about her, in particular where she worked. It was 9.15 a.m. If she worked she was likely to be there already, or on her way there.

Moments later on his screen appeared the words, *About Lizzie Wyman-Bentham, CEO of WB Public Relations.*

He clicked on them and almost immediately a photograph of a smiling woman, with a mass of frizzed hair, came up, together with a row of details to click on for information about the firm. Just as he clicked on *Contact,* his phone rang.

He answered and heard a rather breathless, effusive female voice. 'I'm so sorry, I missed your call – heard it ringing just as I stepped out of the house! How can I help you?'

'This may sound a strange question,' Roy Grace asked. 'Do you have a brother or a son?'

'A brother.' Then her voice changed to panic. 'Is he

all right? Has something happened? Has he been in an accident?'

'No, he's fine, so far as we know. I need to speak to him in connection with a police inquiry.'

'Gosh, I was worried for a moment!'

'Can you tell me where I can reach him?'

'An inquiry, did you say? Ah yes, of course, probably something to do with work. Silly of me! I think he does a bit of work with you guys. He's Garry Starling and his company – well, he has two – Sussex Security Systems and Sussex Remote Monitoring Services – they're both in the same building in Lewes.'

Grace wrote the information down, and took Starling's office phone number.

'I'm not quite sure why – why exactly have you contacted me?'

'It's a little bit complicated,' Grace replied.

Her voice darkened. 'Garry's not in trouble, is he? I mean, he's a very respectable businessman – he's very well known in this city.'

Not wanting to give anything further away, he assured her that no, her brother was not in trouble. He ended the call, then immediately dialled Starling's office. The phone was answered by a pleasant woman. He did not reveal his identity, but merely asked to speak to Garry Starling.

'He's not in yet,' she said, 'but I'm sure he will be shortly. He's normally in by this time. I'm his secretary. Can I take a message?'

'I'll call back,' Grace said. He had to struggle to keep his voice sounding calm.

The instant he hung up, he hurried along to MIR-1, formulating his plan as he strode down the corridor.

116

There was less light than Jessie had imagined there'd be, which in some ways she thought was good. If she was very, very careful, keeping totally silent, she was able to tiptoe a short distance along the gridded walkway and look down at the camper van.

It sat there, cream and grimy, with its side door open. It was the kind of camper van that used to be one of the symbols of the hippy era – flower power, ban-the-bomb, all that stuff she recalled from what she had read about the 1960s and 1970s.

This creep didn't seem much like a hippy.

He was inside the van at the moment. Had he slept? She doubted it. Once or twice during the darkness she'd nearly dozed off, and on one occasion had almost cried out when an animal of some kind brushed her arm. Then a while later, as dawn brought with it a weak, grey haze of light, a rat came and took a look at her.

She hated rats and after that incident her tiredness was banished.

What was his plan now? What was going on in the outside world? She'd not heard the helicopter again, so maybe it hadn't been looking for her after all. How long would this go on for?

Perhaps he had supplies in the van. She knew he had

water and maybe he had food. He could sit this out indefinitely, if he didn't have a job or a life that was missing him. Whereas, she knew, she could not go on much longer without water and something to eat. She was feeling weak. On edge, but definitely weaker than yesterday. And dog tired. Running on adrenalin.

And determination.

She was going to marry Benedict. This creep was not going to stop her. Nothing was.

I am going to get out of here.

The wind was strong today and seemed to be getting stronger. The cacophony of sounds all around was worsening. Good, because that would help cover any noise she might make moving around.

Suddenly she heard a howl of rage. 'ALL RIGHT, YOU BITCH, I'VE HAD ENOUGH OF YOUR DAMNED GAMES. I'M COMING AFTER YOU. HEAR ME? I'VE WORKED OUT WHERE YOU ARE AND I'M COMING AFTER YOU!'

She tiptoed back to her vantage point and looked down. To her shock she could see him, still with his hood off, with what looked like a big red weal around his right eye. He was running across the ground floor, holding a big spanner in one hand and a carving knife in the other.

He was running straight for the entrance of the silo beneath her.

Then she heard him shouting again, his voice an echoing boom, as if he was shouting through a funnel. 'OH, VERY CLEVER, BITCH. A LADDER UP INSIDE THE SILO! HOW DID YOU FIND THAT?'

Moments later she heard the clanging of the rungs.

117

Glenn Branson was already waiting for Roy Grace in an unmarked car at the entrance to the industrial estate. He had the signed search warrants in his pocket.

The map they had studied earlier, in their hasty plan for this operation, showed there were only two possible routes in or out for vehicles visiting Garry Starling's headquarters here for his two companies, Sussex Security Systems and Sussex Remote Monitoring Services. Tucked discreetly out of sight, at this moment, were the vehicles of the team he had organized to carry out the arrest – when and if Starling turned up.

He already had four covert officers in place on the estate, in casual clothes. Parked up a side street, and ready to move in the moment Starling returned, were two dog-handler units to cover the exits to his office building. He had one of the Local Support Team vans, with six officers in body armour waiting inside it, plus four plain cars covering access to the network of roads linking into the industrial estate should Starling try to make a run for it.

Grace left his unmarked car parked in the next street along and climbed into Glenn Branson's. He felt tense. Relieved, yet hurting from the confirmation of Rachael Ryan's death. Thinking through the plan now. Plenty worried him.

'Rock 'n' roll?'

Grace nodded distractedly. The Shoe Man had never left DNA traces. His victims reported he had been unable to maintain an erection. Did this mean Garry Starling was not the Shoe Man? Or that killing Rachael Ryan – assuming he was the killer – had turned him on enough to ejaculate?

Why was he not in his office this morning?

If he had sex with a woman twelve years ago who was then found dead, how were they going to prove Starling was the killer? If indeed he was. What view would the Crown Prosecution Service take?

A million unanswered questions.

Just a growing certainty in his mind that the man who had murdered Rachael Ryan was the man who had abducted Jessie Sheldon. He desperately hoped he could do a better job of finding her alive – if there was still a chance – than he had done of finding Rachael Ryan. And that he would not be disinterring her from a grave in another twelve years' time.

As they drove up to the smart front entrance of Sussex Security Systems and Sussex Remote Monitoring Services, he noticed the cars parked in allotted bays, and the empty one marked CEO. But what he was looking at more was the row of white vans bearing the companies' joint logo.

It had been a white van that had driven off at speed from the car park on Thursday after the failed attack on Dee Burchmore. And a white van in which Rachael Ryan had been abducted twelve years ago.

They climbed out of the car and walked in through the front door. A middle-aged receptionist sat behind a curved desk with the two logos emblazoned on the front. To their right was a small seating area, with copies of

Sussex Life and several of today's papers, including the *Argus*, laid out.

Grace thought grimly that they probably wouldn't be laying out tomorrow's *Argus*, with the kind of headline it was likely to contain.

'Can I help you, gentlemen?'

Grace showed his warrant card. 'Has Mr Starling come in yet?'

'No – er, no, not yet,' she said, looking flustered.

'Would you say that's unusual?'

'Well, normally, on a normal Monday morning, he's the first one in.'

Grace held the search warrant up and gave her a few seconds to read it. 'We have a warrant to search these premises. I'd be grateful if you could find someone to show us around.'

'I'll – I'll get the manager, sir.'

'Fine. We'll start. Tell him to find us.'

'Yes – right – yes, I will. When Mr Starling turns up, shall I let you know?'

'It's OK,' Grace replied. 'We'll know.'

She looked lost for an answer.

'Where do we find your CCTV monitoring section?' Grace asked.

'That's on the first floor. I'll page Mr Addenberry and he can take you along.'

Glenn pointed at the door to the stairs. 'First floor.'

'Yes, you turn right. Keep going down the corridor, into the accounts department and then the call-handling and you'll come to it.'

Both detectives loped up the stairs. Just as they reached the end of a corridor, with offices on either side, a short, nervous-looking and balding man in his early forties, in a grey suit with a row of pens in the top pocket, scuttled up to them.

'Hello, gentlemen. How can I help you? I'm John Addenberry, the General Manager.' He had a slightly smarmy voice.

When Grace explained who they were and about the search warrant, Addenberry started to look as if he was standing on a live electrical wire.

'Right,' he said. 'Right. Of course. We do a lot of work for Sussex Police. CID HQ are important customers. Very.'

He led the way through into the CCTV control room. Seated at a chair in front of a bank of twenty television monitors was a enormously overweight character, dressed in an ill-fitting uniform and greasy hair, and looking far too old to be sporting bum-fluff on his lip, Grace thought. A large Coca-Cola and a giant-size packet of Doritos sat on a table in front of him, next to a microphone and a small control panel, and a computer keyboard.

'This is Dunstan Christmas,' Addenberry said. 'He's the duty controller.'

But Grace had turned his attention away to the bank of monitors. And he frowned as he stared at one in particular. The front of a smart, ultra-modern house. Then he pointed. 'No. 7 – is that 76 Droveway Avenue, the home of Mr and Mrs Pearce?'

'Yep,' Christmas said. 'She was raped, wasn't she?'

'I didn't see any cameras when I was there.'

Christmas chewed a nail as he spoke. 'No, you wouldn't. I think in that house they're all hidden.'

'Why's no one told me? There might be evidence on this from her attack,' Grace said angrily.

Christmas shook his head. 'No, wasn't working that

night. It was down from mid-afternoon. Didn't go back up until the next morning.'

Grace stared at him hard and saw Branson doing the same thing. Was he hiding something? Or guileless? Then he stared back at the screen. The image had changed to the rear garden.

Down on the night she was attacked. The company was owned by their new prime suspect.

The coincidence was too much.

'Do these often go down?'

Christmas shook his head and chewed on his nail again. 'No. Very rarely. It's a good system and there's normally backup.'

'But the backup wasn't working on the night Mrs Pearce was attacked?'

'That's what I was told.'

'What about that one there?' Glenn Branson said, pointing at the blank screen numbered 20.

Grace nodded his head. 'Yes, I was going to ask the same.'

'Yep, that's down at the moment.'

'What's the property that's being covered?'

'The old cement works at Shoreham,' Christmas replied.

118

Jessie knew what she had to do, but as the moment approached her body went into panic mode and froze on her.

He was getting closer. Each clang of the rung slow, steady, determined. She could hear his breathing now. Getting closer. Closer. Nearing the top.

Above her she could hear a sound, like the clatter of that helicopter again. But she ignored it, not daring to be distracted. She turned, holding the knife in her hand, then finally dared to look down. And nearly dropped the knife in terror. He was only a few feet below her.

His right eyeball was at a grotesque angle, almost as if it was peering back into its own socket, half sunken in a gunge of coagulated blood and grey fluid, the whole socket encircled inside a livid purple bruise. The massive spanner protruded from the top pocket of his anorak and he was holding the rung with one hand, the carving knife with the other, staring up at her with an expression of utter hatred.

It was a long way down. Her brain was spinning. Trying to think clearly, to remember her instructions, but she'd never been taught how to kick in a situation like this. If she could plant both feet hard on his face she could dislodge him, she knew. It was her one chance.

In a swift moment, she squatted, fighting off the vertigo as she stared down, trying to concentrate on him and not the long drop below. She took all her weight on her hands, braced herself, bent her knees, then kicked as hard as she could, clinging to the slats of the grid with her fingers.

Instantly she felt a searing pain in the ball of her right foot.

Then, crying out in pain, she felt a vice-like clamp around her left ankle. He was pulling her. Pulling her. Trying to dislodge her. And she realized in this instant she had made a terrible mistake. He had jammed his knife into her right foot, let go of the rung and was now holding both her ankles. He was much stronger than he had looked. He was pulling her. Trying to dislodge her. He was being suicidal, she suddenly understood. Taking a gamble. Either he dislodged her and they both plunged together, or she was going to have to pull him up.

Then she felt another searing pain in the ball of her right foot, followed by an agonizing one in her right shin. And another. He was holding on with his left hand and slashing at her foot with the knife. Suddenly there was a terrible, terrible pain in the back of her right ankle and her foot felt powerless.

He had sawn through her Achilles tendon, she realized.

In desperation she jerked sharply backwards. And fell on to her back. He had let go.

She scrambled to her feet and promptly fell over again. She heard a clatter as her knife skidded away from her and then, to her horror, it plunged through the railings. Moments later she heard a *ping* a long way below her. Her right foot, in terrible agony, would no longer support her.

Oh, Jesus. Please help me.

He was hauling himself up over the edge, on to the grid, the carving knife still in his hand.

Trying desperately to think clearly despite her agony, she struggled to remember her training. This was a better position. Her left leg was still working.

He was on the gridded platform now, only feet away from her, on his knees and getting to his feet.

She lay still, watching him.

Watching the leer on his face. He was smiling again. Back in control. Coming after her.

Upright now, he towered over her, holding the knife, with blood on the blade, in his right hand and taking out the spanner from his top pocket with his left. He took a lurching step towards her, then raised the spanner.

In less than a second, she calculated, he would bring that spanner down on her head.

She bent her left knee, then kicked forward with every ounce of strength that remained in her body, visualizing a point a yard behind his right kneecap, heard the snap as she connected, driving her foot into the kneecap, just as she had driven that hockey stick all those years before into the knee of the school bully.

Saw the momentary shock in his face. Heard his hideous howl of pain as he fell over backwards, with an echoing clang, on to the grid. Then, hauling herself up with the help of the railings and holding on, began to hop, dragging her right foot, away from him.

'Owwww! My knee! Owwwwww, you fucking, fucking, fucking bitch.'

There was a vertical ladder she'd seen earlier at the far end of this walkway. She lunged at it, not looking down, ignoring the height. Gripping the edge with both hands she half-hopped, half-slipped, down, down, down, down.

He still had not appeared above her.

Then, as she reached the bottom, a pair of hands gripped her waist.

She screamed in terror.

A calm, gentle, unfamiliar voice said, 'Jessie Sheldon?'

She turned, quaking. And found herself staring at a tall man with silver wisps of hair either side of a black baseball cap. On the front of the cap was written the word POLICE.

She fell into his arms, sobbing.

119

'You're unbelievable! You know that? You are un-fucking-believable! You know how much evidence there is against you? It's un-fucking-believable! You filthy pervert! You – you monster!'

'Keep your voice down,' he replied, in a subdued tone.

Denise Starling stared at her husband, in his shapeless blue prison tracksuit, with the black patch over his right eye, sitting opposite her in the large, garishly furnished, open-plan visiting room. A camera watched them from the ceiling and a microphone was silently recording them. A blue plastic table separated them.

Either side of them, other prisoners talked with their loved ones and their relatives.

'Have you read the papers?' she demanded. 'They're linking you with the Shoe Man rapes back in 1997. You did those too, didn't you?'

'Keep your bloody voice down.'

'Why? Are you afraid of what they might do to you in the remand wing? They don't like perverts, do they? Do they bugger you with ladies' shoes in the showers? You'd probably enjoy that.'

'Be quiet, woman. We've got things to discuss.'

'I've got nothing to discuss with you, Garry Starling.

You've destroyed us. I always knew you were a sodding pervert. But I didn't know you were a rapist and a murderer. Had a good time on the ghost train with her, did you? You took me on the ghost train on one of our first dates and jammed your finger up my fanny. Remember? Get your rocks off on the ghost train, do you?'

'I didn't go on any ghost train. It wasn't me. Believe me!'

'Yeah, right, believe you. Ha! Ha fucking ha!'

'It wasn't me. I didn't do that.'

'Sure, right, and it wasn't you at the cement works, was it? Just someone who looked like you.'

He said nothing.

'All that tying me up shit. Making me do things with shoes while you watched and played with yourself.'

'Denise!'

'I don't care. Let them all hear! You've ruined my life. Taken my best years. All that not wanting to have children because you had such an unhappy childhood shit. You're a monster and you're where you deserve to be. I hope you rot in hell. And you'd better get yourself a good solicitor, because I'm not standing by you. I'm going to take you for every penny I can.'

Then she began to sob.

He sat in silence. He had nothing to say. If it had been possible, he would have liked to lean over the table and strangle this bitch with his bare hands.

'I thought you loved me,' she sobbed. 'I thought we could make a life together. I knew you were damaged, but I thought that if I loved you enough maybe I could change you. That I could offer you something that you never had.'

'Give over!'

'It's true. You were honest with me once. Twelve

years ago, when we married, you told me I was the only person who had given you peace in your life. Who understood you. You told me your mother made you screw her, because your father was impotent. That after that you were disgusted by women's private parts, even my own. We went through all that psychology shit together.'

'Denise, shut it!'

'No, I won't shut it. When we got to together I understood that shoes were the only things that turned you on. I accepted that because I loved you.'

'Denise! Bitch! Shut it!'

'We had so many good years. I didn't realize I was marrying a monster.'

'We had good times,' he said suddenly. 'Good times until recently. Then you changed.'

'Changed? What do you mean changed? You mean I got fed up fucking myself with shoes? Is that what you mean by *changed*?'

He was silent again.

'What's my future?' she said. 'I'm now Mrs Shoe Man. Are you proud of that? That you've destroyed my life? You know our good friends, Maurice and Ulla? The ones we have dinner with every Saturday night at the China Garden? They're not returning my calls.'

'Maybe they never liked you,' he replied. 'Maybe it was me they liked and they just put up with you as my whingeing hag wife.'

Sobbing again, she said, 'Do you know what I'm going to do? I'm going to go home and kill myself. Will you care?'

'Just do it properly,' he said.

120

Friday 23 January

Denise Starling drove home recklessly in her black Mercedes convertible coupé. She stared at the wet road ahead through her mist of tears. The wipers clop-clopped on the windscreen. A chirrupy woman was wittering away on BBC Sussex Radio about disastrous holidays people had experienced, inviting listeners to call in.

Yeah, every sodding holiday with Garry Starling had been a disaster. Life with Garry Starling had been a disaster. And now it was getting even worse.

Shit, you bastard.

Three years into their marriage she'd fallen pregnant. He'd made her abort. He didn't want to bring children into the world. He'd quoted some poem at her, some poet whose name she could not remember, about your parents screwing you up.

What had happened in Garry's childhood had twisted him, that was for sure. Damaged him in ways that she could never understand.

She drove, way over the limit, along the London Road, past Preston Park, and shouted, 'Fuck you!' when the speed camera there she had totally forgotten about flashed her. Then she turned into Edward Street, drove along past the law courts, and Brighton College and the Royal Sussex County Hospital.

A few minutes later she made a right turn, opposite the East Brighton Golf Club, where Garry was a member – not for much longer, she thought, with some strange, grim satisfaction – let him be a sodding pariah too! Then she crested the hill, swung into Roedean Crescent and finally turned right, into the driveway of their large mock-Tudor house, passing the double garage doors, and pulled up in front of Garry's grey Volvo.

Then, her eyes still misted with tears, she unlocked the front door of her house. She had trouble, for some moments, unsetting the alarm. *Typical! The one time we have trouble with the alarm, Garry's not around to get it sorted!*

She slammed shut the front door, then slid the safety chain across. *Sod you, world. You want to ignore me? Fine by me! I'm going to ignore you too. I'm going to open a bottle of Garry's most expensive claret and get rip-roaring sodding pissed!*

Then a quiet voice right behind her said, 'Shalimar! I like Shalimar! I smelt it the first time I met you!'

An arm clamped around her neck. Something damp and sickly-sweet-smelling was pressed across her nose. She struggled, for a few seconds, as her brain began to go muzzy.

As she lapsed into unconsciousness, the last words she heard were, 'You're like my mother. You do bad things to men. Bad things that make men do bad things. You're disgusting. You are evil, like my mother. You were rude to me in my taxi. You destroyed your husband, you know that? Someone has to stop you before you destroy anyone else.'

Her eyes were closed, so he whispered into her ear, 'I'm going to do something to you that I once did to my mother. I left it a little late with her, so I had to do it a different way. But it felt good afterwards. I know I'm going to feel good after this too. Maybe even better. Uh-huh.'

Yac pulled her limp body up the stairs, listening to the bump-bump, bump-bump of her black Christian Louboutins on each tread as he struggled with her weight.

He stopped, perspiring, when he reached the landing. Then he bent down and picked up the blue tow rope he'd found in the garage, in his gloved hands, and knotted one end firmly around one of the mock-Tudor ceiling beams that was in easy reach of the stairs. He'd already prepared the other end into a hangman's noose. And measured the distance.

He placed the noose around the limp woman's neck and heaved her, with some difficulty, over the banister rail.

He watched her fall, then jerk, then spinning around and around.

It was some minutes before she was completely still.

He stared at her shoes. He remembered her shoes the first time she had entered his taxi. Feeling a need to take them from her.

Hanging limply, looking pretty dead so far as he could tell, she reminded him of his mother again now.

No longer able to hurt anyone.

Just like his mother hadn't been.

'I used a pillow on her,' he called out to Denise. But she did not reply. He wasn't really expecting her to.

He decided to leave the shoes, although they were so tempting. After all, taking them was the Shoe Man's style. Not his.

121

Sunday 25 January

It was a good Sunday morning. The tide was in and the baby on the boat next door was not crying. Maybe it had died, Yac thought. He'd heard about cot death syndrome. Perhaps the baby had died from that. Perhaps not. But he hoped so.

He had copies of all this week's *Argus* newspapers laid out on the table in the saloon. Bosun, the cat, had walked over them. That was OK. They'd reached an understanding. Bosun did not walk over his lavatory chains any more. But if he wanted to walk over his newspapers, that was fine.

He was happy with what he read.

The Shoe Man's wife had committed suicide. That was understandable. Her husband's arrest was a big trauma for her. Garry Starling had been a major player in this city. A big socialite. The disgrace of his arrest would have been hard for any wife to bear. She'd been telling people she felt suicidal and then she had hanged herself.

Perfectly reasonable.

Uh-huh.

He liked it best when the tide was in and the *Tom Newbound* was floating.

Then he could pull his fishing lines up.

He had two fishing lines out, each with weights on them so that they sank well into the mud at low tide. Of course he had been worried each time that the police had searched the boat. But he needn't have been. They pulled every plank up from the floor of the bilges. Searched in every cavity there was. But none of them had ever thought to raise one of the fishing lines, like he was doing now.

Just as well.

The second line was tied, at the end, to a weighted waterproof bag. Inside were the shoes of Mandy Thorpe. Fake Jimmy Choos. He didn't like those fake shoes. They deserved to be buried in mud.

And she deserved the punishment he had given her for wearing them.

But, he had to concede, it had been good punishing her. She'd reminded him so much of his mother. Fat like his mother. The smell of his mother. He'd waited a long time to do that to his mother, to see what it felt like. But he'd left it too late and she was too sick by the time he'd gathered the courage. But it had been good with Mandy Thorpe. It had felt like he was punishing his mother. Very good indeed.

But not as good as punishing Denise Starling.

He liked the way she had spun around and around, like a top.

But he hadn't liked being in custody. Hadn't liked the way the police had removed so many of his things from the boat. Going through everything and messing up his collections. That was bad.

At least he had everything back now. It felt like he had his life back.

Best news of all, he'd had a call from the people who owned this boat, to say that they would be staying on at least two more years in Goa now. That made him very pleased.

Life suddenly felt very good. Very peaceful.

And it was a rising tide. Nothing like it.

Uh-huh.

122

Darren Spicer was feeling in a good mood. He stopped off at the pub, which had become his regular staging post on his way back home from work, for his now customary two pints with whisky chasers. He was becoming a creature of habit! You didn't have to be in prison to have a routine; you could have one outside too.

He was enjoying his new routine. Commuting to the Grand from the night shelter – always by foot, to save the pennies and to keep fit. There was a young lady who worked as a chambermaid at the hotel called Tia whom he was getting sweet on – and he reckoned she was getting sweet on him too. She was Filipina, pretty, in her early thirties, with a boyfriend she'd left because he beat her up. They were getting to know each other pretty well, although they hadn't actually yet *done it*, so to speak. But that was just a matter of time now.

They had a date tomorrow. It was difficult in the evenings, because of having to be back for lock-in, but tomorrow they would be spending all day together. She shared a room in a little flat up off the Lewes Road and, giggling, had told him her room-mate was going to be away for the weekend. Tomorrow, with luck, he reckoned, they'd be shagging all day.

He had another whisky to celebrate, a quality one

this time, a single malt, Glenlivet. Mustn't drink too much, he knew, because arriving back at St Patrick's drunk was a sure way to get thrown out. And now he was getting close to his coveted MiPod. So just the one Glenlivet. Not that money was no object – but the old cash situation was improving all the time.

He'd managed to get himself on to room maintenance at the hotel, because they were short of staff. He had a plastic pass key to get him into every guest room in the building. And he had today's takings from the room safes he'd opened up tucked in his pocket. He'd been cautious. He was going to keep his promise to himself to stay out of prison this time for good. All he took was a tiny fraction of any cash he found in the safes. Of course he had been tempted by some of the fancy watches and jewellery, but he'd stuck to his guns, and was proud of his self-discipline.

In these past four and a half weeks, he'd stashed away nearly four grand in his chained suitcase in the locker at St Patrick's. Property prices had come down, thanks to the recession. With what Tia earned, and with what he could put down as a cash deposit in, say, a year's time, he should be able to buy a little flat somewhere in the Brighton area. Or even move right away to somewhere a lot cheaper. Perhaps warmer.

Perhaps Spain.

Maybe Tia would like to be in a warm country.

Of course it was all a pipe dream. He hadn't talked about any future with her yet. The thought of hopefully shagging her tomorrow was about as far as he had got. But he felt good about her. She gave off a warmth that made him feel happy every time he stood near her or talked to her. Sometimes you needed to go with your instincts.

And his instincts, ten minutes later, as he turned right off Western Road into Cambridge Road told him that something was not good.

It was the shiny silver Ford Focus estate double-parked almost outside the front door of the St Patrick's night shelter, with someone sitting in the driving seat.

When you spent your life trying not to get nicked, you developed a kind of second sense, your antennae always up for spotting plain-clothes police and their vehicles. His eyes locked on the four short antennae on the roof of the Ford.

Shit.

Fear crashed through him. For an instant, he debated whether to turn and run, then empty his pockets. But he'd left it too late. The burly, bald, black detective who was standing in the doorway had already clocked him. Spicer decided he'd have to try to bluff it out.

Shit, he thought again, his dream fading away. And tomorrow's shag with sweet Tia. The grim, green walls of Lewes Prison closing around his mind.

'Hello, Darren,' Detective Sergeant Branson greeted him, with a big cheery grin. 'How's it going?'

Spicer looked at him warily. 'All right,' he said. 'Yeah.'

'Wonder if I could have a word with you.' He pointed at the door. 'They're letting us use that interview room – OK with you?'

'Yeah.' Spicer shrugged. 'What's this about?'

'Just a little chat. Got a bit of news I thought you might like to hear.'

Spicer sat down, shaking, very uneasy. He couldn't

think of any news that Detective Sergeant Branson could bring him that he would like to hear.

Branson closed the door, then seated himself across the table, facing him. 'Dunno if you remember when we spoke – you were giving me the nod about the lock-up behind Mandalay Court? About the white van inside it?'

Spicer looked at him warily.

'I mentioned to you there was a reward, right? Fifty thousand pounds? For information leading to the arrest and conviction of the man who attempted to attack Mrs Dee Burchmore? Put up by her husband.'

'Yeah?'

'Well, I've got good news for you. It looks like you're in line for it.'

Spicer broke into a grin, relief flooding through him. Incredible relief.

'You're shitting me?'

Branson shook his head. 'Nope. Actually, Detective Superintendent Grace, the SIO, has put your name forward himself. It's down to you that we've potted our suspect. He's been arrested and charged.'

'When do I get the money?' Spicer asked incredulously.

'When he's convicted. I think a trial date's been set for this autumn – I can let you know when I have the details. But there's not much doubt we've got the right man.' Branson smiled. 'So, sunshine, what are you going to do with all that loot? Shove it up your nose, right, as usual?'

'Nah.' Spicer said. 'I'm going to buy a little flat, you know, as an investment for the future. I'll use the money towards the deposit. Magic!'

Branson shook his head. 'In your dreams. You'll spend it on drugs.'

'I won't. Not this time! I'm not going back inside. I'm going to buy a place of my own and go straight. Yeah.'

'Tell you what, invite us to your house-warming. Just to prove you've changed, all right?'

Spicer grinned. 'Yeah, well, that could be difficult. If it's a party, you know – like – there might be stuff here. You know, like – party stuff. Could be embarrassing for you to be there – you being a cop and all.'

'I don't embarrass easily.'

Spicer shrugged. 'Fifty grand. Incredible! Fucking incredible!'

The DS fixed his eyes on the old lag. 'You know what? I heard they didn't bother changing the sheets in your cell. They know you're going to be back.'

'Not this time.'

'I'll look forward to the invitation. The Governor of Lewes Prison will know where to send it.'

Spicer grinned. 'That's very witty.'

'Just the truth, sunshine.'

Glenn left the room and went outside, to where Roy Grace was waiting in the car. He was looking forward to an end-of-week drink with his mate.

123

I've started talking. Just for one reason, to get even with you, Detective Smug Superintendent Roy Grace.

It's not great in here on the remand wing. People don't like guys like me in this place. Nonces, they call us. I cut my tongue open on a piece of razor blade that was in my Irish stew. I hear rumours that people piss in my soup. One guy's threatened to put my other eye out.

I'm told it will be better after my trial. Then if I'm lucky (ha) I'll be put into the nonces' wing, as it's known. All of us sexual deviants together. How great will that be! Party-party-party!

Some nights I don't sleep at all. I have all this anger everywhere – all around me in this place and deep inside me. I'm angry at whoever it was who did that rape on the ghost train. It meant that the pier was swarming with police afterwards, completely messing up my plans. It was all going so nicely until then. It just didn't go nicely after that.

I'm angry that the bitch escaped the humiliation that she would have faced, being known as my wife. Something's not right about that. Although I don't really care and I don't suppose anyone else does.

But I have even bigger anger inside me that is directed at you, Detective Superintendent Grace. You thought you were clever, telling the world about the size of my dick. You can't be allowed to get away with something like that.

That's why I'm talking now. I'm fessing-up to all the other times I raped and took the shoes. In particular the ghost train. You won't be able to get me on any trick questions – word seems to have got around about all the crimes the Shoe Man perpetrated – the recent ones – every detail of what he did to the women. Including every detail of what happened in the ghost train.

So I'm briefed!

You didn't understand why I changed my MO, from taking one shoe and panties to taking both shoes. You weren't meant to understand, see? I wasn't going to make your job easy for you by just repeating exactly the same stuff over again. Variety's the spice of life, right?

I'm your man, all right! I'm just going to hope that the creep who raped that woman on the ghost train strikes again.

You'll have egg all over your face, Detective Superintendent Grace.

And I'll have a big grin on mine.

And who will have the smaller dick then?

124

'It's good to see you relaxed, my darling,' Cleo said.

It was the evening now. They'd spent the afternoon together, working on the wedding list. Roy Grace had his feet up, a glass of red wine in his hand, and was watching *The Antiques Road Show*, one of his favourite programmes. Most of all he enjoyed watching people as they were given the valuation of their treasured – or otherwise – heirloom. The look of astonishment when some tatty bowl they'd been using to feed the dog was valued at thousands. The look of dismay when some splendid painting, which had been in the family for generations, was pronounced a fake worth only a few quid.

'Yep!' He smiled and just wished he felt relaxed. But he didn't. Doubt was still gnawing away at him, despite the Shoe Man having been caught. And there were still ripples from Starling's wife's suicide. He'd listened to the prison tape, where she'd talked about going home and topping herself. It had sounded like an idle threat. But then she had gone and done it. No note, nothing.

'I mean,' she said, gently lifting Humphrey out of the way and curling up next to him on the sofa, 'as relaxed as you're ever going to be.'

He shrugged, then nodded. 'At least the Shoe Man's

had some comeuppance. He's permanently blinded in one eye.'

'How sad is that? Shame that young woman didn't castrate him while she was at it,' Cleo retorted. 'All of his victims are maimed in some way and one's dead.'

'I just wish we knew who all of them are,' he said. 'He's coughed, but I somehow don't think he's telling us everything. He's one of the nastiest creeps I've ever come across. His home and office computers are full of weird shit. All kinds of foot- and shoe-fetish sites and chatlines – a lot of it sadistic. And he's got a whole cocktail of sleeping and date-rape drugs in his office fridge.'

'Is he going to plead guilty and spare his victims the ordeal of giving evidence?'

'I don't know. Depends on his brief – good old Ken Acott again. We've a ton of evidence against him. The lock-up's in his name. We've found missing pages from the Shoe Man's 1997 files in a safe in his office. There are links to Facebook and Twitter sites of some of his recent victims on his computer and iPhone. DNA evidence from Rachael Ryan's body.'

He drank some wine.

'But we're going to have to wait for psychiatric evaluations as to whether he is fit to stand trial. Great! Garry Starling's able to run one of the biggest companies in the city, to be vice-captain of his golf club and treasurer of his Rotary Club – but he might not be fit to stand trial! Our legal processes suck.'

Cleo smiled sympathetically. She understood some of his frustrations at the criminal justice system.

'Jessie Sheldon should get a medal. How is she? Has she survived her ordeal OK?'

'Remarkably well. I went to see her at home this

afternoon. She's had surgery on her ankle and hopefully it will be fine in time. In fact she seemed in very good spirits, considering. She's looking forward to her wedding this summer.'

'She was engaged?'

'Apparently. She told me it was her determination to get married that kept her going.'

'So don't feel bad about his injury.'

'I don't. Not about his injury, no. I just don't feel we've nailed it. Not completely.'

'Because of those other shoes?'

'I'm not so concerned about those. If we can get him to talk more, eventually, maybe we'll clear those up.'

He sipped some more wine and glanced at the television.

'Is it the one on the ghost train who's bothering you? What's her name?'

'Mandy Thorpe. Yes. I still don't believe it was the Shoe Man who raped her. Even though he says he did. The forensic psychologist is wrong, I'm still convinced.'

'Meaning the perpetrator is still out there?'

'Yes, that's exactly the problem. If Proudfoot's wrong, then he's still out there. And might attack again.'

'If he is out there, you'll get him. One day.'

'I want to get him before he attacks again.'

Cleo pouted her lips playfully. 'You're my hero, Detective Superintendent Grace. You'll always get them eventually.'

'In your dreams.'

'No, not in my dreams. I'm a realist.' She patted her tummy. 'In about four months' time, our little *Bump* is going to be born. I'm depending on you to make it a safe world for him – or her.'

He kissed her. 'There are always going to be bad guys out there.'

'And bad girls!'

'Them too. The world is a dangerous place. We're never going to lock them all up. There'll always be evil people who get away with their crimes.'

'And good people who get locked away?' she said.

'There will always be blurred boundaries. There are plenty of *good* bad guys and *bad* good guys. Life's not clear and it's seldom fair,' he said. 'I don't want our child growing up under the illusion that it is. Shit happens.'

Cleo smiled at him. 'Shit *used* to happen. It stopped happening the day I met you. You rock!'

He grinned. 'You're full of it. Sometimes I wonder why you love me.'

'Do you, Detective Superintendent Grace? I don't. Not for one moment. And I don't think I ever will. You make me feel safe. You have from the day I met you and you always will.'

He smiled. 'You're so easily pleased.'

'Yeah, and I'm a cheap date. I don't even have one pair of designer shoes.'

'Want me to buy you some?'

She stared at him quizzically.

He looked back at her and grinned. 'For the right reasons!'

AUTHOR'S AFTERWORD

'Stranger rape' is actually extremely uncommon. In Sussex, the county in which *Dead Like You* is based, attacks such as those described are, thankfully, rare. It is in fact the very sad truth that virtually all rapes are committed by men known to the victim. The vast majority of rape survivors describe being attacked by a friend or someone they are in a long-term relationship with. The betrayal of trust caused as a result can undermine their ability to form a new relationship subsequently.

It is impossible to generalize about the way victims will respond to being raped, because there is no 'normal' reaction to such an abnormal act. The trauma can manifest itself in many different ways and there are specialist organizations, such as Rape Crisis, that exist to support victims. One local to Sussex is The Lifecentre, which aims to 'rebuild' survivors of rape. I have chosen to support them because I feel they provide a critical service which, incredibly, is not government-funded. Donations are always welcome. Go online and visit their website at www.lifecentre.uk.com if you wish to help. Thank you.

ACKNOWLEDGEMENTS

As ever, there are many people I have to thank for helping me in my research for this novel.

My first thank-you is to Martin Richards, QPM, Chief Constable of Sussex, who allows me such invaluable access to the world of his police force.

My good friend former Detective Chief Superintendent David Gaylor has, as ever, been a brick, a pillar of wisdom, and at times has wielded a bigger stick than my publishers in keeping me to my deadlines!

As always, so many officers of Sussex Police have given me their time and wisdom, and tolerated me hanging out with them and answered my endless questions, that it is almost impossible to list them all, but I'm trying here, and please forgive any omissions. Detective Chief Superintendent Kevin Moore; Chief Superintendent Graham Bartlett; Chief Superintendent Chris Ambler; DCI Trevor Bowles, who has been an absolute star and a brick; Chief Inspector Stephen Curry; DCI Paul Furnell; Brian Cook, Scientific Support Branch Manager; Stuart Leonard; Tony Case; DI William Warner; DCI Nick Sloan; DI Jason Tingley; Chief Inspector Steve Brookman; Inspector Andrew Kundert; Inspector Roy Apps; Sgt Phil Taylor; Ray Packham and Dave Reed of the High-Tech Crime Unit; Lex Westwood; Sgt James Bowes; PC Georgie Edge; Inspector Rob Leet; Inspector Phil Clarke; Sgt Mel Doyle; PC Tony Omotoso; PC Ian Upperton; PC Andrew King; Sgt Sean McDonald; PC Steve Cheesman; Sgt Andy McMahon; Sgt Justin Hambloch; Chris Heaver; Martin Bloomfield; Ron King; Robin Wood; Sue Heard, Press and PR Officer; Louise Leonard; James Gartrell.

DS Tracy Edwards has been incredible in helping me to

understand the reality of the suffering of rape victims, as have Maggie Ellis of The Lifecentre and PCs Julie Murphy and Jonathan Jackson of the Metropolitan Police, London.

Eoin McLennan-Murray, former Governor of Lewes Prison, and Deputy Governor, Alan Setterington, helped me greatly with the psychology of my suspects, as did Jeanie Civil and Tara Lester, who helped me so much with the psychology of the perpetrators, and barrister Richard Cherrill. I had huge help also with the psychology of the perpetrators from Dr Dennis Friedman.

A special thank-you to Caroline Mayhew, and to the team at the St Patrick's Night Shelter, in particular Emma Harrington, Theo Abbs and Amanda Lane.

And, as always, I owe an extremely special and massive thanks to the terrific team at the Brighton and Hove City Mortuary, Sean Didcott and Victor Sindon. And also to Dr Nigel Kirkham; forensic archaeologist Lucy Sibun; Dr Jonathan Pash; Coroner Dr Peter Dean; forensic pathologist Dr Benjamin Swift; Dr Ben Sharp; Marian Down.

Thank you to my terrific consultants on autism, Vicky Warren, who gave me so much of the inspiration for Yac; Gareth Ransome; Tony Balazs; and to wonderful Sue Stopa, manager of Hollyrood – the Disabilities Trust's flagship autism-specific residential home – and its staff and residential clients.

Thanks also to Peter Wingate Saul; Juliet Smith, Chief Magistrate of Brighton and Hove; Paul Grzegorzek; Abigail Bradley and Matt Greenhalgh, Director of Forensics at Orchid Cellmark Forensics; Tim Moore; Anne Busbridge, General Manager of the Brighton Hilton Metropole Hotel, Michael Knox-Johnston, General Manager of the Grand Hotel. And to Graham Lewis, my lock-up garage specialist! Special thanks to Josephine and Howard Belm, owners of the *Tom Newbound* houseboat. A very special thanks to Steve Dudman, owner of the Old Cement Works, whose kind offer to show me round sparked the idea for

PETER JAMES

the location of the climax. Thanks also to Andy Lang, of Lan-guard Alarms. And to Phil Mills. And also to Anne Martin, General Manager, and Peter Burgess, Chief Engineer, of Brighton Pier.

As ever, thank you to Chris Webb of MacService for keeping my Mac alive despite all the abuse I give it! Very big and special thanks to Anna-Lisa Lindeblad, who has again been my tireless and wonderful 'unofficial' editor and commentator throughout the Roy Grace series, and to Sue Ansell, whose sharp eye for detail has saved me many an embarrassment, and my wonderful PA, Linda Buckley.

Professionally I again have a total dream team: the tireless Carole Blake representing me; my awesome publicists, Tony Mulliken, Sophie Ransom and Claire Barnett of Midas PR; and there is simply not enough space to say a proper thank-you to everyone at Macmillan, but I must mention my brilliant former editor, Publishing Director Maria Rejt, my editor, Susan Opie, and copy-editor, Lesley Levene, and a massive welcome to my new editor, the wonderful Wayne Brookes.

As ever, Helen has been my rock, keeping me nourished with saintly patience and constant wisdom.

My canine friends continue to keep me sane. The ever-cheerful Coco has now joined Oscar and Phoebe under my desk, waiting to pounce on any discarded pages of manuscript that should fall to the floor and dutifully shred them.

Lastly, thank you, my readers, for all the incredible support you give me. Keep those emails, tweets and blog posts coming!

Peter James
Sussex, England
www.peterjames.com
Find and follow me on
http://twitter.com/peterjamesuk